75¢

||||| ||| ||||||| ||| |||| ||| | |||||||||||||||||||||
✅ **W9-CTG-484**

Rona Barrett's
**THE LOVOMANIACS**
IS
THE BIG, BOOMING BESTSELLER THAT
BLEW HOLLYWOOD WIDE OPEN AND IS
SPREADING LIKE WILDFIRE!

"You don't need a scorecard to tell the players in Miss Rona's novel about Hollywood today . . . **THE LOVO-MANIACS** is bound to be a major bestseller . . . It's well-structured, well-paced, well-plotted, and surprisingly well-written."

—TV Radio Mirror

"SLAPS MANY FAMOUS WRISTS."

—Vogue

"UNPUTDOWNABLE—IN MORE WAYS THAN ONE . . . The irresistible aura of secret vice wafts from **THE LOVO-MANIACS**."

—Los Angeles Magazine

"Consider the well-known singing star married first to a comfortable lady who bore his two children and with whom he remains on close friendly terms, second to a ravishingly lovely expatriate movie star, third to a very thin, very young girl. Add the fact that his son, also a singer, gets involved in a dubious kidnapping scheme. And wouldn't you know that this singer is Italian, has a big acting comeback in his career, and knows members of 'the Organization?' And then there's the big-time studio head who hands over the studio to his son, only to oust Junior a few years later when things aren't working out . . . Miss Barrett provides plenty of sex—hetero, homo and auto—not to mention astrology, movie glamour, true love and tragedy . . . And as surely as God made little wormy apples, this looks like a bestseller."

—Publishers Weekly

"**THE LOVOMANIACS** looks like a new bestseller . . . The first printing of 25,000 copies was sold out before publication date."

—Kansas City Star

"Miss Barrett delves deeply into the mire of private as well as public lives to reveal dishonesty, corruption, deceit, chicanery and debauchery . . . [She] has captured one of the major thrusts of Hollywood's     . in group, the stars and executives who wish to triumph at any cost, even to the destruction of those close and dear to them. For those seeking a lurid portrayal of one side of Hollywood . . . **THE LOVOMANIACS** will provide a satisfying experience."

—Los Angeles Times

*To my*
*MOTHER and FATHER*
*without whom*
*there would be no me . . .*

# The Lovo-maniacs

## by Rona Barrett

BANTAM BOOKS
TORONTO · NEW YORK · LONDON
A NATIONAL GENERAL COMPANY

All of the characters and events depicted in this book are purely fictional creations and any resemblances to persons living or dead or to factual events is unintentional and coincidental

*This low-priced Bantam Book
has been completely reset in a type face
designed for easy reading, and was printed
from new plates. It contains the complete
text of the original hard-cover edition.*
NOT ONE WORD HAS BEEN OMITTED.

THE LOVOMANIACS

*A Bantam Book / published by arrangement with
Nash Publishing Corporation*

*PRINTING HISTORY*

*Nash edition published July 1972
2nd printing .......... July 1972
3rd printing ....... August 1972
Bargain Book Club edition published November 1972*

*Bantam edition published August 1973*

*All rights reserved.
Copyright © 1972 by Rona Barrett.
This book may not be reproduced in whole or in part, by
mimeograph or any other means, without permission.
For informaiton address: Nash Publishing Corporation,
9255 Sunset Blvd., Los Angeles, California 90069.*

*Back cover photo of the author by Ron Rubenstein*

*Published simultaneously in the United States and Canada*

*Bantam Books are published by Bantam Books, Inc., a National
General company. Its trade-mark, consisting of the words "Bantam
Books" and the portrayal of a bantam, is registered in the United
States Patent Office and in other countries. Marca Registrada.
Bantam Books, Inc., 666 Fifth Avenue, New York, N.Y. 10019.*

PRINTED IN THE UNITED STATES OF AMERICA

# CONTENTS

# Prime Cusp

*(An Epilogue as Prologue)*

Greetings, everyone . . .

As all dedicated astrologers know, the planetary forces that direct our destinies can never be perceived entirely, though the nets of force they cast about us can be strong indeed, and of an awesome complexity. And so it is with our story tonight . . . an odd assortment of influences, human and otherwise, that began to assemble and interact nearly two years ago, and that affected many lives from the studios of Hollywood to the cells of a Cuban prison.

The story concerns the capture, early today, of the United States Navy's converted tanker, the U.S.S. *Pennsylvania,* in international waters off the coast of Cuba. It also concerns some rather peculiar shenanigans among the high and mighty in our very own Hollywood. Strange bedfellows? Fellows, some beds in this tainted town are stranger than you'd believe.

But first, let me relay to you an exclusive report from an old friend, Johnny Whitelaw, who gave up the Hollywood beat some time ago to become the ace Caribbean trouble-shooter for Reuters. Johnny has been allowed inside the Havana prison where our men have been incarcerated, and his news release has gone out over the wires. But Johnny also talked with our own man in Miami, and here is what we've learned, directly from him.

The U.S.S. *Pennsylvania* is an oceanographic research

1

vessel conducting peaceful scientific operations in the waters between Miami and Cuba—at least, that's what the Pentagon claims. That's not what Fidel Castro says, though. He claims that the *Pennsylvania* is an armed spy ship, that it was engaged in espionage activities *within* Cuba's three-mile limit, and that the officers and crew will therefore be tried as enemy agents.

The only hard facts available at this time are these: The *Pennsylvania* is a converted tanker, 1300 tons, 181 feet long, carrying two 50-caliber guns, one mounted fore and the other mounted aft—not what you'd call heavy armament, but not exactly scientific gear either. It is propelled by a single diesel engine with a maximum speed of 13 knots, which makes it only slightly faster than a rowboat, and it carries a crew of 71 plus 5 officers. The captain is one Lieutenant Commander Burris Howard Dann, a product of Idaho University's NROTC and a specialist in biology. He has been in the navy eleven years.

That's all the Pentagon will release, but after Johnny's visit to the prison where the men are being held, he came away convinced that there is more to this incident than the boys back in Washington are admitting.

Commander Dann and the other officers are being held in maximum security, having undergone what was described as a "lengthy interrogation," often a euphemism for some form of torture. Johnny was not allowed to see Dann or the other officers, so he could not relay any definitive word on the ship's exact location at the time of capture, on the nature of its mission, or on why it was taken without apparent resistance.

But he did manage to talk with some of the enlisted men, and found them confused and resentful. Why had they found themselves out there, like sitting ducks? Why were they told to surrender without a struggle? And where was the sea or air support they'd figured would be nearby? No one knows. They only know that they are here, in this stinking prison, and that they may end up rotting here indefinitely while their government plays games with Fidel Castro.

One man, the electronics mate who doubled as radio operator, swears he got off a Mayday call just before the Cubans boarded the *Pennsylvania*. His name is Hapwood, and he too is bitter about the way they were taken, and about the lack of response to his message. He maintains that he had been told there was a support vessel nearby. And now he wants to know where the hell it was.

Where indeed? Johnny's sources tell him that no U.S. spy ship ever goes on assignment unprotected, and that a serious mission would call for at least one heavily armed surface vessel on call nearby, with specific coded transmissions to be sent in case of trouble. So *if* the *Pennsylvania* is a spy ship, and *if* the radio man did get off an SOS, then where was the support ship?

Hapwood has a theory that the nearest ship was one they passed just hours before their capture. If so, then this story may develop some very strange twists indeed, because Hapwood swears that ship was carrying cameras where its guns should have been, and that it looked like it was filming scenes for a movie. If so, then this could be the scandal of the century in some very high places, both in Washington *and* in Hollywood.

And that, folks, is the report from Johnny Whitelaw, a man who knows his way around both towns very well indeed. Tune in tomorrow for more of this inside story. . . . This is Rona Barrett in Hollywood.

*But there is more to this story than even Johnny could know, and certainly more than will ever be revealed to the gallant men of the U.S.S.* Pennsylvania. *For the very few who could see and understand, it was all right there in the stars. The assortment of influences, human and otherwise, had begun to assemble and interact nearly two years ago. It all seemed so innocuous at that time—except to those expert and dedicated astrologers who could foresee the possible tragic and far-reaching consequences. For the astral interfaces leading to the capture—and to the resulting major disruption of the lives of all who were either directly or indirectly involved—had passed the first (or prime) cusp on Christmas Day and begun their work in the First House of the heavens: the first of the Twelve Houses they would affect before their full and awesome power would be observable to any human being with eyes to see and ears to hear. . . .*

3

# The 1st House

*Destiny in the making:*
*personality, disposition and tendencies,*
*worldly outlook and self-interest . . .*

---

*Forecast: If Johnny Valentine can find a way to throw Irving Dahlberg straight out of the nearest exit of his chartered 707, the better to take control of Dahlberg's studio and to make Dolly Diamond a star, and all without interrupting the flow of Chivas Regal over his velvet vocal cords—he'll willingly sell what remains of his soul to do it!*

*On the other hand, if Irving Dahlberg, the moviemaking mogul who collects and discards starlets like so much Kleenex, can figure out some way of outfoxing Johnny and come up with an explanation to his board of directors of why he's planning to pour $6 million into a film starring a girl no one has ever heard of—he'll gladly give up every one of those foot-long cigars he has tucked away in New York and Hollywood.*

*Such are the disparate dispositions and tendencies of these two giant personalities as they enter the First House to do battle. . . .*

---

### Johnny Valentine

"When were you born?"
That's what she said.
Just like that!

5

I mean, I asked this broad—this stewardess broad—what about having a couple of drinks, see, after the plane lands. So what's the big deal, right? Standard approach question. You get a yes or you get a no-sale. Right? Okay, so what does she say? . . .

*"When were you born?"*

No clue. No cue. No business with the eyebrows, no wiggle in the tail or other action like you might figure from, say, a doll who is trying to make the big impression. No. Just the four words—and a wait for my answer.

What the hell kind of an answer can you come up with?

You tell me! Go ahead . . . call a writer. Get two; see if Kanter is free and check with Reiner. Pay anything their agents want. Give them a week to stage the bit, and what could they come up with?

Plenty of nowhere, *believe* it!

So, I guess I can't rap myself too much, the kind of comeback I finally came back with. . . .

*"Huh?"* I mean it. So help me, that's what I said! Mr. Articulate.

"What day were you born . . . the date?"

Well, you know, there I was still on the hook. So, okay. Fine. Anyway, it got her a second look; a long one this time. *Sandy.* The little nameplate on her uniform blouse said this one was Sandy, and maybe that was what caught my eye in the first place. The plate, I mean, not the name. You know—where she was wearing it. I mean this doll had 'em up there and down there, too, plus a real crazy pair of legs. Funny thing, though, about that. See, the face didn't quite seem to go with the set, you know?

Nothing wrong with the face, now, dig! A nice face; a face you could get comfortable with. Only . . . well, if a guy was, say, an artist, he would lay it on you this way: the nose is a swell nose, only it's just a shade short for the rest of the face. And the mouth is a little bit too wide, especially if you count the corners; they sort of turn up into the cheeks. And the chin's too small, too. Not dimpled; not cutesie-pie or anything. Just not big enough for the rest. And then the eyes.

Yeah. Mostly, I guess, it was the eyes. Green; you know—not the yellow-green you see a lot; and not the blue that looks sort of green if you see the right kind of blond eyebrows with it, and maybe the right eyeliner and eyeshading, the way they do at the studio. But green-green, you know? Green enough I took an extra look to make sure it wasn't trick contacts.

No contacts.

Well—okay. So what's the big . . . oh. Yeah. Weird stuff: the color those eyes are, you don't exactly notice what's really different about the face. Not wrong, exactly. No. But different: those eyes aren't quite in line. I mean, one of them tilts, sort of—the right one. Not much. Not enough you can notice if . . . hey. Hey!

What the hell *is* this?

Knock it off! Who the hell is this bitch, anyway? Just a type: airline stewardess. Blonde. Five-two or five-three. Maybe 100–110 pounds. Take it all in one glance and it comes out production-line model. Quick-and-clean Stew, Model 328-X. Bright-smile attachment optional. They turn them out on a plastics production line. Down in Florida somewhere, probably.

And it's not like they were real live-people. You make the pitch, the bitches expect it. And the answer is "Okay." Or it's "No, thanks—will you have coffee, tea or milk?" And the average is about one yes for every two nos unless you look and/or act like Boris Karloff. Or it's one no for every two yeses if you're Johnny Valentine.

Yeah, baby!

*Johnny Valentine!* Giovanni Valentino. Vanni to friends. Mr. Valentine to the other 99 and 44/100 percent of the no-talent, superklutz world.

So who the hell is she to make *Johnny Valentine* feel like a klutz? What day was I born! What the hell is it to her, and what kind of an answer does she figure to get? . . .

"December fourth."

Oh, brother! I don't know—sometimes I really think I should of spent some more time with that headshrinker, back when Sam was so hot for the idea. Some comeback. A—what the hell do they call it—*riposte!* She asks a question and I come back with the straight-man answer. Okay! All right. Now what's the punch line? . . .

". . . um . . . Sagittarius!"

So that's the punch line? Sagittarius?

*Sagittarius!* Oh, well—hell—*sure!* Of course. The broad's hooked on astrology and it's really getting to her a little in there. I should of spotted it in the first place. Poor bitches.

All of them. Hooked on a lot of weird crap because it's the only edge they can figure on the world. An edge. Sure, baby! What else is anyone looking for?

But it gives me the cue for the next line.

"With Taurus rising."

A-hah! Now it's *her* turn to look. Business with the eyebrows; that one eye—the right one—comes a little bit farther out of line. I bet that's the first time anyone ever picked up on her so quick.

Lucky I got a good memory. And lucky that screwy script girl (What the hell was her name? Aw, who cares. How long ago was it, anyway—four years? Five?) was fouled up the same way and worked out the horoscope crap about rising signs and moon signs and all that jazz.

And now what.

"Thanks, Mr. Valentine." Big, bright smile. Sure, baby —just like they taught her on that plastic assembly line. Yeah, sure, bitch—what time do I pick you up, and where? "Thanks, but I've already got a date. Maybe some other time . . ."

What the *hell!*

". . . would you like coffee? Tea? Something stronger? We have a full bar and . . ."

"You got Chivas Regal?"

"Yes, sir, we . . ."

"On rocks. Squirt of soda—just enough to see a couple of bubbles. Make it a double."

And turn around to give her the back of the Valentine head, while you look out the window at something very interesting. Yeah, interesting. At 30,000 feet, it all looks like a soda cracker smeared with blue cheese. Turn the bitch off. . . .

*Already got a date.*

Where the hell does she get that? Turn me down, okay. So it doesn't happen too often . . . oftener than usual now though, Vanni boy. Oftener than it did back in your hungry years. That's a belly you got there now, not the lumps from your backbone showing through. And your hair . . . yeah . . . only your friendly rug-maker knows for sure.

Bitch.

A kid. Yeah, baby—kid. Remember when you were a kid. And the other kids thought you were . . .

Aw, hell.

Hey, hey! Come on, Vanni baby, Come on! Let's get a little of the old Johnny Valentine going here.

Yeah.

*Yeah!*

Okay. Okay, already—now—what the hell was I thinking about when the little stewardess broad . . . oh . . . yeah. That.

Dahlberg.

Look at him, up there. With his latest hooker. Latest in the long, long line. Stretching back to—who was it? Oh, yeah; Della. I remember, baby. Yeah. I remember. The way he used to sneer at his friends who messed up their lives with bitches. What was it he said to me that time, when I was breaking it up with Angie? "A man who cannot be trusted to honor his marital contract cannot be trusted to honor any other contract!"

*Ohh yeaah.*

And not two years later he brings Della home—to his own *home*, for Christ sake! And sets her up in a bedroom next to his and Margaret's. Hah! What was that line from *Oedipus Rex?* "Count no man fortunate who is not dead".

Yeah.

Now there's a laugh! Johnny Valentine, the big swinger; Johnny Valentine, the Velvet Voice who's got no time for anything but booze, broads, and buddies—that's what the liars say in their columns; the liars—Vanni Valentine, the South Side kid who never got past the first two weeks of high school. *Oedipus Rex,* yet! Doesn't exactly fit the image, does it, baby?

Well, the hell with the image.

And the hell with Irving Dahlberg, too. Offer the old bastard a free ride home to Hollywood for the holidays; my expense, I charter the 707 and pay the freight. Bring along anyone you want—anyone at all, Irving—so who the Christ does he choose to bring?

Gaby duMain.

An out-and-out hooker.

Oh, yeah—sure—she's going to be the next big Monarch Pictures star. Oh, yeah! Sure, baby. Six million iron men. Six million I hear he's got sunk in that thing she's supposed to be shooting with Dave Strauss. *Burn the First Card.*

Ha! Burn six million, more like. Six million. For a *screen*

9

*test!* Never been seen—in Glorious Technicolor, Breathtaking Cinemascope and Stere-o-phon-ic Sound—before. So she's the star of six million smackeroonies' worth of picture?

What a pile of crap.

But say this for old Irving—he may not be able to get it up too easy anymore, but he sure as hell does all right by whatever hooker he's mixed up with at the moment. Oh, yeah. Six million? What's six million. Especially when it's the stockholders' dough and not his own.

Yeah, Vanni baby. And don't forget who one of the stockholders is. Yeah. It's you, Vanni baby. You and nobody else but you . . . *Jesus!* Come on, Vanni boy—stop thinking in old song lyrics already. Shows your age. And you. . . .

"Thanks! . . ."

There she was and there she goes—little stewardess broad and little stewardess rump and little stewardess skirt —down the aisle. And there you sit with the booze and soda in your hand and just time enough to say thanks to her rump because she's a kooky, plastic assembly-line . . .

I wonder what she's saying to Dahlberg now?

Well, whatever it was it didn't do a hell of a lot for the duMain bitch. She's getting up, turning, and marching back down the aisle . . . to me, for Christ . . . no. No. Past me without a look (what a bitch, of the bitch genus) and on. To the john, I guess.

And here comes the plastic stewardess.

Past me.

But with a quick smile.

Oh, yeah. Smile. Smile, plastic stewardess broad. Smile at the nice man who's paying the freight. Smile at all the passengers. Smile at the pilots (I bet she's laying one of them; all these stewardess bitches lay) and smile at everyone. Smile for a living. Smile.

That, by God. That is one thing Johnny Valentine doesn't have to do anymore. No. Talent—that's an antidote for having to smile and that's what Johnny Valentine's got. Talent. And the dough, baby. The iron men. The shekels. The kale. The scratch. The money. *Thirty million dollars* of the money; that's what Sam says and he should know. Christ, he *better* know; if he doesn't, nobody on the face

10

of this world does know. Except maybe Uncle Sugar, and he doesn't really know all about everything either.

Not about the account in Zurich. Not about the account in Nassau.

But what the hell can you do with that money—get a loan against it the way Sam says, maybe? That's how gumbahs do it—and Sam ought to know about that.

And so should you, Vanni. So should you, Vanni-boy.

The gumbahs.

The *padrone*. All those years ago, before it all began; before anyone knew about the Talent. Well, before I knew, anyway. *Mia madre,* she knew, of course. What of course? Of course, that's what of course—because she did, Vanni baby. She did.

Ma always knew everything—especially if it was about you.

Who the hell were you then?

Little, skinny, nothing Vanni Valentino. *Mi bambino Giovanni;* Christ, there I was, sixteen years old, and what does she call me—with me standing right there in front of the *padrone* yet—*mi bambino Giovanni.* Christ! I could of went through the floor. And I guess the *padrone* knew it, too. Always, later, right up until the day he died when he wanted to kid me a little it was *bambino* I got from him. *Bambino* instead of Johnny or Vanni or John.

*Bambino.* . . .

Yeah, but he did all right for you, the old *padrone.* Didn't he always? Bet your ass he did, baby. Ma said I could sing? Okay, I could sing. Never mind what I thought; never mind what anyone else said. I was a great singer as far as he was concerned and that's how it was going to be. And that's how it was, too.

I wonder, did that surprise him, the *padrone?*

If it did, he never showed it. Old boy never showed anything. To anyone. That's how he got to be the *padrone,* I guess. Oh, sure. The smile. Or the frown. Sometimes even the tears; he's a guinea so sometimes it was the tears for everyone to see. Sure. That.

But always behind that face of his you could see it; feel it. The nothing. Always his own. Always the brains. Thinking.

Criminal, the liars called him.

11

Hoodlum kingpin.

Vice czar.

Mafioso. (Don't say that word out loud, *bambino*. Not ever. *Omerta*. Don't say the word and don't even think it.) Mafioso, they called him; the liars. *Calabrese liars*. . . .

Calabrese? Yeah—*mi padre*. From Calabria, his family was; married to Ma, the Siciliano. Calabrese. I wonder . . . how the hell did that get to be a curse word? Funny. I never even wondered about that before; let's see: Calabria was part of the same country once. Kingdom of the Two Sicilies. So how did Calabrese get to be a curse? An obscenity in the mouth of a Siciliano?

Look it up. When you get home, look in that big library of yours and find it in one of the books. History, probably. Sure. And if it's not there tell someone to find out and send you a book about it.

What would the *padrone* think about that, I wonder? Dig the Valentino *bambino* reading books. Laugh? No, he wouldn't laugh. About improving yourself, about finding out things, knowing what was what . . . about that the *padrone* never laughed. Books he had; must of been a million—I can remember I thought that. A million. In that same room where people came when they wanted something; a favor from the *padrone*. The books, all around.

Could hardly read himself, but his kids . . . no, he wouldn't of laughed at me reading and trying to know about things.

"Mr. Valentine? . . ."

Huh?

The plastic stewardess broad again. Smiling.

"Yeah?"

"Can I get you another drink, Mr. Valentine?"

Drink?

How about that—the booze and soda's gone!

"Yeah. Thanks. Another like that one. And . . ."

"Yes?"

". . . and nothing. Thanks."

Turn back to the window and turn her off. Who the hell is she? Just another kooky bitch. What was I going to ask her, anyway?

Balls.

Who the hell cares what I was going to ask her and who

12

the hell cares about her . . . and why the hell do I keep thinking about her?

You know, Vanni baby.

You know.

All right . . . so I know. So I'm thinking about her and about Dahlberg and about Mama and the *padrone* and Calabria and all the rest of it to keep from thinking about what I can't keep from thinking about until maybe I get a couple more Chivas Regals in me, and maybe not then. Because there's no damn use thinking about her. It. Her . . . Dolly . . . no use. . . .

"Here you are, sir."

"Thanks."

Little plastic . . . Dolly. Jesus Christ. All right—*all right, already!*

Dolly.

Drink the drink.

Dolly.

Look out the window.

Dolly.

Think about . . . about . . . Dolly. Oh, god*damn* it! What's to think and what's to do? My God, haven't I already done enough?

*Dolly Diamond.*

Who would believe it—her real name! Dolly Diamond. And who would believe the voice? I got a voice. *Had* a voice, anyway, once upon a time. But never, *never* a voice that could of sung a duet with her. Christ, why couldn't she of been born with pipes out of a bullfrog? Or why couldn't she of been born ten years earlier? Or later? Or anything. Why with a voice like that and why now and for Christ *sake* why . . . *me!*

Voice? Yeah, Vanni baby, but it's more than a voice and you know it. Good-looking? Yeah. Oh, yeah. But there's wall-to-wall good-looking broads around; what's to choose? Besides. She's not really so good looking; not sexy or like that. Too much nose. Too much . . . what? Eyes.

Yeah—that's what's been bugging me.

The eyes.

I guess that little kooky plastic stewardess broad; with the one eye that's off-line with the other one. That reminded me. Dolly—her eyes slant. Both of them, not just one. But they slant . . . and Christ help me if sometimes they don't go cockeyed.

Cockeyed! One up and one down; she could pick up a cigar butt and look at a 707 going over her head all at the same time. Funny. Yeah—funny; funny as a crutch, Vanni baby, and you know it is. What the hell do you do about her? About Dolly . . .

Think.

Think . . . of something else, damn it, before you start kicking and rolling around in the aisles and chewing on the rug. Think. Of . . .

*Dahlberg.*

That goddamn Irving Dahlberg; sitting up there two seats in front of you like he was a regular passenger on a regular flight and who the hell are all these other people? Owns the world. Owns the plane. Doesn't like you, he'll buy the ground you stand on and have you torn down. . . .

Dahlberg.

Well, he doesn't own Giovanni Valentino. And he doesn't own Johnny Valentine. And—by God—he doesn't own Dolly Diamond, either. Shake hands with the man who does, Irving baby. Shake hands with Vanni Valentine! Yeah, Irving baby; sit up there and give me the back of your neck as long as you want to. I set the flight up this way to give you a chance to pitch me a pitch; how much will it cost you—paid how—to get Dolly Diamond for the flick version of *Sadie?* So take your own candy-ass time, Irving baby. Play it as cool as you want.

It's gonna cost you another hundred grand for every goddamn time zone we cross before you start talking!

And maybe you don't get her for the show anyway.

Yeah.

Maybe not!

And maybe yes; what the hell—Sam'll do the real nitty-gritty talking on contract and all that jazz anyway. Christ. . . .

Christ! What became of the booze? Look at that—another booze and soda down to rocks and water. Like nothing. Like air. Where's that plastic stewardess broad, anyway. Can't let the passengers dehydrate. Where's . . . what the hell?

Who's that geek?

Airline uniform. Three stripes on the sleeve. Young guy
—who—hell, he must be the copilot. Sauntering back down
the aisle from the flight deck. To the john, I guess. Funny.
He's got a right to go to the john anytime he wants. The boss
pilot's still up there and you could even leave the airplane
on autopilot and nothing would probably happen. But . . .

But I wish to hell he'd go back and sit down.

*Go back up there, you klutz!*

Get your skinny butt back in the right-hand seat and
do the job I'm paying you an arm and a leg to do for me,
will you? Because Vanni baby's just a wee tiny little bit
chicken when it comes to flying anyway.

What a yock!

Johnny Valentine, the jet-propelled stud . . . queasy
about flying. Bad for the image, Vanni baby. Yeah. Very
bad for the image.

And very damn bad . . .

### Irving Dahlberg

. . . for business if something happened to Irving Dahlberg because some snotnose kid of an airplane driver is
back in the back of the airliner crapping out the liquor
he slopped up the night before. I wonder if there isn't
some law against him leaving the captain alone up there?
If there isn't, there should be.

Monarch Pictures, riding on Irving Dahlberg's shoulders. Five *big* productions, riding on Irving Dahlberg's
shoulders. Seven bankers, riding on Irving Dahlberg's shoulders. Two thousand stockholders, riding on Irving Dahlberg's shoulders.

Always it's like that. On the giants' shoulders, they ride.
To tell themselves in the end that it was all their doing and
they made themselves stars or millionaires or whatever it
was that the giants made them. But the giants know. Nobody tells Irving Dahlberg anything, but Irving Dahlberg
*always* knows. He always knows what everybody wants and
what everybody can do and what everybody has got to
come to Irving Dahlberg to get because he can't get it for
himself. To the giant. To stand on the giant's shoulders!

Irving F. Dahlberg.

In charge.

The *schmuck* who had that office—the very first one,

back at the studio—In Charge of Production he had on the door under his name. And he wasn't a giant, so he failed and they threw him out like the midget he was and put Irving Dahlberg in his office and the carpenters just changed the nameplate over In Charge of Production and that was going to be enough, they thought. Well, they found out. They all found out.

The next day—*the next day*—the phony, lousy wooden nameplates were gone. And there it was. In stainless steel. Big. So nobody should miss it: IRVING F. DAHLBERG— IN CHARGE.

No In Charge of Production.

Just—*In Charge*.

Been a long time (never mind how long), a long time since anyone needed a cockamamie nameplate to tell them who's in charge or who's behind the door in an office where Irving Dahlberg's working. . . .

Want another drink?

No. Want another drink but can't have another drink. What a farce: Irving Dahlberg wants another drink— another lousy drink—and can he have one? He cannot!

Another cigar.

Another cigar, by God, Irving Dahlberg can have any time he wants—and good cigars, too. The best. Made especially for Irving Dahlberg at $3.27 a copy. Wholesale. The best.

Can't have another lousy drink. . . .

Yes, and that's not all I can't have. Damn that guinea son of a bitch to hell—sitting back here, keeping me in sight with those shotgun-barrel eyes of his. I can feel them now on the back of my neck. Waiting for Irving Dahlberg to come to him!

*To him!*

Well, he'll watch me until his shifty mafioso eyes fall out of his head before I turn around. I wouldn't give him the satisfaction. Who in the hell is he? Johnny Valentine— two-for-a-nickel *goyische* warbler. Nothing. Men like me made him. *Made him!* And now he's a Big Man; charter a jet airliner and offer Irving Dahlberg a free ride to the Coast.

Why? Because he wants Irving Dahlberg to come begging. For the *kurveh* who's been blowing him every day since before he bought her contract. Dolly Diamond. Jewish

16

she says she is—Jewish! Blowing that guinea . . . and
Irving Dahlberg is supposed to come crawling to the
mafioso asking can he please pay a million dollars to her
so Irving Dahlberg can make her a star!

Guinea son of a bitch! He'll rot in hell first. He'll kiss
my ass first. He'll starve first.

Bastard.

Bitch.

Nothing but bastards and bitches in this business today.
On the screen—*yentzing,* right there on the screen—what
kind of a way to make a motion picture is that? What
kind of art is that? What kind of story is that?

Pictures that *open*—that *open,* by God—with the people
*yentzing* on the screen! How can you interest anyone—
even a pervert—in a story that *begins* that way?

Perverts. All of them; perverts. That's who's making
motion pictures today. Perverts who couldn't tell a story
to save their worthless lives. And money they get; money
from bankers who wouldn't let their own children or their
own wives go see the pictures made from the money they
lend to them.

"There's only one worthwhile story in this world—and
it's a *delayed fuck!*"

Who said that? Somebody. Some director. Anyway,
somebody.

"Can I get you another drink, Mr. Dahlberg?"

"What? . . ."

The stewardess; yes. Thinking about her before; nice
body—too full to photograph well; the screen puts fifteen
pounds on a skeleton—and the face not quite right. Peculiar
planes. Must have a strange bone structure under there
to have face planes like that. But with the right lighting
. . . and look at the kind of faces they make stars of these
days. Look! Streisand. And Farrow. And Diamond.

Dolly Diamond. . . .

"I could bring some coffee or some sandwiches if you'd
rather, Mr. Dahlberg. Or there's a full steak dinner; very
good. Only take me a minute to fix it."

"No. Nothing. Thank you."

"Well . . ."

Still smiling. They teach them that; if they can teach
them to smile they can teach them to act. Is that why she's
sucking around?

17

I wonder if she fucks?

"Just a moment."

Where's Gaby . . . still out of sight, back in the john? Quick look. Yes. Still in the john.

"Do you have any photographs of yourself, Miss . . . uh . . . Sandy? Sandy, what's your last name, anyway?"

"Hallowell."

"That's a nice name. Maybe it would look good on a theater marquee? Did you ever think of that, Sandy Hallowell?"

"Why . . . no. Not really."

Bigger smile, now. For the giant, Irving F. Dahlberg, who can put that name—Sandy Hallowell—up there on that marquee. Sure, this girl can act.

And this girl fucks, too.

When they smile, thinking about the name on the marquee, they fuck. They all do.

"I'll be out here on the Coast a few days. Why don't you come to see me at the studio? I'll have my secretary make an appointment for you."

Still smiling. She'll come. And she'll fuck.

Well . . . anyway . . . she'll blow me. Save the *yentzing* for where it's needed. Even a giant has got to hoard his energies when he gets to be my age.

"What day were you born?"

Huh?

I'm getting old, Irving Dahlberg is getting old and maybe my hearing is getting bad.

"What did you say? I'm not sure I . . ."

"What day were you born, Mr. Dahlberg? The date, I mean."

What the hell *is* this? Is this little bitch trying to impress Irving Dahlberg with a line like that? What day was I born? What the hell is it to her what day I was born? And what the hell kind of an answer is that when a giant asks you to come to his office? Who the hell does she think she's going to impress? Who?

Well . . . we'll get that nonsense out of her head right here and now.

Look back at her. The face—nothing. Just look. Stare at them without showing anything or saying anything and they always roll over on their backs. Always. Twenty seconds I give this little bitch. Twenty seconds.

18

"Will there be anything else?"

*Anything else?*

I'm staring at you, you stupid little bitch. Irving Dahlberg is staring at you and you want to know if there is anything *else*.

Thirty seconds.

I give her thirty.

"Well . . . perhaps a little later then." And she turns around, still smiling, and saunters up the aisle, through the door, and into the flight deck.

I can't believe it.

People don't treat Irving Dahlberg that way—not when he dangles the Keys to the Kingdom before their eyes. I could make her a star. That crummy, offsides face of hers, I could turn it into a million fan pictures hanging in bedrooms and in army barracks and in . . . in . . . everywhere. All over the earth I could make that face known. I offer her that, *offer* her, and *she* asks *me* a question.

*"When were you born?"* The bitch! She didn't know it but she really got to you, didn't she? Because Irving Dahlberg, the Man Who Knows Everything About Everybody, Irving Dahlberg—*doesn't know* what day he was born.

What day? Irving Dahlberg doesn't know what *year!* Or even what country. Now-country. Not then-country. Was it the Polish part of Russia or the Russian part of Poland? Was it the Pale or in a city? Parents—who? What?

A date they've got in that *verdammt Who's Who!* And a place. Citizen; Irving Dahlberg is a native-born American citizen. Born in Minneapolis, Minnesota. A birth certificate even they got for me, with all on it who I am and who . . . ah, God! Good people. The people who raised us—my sister and me—no children of their own and they raised us because they wanted to and they were good people and I was so happy. Then. Good people—but too honest. They had to be so honest; Orthodox, both of them, and honest before *Adonai*. So honest they had to *tell* me. *Tell* me I'm not who I am. Irving Dahlberg—their name for me; the name they gave me. Never even knew my birth name; never even knew the man who gave them the babies (How old was I? A year, 18 months? How old, damn it?) and said please. In Russian; Russian-Yiddish, they said, so they knew he was a Jew like they were. *Please*, he said to them. *My babies—please, mister, please, missus—*

*please. Don't let Them find the babies. Don't let Them
send my children away from America. They'll catch me; for
me is no matter. Wife's dead. Two days dead; couldn't take
the cold, hiding, in the wagon from Canada. Coughing,
always. Now she's dead and They'll catch me now—the
American* Kazakim*—chased me, yesterday. Fooled Them,
but soon no place to hide. Please, mister, please missus,
please . . . my babies! . . .*

So they took the babies—the tiny girl and the little boy
who could barely form words. One baby they'd had, themselves; a boy, thank God. Maybe a little older than me,
maybe a little younger. Dead, now, and the doctors said
no more children for them. Never again. So for them it
was a gift from God. The birth certificate for their baby—
their *Irving*—mine, now. Their baby's name, their baby's
everything. Their baby's life, even, until . . .

Until they had to be honest! Had to tell Irving Dahlberg the truth. Ah, God. The truth. What's Irving Dahlberg's name? What is my name?

*Irving Dahlberg!* My name is Irving Dahlberg; told
myself that. Starting the next day. Irving Dahlberg. Irving
Dahlberg. Over and over again; no way to find *my* truth.
No way to find *my* name. Only *their* truth, those good and
kind people, goddamn them; so honest they were, goddamn
them. No. God bless them. But couldn't they have been just
a *little* dishonest? Couldn't they have carried the one lie
to *Adonai*—couldn't they have loved me just that *one little
bit* extra—ah, God! Just that one extra little drop of love!

Love. Love me . . . the Big Words . . . Love. To hell
with the Big Words. Who needs them? Who needs love?
Not Irving Dahlberg. Not the giant. A month, it took me;
two, maybe. Not more. *Irving Dahlberg!* I was Irving Dahlberg and I said it over and over and over. I am Irving
Dahlberg. And, finally, I was.

For a week, at first, I was Irving Dahlberg. I was born
in Minneapolis and these were my parents and I was
Irving Dahlberg and I loved them and they loved me and
everything was right. Just like it always had been right. I
*didn't remember* what they said. I truly did not remember. . . .

And then, of course, it popped into my mind one day.

Then I had to do it all over again. *Irving Dahlberg—
Irving Dahlberg—Irving Dahlberg* . . . until it was done

and the world was right. And the next time, it was longer than a week. And then longer than a month. And when I was—what—when Irving Dahlberg was ten years old, it had been a *year* since Irving Dahlberg had remembered he was maybe Isaac Yannowicz or Yakov Sobolenski.

"Happy birthday," she said to me, that dear and kind and gentle lady, my mother. "Happy birthday, my Irving . . . for *whenever* your real birthday is." Ten candles there were on the cake for me, with my school friends around and my little sister there and the rabbi smiling and the gifts piled up to open. And she whispered it, just the soft words, just the whisper so only I could hear, and the strong and fierce hug and the quick kiss on the top of the head. She loved me, oh yes. She loved me.

But not enough to keep from whispering those words.

Ah, God. I hurt her then; I hurt her! Ripped myself away, hating her for all the work she had undone; hating her for all the work of becoming Irving Dahlberg again. For the rest of the day, for the party, and later—when I would have to *pretend* to be Irving Dahlberg instead of *really* being him. . . .

*Enough.* Enough already. . . .

Think of something else (goddamn that stewardess bitch); think of tonight, in bed with Gaby (that bitch stewardess; her questions, damn her), of your son Jack (not even *that* is real; no children for the giant, so Irving Dahlberg has to take his dead sister's child and make *him* a son, even changing his name so that the giant's name will not die—and even Jackie doesn't know the giant's real name, Irving Dahlberg's real name); think of . . . the work. The job. Monarch International Pictures, Inc. Irving Dahlberg's company.

All right.

*Sadie.* A musical—and not even a new theme, for God's sake, but a rehash of *Miss Sadie Thompson,* with an all-new, all-musical approach. Who on earth, even a giant like Irving Dahlberg, could have figured a musical with a book like that would make money—and it's supposed to be the Big Picture for Monarch this year. What a deal I had to give that guinea, Valentine, for the picture rights. What a deal! And why—why—just because that wop son of a bitch put up the money for the Broadway theatrical version. Just for that. Smart? He wasn't smart. He didn't figure a musical like that could make money; oh, no. Nothing like that; nothing you could respect the mafioso warbler for doing; nothing that would make him a giant, too.

For the woman he did it; the hooker; for the Big Blow Job he did it. *Dolly Diamond*. The *kurveh;* the whore!

Married. Since she was sixteen years old married to that crazy *nebbish* David Strauss. Actor. *Actor,* he called himself; I can remember when that word *meant* something. A mumbler, David Strauss—like all the Strasberg stumblebums, a mumbler—and getting nowhere on the stage or in pictures. Getting nowhere because he's a nothing. A bum.

Actor!

Jackie—my dear little adopted son Jackie, that so-called *mensch* with the *goyische kopf*—Jackie, even, couldn't help him. Tried. Friends when they were kids, good friends, even though I never trusted that Strauss—something off, there, something not quite right. And I wasn't the only one to think so. Oh no. Even with Jackie's help he couldn't get a job in pictures in those days.

Mumbler. And married to that whore!

So, to Dolly Diamond the guinea had to go for his blow job. And a Broadway musical he had to put her in with his own money. And it had to be the biggest success in ten years—*in ten years*—and suddenly she's a big star, and her husband has to be a big star, too, because how can a big star be married to a nothing, so the guinea has to help him, too, and suddenly that mumbler David Strauss is in a picture the guinea financed for a tax loss and instead it's a sleeper! A big hit that cost nickels to shoot, and who knows why the audience idiots will pay money to see a pile of trash like that but they did and suddenly David Strauss is a big star too and people are paying their money to see him in anything he can mumble through, and now—dear God, *Adonai,* see what they are doing to me!—in an *Irving Dahlberg* picture, even.

Those bankers. Those fools. Irving Dahlberg, the giant, who was making great motion pictures when they were in knee pants, most of them; Irving Dahlberg tells them Gaby duMain will be a star in *Burn the First Card.* Gaby duMain will be the next great star of Monarch Pictures—they have Irving Dahlberg's word for it. Irving Dahlberg who has made more great stars and more great money

22

for them (the thieves; the cowards; the bloodsuckers) than any other man in Hollywood; Irving Dahlberg says this! And is that good enough for them, those idiots?

"She's never *made* a picture before."

That's what they say.

"She's *untested;* we don't have past records to go by."

That's what they say.

"You haven't even got a *screen test* of her."

That's what they say. To a giant those bloodsucking cowards say this; millions, billions I have made for them. And now to Irving Dahlberg they say this.

All right. All right. So we can work it out, the points for financing. One by one we work those points out for six million dollars until we've got five million dollars. And are they satisfied? Isn't Irving Dahlberg's *word* worth one lousy point?

"Get a star," they say. "Get a star worth the extra point." So who's a star? A *star!*

David Strauss—that mumbler, that nebbish, that nothing David Strauss is a star worth the point; worth the last million to finance an Irving Dahlberg picture!

*David Strauss.*

Well. What does it matter—they'll see. Those bankers. Those no-talent, no-brains bankers. Gaby duMain. That's who they'll remember from *Burn the First Card.* Not David Strauss. I've got the writers. I've got the director. I've got artistic control; personally. The President of Monarch International Pictures, Inc., Irving Dahlberg, the giant, who has better things to do with his time—Irving Dahlberg is down on that sound stage where they're shooting the picture more hours every day than Irving Dahlberg is inside his own office; Irving Dahlberg is watching them. All of them . . .

The time! The time that wastes; the *time!*

A board meeting I've got coming up—a board meeting, where that new one, that *goniff* lawyer of Valentine's, will be sitting and waiting for something he can pounce on—and Irving Dahlberg can't let him have anything. Not a scrap. Got to have a program. Ready to go. All contracts signed, all loose ends tied up; a program only Irving Dahlberg can carry through with any hope of success. Big! That's the way it's got to be: big!

23

Irving Dahlberg is a giant. What one of those blood-suckers could make *any* picture? Any picture at all? Bankers? Lawyers? Accountants? Brokers?

The bloodsuckers.

*Sadie.* It's going to be one of my big pictures. It's going to be big because we're going to *make* it big and when (goddamn him, that guinea, goddamn him) it's finished the bloodsuckers will be richer than ever and Dolly Diamond will be a Big Star in movies besides being a Big Star on Broadway and who will get the credit, who will get the applause?

Dolly Diamond for singing a song and saying the lines out of that imbecile face of hers, she'll get applause.

Johnny Valentine, that wop bastard, for putting up money to make the movie in the first place and for having made sure in his production contract that his name will be up there over the title: "Johnny Valentine Presents" on the first frame. He'll get the applause.

The director, whoever we get, he'll get applause.

And Irving Dahlberg? Irving Dahlberg, the giant who had to scheme and connive and pressure and break his heart maneuvering those bloodsucking directors into a spot where they can't *not* make the picture, what will he get?

More complaints at the next directors' meeting.

What have you done for me *this* week?

That's what Irving Dahlberg will get. Who cares? Irving Dahlberg doesn't care. By the time the *goniffs* are drooling and licking their thin lips over the early gross reports on the hard-ticket roadshow, Irving Dahlberg will be busy making them even *more* money . . . only *this* time, maybe there's going to be a little applause, a little appreciation, for Irving Dahlberg!

*Boarders Away!*

An Irving Dahlberg production. Irving Dahlberg, with a straight producer credit. "Irving Dahlberg Presents," ahead of the title.

"Irving Dahlberg Presents—*Boarders Away!*"

The great adventure of World War II; a German submarine captured at sea by the U.S. Navy; danger, drama, involvement; the first boarding and capture of an enemy at sea since 1815! The *true story.* . . .

Not just your run-of-the-mill shoot-'em-up at sea. No John Wayne heroics. *Real* drama—on both sides!

*Both sides!*

Zanuck did it in *The Longest Day* and *Tora! Tora! Tora!* But neither was really a success. A hundred men, a thousand, a million those pictures were talking about; who could really *know* and *care* about a million men? A million is a number.

Narrow it down.

Let us *know* the people.

Let us *care* whether they win or lose, live or die; let it be a telegram ". . . Navy Department regrets to inform you . . ." being handed directly to every single member of the audience if one of those men on the screen gets killed! Real men, sweating real fear, on the screen; real ships, navy ships, not cardboard cutouts like *In Harm's Way* did it; real action for real emotions from the people who buy the tickets. That will show the bloodsuckers!

That's how it will be . . . *if*.

*If*. Always the *if!* Always and always and always . . . *if* you can make a deal with that guinea for Dolly Diamond to make her picture. *If* you can get the navy to let you use half of what's left of the fleet for *Boarders*. And *if*—the biggest if of all—*if* you can get all this done before the board meeting, and all tied up and the studio firmly committed and the whole matter settled so those bloodsuckers, those cowards, can't start "asking" and "discussing" and "studying" and "assessing" and talking everything to death. . . .

It will work.

It *must* work!

Or they will do it to Irving Dahlberg the way they did it to . . . to . . . *wait a minute!* What the hell is going on here? Where is Gaby? How long since she went back to the women's john and—*how long since that pissant copilot walked back the same way?* Well, we'll see about that! I'll just get up and . . .

No.

Irving Dahlberg can't get up and walk to the back of the airplane to see if his woman is screwing a pissant copilot. Irving Dahlberg is a giant and can't concern himself with such things; the loyalty of Irving Dahlberg's women cannot be questioned!

That stewardess.

Ring for that stewardess—that stewardess bitch with the

25

questions to ask—and send *her*. Tell her . . . tell her . . . tell her to go . . . go back and see if Miss duMain needs any help.

She's been gone a long time.

She might need help.

Irving Dahlberg the giant does not run such errands; besides, Irving Dahlberg is not jealous. Irving Dahlberg is loved. Irving Dahlberg . . .

## Sandy Hallowell

. . . wasn't looking too great; that's why I asked him if he wanted a drink or anything. Anything being coffee, tea, milk, beer, wine, whiskey, gin, vodka or one of the ver-ee see-leckt liqueurs we stock for these crazy VIP charter flights.

Or, anything being the professional services of Miss Sandra Jean Hallowell, R.N. Oh, yes . . . big deal: Registered Nurse! Wow!

He seemed all right, nice looking old guy (I wonder just *how* old he really is; that chick he had with him could have been his granddaughter if I didn't know better, catty little bitch that I am), and in expensively good shape when he came aboard with Johnny Valentine's party.

But after the girl—what's her name? duMain, or something goofy like that—got up and went to the whiffer, it seemed like he got paler and paler, looking out the window for a while and then sitting there with that cigar.

Small wonder!

A big, long cigar like that . . . the way he smokes it—right spang in the middle of the mouth with his lips curled around it like a baby's pacifier—I wonder how many of those he smokes in a day? Poor old man; poor, silly old man with all that money and all that being a big, famous moviemaker since sometime before the world began (for Sandy Hallowell, anyway), the best he can do to make himself happy—the big prize for the winner—is long seegars and having a barely postadolescent girl for a mistress . . . and putting a corny pitch like "I can get you into the movies" on a stewardess the minute Miss Pubescent America goes to the can. What kind of a life can that be for him?

Poor old man!

So I was about to walk past again and have a visual

check of his vital signs anyway, when he rang the stew bell for me.

"Yes, Mr. Dahlberg?"

"Miss duMain, my . . . companion . . . went back to the rest room quite a while ago."

That didn't do much for me; she could turn into a giraffe for all I cared.

"Yes, sir? . . ."

"Well, you know, I was wondering—I know, sometimes, doors get stuck, or—oh—something else goes wrong. She might need some help."

"I wouldn't worry, Mr. Dahlberg; there is an emergency alarm for her if anything . . ."

*(Oh-oh! I get it—that damn Tommy! . . .)*

". . . happens. But all the same, I'll check on her to make sure. Can't have a worried passenger. Be right back!"

"Thank you."

"Of course."

*Of course* my apple-round *ass!* I gave him my brightest Golden Girl smile (filled with Reassurance to the Passenger; stewardess school technical course 21-J; even better if you've got a mouth that's a good deal too wide for the rest of your face) and strolled briskly (at a pace calculated to compete with the four-minute mile while not betraying any sign of undue haste; stewardess school technical course 27-X) toward the rear of the cabin.

Johnny Valentine looked up (he had been staring at the back of Irving Dahlberg's head with an expression that made me glad I can't read minds) and started to make a drink-refill motion at me, but I was past him before it became more than an idea.

That damn Tommy!

Twice already this year the chief pilot's warned him—the surest way for a young and aspiring copilot to find himself selling insurance for a living instead of adding that fourth gold ring to his sleeve is to make a pass at a passenger. Even if the passenger makes it plain that she considers stud service included in the price of the ticket.

That *damn Tommy!*

But I was wrong. The door to the women's midships john was locked; Miss Mammary Silicone Experiment of 1972 was still in there. But the door to the men's john was ajar; I was about to start wondering if he could have been crazy

27

enough to try balling her in the seductive presence of a toilet and tampax-dispenser when I looked farther back—into the unused rear cabin—and there he was, the dear child, sleeping the sleep of innocence in one of the passenger seats, with his uniform cap tipped over his eyes.

For a moment there, I darn near apologized!

But no need. I think copilots—especially young and horny copilots (and when did you ever see one who wasn't both?)—develop the ability to sleep with watchdog circuits engaged and running behind the eyes and ears.

"Hey there, Funny Face," he said.

The head tipped back maybe half an inch, still balancing the cap on forehead and nose, but far enough to let me get the glint of one slit-opened eye under the bill.

"Hi yourself, Sneaky Hands."

"Now, *now*—is that the approved form of address by a Union Airlines stew to one of our heroic and intrepid birdmen?"

"It is when addressing randy idiot-seat warmers who make up dumb nicknames." This was no time to shout nightclub dialogue back and forth with an assistant flyboy. "Where's the old boy's playmate?" I said, all business.

"The Grumper?" He shrugged—just the left shoulder, to show me and the world that it meant nothing to him. "Still in the little girls' room, far as I know."

I grinned at him; the half-face put-down grin I used to practice in front of the mirror before I began to understand that put-downs were not where it was at.

He made an impolite sound with his nose and lips. "She was in the can when I got here and she hasn't come out. I couldn't care less. What's all the curiosity about the Grumper, anyway?"

I couldn't resist. "Why," I said, knowing it was a mistake, "do you call her 'the Grumper'?"

That perked him up a little bit.

"I am an *artiste*," he said, tilting the cap to the back of his head so I could see his whole face. "And an *artiste* sees more deeply—and more accurately—than common mortals. . . ."

"Oh, for Christ . . ."

". . . and communicates his vision to the masses. The lovely young thing currently topping the Great Man's list of Top Forty Talents, Miss duMain to be precise, is not

28

unlike many other young ladies of similar attainments and background. She is exquisite in repose but has not yet learned how to walk."

"Tommy, are your people German by any chance?"

"German?"

"It's an old saying: 'Ask a German the time and he will tell you how to build a clock.' "

"Ah—impatience! 'All youth is impatience,' as the great . . ."

"Tommy, damn it!"

"All right, all right—the chick doesn't know how to walk, so like most, she leads with some part of the anatomy. Some chicks lead with the boobs . . . look like they're falling over frontward. This chick leads with the grumper."

I still didn't understand.

"But what's a . . ."

". . . grumper? Why my dear girl, how sadly your education in the language has been neglected! The grumper, my child, is a portion of the female anatomy. Indeed, some consider it the *most* female portion of that delicious configuration. It is located in the fuselage, just aft of the baggage compartment. . . ."

"*Okay!* Enough already, I get it."

"I just *knew* you would." He was leering now, and—darn my puritan-glanded ancestors!—I could feel myself blushing. But at least I had found out what poor old Mr. Dahlberg wanted to know. I turned back toward the forward section to tell him about it . . . and then stopped again as another question hit me.

"Well, then," I said to Tommy, "if you're not back here to make a pass at Mr. Dahlberg's girl friend—what are you doing, anyway?"

He shrugged and tilted his cap back down over his eyes.

"The kid's sitting in," he answered.

"Kid?"

"Valentine's weirdo son. Thinks he's some kind of Junior Birdman or something. Came up a while ago and stuck his head into the office and asked Malnic if there'd be any chance of his sitting in the idiot-seat for a while."

"What for?"

"Oh, he's had a little time, I guess—had the Commercial Airman's Ticket right with him. Showed it to the boss. . . ."

"And Captain Malnic okayed it?"

"Why not?" he shrugged sleepily. "It's not a regular passenger run and sure as hell his old man's not going to turn in a beef because his squirt flew the airplane for a minute or two."

"I don't think he looks weird," I said.

The eye under the cap opened a bit to look at me again. "Says which?"

"Weird. You said he was a weirdo and called him a squirt. I thought he was kind of a nice-looking guy."

The head and the cap wagged sadly.

"Never," he said. "Never, never, *never* will I be able to understand the vagaries of feminine taste, Funny Face."

"And that," I cut him off, "is just what's wrong with your own little obsolescent, *un*candescent, adolescent mating call—*Sneaky Hands!*"

I turned quickly, to cut off any comeback he may have had in mind, and gave a little extra twitch with the empennage to create a kind of special snap in the miniskirt. Only I cut it out after about one step, when I remembered what he'd said about girls *leading* with one part of the body or another.

Irving Dahlberg might really have been wanting me to go pry "my" copilot off his mistress—but what he'd *asked* me to do was check the john and see if she needed any help. And, thinking about it, I realized she *had* been in there a long time.

So I turned back a step or two, and tapped on the door.

"Miss duMain," I said, loudly enough to be heard through the paneling.

No answer.

"Miss duMain? . . ."

There was a brief pause. And then I heard a faint "Yes?"

"Mr. Dahlberg was wondering if you needed anything." Union Airlines stews are tactful, courteous, and considerate. They also carry out orders . . . on occasion.

"Who . . . is it?" the voice behind the door asked after another pause.

"The stewardess. Mr. Dahlberg wanted . . ."

". . . Oh yes! You're Sandy, aren't you?" The girl's voice seemed to have recovered its strength in the last couple of moments. I wondered how in the world she'd managed to remember my name.

"That's right," I said. "Can I get you anything?"

"Uh . . . wait. Just a minute out there. Please."

Well! How about that? For once the old stewardess instinct had failed; Mr. Dahlberg really *had* wanted to see if she needed some help. Maybe she really had something wrong with her. I made a mental vow to see about changing the Hallowell habit of judging people on short acquaintance and the Hallowell tendency to see subtle, underlying meanings in perfectly straightforward conversation.
. . .

"All right." The exterior handle on the door snapped from *occupied* to *vacant,* meaning it had been unlocked from the inside. "All right—come in. And close the door behind you, huh?"

The door swung inward. I started to follow . . . and stopped in my tracks.

Miss Grumper had been well named. The dear child had arranged a touching tableau for my benefit:

At rise of curtain (or should I say swing of door?) we discover her center rest room, perched fetchingly upon the washbasin. The brief (but oh-so-costly) skirt of her traveling dress has been arranged tastefully about her tiny waist. Her pantyhose (and whatever else she may have been wearing) have been removed and draped gracefully over the toilet. Miss duMain, though technically sitting, is also semi-reclining with head and shoulders propped against the wall in what she must (God bless her revolting little heart!) have honestly considered a seductive pose, the better to expose the pudendum. It was smooth-shaven, and somewhat agape inasmuch as her legs were quite widely spread.

Well sir, then, there, now . . . it is not often, friends and feller Amurcuns, that The Hallowell finds herself at a loss for words. She has well and truly been known to find something to say when being (a) accosted by a mugger in broad daylight on Park Avenue (b) informed by a certain gentleman that he really *hadn't* had a vasectomy, as he had claimed in a moment of heat, and (c) handed a personal astrological chart that contained one bit of information calculated to shake the hardiest of souls.

In all these and many other situations, I repeat, The Hallowell has never failed to find a comeback which could be termed—at worst—passable.

But this time, buddy, I was stumped.

So all the honors went to the charming Miss duMain . . . who discharged them in this wise:

"Do you," she inquired in a low-key husk and with a pretty flutter of false eyelashes, "want to eat it now—or later?"

Hoo-boy.

Say this for The Hallowell: stuck for an answer she may have been. But incapable of appropriate action she was not.

With what I fondly hoped was a firm and professional hand, I gripped the door handle, took a single step backward and closed the door with a solid, but nonemotional click. Then resisting the temptation to search out some means of sealing it up forever, I wheeled calmly about and proceeded with casual élan to walk smack into the nearest bulkhead.

Well . . . gee, fellers.

Gee whiz!

That's why I quit nursing and signed on for stewardess training, right? Glamour. Excitement. Exotic adventure among the clouds. Anyway, something a little more stimulating than a daily routine of bedpan-use reports and overnight-medication orders. New places. Break out of the rut. That was the whole idea, wasn't it?

So . . . what was my complaint?

No complaint, boss! No complaint. Stewardess Sandra Hallowell reports herself in fine condition; all systems operative, commitment and takeoff velocities calculated and checked, ready for taxiing permission . . . only . . . what the *hell* kind of an answer did that drippy little dike think she was going to get from me?

And why *me,* in particular?

A tiny but nasty-feeling worm of suspicion was inching around in the Hallowell psyche.

Lesbian. Sandy Hallowell, *lesbian.*

Well, now: how does *that* sound, honeybunch? No— don't sniff it off. *Think* about it. You're a grown girl, now. God knows, you've probably had the right background.

Yes, the background. Big family, your family. Big—and all-male, except for Little Sister Sandy. Not even a mother around the house for Sandy to talk to; not even a mother to remember, because she died having you. (Did poor Dad resent that; did he feel, even unconsciously, that I was to

32

blame for her death? If he did, the sweet old bear sure made a good job of keeping it hidden. God, but I wish I could talk to him for a few minutes, sometimes. *God* . . . hey, now, Hallowell—cut that out! Stick to the subject!) Just men and boys around the house, Dad and my seven big brothers. Did I, maybe, have a little subconscious thing of my own going there—wishing I was a boy, too?

Did I?

Well . . . no. *No,* doggone it; the truth is I thought it was a pretty good deal for me, being a girl. Dad would *whomp* any of the boys who got out of line, but never once did he raise a hand to Sandy. Not even when Sandy was being especially impossible . . . like the time I wouldn't let him or anyone else kill Tom Turkey (that bird was my *friend;* and hadn't he always told me to defend my friends?) for Thanksgiving dinner. We had eggs for Thanksgiving that year, but Tom lived to a ripe old age. And especially the time I walked in (all of 16 years old, but able to pass for 18 and a good hand at forging birth certificates) to announce that Bob Frampton and I were married. . . .

Poor Dad. How he must have wanted to snatch me across his knee and give me the first—and best—*whomping* of my life! He knew, he *must* have known, what Bob was really like. And what it was probably going to take to get me out of the mess I had managed to get myself into.

But I was a girl—*his* girl—so what was to do about it? Keep the voice down. Keep the words calm and the questions logical. Get at the *truth,* and decide what to do about it. And pay the bills.

For the lawyer, to get the annulment.

For the doctor, to get the abortion.

And for Sandy, to get her into nursing school at the end of summer vacation. All right, then—the abortion and all that went with it. Did *that* turn you off, as far as men were concerned? Did it? *Hah!*

One of the good things about nursing school was that it gave Sandy access to information—and medication—to keep accidents like Bob Frampton from turning into a population explosion. But, turn me *off* with men? Funny. Funn-*eee!* What was that old line of Gypsy Rose Lee's? "I've liked boys ever since I found out I wasn't one."

Yessir. Me and Gypsy. . . .

Dad *did* make one strictly male-viewpoint observation,

though. And it stuck: "A woman's value—to herself—seems to decrease in direct proportion to the number of masculine hands that have gripped her *too casually* by the buttocks."

*Too casually.* That was the phrase Dad stressed, and that was the part that stuck. Odd, the way city people will think a farmer's got to be a hayseed; a rube, a hick, a clod-hopper. Dad was a farmer, sure—a farmer with a master's degree in agronomy; ten years with the Department of Agriculture before he met mother and decided a farm was a better place to raise a family than the city. A farmer who spent one day a week each winter either teaching or taking courses at the state university. A farmer who wrote poetry, sometimes; published in *Harper* or *The Atlantic Monthly.*

So, then—on the question of Sandy the *dike?* Answer: On the basis of the best information available at this moment Sandy, The Hallowell, is nonlezzy and nondikey—recent suggestion to the contrary notwithstanding.

So there.

(And remind me to take a good, long, hard look at myself in the mirror next time I get the chance. Maybe there's *something* I'm doing or wearing or saying that really *does* give people that idea.)

Now then . . . what was I supposed to be . . . oh-ho! Oops!

Excuse it, please, ladees and gennulmen—The Hallowell has been confusing herself with the paying passengers. Again. (Lordy, I have *got* to break myself of the habit of daydreaming on duty!) Poor old Mr. Dahlberg is still sitting up there alone, and probably wondering if the dumb stew he sent to check on his girl friend fell into the same guilty liaison she did. *Get it in gear,* Hallowell! . . .

"Mr. Dahlberg?"

He looked up, almost with a startled reaction. (And where have *your* thoughts been a-wandering, Mr. D.?) I smiled my brightest for him.

"Miss duMain is just fine," I told him. "I spoke to her through the door. She'll be back in a moment or two."

The expression on his face didn't change.

All right. It was the best I could do. For now. Poor old guy—he wasn't *really* going to be reassured so long as Sneaky Hands Newton was back there . . . and I couldn't think of any way on earth to give him that extra little smidgin of information that would allay his concern. So,

34

okay. Next project: get Sneaky Hands back up on the flight deck where he belonged. . . .

Which meant a quick trip up to the Front Office.

I smiled again at Mr. Dahlberg, and started up the aisle for a quick-but-pointed word with Our Esteemed Leader, Captain Malnic. Tough, cynical old pelican, our captain. But any stewardess on the line can tell you he is one. . . .

## Buddy Valentine

. . . hell of a good airline pilot.

Which is a much different thing from just being "a good pilot," or so I have been told by people who ought to know. "A good pilot," my first instructor told me once, "is a man who doesn't blow his cool when the situation seems to be getting out of hand. A good *airline* pilot is a man who doesn't let the situation get out of hand in the first place. The test of a good airline pilot is that he never has any thrilling stories to tell."

And that instructor wasn't guessing. He was a copilot—for United, I think—at the time; picking up some extra money to pay for the Piper Apache he was buying. Finally made captain, I heard. Good for him.

Personally, I would settle—no contest—for a chance to fly copilot, with this captain or any other captain that would have me, on this airline or any other.

Fly?

Face it, Buddy—Buddy baby—you would settle for anything that would get you out of the bag you're into right now, wouldn't you? Pilot. Or baggage handler. Or street sweeper. Or bum. You'd settle for just one month being just about *anything* but what you are:

Buddy Valentine.

Johnny Valentine, Jr., with a big accent on the "Junior." The production model, not the prototype; the follow-on system.

"Let me know next time we pass through our assigned altitude, huh? I like to keep track of these things."

*Oh, shit!*

"Sorry."

Typical. Just typical. Right, Buddy-boy? Noodge in up here and stiff the captain into letting me fly the airplane because I never flew anything with four engines before, and then sit around on my duff, stargazing and letting the airplane wander all over the sky instead of tending to business. Typical.

"We're coming up on Scottsdale VOR. Time to check in with Traffic Control. Get a new clearance; we'll be leaving Victor-19 there and changing altitude."

"Yes, sir."

I went through the standard instrument sweep with my eyes, and then risked a look over at Captain Malnic. He was just sitting there; face telling me nothing. Okay, so ask:

"Want the controls back?"

I tried to make it sound casual.

A shrug. "Want to give them back?"

"No, sir."

"Think you can handle the turn and the descent? It's got to be precise—right on the money."

Take a deep breath.

"Yes, sir. I'd like to try that."

"Oh?" A flicker of expression on that owl face; first one I've noticed. "Well, I got no interest in you *trying*. We either *do* it, or we don't. Which'll it be?"

"I'll *do* it."

"Okay. . . ."

Why the hell is there sweat on my hands? Listen, I've got better than 700 hours, total logged time. A multiengine rating. A commercial ticket in prime shape. A jet rating. Instrument card, all valid and up-to-date. My coordination is top drawer. I do *not* panic in emergencies—well, not anymore than any other red-blooded American boy, according to the instructors—and I am said to have a solid, workmanlike approach to the business of flying an airplane.

But my hands are sweating. And I will bet that before I complete the upcoming maneuver, a relatively simple one under most circumstances, I will have sweat on my forehead and the end of my nose as well. I can feel it coming.

". . . is Union niner-niner-five reporting Scottsdale VOR. Request permission for descent to . . ."

Captain Malnic. Smooth and unconcerned on the radio. I wonder if he's really as cool as all that? After all, if anything—anything at all—should go wrong while I am sitting over here in the idiot seat, whether I'm actually in control of the airplane or not, it's *his* ass. His ass is grass, and here

36

comes the lawnmower. Forty-five, fifty thousand a year they pay him to sit over there in the left seat. That's what he's risking, letting me sit over here on the right.

Time to begin descent; there's the permission from Traffic Control. And here we go. What were those descent power settings again? He had me work them out before he would let me take the airplane off autopilot . . . oh, yes. Okay, now: steady hands on the yoke. Precise turn to the new heading—two-six-oh degrees. Easy; keep off the rudder pedals; this is a 707, not a little Lear. It's not an airplane for rudder control under normal . . . normal . . . normal . . . ah! Smooth as a baby's butt: two-six-oh, now . . .

"Power back to five-five percent."

"Power."

The captain's hand is a lot steadier than yours, Buddy-boy. No sweat, and firmly back. Let your nose drop to descent attitude. . . .

"Flaps, ten."

"Ten."

Hold it there. Hold it. Heavy; but not too heavy. I can . . .

"It's easier if you trim to attitude. We'll be in this configuration for another—uh—seven minutes. But suit yourself."

Hoo-boy. Of course, of course; they put these little goodies in the airplane for intelligent pilots to use. Smart pilots use trim for continued attitudes; dumb pilots use brawn. Where's that pickle-switch? Now: two turns up. There! Easy. See how she rides. Almost; not quite. By hand this time . . . up an inch or two. More. A quarter turn. Half . . . there!

Rate of descent. Altitude. Power. Course.

"Flies like a truck, doesn't it?"

Well . . . glory be! The man can even smile; just half of his face, the half with the cut scar under the eye. And it's gone in a moment. But it really was there. Pin a medal on Buddy-boy! . . .

Rate of descent. Altitude. Power. Course.

"Lots of snow on the Rockies. You notice? Real White Christmas for those people." Quiet tone. Casual. Just passing the time of day with me after he's risked everything he's got on a guess about whether I am an airplane pilot or a four-flusher. No wonder this guy wears four gold rings on the uniform sleeve. That kind of cool is worth every penny of the fifty thou.

Fifty thou. That's a good deal more than they pay Buddy Valentine, the rising young singing star. For sure, man. Club dates for Buddy Valentine. Big publicity push for Buddy Valentine. Special orchestrations for Buddy Valentine. But very damn little money for Buddy Valentine, the rising young . . . *phony.*

Yes, indeedy. That is the word: *Phony.* Capital P. Buddy Valentine has a Voice? Sure he does—sometimes he sounds almost like his Old Man. Almost. Buddy Valentine has special orchestrations? Sure he does—by the same arranger who always did them for his Old Man. And they are almost as good. Almost. And *look* at Buddy Valentine. Look at him! Look how he tries to look like his Old Man, even though he really looks like his mother. And look at the way Buddy Valentine moves. And talks. And smiles. Almost exactly like his Old Man. Almost. Almost. . . .

So?

So . . . why doesn't it ever quite seem to come off?

You know, Buddy-boy. You know. That is the difference between the Old Man and you. That is the difference between Captain Malnic and you. Those guys are real. You are a phony. You are . . . oops!

*Rate of descent. Altitude. Power. Course.*

Coming down on the new assigned altitude. "Power to cruise."

"Power." The captain's hand advanced the thrust levers.

He had been just sitting there. Waiting to see if I'd goof it; let the airplane drop through the floor. Yes, and I would have done it, too, if I hadn't waked up just when I did. There is a response lag on all airliners. Only by the merest chance did I happen to snap out of it in time to make the maneuver look like I'd planned it that way. . . .

Pickle-switch: nose down, two-and-one-half turns.

"Up flaps."

"Up."

Okay, now. Easy. Wait for it to decide; all right. A little fine trim. Attitude correct . . . rate of descent, zero. *Right on* the indicated-and-assigned.

Power and course. . . .

"I'm sorry Captain; could I speak to you a moment?" The blonde stewardess, the one whose legs I had noticed when we came aboard, was bending over the captain's seat. I almost jumped out of my skin. Where the hell had she come from? And how long had she been behind us?

"Sure." The captain seemed casual enough; maybe he'd noticed her earlier. He grinned that half-face grin of his again. "What's the problem, kid? My esteemed junior colleague making with the hands again?"

Well, I'll be damned! I thought I would never live to see the day: a real, live, honest-to-Jesus *blush!*

Well-well-well! . . .

"Something like that." Her eyes made a quick darting motion in my direction (and I noticed, because of the blush maybe, that they were an unusual color; a true green, and deep like the inside of that emerald the Old Man gave Ma two years ago), and I guess that was to indicate she wanted to talk outside my range of hearing. But the captain didn't take the hint.

"Speak up," he said. "Go ahead—no secrets on the flight deck."

She still hesitated. So he laid it out for her.

"He's a professional," he said, quirking his head at me. "Don't treat him like the paying passengers. Talk up, girl!"

Oh . . . wow. I mean: wow! Just like that. "He's a professional." From this guy. So what? Who cares what a dumb-ass airplane driver thinks? What does it matter? I care, man. *I care.* And why? Because, man, it is the first time that . . .

"All right. If you say so, Captain." There was just a hint of extra emphasis on that last word; enough to let the boss know it was on his head, not hers. "I think Mr. Dahlberg is worried about Sneaky Hands making a pass at his playmate. He's getting nervous."

Captain Malnic nodded judiciously. "I can see where he might," he said. "Does he have any real cause for alarm?"

I'll be damned if the girl didn't blush *again!*

"If you mean, has Sneaky Hands put the make on her yet, the answer is no. She's been locked in the women's john ever since he got back there."

"Uh-huh." The captain nodded again, but said no more. He seemed to be waiting for the girl (her nameplate said she was "Sandy" I just *happened* to notice by turning my head so far to the left I was afraid I'd get a permanent kink in my neck) to say something else.

"And," she went on finally, "if you're wondering whether or not he'll score when she does come out, I would have to give you a fairly definite 'no' there, too. In fact, a very definite 'no.' She doesn't go for . . ."

Sandy stopped herself, with another glance at me.

"Speak up. You're among friends." The captain still seemed unperturbed, staring out at the horizon through the windscreen.

"Nothing." It was something, all right; but Sandy-the-stewardess had said as much as she was going to say.

The captain raised and lowered his brows and took a deep sniff of air through his nose. He expelled the air as an audible sigh. "But," he said then, "Dahlberg the Great is still uneasy. All right. Go back and tell Superwolf Junior to drag his tail back up front."

Sandy smiled at him. And then at me. And let me tell you, boys and girls, that was some kind of smile, all right. *For sure!* They say my Old Man's smile is like that; his face opens up and you forget what he looks like, really, and the room kind of gets brighter. Truth: I never did really notice it, myself, though I would rather he would smile at me than just—well—*look* at me, the way he usually does. But this smile from Sandy-the-stewardess was like that smile is supposed to be; yeah, just like that . . . plus two pitchers, a catcher, and a utility outfielder.

I just sat there, looking at the empty space where the smile had been, after she had turned away and disappeared through the door back into the cabin.

Then I concentrated on flying the airplane for a while.

Of course, it didn't make one damn bit of sense for me to be flying it—I mean, *really* flying it—in the first place. Once you've reached an assigned altitude and normalized heading and power, it's SOP to engage the autopilot; it can hold the ship on course far more expertly than anything that breathes or thinks. The captain was just being nice and charitable, letting me sit in the right seat and play intrepid birdman with a bigger and heavier (and, probably, faster) piece of equipment than I could ever hope to guide on my own.

And that bit about "professional." That was a *real* exercise in tact and charity. Buddy Valentine, "professional pilot." Buddy Valentine, professional . . . self-kidder. But still it was nice of . . .

*"Tired of flying, friend?"*

The copilot had entered the flight deck quietly; I hadn't heard him come in. And the words were innocuous enough, in themselves. But there was something in the way he said them; something that made me almost believe he had been able to read my thoughts for a minute. I forced myself to keep my eyes front; check the horizon, scan the instruments. *Altitude. Power. Heading. . . .*

"Nope. Not a bit."

The captain didn't say anything. But the copilot kept leaning, breathing on my neck. I got the picture, and snapped the armrest up to let me get out of his seat.

"No hurry," the captain said then, not putting a plus or a minus on his tone and not looking in our direction. "Tommy can sit in the engineer's position."

Well, it was a temptation. *Buddy Valentine, Intrepid Birdman.* I'm not proud; I would like to have stayed up there, kidding myself, for as long as I could get away with it. But . . . hell. If I did, I would know the copilot was sitting behind me doing a slow burn and criticizing every single move I made. And I get plenty of that in my life without looking for anymore. Besides, why turn a good experience into a bad one?

"No. I think I'll go back and rejoin the troops." I hope I kept the tone as light and unconcerned as I had intended it to be. "Thanks for the . . . everything."

I got out of the seat and edged past the copilot. It was over.

"Don't mention it," the captain said. I started to move aft. But he wasn't quite done. "By the way," he said, with plenty of nothing still in his voice, "if you've got your logbook with you, I'd be glad to sign you off for an hour's dual in the equipment."

Nothing special.

Just a simple, straightforward offer—like from one pilot to another. Just a simple little thing like that.

Well, I *didn't* have the logbook along. And I knew I didn't really rate confirmation of an hour's dual instruction on the 707 either. And the captain knew that, too. But what he'd said didn't have anything to do with any of those things. It was nothing, and it was plenty. And he knew it. And I knew it. And he knew I knew it.

"Thanks," I said. And I almost had to duck down getting out the door from the flight deck to the cabin because I was, all of a sudden, ten feet tall.

Oh, yeah.

For sure.

And out there, facing the door as though she had been waiting for me, just to make the day complete, was the Sandy-stewardess.

Well, hell.

What does a man do when he's ten feet tall and has got the world by the tail and it is the morning of Christmas Eve and a gorgeous girl with a light-up-the-room smile and a really great bod is waiting for him after he gets done slaying the first dragon he can remember putting down in many-too-many years?

Does he say, "Hey, baby! Let's you and me slosh down a little quick booze at the terminal when we get down and then go and offend the fates of Christmas Eve by throwing billiard balls at the moon and flying kites in two-room apartments. Like, say, *my* apartment! . . ."

He does, if he's my Old Man.

Johnny Valentine, the Velvet Voice, the superstud of Superstudsville . . . he could deliver the line and the answer would be yes. Even if he was half-drunk and the chick had something else lined up for Christmas Eve, the answer would be yes. Sure. You know it, baby.

So what does *Buddy* Valentine do? Smooth, suave, assured, talented scion of wealth and advantage, what does Buddy Valentine do? What else: he smiles a smile at her that feels like half-melted ice cream on the nose and chin, draws in a deep breath and closes the throat a little (to be sure of sounding *just* like his Old Man), takes a step toward that lovely thing and . . . trips over his own feet.

For a wonder, I didn't fall flat right there in the aisle. But what I *did* do was catch myself on the side of a seat and ricochet in the Great Circle navigational manner—a full half-orbit that ended, God help me, with a solid 165-pound head-on comic-strip-goat-*butt* into the lovely midsection of the Sandy-stewardess.

Unfortunately, she wasn't exactly expecting an approach like that. I mean, it caught her off-guard and unbraced, with the result that we landed in the passenger seat next to where she had been standing. With me sitting in her lap.

Oh, wow.

As pickup technique goes, you know, I have got to say it did obtain her undivided attention. For sure. Whatever I said, my next words would register. So what sexy, compelling phrase did I utter? What surefire score line? What gem of sophistication?

"Ghoor!" I said.

Oh-well-for-the-love-of-Christ, Valentine! *"Ghoor!"* Who in the hell ever told you that you were a swinger? Who in the hell ever told you that you were . . . *anything* . . . except a goddamn slapstick comedian?

"Excuse me, sir," said the Sandy-stewardess, "but will you have coffee, tea . . . or me?"

Oh, lady.

I couldn't help it. I started to laugh; damn it, there I was with several crates of egg on my chin, my full weight obviously crushing the poor girl to a paper-thin pulp, and I burst into a cackle of laughter clearly audible at the next cleared-altitude level and varying in pitch between baritone and castrato soprano. Sometimes, I mean it, I think I must be some kind of a maniac.

Weird thing, though: she was laughing, too.

And there we sat, for God's sake, for at least a minute or so (if you want to know, it would have been a lot longer if I could have arranged it) laughing like idiots.

Finally, of course, I got it together enough to manhandle myself up and off her and back onto my feet. I even managed to stand on them without some new kind of clown business, and to say something intelligible.

"I'm terribly sorry," I said, offering a hand to get her up on the chance that she wasn't permanently disabled. "I hope you're not hurt."

"Me? Not a bit." Her hand was warm and dry and firm on mine, and I was sort of relieved to notice she didn't really need its help getting out of the seat.

She stood up, took a deep breath, grinned—not a wide, light-up-the-room grin I'd noticed earlier, but a nice grin all the same—and straightened the jacket of her uniform.

"Us stews," she said, "are built for durability. If we

weren't, we wouldn't last long. Really, though . . . is there anything I can get *you?*"

Yes, lady, I wanted to say. Yes, lady, you can get me a date with you tonight, for Christmas Eve, and I promise I will not knock a bowl of eggnog into your lap.

Yes, lady, you can get me a magnum of self-respect and a jeroboam of confidence and just a shot glassful of brains to go with them.

Yes, lady, you can get me a career where I don't feel like an imitation and a phony and a midget all the time, one with a future I can give a real damn about, and see myself enjoying.

Yes, lady, you can get me a different family and a different background and a different Christmas Day to look forward to from *this* one, that makes me wish for January.

Yes, lady, and while you're about it . . . you can get me a personality that lets me do something about a pretty girl besides knock her down, sit in her lap, and say "Ghoor!" to her.

All that thought, of course, took about half a second.

I must have mumbled something at her, because she gave me a little nod, and the same grin again, and said, "Well, all right then. If you're sure. But let me know if there's anything."

"Coffee, tea, or . . . anything?"

Well! Not much of a line, but that much I *did* manage. And she picked up on it.

"Well," she said, and this time the smile was the big kind, "well, *almost* anything. . . ."

And she turned away. And was gone.

Okay.

Okay, Buddy-boy, okay. You acquitted yourself in your usual manner. Now let's see if you can find someplace to sit down without breaking someone's leg. . . .

The little scene in the front part of the cabin hadn't gone unnoticed by any of the others, naturally. The duMain cooz had apparently found her way back from the john while I was still up front; she and Dahlberg had their eyes on me like a pair of shotgun barrels.

I walked past them, and the Old Man was looking at me—with a great deal of *nothing* in the famous Valentine face, as is usual when he is looking at his only son. He made that swirl gesture with the ice in his glass meaning, I think, that he expected me to sit down beside him. Normally, I would have been sort of flattered; the Old Man does not generally seek out the company of his son-and-foremost-imitator.

Only, for right that moment, the hell with it.

And all of them.

I kept moving until I was several seat ranks behind, where they'd have to turn their heads if they wanted to keep on staring, and sat down in the seat nearest the window to make myself invisible. All right, then; all right, Buddy-boy. Now: what was all that stuff you were thinking, back there a couple of seconds ago?

Sort it out:

*Self-respect.* I have self-respect, don't I? Sure I do. Sure. But . . . do I? Listen, I'm not a swinger and a household name like the Old Man yet, but I'm coming along okay. It takes time—that's what Sam LoCicero always says to me—it takes time; to build the image, time to . . . to . . . what?

Sam is my godfather. My *padrino.* Also, he's the Old Man's lawyer and business manager and, I think, best friend. So would the *padrino* lie to me? Would he?

You bet your sweet ass he would.

You, Buddy-boy, Buddy-baby, Buddy-love, *you* have about as much chance of making it to the top in the music business—as a singer, anyway; the Kinfolk thing could be a new start—as a tone-deaf pygmy with laryngitis. Face it; you're a singer because everyone expected you to be one (well, Ma anyway, and in my family that means everyone). And they hire you, even the toilets Sam the *padrino* has been able to book you into, only because you are Johnny Valentine's son. On your own, you'd be playing the swank elevator shaft of the Nowhere Hilton, in beautiful downtown Ulan Bator.

How in the hell can anyone—you included—respect a slob like that?

All right. What else?

*Family and Christmas.* I love my parents and they love me; I am flying all the way across the country and paying some stiff appearance-clause penalties to the club so I can spend Christmas Day with them. It'll be great to have us

all together again. Ma. And the Old Man. And the *padrino*.
Joy to the World; God Rest Ye Merry; Gloria in Excelsis
. . .

Crap.

Christmas with the Family will be like last year and the
year before that and all the other years I can remember:
Ma will be doing the cooking, good, traditional Italiano
Christmas stuff, because the Old Man's going to be there,
and she'll be wearing half of some overpriced store's stock
of overpriced jewelry because the Old Man gave it to her
and she wants him to know she appreciates it, and he'll
already have had all the presents sent over from every store
in Beverly Hills and he'll get there a little bit late and
watch like a king while we all tell him how great he is and
what a wonderful father he is and how terrific and thoughtful the presents are and Buddy boy will be right there
slobbering it up. Why would *this* year be different?

Only it will be. Because Ma and Sam, they know what's
going on back in New York (how could they *not* know?)
with him and Dolly the blue-and-white Diamond. And
Ma will be looking for some edge, some opening to stick
the knife into *that*, because for what else, for Christ sake,
has she prayed to the Madonna and her Son for every night
for nearly twenty years but that the Old Man will remember he's her husband, like she's never forgotten she's his
wife, no matter what the court and everyone else in the
whole damn world says. And the Old Man will tell her it's
not true; just rumors and doesn't she know enough not to
listen to a lot of rumors from the liars.

If I didn't love them. If I didn't feel anything for them.
If I didn't care what happened to them—Jesus, if only I
didn't—if only, if only. But that is how it is going to be and
I have been careful not to think about it for a month, now,
and I wish it was January.

There goes the Sandy-stewardess again, up the aisle with
another belt for the Old Man. Chivas Regal and soda. For
sure. Hand him the full one; take back the empty. A little
casual chatter from him, that I can't hear, but we've been
in the air now how long . . . three hours? nearer four . . .
so at his standard computed rate that means he has had
six stiff ones. And no breakfast because we took off early
and I know how he looks when he's had a long shower and

six cups of black coffee and a shave from the hotel barber instead of sleep the night before. As usual. So the diction will be a little more precise and the early-sixties jive talk will be a little thicker (for the Old Man it will always be the early sixties) and she will smile that big smile for him and that will be the ball game because he is sure as hell going to be at loose ends tonight and he'll ask her to . . .

How about that!

No big smile from the Sandy-stewardess; no nod of the head to him. Just the turn-around and back down the aisle with the empty glass in her hand. *Get up, idiot! Get up and* . . . aw, hell. I heard the voice yelling in my head. I knew what to do. But did I do it? . . .

What is it, Buddy-boy? What is it about that chick? Great legs; great bod. Kind of a different face, pretty, but not Monarch Pictures pretty, not enough nose, too much mouth maybe, kind of a tilt in that green eye. What?

With chicks I'm not always a cipher. What the hell, one big favor the Old Man did for mo  and at just the right time, too; when I was first beginning to notice a little extra nervousness, a little heat in the groin when I was around them—he showed me about chicks. At least, he showed me what can be shown. That bim he set me up with, the one from Vegas, she looked like she couldn't be more than a couple, three years older than me (I found out later she was *thirty;* wow!) but she knew it all. Had to tell Ma we were going off camping (camping, for Christ sake; what a picture, the Old Man in a tent in the woods!) so I could have time to get rested up. She would have raised hell and jammed a prop under it if she knew I spent the week shacked at the Tahoe cabin. But it did the work; like the Old Man said, that bim turned me *out!* . . .

From that time on, there was never any big hassle about getting laid, you know? I knew the score; not even a problem about money. You can't hack a habit like chicks on the kind of allowance Ma would give me—not with the ideas *she* had about money and age—but the Old Man was always there, at the other end of any telephone line I had to use, long-distance or local; tell him the problem, describe the chick (he always wanted to know what the chick was like) and bang! Go over to the *padrino's* office and an envelope would be waiting.

47

Funny: You tell some straight-arrow about that, he'd start using words like "corrupting youth" and "juvenile delinquency." What a lot of crap! The Old Man knew what he was doing. And, wow! Didn't I have proof—didn't I?

How many guys do I know, guys my age or maybe younger even, got into a big screaming hassle, two families pulling and hauling, over some high-school chick. She'd get knocked up, or have hysterics all over her mother about how she was "ruined" by so-and-so and, Christ, you'd think the sky was falling down.

"Stay away from *them!*" That's what the Old Man told me after that first time with the bim, there at Tahoe. "Stay away from the little high-school dollies. I know—they're ready, and they look like they'd be a hell of a lay. The young cooz always looks like that, and, I guess, maybe, some of them would even be as good as they look.

"But they're *trouble*. They take that kind of jazz serious; you say something and they think you *mean* it. Their mamas coach them—trade it in for a lifetime meal ticket. And that's what they're thinking about all the time you're in the kip with them. *Nice* girls, see? Nice girls . . . hell, yes . . . and some day you'll finally even *marry* one of them, because that's the kind you marry. And that's just exactly why you don't put the make on them now, you dig? Right! So stick to the other kind. And don't go all baby-faced on me, sonny-boy; you know the difference. . . ."

That's what he said. And he knew. For sure.

(Funny. You know, that's the same damn thing Ma laid on me, four years later, when she got to worrying because I was having a lot of dates with that one chick—the director's daughter—and she was afraid I might try to ball her, I guess. "She's a nice girl," that's what Ma said. "She's a nice girl so you be a nice boy. If you got to be something else, find a girl who's *not* nice!" Yeah, funny. Who'd have thought the Old Man and Ma would agree about anything.)

But they were right. And it's always worked okay for me—so what the hell is so different about this Sandy-stewardess chick? Why the hell do I go acting like Bozo the Clown around her? How come I can't just pitch her for a couple of drinks when we get down?

*You know why, Buddy-boy. Buddy-baby. Buddy-love. You know. . . .*

Yeah, I know. Sure I do—not all of it. Not enough to stop it. But I know. With hookers, with semipros, with the sleep-around chicks I meet all the time; with them, I'm okay. No sweat. No stumble. No *"Ghoor!"* Not with them.

But with this Sandy-stewardess—with her, and with every other chick I ever met who didn't look and act like the finale number at the Pink Pussycat; with any chick who comes on like a grown-up woman instead of something out of a Playboy gatefold; with any chick who comes on like *people*—I automatically blow it. I automatically come on Slob. I become Instant Clown. Instant fourteen-year-old clown. . . .

Listen: here she comes again. Past you and down the aisle with a tray of little sandwiches and a drink—for the duMain cooz, it looks like. Yeah. All right! And now she's walking back on those far-out legs of hers. Walking by . . . Okay, Clown, up!

"Uh, *Sandy?*" Oh, wow! Now there is a great start, man. Great. But at least this time you didn't butt her in the belly; that's something. "What's your last name, Sandy?"

Another gem, but at least it's better than "Ghoor!"

"Hallowell." The small smile, not the big one. But who's complaining? "Why?"

"Well, I've got this rule, see. I never invite a stranger to a funeral, a wedding, a bar mitzvah—or to have a drink with me when the plane lands."

Another smile, but still the small one.

"Well, I guess I'm not a stranger, if you know my name."

"So consider yourself invited."

The smile got bigger.

"To all those things? Whew!"

"Well," I said, "maybe just the drink. For a starter. Hold the wedding and the funeral for later; the bar mitzvah, I can't guarantee. On the other hand, seeing it's Christmas Eve and all, maybe some dinner and a club or two would be a better idea. I—uh—don't invite strangers for that, either."

And this time I'm getting the big smile. Sometimes, Buddy-boy, I begin to think there *is* hope for you after all. . . .

"It sounds wonderful." The head on one side, but the big smile still not gone and the green-green eyes still aimed straight at me. "Tell me one thing. . . ."

"Sure."

". . . what day were you born?"

Huh?

"What—day?" I stammered.

"The date, I mean."

"Yes . . . uh . . . well, it was . . . uh, January 16."

"Oh." Just the syllable. No inflection. Followed by a one-beat pause while the eyes were still on me but not looking at me and I could almost hear clickity-clickity-click as she ran something over the course in her mind. I couldn't pick up on any of this. At all.

"Capricorn," she said finally, and the eyes were looking at me again and the big smile still hadn't slipped. "Thank you very much. It was a sweet offer . . ."

(Yeah. Sweet. But. I could see it coming—the next word just *had* to be "but.")

". . . but I really did promise to do something else to-night . . ."

Sure. And there stood Buddy-boy, the noted clown, with mixed egg and custard pie on his face. No sale. After all that, no sale. Wow.

"Sure," the clown said, and I could hear the fourteen-year-old in his voice as he tried to sound casual as hell. "Sure; I dig. Christmas Eve. I should have thought of that. Funny, in showbiz you kind of forget what time of year it is unless you're a comic and need seasonal material. I don't. In fact, I can't sing Christmas stuff; leave it to old Crosby records . . ." (*Jee-sus!* I was chattering away like an idiot. I couldn't seem to stop!) ". . . and the King family, right? Well, catch your act next time, beautiful! Have a happy and a merry-merry. . . ."

I finally got my mouth stopped. If there had been any doubt in her mind about Buddy-boy being a grade B phony, the doubt was sure gone by now. What a lot of juvenile crapperoo! *"Showbiz,"* for Christ sake. *"Catch your act next time."* Wouldn't blame her if she laughed herself into a permanent state of hiccups!

But she wasn't laughing.

Instead, the eyes were still looking at me and I couldn't

50

quite read the expression in them. It was—almost—sort of like Ma used to look, sometimes, when I was just a kid and I'd hit my . . .

". . . two of my brothers," she was saying; for some reason I hadn't really caught the first part of the sentence, "and it's the first time we've had a chance to see each other in three years. They're stopping off on their way back from Vietnam. In fact, I volunteered for this charter in order to get to Los Angeles at just the right time."

It took a minute to get the words through my head.

And then, for a wonder, it finally clicked: this Sandy chick was for real. That wasn't just a brush line she'd handed me, she *did* have something else she'd promised to do. And she was interested enough to try and get the point across to Buddy-the-clown. Who almost took too long to figure it out. . . .

She was just shifting the sandwich tray to turn away when I got it together enough to stop her.

"Look," I said, "how long are you going to be in L.A.?"

"Until day after tomorrow," she said, and the smile was back. "This special got me off the regular schedule."

"Great! And will your brothers be here all that time, too?"

"No. They're on orders and they want to stop off and see the rest of the family before they have to report, so they'll be on a late flight tonight."

"Well, then, how about spending Christmas Day with me?"

"But . . . won't you be spending it with your family?"

"That's what I mean" (Ma was going to have a nine-day-trembling-fit at me; so let her). "With us. Tell me where you're staying and I'll be over to pick you up in the morning. You ever have Italian cooking on Christmas?"

"No. . . . But—!"

"No buts! Nobody should be alone on Christmas Day." (Except maybe you and me, lovely; except maybe you and me, but this is the best I can do on the spur of the moment.) "Where are you staying?"

She was still hesitating.

"Please," I said. "I don't want to be alone either."

I don't know where that came from; it just popped out.

"But you'll be with your family! . . ."

51

"That's right." I didn't take my eyes from hers; I couldn't. It felt like there was something I had to get across to her. Something I couldn't put into words. I'm not even sure what it was, but she seemed to feel it, too. "That's right; that's what I said. I don't . . . want to be alone. . . ."

The green eyes changed, then, and she nodded a little nod. But she still didn't say anything.

"Besides," I said, "I'm a Capricorn, right? You said so yourself. Doesn't that count?"

I guess it was the right thing to say.

She laughed.

And it was settled. She was staying at the Airport Marina Hotel; I would pick her up there at ten o'clock and bring her back in time to get comfortable before the Old Man made his Entrance. (I made another mental note to go out sometime after we touched down today and grab a couple of presents to stick in with the rest of the loot pile, for her.)

Okay.

All *right!*

She flickered off to get the Old Man another booze and soda, and Buddy-boy sank back against the seat cushions to relax, feel ten feet tall again (for the second time in one day! That was a kind of a record, you know? Most unheard-of thing I ever heard of!) and damn near forget to snap his seat belt as we began final letdown for the landing at LAX.

Looking out the cabin window, I could see Los Angeles unrolling ahead of the leading edge of the wing. There must have been a little wind, because the air was clear, no smog, and you could see the whole basin, from the Santa Monica mountains down to the Palos Verdes peninsula and over to Catalina Island.

The Airport Marina Hotel was dead ahead, hard by the runway we would be using to land.

I grinned like a fool. I couldn't stop it, even when it began to hurt. The landing was a real greaser; the captain must have been pretty pleased with himself, bringing it off like that in the crosswind I'd heard him warned about while I was sitting in the idiot seat. I wanted to go forward and congratulate him; shake his hand and maybe buy him a cigar. And one for that jerk of a copilot, too. I wanted to go up to where Dahlberg and the duMain

52

cooz were sitting and tell them they were beautiful people and I hoped they had enjoyed their flight. I wanted to pour an extra slug into the Old Man's booze and soda.

The cabin Muzak clicked on as soon as we were down and rolling off the runway toward the terminal buildings. It was playing Christmas carols; Union Airlines is nothing if not perceptive about the calendar.

But don't ask me which Christmas carols they were.

I was hearing my own.

Joy to the world. . . . Joy to the world. . . .

# The 2nd House

*Financial prospects, monetary affairs, material gains or losses—depending on the positioning of the planets on one's chart . . .*

---

*Forecast: With the moon in Cancer and Neptune touring Aries, it won't be long before everyone's pockets will either be weighed down with gold or so empty that the streets will be crowded with panhandlers.*

*David Strauss, star of stage, screen, and ESP, has longed for fame and glory from the moment he could read a marquee. But having finally reached that zenith, he finds himself searching for an elevator that will take him on an express trip down.*

*Now, as he enters the Second House, he may find what he's been searching for. . . .*

---

### David Strauss

The Scotch was good and went down easy, but it might as well have been colored water, or kerosene, as far as I was concerned. Some nights it just doesn't do the work. And this was getting to be one of those nights in one hell of a hurry.

I signaled the bartender for another.

Three hours I had been in here, in this nothing little bar a block back from Columbus Circle. And what had it got me?

55

Nothing.

I looked at my face in the bar mirror; the way I was sitting, my face just fit inside the Christmas wreath the owner had hung there. Send a Christmas card to a friend, friend. *David Strauss, star of stage, screen, and ESP, invites you and yours to have a merry, merry Christmas.*

See what a merry one he's having?

> God rest ye drunken gentlemen
> Let nothing ye dismay,
> You're gonna have a hang-o-ver
> All through your Christ-mas Day.

The empty glass changed places with a full one on the soppy cocktail napkin under my chin.

Have another Scotch-rocks, David, darling.

And merry Christ-mas.

### Bingle Jells.

The holly-wreathed face in the bar mirror turned away from the sight of itself and the head screwed around to look over a shoulder at the rest of the drunks in the room. There were plenty of them. And not a single face I recognized, or that recognized me. Which was great. Which was why I had picked the dump in the first place.

> Deck the halls with boughs of holly
> Fa-la-la-la-la-la-la-la-la.
> I'm in drag, and so is Dolly
> Fa-la-la-la-la-la-la-la-la.

Have another Scotch-rocks, David, dear.

Thank you, Doll, don't mind if I—huh? Now what the hell is going on? Damn glass is empty. Just the rocks and a little water. What? . . .

I didn't drink that.

Did I?

The head turned back around and framed itself again in the bar-mirror wreath. *David Strauss, star of stage, screen, and ESP, invites you and yours to go fuck yourselves.* Merrily. For Christmas.

The bartender caught my signal and brought—no—this time he brought the bottle over, poured the empty glass full, rang up the sale on my tab with his other hand. I started to lift the glass to my mouth, but couldn't quite get it framed right in that wreath on the mirror. It wouldn't fit.

Nothing ever fits.

A fleeting sensation of cold on the tips of my fingers told me I was spilling the Scotch. And acting like a ding.

> *Hark, the herald angels sing,*
> *David Strauss, the well-known ding.*

Have another Scotch-rocks, David, darling.

Thank you, Jack.

Jack! . . .

I tossed the cold Scotch down into my cold stomach (it wasn't cold a minute ago) and wished the damn bartender had left his damn bottle where I could get my damn hands on it.

Jack.

I looked at the face-in-the-wreath and looked away and looked at the other drunks in the bar and looked away and concentrated as hard as I could. On Dolly.

Only, it didn't work.

That's the bad thing, the worst thing, about it, I told myself, while another part of my mind (don't mind me, mind; just crack into as many pieces as you need) went searching through a list of faces to find one to stick in the empty place in the album of my mind where the picture of Dolly was missing. That's the worst thing about breaking up. I can't think of Dolly, that way, anymore. I can't use her to get rid of . . .

> *I'm dreaming*
> *Of a blight Christmas.*

Have another Scotch-rocks, David, dear.

Thank you, Dolly. Jeanne. Hulah. Mamie. Marilyn. Barbara. Natalie. Thank you. I don't mind if I do.

*David Strauss, star of stage, screen, and ESP, invites all of you to come and get laid.* All but you, Dolly. The hell with you. You don't get any nookie, because you have got better things to do with your time, don't you. Like a knob job for the Velvet Voice. . . .

For me, no.

For that guinea, yes.

57

Why?

I looked down and noticed the pattern of the rings on the bar top. Almost like that five-ringed (seven-ringed?) pattern they have for the Olympics. I studied the rings for a minute and then moved the glass to try and even them up. Tidy. That's David. Like to have everything just in order. Jack used to tell me . . .

No, damn it. No!

Suddenly it was time to get out of there. I fumbled in a couple of the wrong pockets for money and finally fished out a twenty. It was too much, of course, even at the rate I had been throwing the stuff down. I dropped it beside the still-full glass and gave the face in the wreath a big wink. It winked back—and my heart stopped for a beat or two because it was the wrong kind of wink. The wrongest I could possibly have seen right then. I knew that wink. I knew the smile that accompanied the wink.

Down on Times Square, that wink makes money. That wink and that smile.

It keeps conversation to a minimum. The young man winks that wink and smiles that smile at the mark, the older guy who cruises down there looking for an understanding soul he can take home with him. The only thing that gets said, the only word, is when the mark quotes the price. The young man can nod, then, or he can walk away, or he can smile a little more and wait for the price to go up. And sometimes it does. And sometimes it . . .

*Silent Night, Times Square Night,*
*See the fags, young and tight!*

Outside, the cold of the night hit me like a ton of frozen chicken fat. I thought of ducking back into the bar. But the wreath and the face and the wink would be in there, waiting for me, and I decided I would rather freeze to death.

Maybe a cab?

Hah. Fat chance!

Past midnight. How *far* past? Don't ask me, friend, I don't even work here. I'm a stranger in town myself. Past midnight in newyorkcity, borough of Manhattan, and now it is early hours of Christmas Day when all the world snuggles warm and rosy all safe in its bed while visions of sugarplums dance in its head. And the one, the only

David Strauss flounders along on ice-covered sidewalk with cold air cutting his larynx to ribbons.

Eyes front; keep the mind on the business at hand; concentrate on staying vertical to the plane of the earth. And finally I made it—the big goal—to Broadway.

Big deal.

If there was a cab, parked or moving, anywhere along the street, I couldn't focus on it.

I looked down the street in the direction of Times Square.

There just *had* to be a cab in Times Square.

And even if there wasn't, it was somewhere to go. A destination. Better than standing still in the cold and winding up after Christmas as a statue in some park.

For another two blocks, I managed to keep my mind disconnected.

Just one step at a time. *Step.* Move the other leg. *Step.* Move the other leg . . . *uff!* The next step was a little off-center and the new snowfall had covered a piece of ice some property owner should have got sued for and my foot slipped and I went through a quick series of morning setting-up exercises. I ended still on my feet, but at a dead halt. I looked around. Still no cab.

## DAVID STRAUSS

The movie house was dark and the cashier's cage was empty and the doors had a locked look, but the exhibitor had left the marquee lights burning. It made extra light on the soft whiteness around me and I looked at my name, up there, in the night.

> *Fame and fortune,*
> *Burning bright,*
> *In the forest*
> *Of the night.*

Have some fame and fortune, David, darling.

*Thank you, but I already have some.* Well, it was what you wanted, wasn't it? What you came for? Fame and fortune. Your name on the marquee. In lights.

Wasn't it?

I took a deep breath (I think my larynx is frozen; it doesn't hurt anymore) and started to move myself again when I noticed the other marquee, diagonally across the street.

59

Have another picture, David, dear.

Thank you, but I already have one, and it's running competition to the picture I made five days after I finished shooting the first one. What kind of nonsense is that?

Smart business, for all I know. David Strauss is suddenly a hot item on the movie marquees; if the competition is showing the first run of a David Strauss picture, why not nab onto the second run of a David Strauss picture and show it across the street to rake in some trade that wouldn't wait in line for . . .

*Stop that, Strauss!*

Stand here another minute, looking at marquees with your name on them and you'll . . . what?

I turned the mind off and moved again.

*Step.* Move the foot. *Step.* Move the foot. *Step.* Move . . .

The corner marquee—a theater with plenty of space for itself—was dark, but the lights of the street, with the reflections from the white of the snow, caused the block lettering to show up stark and plain as noon, and informed me that I was appearing in another big box-office flick.

Another fragment of David Strauss was competing with two other fragments of himself. Again. *David Strauss, star of stage, screen, ESP, and the American Free Enterprise system, invites you to collect little pieces of him.* A fragment a month. Join the David Strauss Collectors' Club. For just two dollars and fifty cents (second run, only) collect a full David Strauss. A cold cut a month from all over! Be the first one on your block to have a life-size David Strauss for your home. It walks. It talks. It glows in the dark! Send your . . .

Walk!

Move!

Don't think!

*Step.* Move the foot. (What foot? I can't feel anything in that foot anymore. It's not mine. It belongs to the statue; the one the collectors' club is cutting up for a big profit.) *Step.* Move the foot. *Step.* Move. . . .

A cab! Something alive, moving; I must be getting closer to Times Square. Something besides me is still alive.

"Hey! . . ."

Right by me. Slosh. Right by me and away, leaving two

black and dirty lines in the new snow of the street. Between the buildings, between the marquees. Davidstraussdavidstrauss. It's me, you putz! Meeeeee! David Strauss. Me. Not up there on the signs. Down here. Freezing. I need a cab, you slob-faced sonofabitch and you . . .

*Step.* (Move, damn it!) Move the leg, the foot will come along if it hasn't fallen off (I'm almost afraid to look) and again you *step!* Move the . . .

What the hell? David Strauss in *that* dog? *David Strauss?* You idiots; I had two fucking scenes in that flick; six lines, I had, and billing in type you couldn't find without a magnifying glass and screen credit you would miss if you blinked. And now you're selling that picture, that unredeemed waste of film, by putting my name on the marquee?

No mention of the real stars.

No nod to the reviews that told the world it was a bomb.

No mind.

No morals.

Just sell the picture, release it again and kid the people. It's a David Strauss picture, now, so click-click-click, change the marquee billing (did they change the poster billing, too? damned if I'm going to look, damned if I will) and click-click-click it will finally make enough money to get back the negative cost before we sell it to television. Click. Click-click.

This one's still open. This one's an all-night theater and it's still open; no cashier in the box (she would freeze to death; maybe she already did and they took her away) but the punk in the monkey suit is standing in there, warm and sleepy, waiting to take the admissions and tear up a ticket (or maybe not tear up the ticket and stick the admission money in his own pocket the way I used to do when I was a kid and had a job like that) so that any bastard with two bucks in his pocket can wander in out of the cold and get his feet warm and maybe go to sleep while David Strauss postures for him in flickering color and says the lines without really knowing what they mean anymore because when he made that one, David Strauss was tired and he couldn't always remember which picture he was in this month. Wasn't that the one where you had the overlapping shooting schedule and you were getting a call from Abe-the-agent every morning to remind you which studio you were supposed to go to in the morning and which you were supposed to go to in the afternoon and which lines you were supposed to know for which part in which picture and what the hell did it matter, it was the big time at least so what did it matter, when you're in the big time and you're a hot property you grab it while it's there, baby, and take the money and run bay-bee and . . .

*Step.*

Get out from under that marquee because it's going to fall on you if you don't. . . .

*Step.* Get away. Away! Away. . . . *Step.*

Have another step, David, darling. Have another part. Have another picture. Have another Scotch-rocks. Have another piece of Dolly. Have another piece of Julie. Have another piece of what-the-hell-was-your-name, chickie baby? Have another slice of everything, and don't chew, just swallow it, because if you chew you won't have time to take the next slice and you have certainly-certainly got to take the next slice, haven't you, David, darling? Yes, indeedy. You do truly have to have the next slice and the next slice and all the next slices you can get, because you are nothing but a little . . .

"Got a cigarette, mister?"

Who? . . .

"Cold morning, isn't it?"

*A boy.* Standing on the street a block off Times Square, wearing tight-tight Levis and a windbreaker around his big shoulders, with a stray trace of snow on his curly blond hair (too blond, it has *got* to be bleached) and a pair of ski boots half-buried in the sidewalk snow but plainly more expensive than the total of everything else he was wearing; Abercrombie and Fitch, or my name's not . . .

". . . David Strauss. Aren't you?"

What? What is he? . . .

"It must be *wonderful* to walk along here and see your name on the theater signs. I'd just stand there and *look* at them if it was me. Even as cold as it is."

"Uh . . . yeah. Sure,"

"*Do* you have a cigarette for me, Mr. Strauss? I simply *can't* seem to . . . oh, *thank* you. Do you have a *match?*"

Holding the cigarette up, like an ad for the brand, he looked at me with a little smile at the corners of his mouth and—something else; something knowing and old and shrewd—something challenging in his eyes.

"Yeah. Match. . . ." I fumbled into the pockets of my duffel coat and found my lighter, the one Dolly gave me a year ago ("Merry Christmas, darling. I wish I could be out there on the Coast with you, but I just *can't* get away. The understudy simply isn't good enough to fill in. But Merry Christmas. We'll spend the next one together. Won't we?"), and hit the roller a couple of times before I could get a flame. The wind blew it out (and all the time, the guinea was with her; she was calling me from bed, that's what she told me the next month, from bed where she had just given him a knob job after balling him all night, and it was him who had to remind her to call me for Christmas) before I could get the fire to his cigarette, and then I finally got it and shielded it with my hand.

He put his hands on mine, to get the flame to the end of the cigarette. But he wasn't looking at the flame. He was looking straight into my eyes all the time, and his fingers worked on mine and held on even when the tip of the cigarette was glowing and I could see the reflection of the flame, in the depths of the eyes that were on me and his forefinger moved, inside my palm and then . . .

"Take off, asshole!"

He just kept on staring at me.

"Take off, you motherfucking fag hooker before I beat your lousy face in!"

"Oh, *goodness!*" He still had the little smile; he didn't move; the eyes were still on me. "Goodness—I didn't know you were rough trade, David."

"You . . . !" I started to move toward him and I guess he finally got the idea. He knew I meant it. He dodged, still smiling, and danced a few feet away. I kept coming.

"Don't blow your cool, David," he said over his shoulder, turning to get more speed. "You don't have to prove anything to me. I'll be around . . . when you're in the mood."

He was gone. Around the corner and out of reach; making better time on those Abercrombie and Fitches than you would expect with the snow and the cold. I didn't follow. All I had wanted was to get him out of there. Away from me. Out of . . .

"Oh, *God!*"

63

I said the words aloud. To myself, but aloud in the silence and blackness and whiteness.

A fag; a fairy, and a fairy whore at that.

And he knew you, Strauss.

He knew you—how? Something in my face? Something else about me? Or was it something he'd heard? Did the young men and the out-and-out queers around Times Square tell each other David Strauss was a member of the club? A mark for them?

Not true.

Not *true!*

How long had it been—how long? Years and years. And nobody, but nobody, knew about that. Not from you. And sure as hell not from Jackie. Jack. No, he couldn't have heard anything. It must have been . . .

*Step*. Move the leg. *Step*. Move the leg. *Step*. . . .

I got myself moving again. Maybe, somewhere along here there was a bar. Or a café. Or a stand. Or something —anything—still open besides a theater. Somewhere I could . . . The tune to "Daisy, Daisy" started running through my head. A bisexual-built-for-two, yessir, that's me. . . .

> *David, David,*
> *You have become the rage;*
> *You're a Big Star,*
> *Screen, ESP, and Stage!*
> *You've got all the girlies yearning,*
> *And all the boys are burning;*
> *For you can please*
> *Both hes and shes,*
> *You're a Bisexual-Built-For-Two!*

I stopped walking and clenched my mind.

Have another song, David, darling.

Thank you, but I think I'd rather stand here and freeze to death and become a statue and be shat on by pigeons. I think I would rather stand here and not think. I think I would rather clench my mind and my eyes and my face and . . .

Hell, what good is it doing?

What good?

*Step*. I moved the other leg. *Step*. Just keep walking and concentrate on the motion, and you won't have to think about any of it. If you walk far enough, you can stop being David Strauss. If you walk far enough. What the hell does a homosexual prostitute think he can see in David Strauss's face, anyway? Who is he, what is he, the fucking fag.

Nobody else sees that in David Strauss's face.

Do they?

*Do they?*

Hell, no. Hell, no, they don't because if they did it would come across on film. It's not there; it's not there.

Oh, my God.

Oh—my—God! A billboard this time. Enough already. I've got to get out of here, to get away from these pieces of my name and my face and myself.

How many? *Step.* How many? *Step.* How many pieces *(step)* of David Strauss are there? How many pieces, how many fractured sections, how many David Strausses broken into how many pieces on how many theater marquees and how many billboards on how many streets in how many towns in how many—Christ almighty, think of it—how many *countries!*

*Step.* Move the other leg. *Step.* Move the other leg and don't try to count because that is a numbers game and nobody can win a numbers game, don't you see it's all a racket and it's rigged and nobody can win in the first place how many pictures jesus my balls are cold have I made I can't even count them anymore but each one makes David Strauss a bigger and bigger Star of Stage and Screen and ESP and Theater Marquees and Billboards and ads in the *Reporter* and *Daily Variety* and stories in *Photoplay* and *Motion Picture* and every—Christ-how-many-are-they—one that makes David Strauss bigger also makes *davidstrauss* a little bit smaller because it cuts him into tinier and tinier bits (for distribution rights both foreign and domestic; for exhibition whether in theaters or via electronic media) and each of those pieces is broken up, too, between his agent and his business manager and his public relations counsel and his tax man and his lawyer and who else is there, how the hell would I know who the hell keeps track of all those names and all those faces anymore, not me, that's for sure because I have enough to do just trying to keep track of davidstrauss, he's getting harder and harder to find (step right up, ladeez and gennulmen, see the Incredible Shrinking Man; he used to be an actor named David Strauss but now he's a property and he's davidstrauss and he's getting smaller and smaller before your very eyes) and now, today, on this Christmas morning I can find all these little bits and pieces of him but I am not really sure I still know where or how to find davidstrauss.

## DAVID STRAUSS & DAVID STRAUSS

in

*NO!*

No!

No.

There are *not* that many pieces of me. I did *not* play any part opposite myself and I will *not* look at any lying theater marquee that tells me I did. I know I didn't.

I won't look.

*Step.*

I . . . will . . . walk . . . right . . . under . . . the . . . sign . . . and . . . I . . . will . . . not . . . look. Under it. And past the theater. Without looking. And now it's past and behind me and I am not looking back. See, world? See, theater? I am not looking back. I am not looking back. No. Eyes front to the . . .

Bar.

For God's sake—will you look at *that!* A bar. Open. On Christmas Day, before dawn. There must be a God somewhere. Somewhere. *Step.* Touch the door. *Step.* Push it open—and it does move!

Have a drink, David, darling.

You bet your sweet ass. You bet your sweet . . . no . . . wait a minute, wasn't there something you . . . oh, yes! Telephone.

Oh, yes. Oh, yes. Oyez! Where there is a bar in newyork-city there is also a pay phone. And where there is a pay phone, there is a chance for davidstrauss to collect at least one of the many, many pieces of himself that seem to be strewn around the world in unlikely places these days. There was a chance of loose change in the bottom of my duffel-coat pocket; I wouldn't even have to break a bill. Which left me with only one problem. A choice. One more little decision to be made:

Which?

Which piece of davidstrauss do I collect first? Which has

66

priority? The pay phone was just where I thought it would be. Back of the bar. Between the two crappers.

Which?

I managed to get the change out and keep it in my hand; feeling was coming back, but not fast enough. It seemed like one of the labors of Hercules, getting the fingers on a dime and getting it up to the coin slot.

Which? Who-which-who?

In the end, it was the phone itself that made the decision for me. I stuck a finger into the dial but it was too cold to follow orders.

Twice I got halfway through Dolly's unlisted number, the straight line to the phone beside her bed, the one that didn't have to go through the switchboard in the lobby. Twice I got halfway through dialing it. And twice the tingling finger slipped and stuck in a wrong digit and I had to . . .

The hell with it.

That piece will wait, that piece of davidstrauss will wait until his fingers are on speaking terms with his brain again. Have a different piece of davidstrauss, David, dear.

Thank you, I don't mind if I . . .

"Operator. Can I help you?"

"Uh . . . yes, operator. I . . . uh . . . want to place a call to . . . uh . . .Beverly Hills, California.

"Do you know the number, sir?"

"Yes. Yes I . . . uh . . ."

*Number.* Oh, my sweetjesuschrist, do I still know Jackie's number? Sure I do. Sure I do. Sure I do.

". . . Crestview . . . uh . . . six . . ."

And there I stuck. The rest of the number wouldn't come. I could feel the nails of my left hand digging into my palm, the fingers clamping like a . . .

"I'm sorry, operator."

I cut off her reply, hung the receiver back in its cradle and clung to it, resting my whole weight on the hand that held it. The impersonal blackness of the pay phone felt cool against my forehead. Cool and hard and unimpressed with the remaining fragment of davidstrauss standing there and supporting himself, hanging like a drowning man with one hand clamped around a lifeline. Hanging like . . . like . . . a child clinging to its . . .

Dolly.

I forced myself to stand up. Forced the left hand to re-move the receiver from the cradle; forced the right to the dial again. Slowly, carefully, deliberately curving out the numbers of the private-and-unlisted . . .

## Dolly Diamond

. . . telephone right here beside my bed. And I've got these nice clean black-satin sheets for the bed. And I've got that nice clean smoky-tinted mirror above the bed. And I've got that nice clean Merry Christmas music playing on the nice clean eight-track stereo.

And I've got that nice clean . . . *body,* looking back at me from the mirror.

And I've got this nice clean ashtray all red against the black of the sheets.

And I've got this nice clean reefer all started, with the lilac-flavored paper all green against the red of the ashtray.

And if that isn't a lovely, beautiful, darling Christmas color scheme I'd like to know what is. Come on, tell me something nicer for Christmas—tell me something nicer, some Christmas present that would be nicer for Dolly the blue-and-white Diamond than a little color scheme like that.

. . . *colors are fading out* . . .

I brought the tiny green cigarette to my lips and took a long, careful drag—letting in just enough air at the same time to keep from gagging—and held it, down where it could do some of the good—and held it—and held it—and held it. . . .

The telephone chimed.

I let the smoke out in a long *ahhhhh* and the long, white, beautiful girl in the overhead mirror twinkled her cute little nose at me and giggled a little as the colors came back up to sharp and her toes wriggled happily and her little pink tongue licked out and curled like a kitten's.

The telephone chimed again.

It was funny. The chimes were funny because they made little multicolored motes in the air between me and that beautiful child up there in the mirror and then they ex-ploded—*pop pop pop*—one by one in the air and the air shimmered where the motes had been. The girl in the mirror giggled and moved the joint back to her mouth for another drag.

Deep, deep into the girl. Deep, deep, deep *down* and suddenly I could *see* that smoke going down inside her; like a ghost of a ghost, filling the cavity behind the tiny, perfect, bud-tipped breasts (hi, bud! hi, bud! Stand up there. Stand up and be counted—one, two—hi, buds!) and down the milk-white slimness, past the belly (see how it slopes in, below the ribs, beautiful and white with the faintest touch of freckles) and down to the flare of the hips, like boyish parentheses enclosing the triangle of the pubis (the inverted, blunt-topped triangle; warm, now and becoming moist) and down and down and down the softness of the thighs and the knees and the sweet curve of the calves to where the toes curl back and wave at you as the happiness touches them.

A thousand million billion trillion cells and lovelinesses of that girl, all filled now with the ghost of the happy-time cigarette, and the telephone chiming its notes of joy to float and hang and burst in the shimmering air . . .

*Who the fuck could be calling you at this time of day?*
. . . the feeling and the ghost-filling and the tingling and the girl in the mirror—beginning to fade—but the joint is almost down to a nub and all that is left is the notes of joy, hanging and bursting and leaving a mote-dust of bright colors now like a mist in the air between me and that wonderful, lovely, desirable, pink-and-white-and-cream girl in the smoke of the mirror. But the telephone color notes aren't notes of joy anymore. And the fire of the cigarette has gone out. And it wasn't enough (I *knew* I should have told Rafael to bring me *charas* this time, or at least some hash; the straight weed is nothing when you've been turned on to *charas*) and now I can hear the telephone but I can't see the notes any . . .

"Hello?"

The hand holding the telephone looked like mine, but I knew it belonged to someone else. I hadn't moved it. I hadn't told it to reach out and pick up the telephone.

"Who is this? . . ."

Nothing.

No answer from the telephone. I held it closer to my ear, watching the girl in the mirror do the same things, imitating the motions and rolling on her side to strike a glow and a glitter from the blue-white strands of the long, long perfection of the hair fanned out on the background of the black satin beneath her.

*"Hello? . . ."*

I could hear something. A sound. I closed my eyes to see what color the sound was. It was brown-and-black, hairy like the coat of a bear. It was the sound of breathing, and—very faintly in the background—I could hear music; something about that music (what? what?) that reminded me of something.

*"Listen, say something. Don't just breathe at me, say something or I'm going to hang up on you."*

. . . the color of the music was pink and white and cream and topped-and-surrounded by a halo (like an angel's halo, only all around) of blue and white. My voice. I couldn't recognize the words. I couldn't be sure what song. But it was my voice; the voice of that beautiful, perfect girl in the mirror. . . .

*"All right!"*

I dropped the phone back into its cradle and started to roll back to look at the girl in the mirror. Another joint. I needed another joint.

There was the ashtray. And there was the roach—the last eighth of an inch of the just-smoked cigarette—lying green-lilac against the Merry Christmas red of the ashtray. I picked it up and put it in my mouth, tasting the green-lilac of the paper and mixing the flavor with the harshness of the weed, chewing it all to get the last of the good and then swallowing and twinkling at the beautiful girl in the mirror who was having a beautiful Christmas morning for herself. She twinkled back at me and her toes curled again and reached up to the head of the bed to get another paper, a strawberry-flavored one this time (maybe I should get a green ashtray; that would be just as Christmasy as the red ashtray and the green paper) and rolled it around another helping of the weed (good stuff Rafael brought this time, no dirt and no seeds just the real gold) and lay back, beautiful and naked and alone with the girl in the mirror; lighting the end and taking a deep, deep . . .

Pop . . . pop!

The little color balls were bursting again in the air

between the mirror girl and the bed girl, spraying their tones of joy into a haze of color-sound to screen us from each other, and I knew the telephone was ringing. Again.

Pop . . . pop!

I took a deep-down lungful of the happy-time and held it, waiting for the sound-haze to go away. (Who could it be, breathing at me on the telephone at this time of the day? Johnny? No, not Johnny; he would have said something *"Hi, baby! 'd I wake you? Listen, I wanted to call you up and tell you you're the greatest. I mean it really the greatest!"* so it couldn't be Johnny. No. Mmmmmmmm).

Pop . . . pop!

The little color balls were fading, but not quickly enough. I couldn't see the happy ghosts descending through the girl in the mirror. I could see her touching her neck—lightly, lightly, so lightly—and stroking downward with the ghost, across the tiny-tender rose of the breast and down, down, to the . . .

Pop . . . pop!

. . . tiny rise-and-dip of the navel and then (just a phone-freak pervert? Calling up to breathe? No . . . it almost couldn't be, because that number's unlisted; he'd have to have dialed at random, just getting my number by chance. Plenty of obscene-telephone-call freaks in New York; it could happen. But it's just not . . . ).

Pop . . . pop!

Now the happy-time ghosts were visible again, following the hand as it stroked, and stroked and stroked, just like (David! I know it—that was David! Who else could it be but David, telephoning me and then breathing instead of talking. It's got to be David! That silly half-queer husband I had, swinging and chewing on me like a big, soft hairy baby. David! It's bound to . . . )

Pop . . . pop!

The girl on the mirror-bed handed the strawberry-paper joint into the stroking hand and reached with the other to pick up the telephone. She didn't bother putting the receiver to her ear. She just held the mouthpiece where she could talk into it.

"David," she said, in that sweet, husky voice that makes the song lyrics so warm and intimate, "try a different telephone number, David, dear. Have a nice Christmas, David,

71

dear. Have another drink, David, dear. And phone some-one else. You're a fucking bore, David, dear. *You're a fucking bore and a boring fuck!* . . ."

I dropped the phone back on the cradle and then, as a very, very smart afterthought, lifted it off again and shoved it under a pillow where I wouldn't hear anything it did (no more bursting color-motes of sound; no dial tone, no howling from the telephone company, no more distractions) until I was ready to let it out. Which might be never.

The pillow, billowy foam under zebra satin, felt soft and cool as I slipped the telephone receiver under it and my hand was still empty as the girl in the mirror raised the strawberry joint to her lips for more happytime, and I giggled at her.

She was so funny, that girl.

Because she was fumbling, catching the corner of the other zebra-pillow with her fingers and dragging it down, down the black satin bed to where her darling boyish hips moved and moved and moved and then bucked upward in the wonderful, enticing first motions of the love dance and she shoved the pillow under them to hold them in that position as the ghost of the happy-smoke eddied and waited in the parentheses and she took another deep drag and held it and all the colors of that beautiful body swirled and moved and shifted, and shifted again . . .

The free hand was still busy. Searching. On the stand. Then in the little drawer at the head of the bed.

And then she had it. Her hand had it, curled around the cool hardness, brought it out. Touch the button . . . *wrrrrrrr* . . . let the button go. Deep, deep, deep filling of the happy-ghost, moving down and down, but see the toes curl and writhe, they're not getting any of the happy-ghost now, it's all stopping at the parentheses . . . slow, slow, slow . . . colors and cool and warm. Warm it. Warm the end, the hard-hard pink end of the vibrator with your hand, it mustn't be cold for the girl in the mirror, warm it.

Another deep lungful.

Gone. All the happy-ghost-making sweet-strawberry gone, but not gone, a ghost, see it and feel it going down and down to stop at just the right place. Hear the colors. See the sounds. Move the warm, hard pink Lover down to the snubbed end of the triangle while the long, loving, beautiful legs turn and yield and spread. Feel the warm,

72

The soft. The moist readiness of the triangle as the hard Lover touches and tilts and strokes and *enters* and deep, deep, deep, deep, *moves*. Back and forth, back and forth, exploring and probing and now . . . now . . . now . . . *now!*

*Wrrrr.*

Oh. Oh, yes. Yes! See the beautiful, enticing, adored, loved, idolized, desired, wanted, needed, worshiped girl on the bed. See her move from side to side. See her legs jerk and bend at the knees and stretch outward pushing the soles of the feet together so the happy-ghosts can't escape. . . .

*Wrrrrr.*

Yes. Yes. Yes! And it's . . . there! Yes! And . . . again! Yes! And again. . . .

*Wrrrrrr.*

To *hell* with you, Johnny, to hell with you, spend your Christmas with your goddamn family and throw a mercy-fuck into your dagobitch ex-wife or get . . .

*Wrrrrrrr.*

To *hell* with you, Daddy, to hell with you for dying when I needed you most and to hell with your bad heart and to hell with you for kissing me and stroking me and whispering to me all the time when I was a little girl and making me think you were so wonderful until the night Mama had been so sick for so long and you got so drunk and you kissed me and held me and then when I went to bed and it was dark you came in and there were your hands on me again and you were in bed with me and you were naked and you put my hand on your . . .

*Wrrrrrrrrr.*

To hell with you, David, you boring, limp-hanging, pansy-loving, tit-chewing baby, to hell with you and your career and all the times you tried and couldn't and to hell with your talk-talk-talk and to hell with your pint-size fairyboyfriend. You couldn't kid *me,* every time you *did* make it with me it was him you were thinking about. . . .

*Wrrrrrrrrr.*

And to hell with all you so-called men everywhere—all you unmen who used me and use me and want to use me—for *what?* For a *pot!* For a *jug!* For a *receptacle!* To hell with all of you who'd be just as happy if I were your goddamn hand. . . .

73

*Wrrrrrrrrrrr.*

To hell with all of you who aren't Daddy, none of you big enough or warm enough or hard enough or needing enough or wanting enough or close enough—to hell with you and I'm *glad* my daddy made love to me I'm *glad* my mama died and left him with me . . . I'm glad, I'm glad, I'm glad, I'm *glad!* . . .

*Wrrrrrrrrrrrrrrr.*

To hell with *all* of you. *All* of you. Dolly's got what *she* needs. Dolly the blue-and-white Diamond is having her own Merry Christmas, having her own happytime, her own funnytime, here with the warm and the color and the moist and the beautiful, desired, desirable girl in the mirror who is . . .

*Wrrrrrrrrrrrrrrrrrr.*

Yes! More . . . again . . . more! Yes! Please . . . *please* . . . once more. Just once more for Dolly. It's not enough. It's not fair. *It's not fair!* It's never enough even with the Lover, never-never-never enough! . . .

*Wrrrrr!* . . .

Oh.

God, why can't it ever be enough for me?

Listen—to the silence.

Listen.

Wait! Wait there, girl-in-the-mirror. Wait there, and we'll try it again in a minute or two. Wait, beautiful pink and white and cream and silver girl in the mirror, flat now and spent and motionless, with the pink palm half-hidden but not holding the Lover . . . wait.

Listen to the silence.

Christmas morning.

Listen to the silence.

David. That idiot, David. Well, he can't phone me again. Nobody can ring my telephone again until I want them to and I don't want them to. Not for a long, long time. That idiot, Johnny. Why can't he be daddy, the way I want him, why can't he be daddy and stay here, in this black-satin, to love me and to let me love him the way I want to love my daddy, watching that other girl and her daddy balling and playing turnabout and loving, why?

What's wrong with them, all of them?

Why can't they be men? Why can't they be daddies like they are supposed to be? Why can't they love me and kiss

74

me and be inside me all the time, *enough* of the time, until it's really good and warm and safe and the way it was . . . the way it was . . .

David.

Damn him! Damn David. Why did *he* have to be the baby? Why couldn't he let *me* be the baby? *I'm* the beautiful, loved, adored, protected, wonderful baby. My daddy loves me. My daddy wants to be with me. With me and not . . .

*Damn* David!

Balling with me and all the time, all the time, no matter what we were doing with each other, no matter what he was saying, no matter what, his mind was always . . .

### Jack Dahlberg

". . . and always, and always on nobody but Jack Dahlberg, the *world's shortest giant!*"

I made a conscious effort to relax.

I unfolded the fist my hand had turned into without any known or remembered effort on my part. I stood perfectly still. I kept my mouth shut. I did not respond.

"Well—what are you going to do about it, Jack?"

Nothing. I am going to do nothing.

"Aren't you going to hit me?"

No. I am not going to hit you.

"Aren't you going to tell me again what a pig I am and how marrying me was the mistake of a lifetime and how you can't stand a drunken woman? Aren't we going to play through that dreary little scene again? Maybe you can get more out of it this time. Some extra production values. That's what you're forever screaming for, isn't it? More production values. . . ."

"I don't scream, Clara."

She laughed and made a pseudodramatic gesture. It didn't quite come off. A gesture like that has to be precise and neat. The neatness was ruined, in this case, by the drink in her hand. It spilled some of its colorless contents on the rug.

"No, say that for you, Shorty. Scream you do not."

She laughed and spilled some more vodka.

"Clara, listen, It's past midnight. Can't we . . ."

"What's that?" she broke in. "What's that you say,

75

Shorty? Speak up! I can't hear you, 'way down there, Shorty!"

She was mean-drunk, all right. Mean-drunk enough to be taking dead aim at my jugular; she knew I hated that nickname. Shorty. They had gotten away with calling me that, once. A long time ago. When I couldn't defend myself. I took a breath and kept another tight hold on myself.

"It's past midnight," I repeated, keeping my voice as level and toneless as possible. "We've got to be up bright and early in the morning. So let's get to . . ."

"Go screw yourself," she said. "Go screw yourself, Shorty. Little Clara's going to have herself another drink. Go screw yourself—because yourself is the only screwing you're going to get. Tonight, or any other night, Shorty."

I looked at her and wondered, not for the first time, how the timid little actress I'd met on the studio lot on a long-ago day I'd since come to regret had turned into the slovenly shrew I saw swaying before me. It was the booze, I knew, but *why* the booze? What had made Clara retreat into that alcoholic daze and turn against me? I didn't know —I only knew I had no patience for her anymore.

She tipped her glass up, craning her head backward to let the last watery dregs of the drink trickle down her throat.

"Clara," I said. "Please, let's—"

The phone rang, interrupting, and I turned away in relief to answer it.

"Hello? . . ."

"Jackie?"

The voice didn't register. But I had the feeling that it ought to.

"Who's this?" I said, shifting to the I'm-Jack-Dahlberg-and-who-are-you-to-disturb-Jack-Dahlberg's-train-of-thought set of gears, modeled after the past master of frostbite, my father.

What I got in return was a silence. And breathing.

"Who *is* this? . . ."

More breathing. It was beginning to annoy me, now. Not that I hadn't been annoyed enough in the first place.

"Listen . . ."

". . . it's me, Jackie! It's *David*."

Sure enough. I should have recognized the voice, all right. And I knew why I hadn't. It wasn't a voice I wanted to remember. David. Well, that made the night complete.

76

"Listen, David, call me back in the morning, will you? Or at the office, after the holidays. Things are kind of . . ."

"Jackie. Jackie . . . it's *me*. . . ."

My heart was pounding, but I tried not to let anything show in my voice.

"Where are you, Dave?" I said. "Where are you phoning from? Are you here? In town, I mean?"

"I'm in hell, Jackie. I'm calling you from hell."

"Sure. Sure, I know, David." Suddenly I wanted a cigarette. I patted the pockets of my jacket, but they were empty. "Sure," I said, "but what part of hell, Dave? The New York part of hell or the Hollywood part of hell?"

"Jackie, please. Don't call me that, Jackie."

Christ, wouldn't you think a man could find just one . . . !

"Don't call me 'Dave,' Jackie. Be nice to me. I'm in hell, Jackie. I tell you, I've got to talk to you, Jackie."

"All right." I gave up on the cigarette and sat down. "All right, all right, David. You're in hell, so now you want to talk to me. So talk."

"It's cold here, Jackie."

"Uh-huh."

"I'm cold and I'm in this bar and I just phoned that bitch, my wife, ex-wife I mean, and she said *that* to me again. . . ."

"You phoned Dolly?" I said. I leaned over and rested my forehead on my free hand. "At this time of the morning you phoned Dolly? You've got to be drunk, Dave."

"David, please. *David!*"

"Okay—David. You're drunk, David. Go to bed and sleep it off. Call me when you're sober."

"Merry Christmas, Jackie," he said. "Merry Christmas to you from my little corner of hell."

"David—please, David—as a friend: get some sleep. All right?"

"Merry Christmas to you . . . Merry Christmas to you. . . ."

He was singing, and I could hear music—some kind of music—in the background. That made it a bar. He was drunk and singing in a public bar. Oh, God.

". . . Merry Christmas, dear Jack-ie. Merry Christmas to . . ."

". . . all of you from both of us," Clara's voice cut in

from the extension. "It was sweet of you to call, David, dear, and I want you to know we both were waiting for—"

"Clara, get off the line," I said, making it an order.

"Go fuck yourself," she said. "Or better still, go fuck each other—serve both of you fucking well right—"

There was a click as she hung up.

One down, I told myself. One down and one to go.

"I don't think she *likes* me." David's voice had the petulance of a rejected child—and, suddenly, it was all too much. Too entirely damn much.

"Goddamn it," I heard myself yelling into the phone, "goddamn it, Strauss—!" But there wasn't anything I could hang on the end of that, so I compromised and banged the phone down as hard as I could on its cradle.

There, now, I jeered at myself from deep inside; there, now! The little man's had his little tantrum and taken it out on the little phone. And now it's all better.

Well . . . isn't it?

Of course, the little man is supposed to be an adult. A grown-up. Executive vice-president at one of the biggest motion-picture studios in the world. One of the two or three most powerful individuals in Hollywood. A man like that, if nothing else, he ought to be at least a little bit in charge of himself. Not to mention his wife.

Well, what about it, little man?

*Little.*

The antiqued-glass mirror panels of the living room told me again the truth that I didn't need to be reminded of. Five feet not-quite-five inches. Five feet five if you give me a minute to stretch and relax the muscles in the back. Sixty-four and three-quarters inches if you don't.

*Little.*

Well, hell. Papa himself was no basketball star. No Gary Cooper. No Jim Arness. Physical size needn't be a handicap. Look at Napoleon. Look at (go on, Dahlberg; say it!), look at Hitler. Small men. Little. But history will not forget them; good or bad, hero or villain, they will be remembered.

*Little.*

I remembered the day I knew for sure. That this was the way it would be. All through the summer I had worked out. At the studio, where Papa had me on the payroll of the messengers; the Boss Messenger gladly looked the other way while Irving Dahlberg's son spent every afternoon in the studio gym, working out with the weights and the rings and the other equipment. Four-five hours a day I was at it. Even on weekends. All to be ready to play football when I got back to school.

And I was there an hour ahead of time, for the fall try-outs. Suited up. Ready to go. (Jesus, the football equipment itself should have given me the answer. The smallest they had was still way too big.) I had the reflexes. I had the brains. I had the guts—and I never got as far as the edge of the field.

"Look, Jackie," the coach said ("Jackie" even then; Jesus, wasn't it bad enough what he was going to say to me? Did he have to throw in "Jackie" for a bonus?). "I just can't let you do it. Last year it wasn't so bad. Freshman ball, okay. But this year . . ."

I didn't understand. "But I've been practicing all summer," I told him. "I'm a lot better than last year. You'll see."

"What I'll see, I'll see you get killed—and I'm not hired to get you kids killed. Jackie, you're just not big enough. . . ."

"I'll grow."

"No." I'll never forget the look on his face. Sad. So sad. I guess it was as tough on him as it was on me, in a way. "No, you won't grow, Jackie," he said. "You're through growing. You're as big as you're ever going to be."

"I am *not!*"

"Jackie . . . hold up your hand."

I held it up, palm first, like an Indian in a B-budget Western. He held his hand against it. Flat. Every one of his fingers was at least an inch longer than mine. I still didn't understand.

"It's elementary anatomy, Jackie," he said then. "You can always tell pretty much what size a kid will be from his hands and feet. They grow first; the rest of the body catches up. You see some kid who looks just average size, maybe even a little small for his age, but his hands are real big and his feet—there's a kid who is going to do a lot of growing in the next year or two. You see a kid the same size, even bigger maybe, but the hands and feet are the same size as the rest of his body—forget it. He's done all the growing he's going to do."

"Some people . . ." there was something thick and gluey

79

in my throat and I had to take a second to swallow it, ". . . just naturally have bigger hands and feet than others," I said. "In biology—genetics—they taught us . . ."

But he just shook his head, still looking sad at me. "Since last year," he said, "in the past twelve months, Jackie, how much did you grow? How many inches?"

"I . . ."

I stood there. My mouth must still have been open, but I didn't answer. I wanted to tell him I knew lots of people who grew a lot after they were my age. I wanted to tell him I would *make* myself grow. Because I wanted to so much. Because I just *had* to play football.

But I didn't say anything at all, because suddenly I knew he was right. I looked at the ground, at the toes of the football cleats I had almost overlapped getting them tight enough to stay on my feet. Shorty Dahlberg. They had started calling me that last year—and they would be calling me that for the rest of my life. This was how I was going to be. Forever. I would never look at the ground and see it from any greater distance than I did right then.

And nothing, *nothing* I could do would change it.

I looked back at the coach, and I guess everything I had been thinking was right there in my eyes.

"Look, kid," he said, "it's not the end of the world. Football isn't the only sport there is. Sports are for everyone . . ."

I didn't answer.

". . . short, tall, or in-between. There's golf; plenty of short men make it big at golf. Tennis; you're fast and your reflexes are quick. Diving—what about scuba diving? I know that's something you've had a whirl at. And there's skiing. . . ."

He trailed off, and I didn't help him any. I just stood there, looking at him, with something black and sour and full of venom building up inside me.

"You left out horse racing," I spat out, with a coldness that surprised even me. "I could always be a jockey. Right, coach?"

And I turned around and went off to the locker room without giving him a chance to answer. I didn't run. I walked. I made myself walk. And I didn't cry; not then and not later, when I was alone in the room, waiting for David to come back from football practice. He was my roommate, scrimping along at school partly on a scholarship and partly on money from his uncle; I knew his family was nowhere near as rich as mine, but right then I would have traded places with him or anyone else who was allowed to go out for football.

He did all right that year, David. Sure. David Strauss, captain of the football team. Well . . . I was head cheerleader, wasn't I? And I got pretty adept at diving that summer, too. Not to mention becoming a champion ping-pong player.

Jesus . . . ping-pong!

I never even mentioned that to Papa; the name—ping-pong—sounded funny and somehow effeminate to me. What a laugh, thinking about it, now. Ping-pong! A lightweight amusement rather than a sport until, suddenly, it became embroiled in international politics. What a twist!

"Admiring the view, Shorty?"

I hadn't heard Clara come downstairs. She was pouring herself a fresh drink—more vodka on the rocks—and eyeing me with that phony Marlene Dietrich one-eyebrow-cocked pseudosophisticate expression that must have been one of the few things she learned at the studio acting school. But this time the look got to me, even knowing how phony it all was. And how alcoholic.

I wondered how long I had been standing there, surveying myself in those mirror panels.

"Clara," I said, with a lot of careful-executive-calm in the voice, "I'm asking. Not telling . . . asking. Please. No more tonight. You know how bad it's going to make you feel tomorrow. . . ."

". . . and we've all got to be bright-eyed and bushy-tailed for Papa, right, Shorty?"

Brief pause for control. Keep the voice level.

"Irving Dahlberg," I said, when I was sure I was ready, "is my father, yes. And he is also my boss. My immediate superior. The president of Monarch Studios, to whom the executive vice-president is directly responsible. You know how important the next few days can be for everyone. . . ."

"Christmas," she said, lifting the refilled glass in a mock toast. "It's Christmas. So here's to peace-on-earth and business-as-usual. Right, Shorty?"

It was a lost cause. I knew it, but for some reason I just couldn't stop trying. Somehow, I had to make her understand. To realize that this underground battle that was being waged between Papa and me would soon have to come out in the open and when it did all hell was likely to break loose. That having a drunken wife going at me all the time didn't exactly help my frame of mind. Somehow I had to get all this through to her. Somehow.

". . . because the whole schedule of production for the coming year has to be approved before the directors meet again. Papa wants to make big pictures—whopping budgets and major stars and long shooting schedules—because that's the kind of thing that built Monarch when he was out here and running production."

She grinned with half her mouth, the Dietrich eyebrow still cocked, and sipped the vodka.

"Who," she said, "ever suggested he's not *still* running it?"

Another pause for control.

"Clara," I said, "what happens this week—in fact, the next twenty-four hours—is going to make or break me. *And* Monarch Pictures."

Was she listening? Was she? I couldn't tell. But I kept going, in the hope that she was.

"If I can't convince Papa, he'll go ahead with *Sadie* and *Burn the First Card* and that other thing, *Boarders Away!* and we are cooked. If any of those pictures *ever* makes money it will be ten, twenty years from now when they've been rereleased two or three times and finally sold to television, and by then it won't make a damn bit of difference to any of us."

I still couldn't be sure. . . .

"All the directors'll see is another big loss on the books, because even *Sound of Music* didn't get back the negative cost in a year. The road-show hard-ticket routine just doesn't work the way it used to, not with the audiences we have today. The guarantees we have to make to the exhibitors will just make it worse; you can't *make* a profit anymore when you spend the kind of money Papa wants to on a picture."

Still just standing there. With the drink. Looking at me.

"Now my way will work. You make a good picture, aimed at today's audiences. But hold down the budget. And that makes profits. That's what I've got to get across to Papa when we see him tomorrow, and that's why we've both got to be in—"

"Top condition," she finished the sentence for me. "Sure, like athletes. Top condition. For another gala Christmas dinner. Uh-huh."

She flung me a look filled with contempt, then slowly left the room, fresh drink in hand. I heard her climbing the stairs slowly, one by one, as I stared absentmindedly at the phone. Suddenly, it startled me by ringing. I gathered myself together and picked it up.

"Hello."

"Jackie? . . ."

Papa.

What the hell did he want, at this hour? I shifted the telephone from one hand to the other and got a cigarette out of the box on the table. "What was it you wanted, Papa?"

"Oh. Yes. Jackie . . . it's about tomorrow. Today, I mean. You'll have the full scheduling, the month-by-month breakdown for the year? You've got that ready for me to see?"

"Well, yes, Papa. As much as possible, anyway. You know we can never be more than a few months ahead, but it's all there—the tentative, you know."

"Yes. That's good enough. I just wanted to be sure."

And for that he phones me at—what?—one o'clock in the morning?

"Was there something else, Papa?" I asked.

"Well . . ."

That surprised me; he actually seemed hesitant. I couldn't remember when I'd ever heard him that way before. Yes. There had to be something else. I waited for it.

"The Dolly Diamond contract," he said. "You've been talking to her people out here. You made any progress?"

"Why—no. Not really. I've been leaving it pretty much to the producer and director. It's their job to get her and to settle the price. Besides, I thought most of it was being handled on your end. Am I wrong?"

"No . . . no, not really."

There was a long pause on the line. Somewhere, far away, I heard a sound I thought I ought to be able to identify. A soft, almost liquid pop-popping. I groped for the memory it seemed to want to trigger. It sounded . . . it sounded . . . yes. The picture was suddenly clear in my mind. It was . . .

## Irving Dahlberg

. . . a man lighting a cigar. Do it right, and you're good for half an hour of decent smoking. Do it wrong, you're just another chewer-chomper wiggling a piece of rope back and forth in your mouth.

Irving Dahlberg does things right.

Irving Dahlberg attends to details so the big things go right, too. That's what makes him a giant. Why can't these kids—Irving Dahlberg's klutz of an adopted kid in particular—seem to grasp such a simple fact as that? Is it because he's not really my kid? Because he's the son of some pipsqueak who married poor little Ruthie, Irving Dahlberg's sister that he tried so hard to take care of? Some little nothing who married poor Ruthie and planted a kid in her before he died and went to wherever nothings go. Poor Ruthie, the giant's little sister who had no brains and no guts and not even the will to live, even after the baby came. *No!* Jackie is Irving Dahlberg's son because I *made* him my son, because I took him and gave him my name and raised him as my son, and no one except Margaret ever knew. *Irving Dahlberg's son!* He is that because the giant decided he would *make* him that. But even Irving Dahlberg could not make Jackie a giant.

I heard Jackie breathing on the other end of the line. Waiting for Papa to say something. Always he waited for Papa to say something.

"But you know how important it is," I went on when the cigar was right. "This picture, *Sadie,* it's going to be the big picture for Monarch. Very big."

"Yes." There was something flat in Jackie's tone. Something I didn't like. "I know it's what you have planned, Papa—"

"It's how it's going to be."

"Yes. . . ."

Something wrong. Irving Dahlberg always knows. Especially with the kid, Irving Dahlberg knows.

"Jackie," I said, very carefully, "what's been going on

back here? I get some strange reports in New York. Very funny reports."

"Funny reports, Papa?"

"Not funny ha-ha."

"I don't know what you mean, Papa."

The hell he didn't. But drop that for now. Another time we'll take it up. Another time. "Maybe," I said to him, "the guinea isn't after more money for Diamond. Maybe it's something else."

"What else, Papa?"

"That television deal we made for him. That was part of the contract on *Sadie* we made, you remember, Jackie?"

"Oh!"

So finally, "Oh." Grab him by the ear, twist and shake. And finally Irving Dahlberg gets an "Oh."

"Yes, of course. That. Well, about that we've been doing it just the way you said, Papa."

"The offices, the furniture, telephone, the rest of the service services—they've been okaying them and stuff, just the way it was agreed?"

"Yes, sir."

"And . . . nothing else."

"No, Papa. Nothing else. Just the way you said. They make up their proposals and send them to Bill. He looks them over, tells them they sound just great. Just fine. . . ."

". . . and after that, nothing happens?"

"No, sir. Just as you said."

"Uh-huh." I took the cigar out of my mouth and let my eyes focus on the lights outside the window. It was a clear night. From the twelfth floor, from the highest window in Beverly Hills, you could see a long way. See the lights. But no people. Good. On the screen you need to see people. But, in life, they just get in the way. All the time. In the way. "They complain yet?" I asked. "Say anything to Bill? Anything to you?"

"Not to me, no, Papa," he said. "To Bill . . . well . . . I don't think to him, either. He hasn't mentioned it if they did."

"What do you think?"

"Well . . . as I say, Bill hasn't had any—"

"*You*, Jackie. You. What do *you* think? I want to know."

He didn't say anything for a minute. Thinking, maybe.

The kid; Irving Dahlberg's kid, thinking. For him, thinking takes time.

"No," he said finally, when the thinking was done. "No, I don't think that is what Valentine's got on his mind, Papa. It's too early. They couldn't be sure, yet, what's happening."

"Um . . . yes. Maybe. Still, Jackie, it could be something like that. They know we didn't want to make a television production deal for them. Even for the specials, let alone for all the things they have in mind."

"Yes, sir. I know. Valentine is no fool. . . ."

"Valentine is a *schmuck!* A warbling wop. He wouldn't know if we burned those offices of his to the ground. Or care. What does he know about, him, except for his liquor and his gambling and his singing and his *nafkas!* It's the other one, that Sam. That Sam of his, that is one smart Jew he's got himself there. . . ."

*"Sam LoCicero?"*

"The lawyer. Sam! Who else?"

"Papa—Sam LoCicero's Italian, too. Not Jewish."

Kids. You have to lead them by the hand. By themselves, they would get lost.

"His father," I said, slowly and quietly, so maybe he would remember. "Sam LoCicero's father, he was a wop. Yes. But his mother was a Jew. From her he got his brains."

There was a little wait, a little silence. And then—that idiot—he laughed! Funny. Very funny, he thought it was funny, Irving Dahlberg's kid. The idiot.

"Papa, is there anything in this world you don't know about the people we have to deal with? Any tiny little fact they can hide? Anything at all? . . ."

Kids.

You can't explain anything to kids. Can't make them understand. Tell them something true. Tell them something that is important. Something that ought to mean something to them, they laugh. A joke. They think everything is some kind of a joke.

And so what? We were getting off the subject.

"Tomorrow," I said, to pull him up short. "Tomorrow, we'll talk more. About that. One other thing tonight. . . ."

"Yes, Papa?"

"That navy guy, your friend from college. The one who's

out here, now, with navy public relations. You talked to him?"

"About what, Papa?"

"About *what!*" Sometimes. Sometimes, even for the giant, sometimes it's too much. "About what the hell do you *think?*"

"Oh. Yes—the picture—"

"About the picture *Boarders Away!* About that . . . did you talk to this what's-his-name about the picture? About getting the navy to cooperate with us in making it?"

"Well, Papa—"

"Don't 'Well, Papa me!' Did you or didn't you talk to him?"

"We've been awfully busy, Papa. You know that. Putting together the schedule you wanted. For next year. I haven't really had . . ."

"You eat?"

"Yes, Papa."

"Lunch?"

"Yes, Papa, but, this last week, only something sent up. To my office. So we can—"

"Dinner?"

"Yes, Papa."

"You couldn't invite him—invite your old friend what's-his-name—to have lunch with you? In your office? Or dinner? At your home?"

"I don't usually go home for—"

"Then *anywhere!* Who cares where? Chasen's. La Scala. Jean's. That new place . . . what is it? The Bistro! You couldn't invite him to have a nice meal with you at the Bistro? A nice friendly meal where you could ask him, as an old friend, and it would be good public relations—that's what he's in, isn't it? Public relations?—good public relations for the navy, to put a good navy story on the screen, to help get the navy to cooperate?"

"Papa—"

"They cooperated with Zanuck! Sure. For him, everything; they cooperated. And for what? To make *Tora! Tora! Tora!* a picture where the navy gets its balls cut off at Pearl Harbor! For that, they help. But for *Boarders Away!*—to tell a story where the navy is a winner—for that, can I even get my own son to . . ."

87

*"Papa!* Please—!"

All right. Enough. When emotions get mixed up in anything, it's enough. In business, it's murder. Don't I know that? After forty years—more than forty, by God—doesn't Irving Dahlberg know that?

"We'll talk," I said, and I had my voice under control again. "Tomorrow . . . today . . . when I come over, we'll talk. Clara, she's going to cook?"

"Uh . . . yes, Papa."

"Good. Get some sleep, then, Jackie. Good night." And I hung up the phone and took a deep lungful of cigar smoke. You're not supposed to inhale them. I don't usually. But it was good, and it was late and Irving Dahlberg was tired and the lights twinkled. Far away.

A good place. Not like New York. Here I could stand, on the twelfth floor, not the fiftieth, and smoke the cigar with the window open. On Christmas morning. No snow. No cold air to tear up your lungs and freeze your nose. Just the lights. And the night air, to blow the cigar smoke.

"Always business," she said.

I turned away from the lights to look at her. Irving Dahlberg's woman. One strap of the shortie nightgown I had given her had fallen off her shoulder. The boob out, almost, down to the nipple; not that the fabric of the gown covered anything, anyway. Her hair was tousled and there was a sleepfold on one side of her face. But the eyes were bright. Wide awake.

"I thought you were asleep," I said. "You were tired when we came up. You said . . ."

"I was asleep. But you woke me, talking. Was that Jackie?"

"Yes."

"Has he seen the rushes? Of my scenes?"

I walked back over to the bed and sat down on its edge, turning my head, looking at her. "Yes," I told her. "He's seen them."

"Well?"

"Well, what?"

"What did he think? Of them? Were they all right?"

My woman. Irving Dahlberg's woman; all boobs and questions like that, at one o'clock in the morning. I felt tired. Very tired, suddenly. I wished she had stayed asleep.

"They're all right," I said.

"He liked them."

I shrugged. "What's *not* to like?" I said. "It's just bits and pieces so far, Gaby. A few lines in those early exteriors, and then the parts from that scene with Strauss. In the bed."

"But he *liked* them?"

"Sure. Of course." I wondered if Jackie really *had* seen any of the rushes. Maybe so. After all, wasn't Irving Dahlberg, himself, spending time on the set; wasn't Irving Dahlberg almost personally directing those scenes? But I hadn't asked him. I couldn't bring myself to.

"And *you* like them."

"I told you I did. Of course. Wasn't I right there, right on the set, to see that they were right?"

She giggled. That was one thing about her I hated, that giggle. Irving Dahlberg's woman shouldn't giggle.

"That wasn't why you were there," she said.

"What?"

"Why you were there. To see the scene was right. You didn't come down to the set for that."

"Why, then?" I said. "For what?"

She giggled again. "You know why," she said, "It was a sex scene. With David Strauss. The two of us. Making it. In the bed. You came down for that."

"What?"

"Come on, honey. Come on! It was supposed to be fake. *Look* like we were really making it. *Sound* like we were really making it. But really be just acting. So you had to be there."

"I had to . . ."

". . . run over. Every single time. Between every take."

"To make sure the sheet was right. For the camera angle. So it would show you off to the best . . ."

"To *check*." She wouldn't shut up. Wouldn't let it alone. The giant's woman. With the mouth. "To check," she went on, "with your hands. Under the sheet. Every time. Don't think I didn't notice. To make sure David Strauss was limp. Not up. To make sure he wasn't really getting any. Wasn't really putting it *in*—"

"Not true." *Not* true.

"True."

I turned away from her and shrugged out of the robe. I had had enough of this ridiculous discussion. And I was tired. Sleep. Irving Dahlberg needs his sleep.

"True. You ran your hands between us. Every time. To make sure. To see that he didn't have a bone on. To see we weren't really balling. . . ."

All right. Have it your own way. Irving Dahlberg needs sleep.

I tried to hold in the belly, leaning back to lie on the bed. That's the worst thing about the years. They put a belly on you, no matter how much care you take. Even on Irving Dahlberg. A belly. But it doesn't show much, when you lie on your back. I lay on my back. Beside her. With the cigar.

"You needn't have," she said, and her hand was on me. "You needn't have. Not for him. Not for David Strauss."

I didn't. I didn't! Irving Dahlberg, the giant, doesn't—but her hand was on me, massaging me, caressing me, and the nails were trailing. Digging, letting go, digging again.

"David wasn't trying," she said, and the hand moved down and inward. "David wasn't interested. Not him." Under me. The nails coming up, probing. Digging. Letting go and trailing again, upward. "But *you're* interested," she said. "You're interested, aren't you, honey? . . ."

And I was. God—ah, God—God help me, I was. Yes. Irving Dahlberg's head was interested. His belly was interested. His hips and crotch were hot, with pressure rising. Irving Dahlberg was interested—all but his equipment. All but that. The equipment was still ready for sleep. Still limp and ready for sleep.

That's another thing the years do to you.

I fumbled on the nightstand, putting the cigar aside. A half-hour smoke. I hadn't finished most of it. I put it aside in the ashtray and reached my hand over to her head. Touched the tousled hair. Felt the skull under it. Pushed her head, gently, gently, gently, down. Toward the heat. Toward the pressure. Toward the sleeping equipment. . . .

"Yes," she whispered. "Irving's interested. Irving's real interested." She moved her head toward the equipment. Touched it. Teeth. Tongue. *Yes! More! Oh, yes!*

And then she was gone.

So quick. Gone. Her head, from under Irving Dahlberg's hand. Her hand, from under Irving Dahlberg's body.

The radio snapped on.

Music.

"Yes," she said, still in a half-whisper. "Irving's real interested . . . so . . . let's see Irving *dance!*"

Ah, God. I wanted to kill her.

"Gaby!"

"Come on," she said, sing-songing the words. "Come-on. Come-on. Come-on, now. Irving knows what Gaby wants. Gaby knows what Irving wants. So let's see Irving *dance!*"

"Gaby. Not this time. Not tonight. Please."

"*Come*-on. *Come*-on. *Come*-on, Irving daddy! Come-on. do that dance for Gaby. Do that cute little dance you do. All naked. *Come*-on! Swing back and forth, Irving, daddy. Swing with your legs apart, that cute way you do, daddy. You know it turns me on. You know what it makes me want to do to you. Swing yourself back and forth, Irving, daddy. Make it swing in a circle!"

I got up.

Irving Dahlberg, the giant, got up. Irving Dahlberg, the giant, standing in his hundred-dollar-a-day suite. Irving Dahlberg standing naked, with the belly he can't quite hold in anymore. Irving Dahlberg, the man of *power*. The *giant*.

Irving Dahlberg began to dance. . . .

Ah, God!

I wanted to kill her.

But Irving Dahlberg began to dance. To the music. I hated her. I hated myself. I hated the years. I hated the equipment that needed what she could do . . . *needed* it . . . so badly that Irving Dahlberg would dance to the woman's tune. Swing himself. Back and forth. While the music . . .

That *music!*

Ah, God. What else would it be? Who else? Irving Dahlberg, the giant, was swinging himself, naked, to the music of . . .


## Buddy Valentine

". . . Mr. Johnny Valentine, doing an oldie but a goody, back when Johnny was really the Velvet Voice. And where else but here, on the Big Records Station, can you hear anything like that today? We'll have another of Johnny's records—something more recent, this time—right after this announcement."

I snapped the set off, and hit the stop on the tape.

Then I backed it up to the beginning and played it through once again, to make sure it had picked up both ends of the stereo.

It had.

*Buddy Valentine, boy engineer.* I sat back, resting my head against the chair, and listened to the Old Man sing. The Velvet Voice. For sure! The Velvet Voice—he really *had* a voice in those days. Oh, for sure.

*"But we were still singing,*
*Which gooo*            *show/that music hath . . ."*
      *o*
      *o*
      *o*      *to*
      *o*
      *oes*

For sure.

That's where it was, all right. Even then, before he really had to learn to sing, he had that. The sudden off-pitch drop. Following the note—all the way down to where the *money* is at, in those deep places—and then back up to the pitch again.

For sure.

Like the little warble catch Crosby'd had in his voice, when he was a kid. The signature. The something special. The extra quality in a performance that makes it uniquely your own.

Even when the Old Man's voice wasn't so great anymore (what, a two-note range, now? Would you believe one-and-a-half?), it was there. Not just that he'd learned to sing. No way. More than that, because it was still Valentine, and you couldn't mistake the style.

And he did learn to sing.

That was another thing. When the chips were down and he had to, he did learn. Wow, if only he'd really learned before the voice went. If only he had.

Sure. And if Buddy had been born with wheels, he'd have been an XK-E.

Or, anyway, a Datsun.

I listened to it all the way through twice more. Then I tried it through, myself, beating time with my finger on the edge of the desk and trying to hear myself and the Old Man at the same time. It wasn't too successful. It never was. But how else? . . .

The next time, I rewound the tape for playback, keeping the stereophones on, and snapped the little monaural cassette recorder to record.

Then, with the Old Man's version coming in through the phones, I sang it through myself for the tape, concentrating on making the big try at that tone-drop trick.

It sounded okay, from inside.

But when I switched over to play the cassette through the amps, it was nothing. I mean, nothing at all.

The voice? Oh, sure, the voice was okay—nothing great, not the Velvet Voice of Johnny Valentine; not like that—but acceptable. Very acceptable, if you like that sort of stuff. I have a good, average voice; good rhythm sense, fair tone quality. And I know something about singing. More than the Old Man did when he was making that record, twenty-five, twenty-six years ago.

But it was still nothing, and halfway through I couldn't stand it anymore and switched it off.

Not soon enough, though.

"Buddy? You're not sleeping. Why aren't you sleeping?"

"Sorry, Ma."

She poked the door open, just enough for me to see her eye through the crack. The hallway was dark, but I could see she was wearing the flowered-silk dressing gown. The one the Old Man had given her last June. On their anniversary. Their *anniversary,* for Christ sake!

"What are you doing, Buddy? In here, all by yourself. Was that you I heard—singing? Is that what you're doing?"

"I'm sorry, Ma. I didn't mean to wake you up. I was just—"

"You didn't wake me up." She came into the room, pulling the robe close about her. "I was up anyway, making sure about the table . . . and . . . making sure about things. You're cold in here, Buddy. You should keep warmer."

"Ma, please, don't be a Jewish mother!"

It was a joke. I meant it that way; a joke. But I forgot. My mother has no sense of humor. None at all. So naturally she took it for what the words said.

"We're not Jewish," she told me, looking at me like I

had maybe lost my mind. "We're Americans, and don't you forget it. And . . ."

I held up my hand, to try to explain. She ignored it.

". . . if we're anything else, it's Italian. Sicilian. We're Italian-Americans. And we're proud of it. Don't ever let your *father* hear you . . ."

"Ma," I said. "Ma, it was a joke. Just a joke."

"Well, it's not funny."

Okay. All right. Enough, Ma. Good night.

But, no.

"This girl," she said. "This . . . stewardess . . . Mandy, you're bringing. Tomorrow. Is *she* Jewish?"

"Her name is Sandy, Ma. Not Mandy!"

"Mandy. Sandy I never met her—but is she Jewish?"

"Ma, how would I know?"

"Not that I care," she said. "You know that, Buddy. You know I don't care if she's Jewish."

"Ma . . ."

"I just wanted to know. For myself. I wouldn't want any of us to say anything—you know—*wrong*. She'll be a guest. I wouldn't want to embarrass a guest. You know that, Buddy."

"Ma, she's just a girl. She could be Jewish. She could be a Moslem. She could be a Buddhist or a Freethinker or a Sun Worshiper or an African Methodist. . . ."

*"African Methodist!"*

Oh, Lord. Will I *never* learn; no jokes? For sure, she picked up on *that*. For sure!

"You didn't tell me . . . is this a *black* girl, Buddy? A *Negro* girl? Not that I care, of course. I don't. Your life is your own. But you didn't tell me. . . ."

"Ma—please? Her name is Sandy Hallowell. She's a stewardess on Union Airlines. She's a pretty girl. She's a nice girl. She's got a kind of kooky sense of humor. I like her. She's a white girl. She might have a grandfather as black as the ace of spades for you not to care about. She might be Jewish for you not to care about. But if there are any of those things for you not to care about, I don't know. I didn't ask her."

"All right! All right. . . ." She held up her shoulders and looked at the ceiling in that way of hers that means her only son is misunderstanding her as usual and being impossible as usual, and heaping coals of fire on her head as usual.

So, as Sam the *padrino* says, what else was new?

"I'm just trying," she said, "just trying to make sure we make a good impression on this girl you're bringing home."

Sure. Sure, Ma.

"The way you're saying that, Ma, you'd think I had proposed to the chick or something. This is . . ."

"Buddy, please! I've asked you a million times, don't use words like that."

"Like what?"

"Calling her a 'chick.' It's not nice."

"Ma, *chick* isn't a dirty word. It's just . . . well . . . chick. A word. For a girl. For a young girl like . . ."

"It's not respectful."

Ma, I'm respectful. Good God in Heaven, I am so respectful. Ma, I am so respectful, like you taught me to be respectful, Ma, that I fumbled, and bumbled and tripped. With hookers I can be at ease, Ma. But with "nice" girls I am a clumsy oaf, just like you taught me to be, Ma. That's how respectful I am.

"I'm sorry, Ma."

"I should hope. Be nice, Buddy. Like you used to be. Your father is a wonderful man, I've always told you that, a wonderful man. But don't be like him, where girls— women—are concerned. You don't want to be like that."

Like *hell* I don't want to be like that.

"Sure, Ma. I'll remember."

"Good. That's my Buddy."

She started to go out of the room, but stopped again by the door. I could see what was coming. A mile away. Talking about the Old Man, that had done it. Now she was going to be very subtle. Very casual. Very unconcerned.

"By the way, Buddy," she said, very subtle, casual, and unconcerned, "how *is* your father? You see a lot of him, back East?"

"No, Ma. Not much. Dad is busy—so am I. We don't get much chance to—"

"But you hear about him."

"Well, sure."

"His health's good? The cold back there, it was always hard on him. Even when we were younger."

"He's fine."

"Good, good. That's good." She didn't seem to have any more questions. But she didn't seem to want to go out the door, either. So I told her what she wanted to know.

"Only time I saw him," I said, "before on the plane, today, was the time at the party for Dolly Diamond. On the second anniversay of her show; you know, *Sadie*. Dad asked me to come, so I went. He looked fine then, too."

"Oh, yes." Still very casual. Still very unconcerned. And as subtle as a rhinoceros charge. "*That* one. Dolly Diamond. The flat one, skinny-flat, like a stick. I've seen pictures."

"Yes," I said. "Dad owns the show, you know. Put up the money. I think he sold it to Dahlberg the Great. He was on the plane, coming back from New York."

She wasn't listening.

"I heard somewhere that your father was going to marry this girl. This Dolly Diamond. That's a *lie*, isn't it, Buddy?"

"I don't know, Ma." I made it as convincing as I could, without any direct lies. "Like I said, I don't see much of Dad. We're both too busy. But I don't think anyone's said Dad was definitely going to—"

"He wouldn't." She was so firm, I knew she was scared. So sure, I knew it had been eating her up for weeks. Poor Ma. "He wouldn't—he *couldn't*—do that to me. To us."

Poor Ma.

"Sure," I said. "That's right. He wouldn't."

Poor Ma.

"Get some sleep, Buddy," she said, tightening the dressing gown again. "You don't want to be tired when your father comes. Or, you're going to pick her up, that girl, at some hotel, early, aren't you?"

"The Airport Marina. Yes, Ma."

"Well, you don't want to be all tired for that. Or red-eyed. Let me see your eyes." She bent over, putting her face close to mine, and pulled at my cheeks. "Red!" she said. "I knew it. You sleep, now, Buddy. And don't get it so cold in here."

She went out.

Poor Ma, praying every night that the Old Man would come back someday; poor Ma, dying a little every time he was seen around with another chick.

Poor Ma.

And poor Dad; poor Johnny Valentine, the big swinger with the brass balls, the Velvet Voice, the all-American stud.

And poor Buddy, the half-talented imitation, Buddy-boy Valentine.

Poor all of us.

Poor unfortunates—the Poor Unfortunates—all of us. Every single one . . . .

*And the hell with us.*

I picked up the stereophones again and put them on my head.

I snapped the playback, and I listened.

Not bad. Not bad at all. A singer, a Velvet Voice, Buddy-boy might not be. But an electronics engineer he was. They had done a good job rerecording that old monaural record of the Old Man's; I had the record, of course, but on stereo it sounded better. And my own tape of it, right off the air, with no distortion, no hum, no nothing. And I had built this rig myself.

A good job of work.

*Poor unfortunates . . . all of us. . . .*

Yes. For sure.

*Poor unfortunates. . . .*

But it was just too late at night, or too early in the morning, to stay bent out of shape that way. The hell with us. I replayed the tape one last time, hearing the tone, the quality. And it was . . .

## Johnny Valentine

. . . better than ever. Yeah, baby! Better than ever.

The Valentine pipes might be gone, but the Valentine talent was still right in there. You know it! The Valentine talent and the Valentine pizzazz and the Valentine zinga-roo!

Right *in* there.

So why in the hell hadn't the platter sold?

And what in the hell was wrong with the albums? . . . What kind of a kick-in-the-balls were these people giving me? The Organization?

*Think about that, baby.*

Could the Organization be doing it again? But why,

what for? The old trouble—that was ancient history. Past. So they taught a lesson, already. So Vanni got the message, right?

You know it, baby.

Catch me making a mistake like that again! Not in *this* world! I squared it, didn't I? Apologized, to the *padrone* and to old Angie's folks, the way the *padrone* said, I did all that stuff.

And even that wouldn't of been enough, if Anne hadn't——

*Cut it out, Valentine!*

Hey . . . hey! What's all this, anyway? The Organization, what the hell could they be giving me the business again for? I been careful, haven't I? Sure I have. Very, very damn careful. If there'd been anything at all, Sam would of given me the word. Sure he would.

*So why the hell isn't it selling?*

Who knows?

Who can tell about music, a record, in particular. It's all a kind of a—yeah, and you can cut that crap out, too, baby. Remember the last time you had to tell yourself a line like that? Sure you do. When the pipes went; when the engineers started sitting on the hands instead of snipping you together to sound like Johnny Valentine, and you sat around, you followed Anne around like a lost pup and everyone was calling you poor-Johnny-he-used-to-be-so-big. That's when.

And what was the truth, then?

The truth then was exactly like the truth now; it was all up to the Organization. Oh, sure, the pipes were bad. Bleeding, sometimes. And maybe the material wasn't the greatest either. (And who did *that* turn out to be? Who was making sure you never got a stab at the good material? Who?)

The Organization. They can make or break any singer. Any musician. If they're not right in there, making sure the distributors and the jobbers and all the rest, all of them, are pushing your stuff, if they're maybe getting the word around about how you're getting too big, all of a sudden, that you don't listen to the good advice anymore— how long does it take for you to be a whatever-became-of? A complete stranger? A no-name?

The stack on the turntable was played out and it shut

itself off and I hadn't even heard the last two. Or three, maybe.

Time. I started to look at my watch but the hell with that, who cares what hour, what minute, what second? Who cares which one of them is moving by. Time? Nighttime, Dad. Nighttime. Thinktime. Remembertime. Nowheretime.

The Chivas Regal bottle was sitting beside the chair, open. And the ice bucket. I started to lift the record stack and let it play through again but stopped with my hand on the records.

Have another blast of the booze.

Just one rock, this time—it's late and the stuff's not hitting me right.

Another blast.

With the glass refilled and a lot of silence around me, I wandered into the dining room. Dining room! A house like this, in Bel Air; a class house like this (what did it all cost? Two hundred grand, three? Hell, I can't even remember, now) and how many times had anyone ever eaten dinner in the dining room?

Yeah, in the bar or the Room or, no, not in the Room; nobody but you and sometimes Sam, ever, in the Room, but never in the dining room.

The Room. Now how did I get here?

What a laugh. What a farce. What a yak—turn your mind off for five seconds, Vanni baby, and where do you wind up? Still the Room. Well, hell, what did you expect? You knew. Didn't you know? You knew. The hour numbers get small, and Vanni winds up standing in the Room. Alone.

Yeah. Alone. But not alone.

There it was, across from me, across the Room. I had been staring at it for—how long?—a long time. And seeing it, in my head. In my head all the time whether I'm in the Room or on the other side of the world.

Christ, what a bitch. But what a beautiful bitch. A loser, yeah, a loser in spades. When I had that portrait painted, what was she; the biggest and the brightest and the hottest star in the business, that's what.

Just another bitch. Like a million bitches. Just another bitch, but on the screen, wham! Like a roll in the hay, just looking at her. Just watching her move. Everything. The voice, the eyes, everything. Like a roll in the hay.

And she was mine.

Vanni Valentine—she belonged to Vanni Valentine. Johnny Valentine and Anne Morgan (anyway I got top billing) made the big headlines all over the world. The two big stars. The Velvet Voice and the Golden Girl except, hell, Anne's hair was black (I wonder what color it is now? Gray? White? What?) and spread out on a bed, it . . .

*Stop that.*

I made the effort. But what was the use. What?

I sat down in the chair, facing the picture.

*Anne.* More than ten years, now—ten—hell, more like fifteen. Almost twenty. Where the hell was she, right now? Where? The phone, the private line that gets its number changed on a regular schedule to make sure it doesn't ring unless I want it to ring with a call from someone I want to call me, it was right under my hand. A wire, from that phone to anyplace in the world; I could call Anne, just wish her Merry Christmas, just talk to her a minute and hang up. I could do that. I could.

Like hell I could.

All right, then, let's try something. I got up, leaving the drink on the table beside the chair, and went over to the hi-fi setup. Prowled through the tapes there. Didn't find what I wanted and went back to the game room to get it.

All right. Now. . . .

The top of the eight-track cartridge stuck out of the player like a tongue, giving me the razzberry, but the sound from the tape was smooth and rich, a tone that said a lot of things; things that maybe weren't even there for the singer, but the kind that let you turn the sound into pictures in your head. Pictures of—*not* Anne. And *not* Vanni-baby, either. Pictures. . . .

Of *Dolly.*

I sat down in the chair again and took a deep one from the booze and looked straight at Anne's portrait. Waiting. Letting the two parts of my head fight it out between themselves. Dolly, coming in my ears. Anne, coming at my eyes.

Weird. Crazy. Nutty.

Love.

Love, I told myself, looking and listening; love—*amore.* Crap, Vanni baby. Crap! You are fifty years old, I told myself. Fifty, Vanni baby. Five-oh. Love? Listen, what the hell *is* love, anyway? . . .

I love my kids. I love the sun. I love the desert. I love looking at stars. I love hearing good music. I love—me? Yeah. You know it, baby—I love me! Vanni Valentine. Johnny Valentine. I love me.

So what about these two broads?

Anne? Dolly? What about them? Love them—well, come on, the truth—love *them?* Either of them? Both of them? *Love?*

And suddenly the sound stopped and I was alone. A fifty- (five-oh, baby!) year-old man alone in silence in a Room that I had once decorated, a Room I used to kid myself in about a lie, and who the hell needs that?

Too much. Too much future and too much past. Some gin. Call Sam and get him to play some gin with me to get me through the night. I reached over and picked up the phone and dialed a number I never have to look up.

He answered on the second ring.

"Hey, Sam! . . ."

"Wha'?"

"Hey, look, Sam—you asleep?"

"Oh . . . Vanni! Christ. *Merry Ex*-mass, baby. How was the flight from the East?"

"You were awake."

"Well, yeah; some stuff. I wanted to get it all looked over and checked tonight. You know. To get it done and have it offa' my mind. Before I come over—you know—to Angie's. You're gonna be there, right Vanni?"

"What? Oh. Yeah. Angie's. Sure, Sam. I'm—"

"Good. Couple things I wanna kick around with you. No big deal, maybe. No sweat. But—"

"Hey, Sam—"

"Yeah?"

". . . come on over. We'll play some gin."

"Christ, Vanni, it must be three in the—"

"So it's three in the morning, come on. I got you down seven thou for the last four months, give me a chance to make it an even ten."

"Vanni—"

"What's the matter, Sam baby? Getting old?"

"Yeah. And so are you. Look, Vanni—"

"What's to look? Come!"

"Naw, I can't. Really, Vanni. The stuff I got piled up here now's gonna take me the rest of the night."

"So put it off. It's Christmas."

"That's *why* it's gotta be done now." There was a little pause, then I heard the end of a yawn. "Look, keed, I really can't come. But as long as you're all wide awake and hot for action, what about a little talkie-talkie right now?"

"You don't *love* me anymore!" I put the fairy-whine on it. Sam loves to kid around about crap like that.

"Fuck you!"

"Promises, promises! . . ."

Sam laughed. One thing in particular I like about the guy; when he laughs you know it's for real. An honest guy, Sam. When he's on *your* side, anyway.

"No kidding, though," he said when the laughing was *finito*, "you got any listeners? I mean, is this on the special line?"

"Sure."

"Okay—lemme fill you in on a couple things you can be running over in your head between now and when I see you at Angie's."

All right. Okay. So, no gin game. A real worker, that Sam.

"Yeah. Shoot."

"First about the deal at Monarch: I think Irving baby's trying to give us a screwing, Vanni."

"How?"

"You know how the deal was set up: part cash for *Sadie* and part percentage on the picture's gross, part deferred cash, and part a coproduction agreement for TV?"

"Yeah?" Well, I guess I *did* know, all right. In a sort of a way; Sam handles the details. Just tells me the highlights—what to sign, what not to sign. Who's got time for all those clauses and all that fine print, right?

"Okay. So the money, the deferrals, the percentage, okay. On the button. But the television production deal—*zilch!*"

"*What?*"

"They're dragging their feet, Vanni. Remember we had a little trouble getting them to go for the TV setup to begin with? Because we aren't risking anything. Monarch pays half the most of anything we make; a network— whichever one we go to—picks up the other half of the tab. And the studio's stuck, too, for our office and other expenses there."

"They agreed to it, didn't they?"

"Yeah. Sure. They'd of promised you the torch offa' the Statue of Liberty, too, if you'd asked hard enough. Dahlberg was that hot for the *Sadie* rights. But, like you said, *'Promises, promises!'*"

I was beginning to see how it would be. Yeah, move our people into the offices, pay their hired help, but make sure you never have to put up your half of the production money. Yeah! And that money *would* crimp Dahlberg, too, right now; television had been a loser for the studio for a couple of years. His directors were going to be hitting him with questions if he sank upward of half a million in another television deal.

". . . so, no matter what we come up with, or who we take it to," Sam was saying, "we get the smile, the thanks, and the 'We'll let you know' routine. It's sour, Vanni."

"That rotten bastard."

"Who—Dahlberg?"

"Who else? Sitting a couple of seats from me on the plane, all the way out here. And never a word out of him. No wonder! He probably thought I already knew what was going on about the TV deal and wanted to rack him about it."

"Maybe," Sam said. "Maybe—maybe not. You didn't talk to him, did you, about Dolly Diamond signing for the flick?"

"No. I *would* have. Sure. But he just sat there. In fact that was why I asked him on the flight, so we could kick some jazz around about her contract. Not that I'd sign anything without you, Sam. You know that."

"Yeah." He shut up for a moment. Thinking. I was thinking, too. That Dahlberg! That old creep! "Well, in that case," Sam said finally, "maybe we got them by the balls."

I couldn't see it. "Maybe I missed a couple of frames," I said, "but to me, it looks the other way, Sam. . . ."

"Not necessarily." Sam had that cautious sound in his voice, now; the one I knew so well. It meant here-comes-the-wienie. "I kinda think Irving baby has outshrewded himself this time."

"How?"

103

"Well, two things: first, aside from the financial crap, that was a pretty standard legit-movie contract we gave them. Standard restrictions and all that. Standard enough, maybe Dahlberg the Great—*and* his cutesie-pie legal staff —didn't pay much attention."

"So?"

"So *this:* that contract contains a clause forbidding them to *release* the movie—not *produce* it, mind you; just forbidding them to *release* it—until the show, the legit stage show, is folded."

I still didn't get it.

"Sam, I talked to the theater people when I was East. They said six months more, maybe. Hell, it's already set a couple of records for that house. It folds in six months, Dahlberg has the green light."

Sam laughed. Not the belly-happy laugh; the dirty one. The kind he gives me when he puts down gin.

"Yeah, baby," he said. "On *Broadway,* it folds. But a *road company*—that could still make money, no?"

"Well, sure. I guess so."

"Uh-huh. And as long as we got a company on the road, Vanni, it's still covered by that clause. They *still* can't release!"

I was beginning to see it now. But there was something I thought maybe Sam had missed.

"Okay," I said. *"Fine.* But—Sam, I don't know how you're going to like this—I kind of promised Dolly, see. She said she doesn't want to go on the road with the show; I guess someone already mentioned it to her (and the someone was *me,* baby) so she—well—you know how it's been, Sam, with Dolly and me. And—"

"Vanni—*Vanni!"* Sam almost sounded hurt. Almost. "Vanni, this is *Sam,* baby. Sam! Would I miss a point like that?"

No. Not Sam.

"That contract," he said, "doesn't say a fucking word about Dolly Diamond, or anyone else, having to be in the road show. Not even about the Broadway production. She could leave tomorrow. . . ."

"Sam, you're the *greatest.*" And I meant that.

". . . and while the show continues its run, they're still hung up. Hell, baby, you could get Whistler's mama for

104

the lead. Tomorrow, if you feel like it. And nothing's changed, as far as our deal is concerned."

I don't know. With a cat like Sam on the team, why the hell do I ever worry about anything. Tell me—why?

"Okay," I said. "That's one ball we got them by. And it's a dinger. It's a business to do pleasure with you. Still, don't forget, Sam, I really *would* like to get into that TV production deal. Maybe direct some of it, even; I always wanted to have a real hack at that."

"I know." The words came out flat, but there was an extra in there. Somewhere. Like another laugh he didn't want to laugh, yet.

"If we put it to them," I said, "lay it on the line with Dahlberg, maybe we can squeeze enough to make them go ahead with the television?"

"Uh-huh," he said. "Funny thing, Vanni, you know, I kinda thought that's how you might feel. About *really* going into the production thing. You been talking about it more and more, lately"

"I have?"

"Yeah, you have." He stopped to yawn again. Poor bastard, I guess he really was bushed. "So I did a little looking, a little checking, and I sorta' think I came up with a gimmick that's a winner."

What else, with Sam?

"Who do I have to kill?"

"Nobody—maybe." It was supposed to have been a gag line, but Sam wasn't laughing. "It depends. Vanni baby, how'd you like to own a whole studio?"

"*Monarch?* Hey, Sam, what've you been smoking? You know we—"

"Not Monarch," he said. "At least, not yet. But a big studio; a major."

He just let it lay there.

"Okay," I said after a minute. "Okay. What do we play, Twenty Questions? Drop the other shoe, already."

"How about—oh—say, Priapus? How would that do, Vanni? Just for an easy start, I mean?"

Say this for Sam: when he flips his wig, he doesn't mess around. He flips it all the way.

"Sam," I said, "Sam, go to sleep, huh? You're tired. I shouldn't have called . . ."

"I said Priapus," he made every word clear and exact, "and I meant Priapus. Do you, or don't you want it?"

"Hey—you're not *kidding!*"

"I'm not kidding."

"Old Steve Pappas wants to *sell?*"

I couldn't believe it. Pappas was one of the few old-time moviemakers to survive into the second half of the twentieth century still in absolute control of his own studio. Sure, it was a corporation; sure, he had a board of directors. Sure. But his stock was controlling; his grip on Priapus was firm. And he was proud of it—proud of being the last absolute studio boss in town. In the world, in fact. *Proud,* baby!

No. Old Steve wasn't going to sell; I was sure of that.

And I was right.

"Not sell, exactly," Sam said.

"Yeah, well, then?"

"He's looking for a merger, Vanni. Looking for just the right kind of a merger—and Vanni, baby, *so are we!*"

"You're out of your head," I told him. "No *way* do I walk into that old spider's parlor! You got to be kidding, Sam."

"I'm not," Sam said. "And neither is old Steve. Listen, Vanni—you know why he wants it? The merger?"

"No, and I—"

"He wants it because he's had a consistent loss record on the studio and all its subsidiaries for two, three years, now."

"He could ride that out. He—"

"Why, though? Why, when he can make a deal that gives him a whopping loss *this* year—and shoves him back into the heavy green again next year?"

That was a stopper.

"Huh?"

"Lullaby, Vanni," Sam said. "Lullaby Records! Our company—our little gold mine that struck a bum vein this year."

"Sam, I don't want to do it."

"Yeah, yeah, you do, Vanni. I know how you feel about the record company. When you put that one together, it was because you knew you'd been getting shafted on record deals for years while you were with Foremost."

"Too right, baby," I said. "And I'm not taking a chance like that again. So forget it."

"Vanni, will you listen? Just a minute, for Christ sake,

will you listen to your ol' Uncle Sammy? Lemme lay it out for you; then if it's still no—okay. We don't discuss it again. All right?"

I didn't want to. I guess I got a lot of memories I don't like. Most of them, though, I can kind of shove back, far into the mind, right? Where they don't keep scratching. But one I never put back there—the part those Foremost bastards had in damn near breaking me. Grudge? Maybe. But just the idea of taking any chance like that again, just the idea, was enough to give me the creeps.

Still, Sam is Sam.

He hadn't given me a bum steer yet.

"Okay, Sam," I said. "Let's hear it."

"Good. To begin with, the record business has changed a hell of a lot the last few years. You know that as well as anyone. This new sound—acid rock, all that crappola—that's what the kids are buying. The records that woulda been surefire a few years back—zilch."

"Well, yeah," I said. "Funny thing, I kind of wanted to talk to you about records anyway, Sam. That last album of mine . . ."

". . . was a loser that shoulda been a winner. Right! Look, Vanni, who buys records? Who, the geriatric set? The people thirty-five to forty?"

"Some," I said. "They buy records, mine, especially. Hell, most of those people, they grew up with me."

Sam laughed. "You putz," he growled. "Who in hell said you ever grew up? Sure, Vanni, some records they buy. And yours are big with them. But you know and I know that the big hack is just what it's always been—records sell a million only when the kids go for them."

Yeah. That was the hell of it. I knew.

"So right now, Lullaby is in trouble," Sam went on, "because most of the talent we've got just can't make it in this New Sound thing. They swing, yeah. But, face it, baby, for the moment, we're sucking hind tit. They're great, but not hot. Not no more."

"So we switch," I said. "Any talent we got, me included, who can't dig the New Sound—aus mit! And we nab off a couple of the big acid rock groups (when did we ever have trouble pirating, Sam?) and maybe develop some of our own. Buddy even; he's got some new group he wants to record. No problem."

"Right!" Sam surprised me. "That's what we do, right! Hell, we're already doing it. I'll lay that on you tomorrow. But meanwhile, you know we still got another hassle—distribution. Since the first, that's been a pain in the butt."

"Well?"

"So check this action, Vanni," Sam cut me off. "Everybody knows old Steve Pappas's platter arm, Priapus Records, has always been a big loser for him. If Lullaby is having New Sound problems, Priapus never even made it with the Old Sound. Their talent—wasn't."

"Give that man an exploding cigar!"

"But, Vanni baby, don't forget: talent they might lack, but organization they got! They can distribute, Vanni. Now, here's how I figure it. We merge with Priapus, on condition that old Steve drops the whole Priapus Records A and R program; that's our baby, from Day One. He keeps Priapus distribution, for use by Lullaby, with full audit and bookkeeping under our thumbs . . ."

"You bet your *ass* it'll be!"

". . . and we are holding, to start with, board representation for the Priapus stock we pick up on trade in the merger—*plus* (and here's the brass ring, baby) a profit-purchase option on Steve's entire Priapus holding, based on annual return."

*That passed me on the turn.*

"In English, Sam," I said. "What's it mean?"

"It means that, year by year, we pick up more and more of Priapus until, when Steve's finally ready to get out, or if he dies, we own the joint."

I still wasn't sure.

"How long?" I asked. "How long does it take, this way, for us to climb into the saddle?"

Sam sighed.

"It could," he said, "be as long as six, seven years. More, even, if business stays bad. Sure, Vanni, that part's a gamble. But at least, even at the beginning, we have a combined loss picture that makes the deal profitable on both sides. And we stay in the saddle with Lullaby, too, plus picking up a first-rate distribution organization."

I closed my eyes.

Christ, who could know? The idea of owning a studio, a major at that, was a daydream. One I hadn't figured could ever be. But the old bugaboo, losing control of my own records, was right in there doing business, too. And the time angle. Seven years, maybe!

*Who could know?*

"Sam," I said, with the eyes still closed, "I got to say it's worth a look. That much, yeah."

"One other thing," Sam picked up, still selling hard, "about old Steve. You know, Vanni, the guy really is a lot older than those studio biogs claim."

"Who isn't?"

"So, it might *not* be seven years, too."

I wished he hadn't said that.

"Yeah, sure," I said. "But let's don't figure it that way, huh? It's—well—it's wishing a guy dead for his money."

Silence from Sam.

"You know I don't go for stuff like that, Sam. I mean, you know . . . I feel *wrong* about it."

"I know," Sam's voice was tired again; but warmer, too, some way. A funny guy, Sam. "I know how you feel about that, Vanni. The Commandment, right? You, Vanni—from anybody else, anybody in this frigging town—a line like that would be a phony. A put-on. But not from you."

A kind of a laugh, he ended it with; and some sad in it.

"I just . . ."

"Forget it. Pay no attention. Who would believe Giovanni Valentine, the Chicago altar boy, still is walking around inside Johnny Valentine, the big swinger, ready to make the *contrito* because he *coveted!*" A big yawn, this time, into the phone. "Anyway, you're a hard guy to figure, sometimes. Like a helluva lot of other people. Including the big-shot lawyer, who is now going to get some sleep, Mr. Valentine, sir, if you do not mind."

"Yeah," I said. "Okay. Good night, Sam."

" 'Night—oh, and Vanni . . ."

"Yeah?"

"You don't have to make up your mind on the Priapus deal right now. We got time. Kick it around, walk around it and look. Take your best shot. Right?"

"Right."

"Later, keed. . . ."

And he hung up.

Well, hell. A long conversation for a long morning; a lot

of heavy thought to lay on a guy. A lot, particularly, in the early hours of Christmas. A lot to think about. Too much, I tell you true, for sleep.

Suddenly I realized I was still standing with my eyes shut. I opened them.

Suddenly I realized I was cold.

I slugged down the booze.

Suddenly I realized I was staring at Anne's picture.

I turned away.

Suddenly I realized I was all alone. . . .

Walking fast, but not running, I cut through the game room to pick up the bottle and grab a fresh glass, and headed for the special iron spiral staircase in my bedroom. Up the stairs, two at a time, wrestle with the catch on the trap (damn it, why couldn't I ever remember to get that thing fixed?) and then onto the roof.

Across the special board-lattice walk.

To the Shack.

Most of the really bright lights of the city were screened by the hills and the trees, but the trees and hills were a drawback, too. They cut off the sides of the sky.

Still, there was a good arc of vision.

I opened the shutters and pedaled the Shack around part of its traverse, peeking through the Spotter.

And there it was. . . .

I wound and locked in the timer-tracker and sat down.

And the rings of Saturn posed for me; smooth and beautiful, like a kiss from the soft blackness around them. A perfect thing; a fire opal set in crystal.

The far place. The dream place. The unknown. The Eye of Satan.

*The anodyne for all-alone.*

I looked away long enough to tilt the Scotch and savor the rush of it down my throat; the warmth for the gullet, the explosion down below.

And then I . . .


### Sandy Hallowell

. . . landed on the outer ring and it was like the old wooden Whirlaway ride that came to town every summer. It was turning, faster and faster, and I did my best to hang on but in the end it was too much and I felt myself slip-

110

ping—slipping—off into the cold black of space. Only it wasn't space anymore. It was water; the ice-cold water of the sea, waiting to take me, reaching for me with foam hands to . . .

*Whump!*

I landed, flat on the Hallowell derriere, beside the too-narrow hotel bed—and felt better right away. Say what you will, ole buddy, a wroggle out of bed and a bump on the empennage beats a tussle with the Hallowell Special sea nightmare every time!

Grappling valiantly with the bedclothes and rising in the process to semisitting, I fumbled in what I fondly hoped was the direction of the bed lamp. And stopped, too, before any real damage could be done.

The stew in the other bed was a light sleeper, and she had a flight at oh-six-hundred.

A good kid she might be, and an old friend as well. But hell hath no fury like a stew whose sleep is chopped up by a restless roomie. I untangled myself in the darkness and managed to get back into bed; the covers would just have to live their own life. Certain tactile irritations informed me that the sheet was apparently atop the blanket. Let it be.

*The sea dream again. . . .*

Well, so what? It had been a long time, now, and I guess the time was ripe. Christmas. Seeing Bob and Mickey again. And now this thing coming up with Buddy Valentine. Of course. What did you expect, Hallowell? All that in about twenty-four hours and then you let your leg stick out from under the covers and the room is too cold (whoever said southern California is a warm climate? Hoo-boy. He must have been someone who never left his nice warm cave after dark in winter!) and so you were heading for the sea again. . . .

*Well—that's what the chart said, isn't it, Hallowell?*
No!

"Astrology is not a doctrine of fatalism. It provides us with an inventory of the working materials with which we are endowed at birth. . . ."

"How we use or neglect the tools remains within our own jurisdiction. . . ."

". . . improve our fate by complying consciously with nature's laws instead of violating them. . . ."

"Wisdom puts an end to pain."

111

*You betcha!* The chart only showed me the danger: good, strong, reinforced air signs; dangerous, weak, hairy water signs. Work with the one, avoid the other. What could be simpler?

*Absolutely!*

Only I've been scared spitless of water, anyway, ever since that time at the lake when I was just four years old and that little bully rotten Wally Reed, threw me off the boat dock and laughed because that was the way to teach a dog to swim. Darn him! Oh, he got *his* all right—did he ever. First from my brothers, and later from me, as soon as I figured out a way to catch the dirty sneak alone. That rock I was carrying made up for the fourteen months and ten pounds difference.

*I'd like to go back, right now, and sock him again.*

No.

Not really, I guess.

But I still wish he'd stuck to dogs. . . .

*Think about something else:* be smart, Hallowell, and think about getting some sleep, maybe!

Boy, are you ever going to be a prize package when Buddy picks you up in the morning. (I don't like that name; it doesn't fit him; what's his real name, I wonder? John, maybe? For his father?) He'll probably scream and run out the door. . . .

*Funny-Face. Odd that Sneaky Hands Newton would come up with that* one.

It's been a long time since anyone called you that— where you could hear them, anyway.

Oh, *God,* but it was good to see Bob and Mickey again! They can call me Funny-Face anytime they want. Just so they're safe. *Funny-Face.* That used to hurt, didn't it, Hallowell? Yes. That hurt. Why so much, I wonder?

Well, check out the inventory: coloring, passable (more than passable, maybe, if you count the eyes; that is some swell shade of green if I do say so myself) and configuration up to specifications. (Be honest there, too, chum: that is a little jim-dandy of a bod, not only a visual asset, but quick of reflex and durable of construction—and you know how well and how quickly it was able to learn its primary function, and how direct and certain it can still be, given the proper programming.)

But the face. . . .

112

*Funny-Face.*

Nothing really wrong with that face (except that one eye is level and the other isn't, quite), nothing at all (except that the mouth is too wide and the nose is too short and whoever assembled the parts must have been new on the job and didn't know enough to demand an exchange on the chin; it would fit a baby a lot more handily than a grown-up woman named Hallowell).

*"Sandy's never going to be the beauty in the family, no. Not the way her mother was. Takes after my people, poor kid, poor little Funny-Face. . . ."*

You never knew I heard you say that, did you, Dad?

Or that I could have understood. Only five years old. Sneaking out of bed to spy on the grown-ups, still sitting up and talking down in the parlor after my bedtime. You never knew I heard it.

*Funny-Face.*

But the boys didn't seem to notice about that when the time came for them to start to notice. Only the other girls, and only when The Hallowell would win something from them: Homecoming Queen, that last year in high school; Head Cheerleader the last two years; Class Valedictorian (not bad for a kid who went to school where they skip you a grade or two upward if you're bright, so that I was two years younger than anyone else in the class). Only, of course, I didn't get to give the graduation address, because of Dingy-Bob, The Frampton, and a little too much time alone with him coming back from the basketball game in Evanston. . . .

*Funny-Face.*

So why did it hurt so much? . . .

*It didn't!*

Yes it did, too. Be honest, Hallowell. It *hurt*. Yes. But . . . but not always. Not from everyone.

From Dad, that first time, it hurt.

But not from the girls I knew in school. Not from guys I knew there, or even dated. From them, it came on as sort of a nickname, the kind they don't call you if they don't like you. Friendly, but not—well—important. Not even an opinion, really. Or anyway, not an opinion that meant anything.

From your brothers, it sometimes hurt.

But it didn't touch me, one way or the other, when Bob Frampton said the name to me. No, indeedy. And that alone should have warned me I didn't care a darn for him.

Yessir. That's it, isn't it, Hallowell? The nickname only hurts when someone you love says it.

Yes.

And that's why it hurt when John Dryfuss called you Funny-Face. Of course, you kind of walked into it, didn't you? Doing The Act. It was *supposed* to be funny, wasn't it? Sure it was. A psychiatrist—a headshrinker—would call The Act a defense mechanism. And he would be right: you put it together deliberately, chum; with malice aforethought, to be funny.

The guitar lessons. First thing you bought when you went to work at the hospital. And it turned out The Hallowell had a little talent. Not a lot. No Joan Baez—not even Buffy St. Marie. But a little. The voice, sort of husky and breathy on the vocals. But true on tone and good diction; you could understand the words.

Especially if the words were my own. And funny.

The Act: Sandy Hallowell, girl comic. Music by just-about-everybody, but lyrics by Hallowell—sometimes even ad lib, on the spur of the moment—accompanied by guitar and comedy expressions. They laughed. Darn right they laughed; The Act was funny and The Hallowell was funny and it got to be a kind of standard after-shift or coffee-break deal . . . go down to the doctors' lounge and have a good laugh listening to Sandy's songs.

*Funny-Face.*

I guess John meant it as a pet name; a term of endearment. And naturally I couldn't tell him not to call me that, could I? Nope. Because if I did, it would have been admitting, to me as much as to him, that he meant something to me. Dr. John Dryfuss, the noted surgeon. Dr. John Dryfuss, the nurses' delight. Big, tall, curly-haired, casual, friendly, brilliant, gentle Dr. John Dryfuss. Of course every nurse in the place had a crush on him. What else?

But it was Funny-Face he talked to. Spent time with. Kissed. Touched. Held. Made love to.

*Stop it, Hallowell.* Go to sleep.

Yes, and it was Funny-Face who cried herself to sleep when his letters stopped, after he'd finished his internship and gone on to Johns Hopkins for the surgery residency. And Funny-Face who quit the hospital—telling herself she was bored with the routine—when word trickled back from

Baltimore that Dr. John Dryfuss was married—very suddenly, the word was—to one of the nurses there.

One of the nurses. Uh-huh.

One of the nurses who was *just a little bit* smarter, and probably a whole lot prettier, than The Hallowell, that kooky, guitar-playing kid back where he spent his internship. I wonder if he ever mentioned Funny-Face to the new Mrs. Dryfuss?

Oh—*stop* it, Hallowell!

Anyway, the words haven't hurt since then, have they? Funny-Face. They still call you that, even brash copilots.

But it doesn't hurt, really. Not since John Dryfuss, the name hasn't meant a thing. So why are you lying here, losing sleep? Could it have been different? Could anything really have been much different for you, Hallowell?

No.

Yes.

Maybe . . . if I'd had Understanding book then. Maybe.
And how I fought against it. Told myself it was just superstition. Just a new edition of an old idea; a fad that couldn't really tell you anything. After all—*astrology,* for Pete's sake!

But you couldn't let it alone.

First the talk. To the woman passenger who wanted to know the date and hour and place you were born. Five hours, she had, on a transcontinental flight, and she worked out that first tentative chart for you (but she was an amateur; the figures were off on one part) and told you things about yourself she couldn't have known even if she'd been a private detective.

And then later, when the mistakes she'd made were corrected, when you finally broke down and went to a professional who showed you where her work had been incorrect, and how right-on-the-button the chart could be if it were done properly.

Even to correcting your time of birth.

That was the clincher, wasn't it, Hallowell? The convincer. Because Dad had always told you that you were born at 2:15 in the morning, or pretty close to that, only the chart didn't quite work out that way; to make it come out right, for every single thing that had happened to you so far in your life, it would have had to be almost an hour earlier.

And finally you asked him again—and he rustled up your birth certificate and discovered he had made a mistake. That you *were* born earlier, right around the time the chart said it would have been, and the time he'd said was really the hour that your mother died. A little more than an hour after you were born. . . .

Poor Dad.

Oh, I wish—I wish—I wish a lot of things. For him. For me. For all of us. But anyway Mickey and Bob are safe, not dead somewhere in a rotten jungle halfway around the earth. Of course I knew they wouldn't get killed. I had the Understanding. I worked out their whole charts before they went overseas, didn't I? And it showed some danger, but not death. Not in that part of the world and not by accident or the act of any other person. A natural death for both of them. Something in the blood or the circulation. Sudden, but natural.

Strokes, probably. Like Dad. And a long, full time away.

But you worry anyway. Sure you do. Why? Because, even with all the proof, you still don't trust it entirely, do you?

*I do.*

You don't. Or you wouldn't have worried.

*I do.*

All right, then, Hallowell. Have it your own way. You do. So it's panic time again. Uh-huh.

*Capricorn.*

Buddy Valentine is a Capricorn. *The* Capricorn, Hallowell? No. That doesn't make sense. He's just a man I talked to a few minutes on the plane.

*You're seeing him tomorrow—today, it is now.*

And that will be that.

*Will it, really?*

Of course. I'll be back on schedule a few hours afterward and flying East. Three days from now, the schedules all change. You're still not senior enough to call your shots every single time; you'll probably wind up with some other run. Something that will make sure you never see or hear from Mr. Buddy Valentine again.

*Uh-huh.*

Still, it might just be a good idea to see if I can't find out the exact hour and place he was born. Just to . . . to . . . keep in practice working out charts. So the mind muscles don't get flabby.

116

*And if it turns out he's the Capricorn?*

It's not inevitable. Nothing really is. Just indications. Just things to be careful of. Like you've been careful all this time; making sure the airline you work for has no overocean flight schedules. Because . . .

*The chart shows it very clearly.*

Death by mischance. Accident. Outside agency. But before death—or the extreme danger of death; it's *not* inevitable—the *Capricorn*.

*So . . . ? Even after finding him, you could have turned him off. Why don't you, now?*

Because he—because Buddy Valentine seems like such a sweet guy, and he knows how to laugh and that's pretty darn unusual, especially if the laugh's on him, and he . . . he . . .

*What?*

None of your business.

*Oh, come on, Hallowell. Stop evading!*

I won't, and you , , ,


## David Strauss

. . . can't make me do anything I don't want to because it's my life and I'll live it as I please . . . please . . . please . . . *please* let the morning come. Let the light come. Let that window to the street show something besides black.

*"Sure you want another one, buddy?"*

The screaming in my head cut off abruptly and I looked away from the little sign hole in the front window of the after-hours bar, where the world outside remained so dark and frightening, and looked at the bartender.

Type casting.

A heavy fellow, with about ten strands of what looked like dyed black hair combed carefully over his bald head and a cigar clenched, but not burning, in the side of his mouth. Holding the Scotch-rocks I'd ordered, but not putting it on the bar in front of me.

"Sure I do. I ordered it."

"Maybe what you really need is to go home. I could call you a cab."

"But I'm *not* a cab!"

Bad line, David, dear. Bad line—it didn't convince him,

117

and he didn't even pretend to laugh at the gag. Keep it serious. Keep it straight. He could eighty-six you—and where in hell would you find another bar at this unearthly hour?

"Honest," I said, gathering myself together and turning on the well-known Strauss charm. "Honest, I'm okay. I only make bad jokes on Christmas morning."

Another moment's hesitation.

And then the shrug, and the drink set down in its proper place, in front of David. And he walks away.

Have another Scotch-rocks, David, darling.

"Thank you, don't mind if I do."

*Watch it, Strauss!* Now you're saying lines out loud, in those clear, ringing tones that are designed to carry to the very back of the theater. People are going to start looking at you. (Well, that's what they're supposed to do to an actor, isn't it? Look at him?) *David Strauss, star of stage, screen, and ESP, invites each and every one of you to Look At Him.*

All except the bartender.

He's new. New since I was in here, earlier, since before I walked up to Times Square and got littler and littler, and made those telephone calls to tell people I love them and Merry Christmas and got shat on (right through the earpiece!) by both of them, and then walked back here (carefully keeping my eyes away from all the theater marquee signs; carefully not seeing how many tiny little pieces of davidstrauss they contained) and came in again because there was no place else. No place else. No place . . . that is safe.

Have another fear, David, dear.

Thank you. I mind terribly if I do. But this isn't another fear. This is the same old fear as always. Mugging? Not a chance, not in all this cold. The only mugger fool enough to be up and around at this time of morning, in this kind of cold, in this part of town; the only mugger like that would have to be a drunk and a slob that David Strauss can handle with one hand. No. Not mugging; I don't have to be afraid of mugging this morning out of all the possible mornings of the year.

What, then?

Who, then?

*David Strauss, star of stage, screen, and ESP, invites you and yours to notice the trembling of his buttocks, the shivery spasms in his back, the tremor in his hands.*

It could be just the cold.

It could. . . .

Suddenly I looked up, flashing back in my mind to the time a few hours ago when I sat fitting my face into the wreath behind the bar. The wreath hanging in just the right position, against the mirror, to frame the face of davidstrauss.

The mirror was there, but the wreath was not.

*Is this the same bar?*

Yes.

It's the same bar. So—what became of the wreath? That bartender, the one who was here before, was it *his* wreath, maybe? His own wreath, so he took it home with him for Christmas? To his own warm home-and-hearth?

This new bartender doesn't look like anyone who'd have a home-and-heart. Excuse me: *not* heart. Hearth!

> *You belong to my hearth,*
> *Now and For-never!*

How about that?

At least I'm not making up dirty Christmas carols anymore. Just bad lyrics for old sons. Excuse me: *not* sons. Songs! Songs. Songs like that one: *"Solamente una vez. . . ."* Ah! *Si!* David Strauss, start of—excuse me: *not* start. *Star!*

Star! davidstrauss is a *Star!*

David Strauss, however, is sitting here in this bar (where a wreath's mysterious disappearance has just been noted in the great detective's mental notebook) remembering for the first time in howmanyyears that he can speak Spanish. Well, Cuban Spanish, anyway (everyone else in the Spanish-speaking world hates the way Cubans talk Spanish; they say they make it sound like German, deep and guttural and harsh, like the way Americans speak English. Maybe that's why I had no trouble learning it, after all I could speak German—low German, with enough admixture to make it Yiddish—before I could speak English, couldn't I?).

Of course I can speak Spanish.

Learned it from listening to the Cuban kids in my old neighborhood, before my uncle shlepped me away and out to the Coast to school. Out to where I found Jackie.

119

*Jackie.*

*Why did he have to be so mean to me? Why?* Why did he have to be so mean when I just called him up to say Merry Christmas and I love you, Jackie, darling. I've always been true to you, Jackie, darling. Never with anyone else. Never with any other boy. . . .

Never.

Only with girls, Jackie! And you know that doesn't count. We agreed about that, didn't we? We agreed about that.

Then why was he so mean? I was true to you, Jackie. Kiss me, Jackie. Love me, Jackie. Love me. *Love me!*

*Damn* you!

*Love* me!

Have another drink, David, darling.

No.

*Have another . . . lover . . . David, darling.* Have another lover! Show Jackie you don't care. Prove it to him. Prove it to yourself. Another lover. *Love!*

Yes.

This is Christmas, give yourself that gift, David. Give yourself that! *Love.* Leave now and . . .

No.

I won't. It hasn't happened, not since Jackie, it hasn't happened. Not with anyone else. Only girls. David Strauss is straight. David Strauss is a well-known stud! Oh, yes. Well known. Well.

David Strauss is a *well*-known . . . cuckold!

Oh, come on, now, Strauss. What kind of a word is that? What page of Shakespeare, what part of Lee Strasberg's Jungle Book, what semester of Early Drama did you find that word in? Cuckold. Forsooth and gadzooks!

David Strauss: cuckold.

Wearing—in good health—the gift from the guinea.

David Strauss: stud turned cuckold.

Because he bored his lovely, boyish, talented, powerful, compelling, frigid, rejecting, bitch-of-a-wife. *Bored* Dolly!

"You're a fucking bore . . ."

Eat *that,* David Strauss!

". . . and a boring fuck!"

Eat *that,* davidstrauss . . . because she finally said it, said what you could see in her eyes, day after day after day, when you were married to her; thank her for that, thank

120

her for your Christmas present, David, darling. Thank her for finally telling you the truth.

Merry Christmas, Dolly, from your loving, boring, cuckolded husband.

Merry Christmas, Jackie, from your adoring, true, rejected love. . . .

Merry.

*Merry!*

. . . and suddenly I had to get out of there. Not like the first time I left. No. This time the fumble for money was no fumble. I checked the tab (my eyesight was clear; twenty-twenty) and added it twice (no sense letting this cigar chomper take advantage) and counted out the exact amount and then threw down one buck—one lousy buck—for the tip. And walked out.

It was still dark.

Why had I been fighting it? Sitting there and letting my eyes steal sneaky looks at the window hole, to see if dawn—and safety—had come? What for? Who for?

It was still cold.

But that made no difference to me; a warmth, full of urgency and excitements I had denied for too long, for *far* too long, filled me with tropic heat.

Around the corner. Along the street (no theater signs here to break davidstrauss into smaller davidstrausses!) and around another corner. Across the street. Across the Circle. Across another street.

And to the fringe of the park.

Yes.

Yes, there they were! As I had known they would be. Danger? Sitting back there in the bar, I had told myself they were danger. Walking the other way along Broadway to that damnable, that destroying telephone, to make those damnable, destroying calls to those damnable, destroying people, I had told myself they were danger.

Danger?

I walked toward them.

I walked past them. Slowly. Letting my eyes tell my story to those who would see. Feeling the heat and the trembling become more and more intense.

They saw.

They knew.

Turn. Into the park! Past the path and the bushes. Past

. . . yes! Past the couple I could dimly make out in the darkness, grabbing frantically at each other, together, only a part of their clothing removed or opened; a crushed intimacy of mottled shadow, one on his stomach in the snow and the other astraddle him, deaf and blind to the danger that might have been in the sounds of my approaching footsteps, blind and deaf, in that last moment of exiled excitement to the fear of detection.

*Be happy!*

*Merry Christmas to you both!*

My ears seemed to extend like the antennae of a questing insect, checking, making sure, confirming the soft sluff-shush of other feet, other footsteps, following and pacing my own. Eerie, dappling light from the occasional and distant lamp. Across the dark and twisted lanes.

A sudden patch of blackness. Enough light only for me to see. To be sure. Don't give it all away! A wary instinct of survival whispered, and I removed a single bill—I think it was a ten—from the rest of those in my wallet; hid it in my coat pocket.

Love.

I'll show you, Jackie! Reject me. Say those words to me, I'll show you.

A tree.

And a little light. Not much. Enough. *Just* enough. Just enough for *them* to see. . . .

The wallet, in plain view. With the money.

Visible only at close range.

And . . . wait. . . .

Across the patch of light just beyond the tree, those following figures come to a halt. How many? Five. Six. Seven?

An exploding, almost unbearable excitement within me. Mixed, now, peculiarly, with an unexpected and inexplicable sense of panic. Are they? *Will* they? . . .

Waiting, not breathing, I stand beside the tree.

One of the night figures (I recognize him now in the patch of light; he was on the benches I passed) advances, smiling, one hand extended.

A bill leaves the wallet, vanishes in that hand.

Moving to me. Touching me. Both hands—pressing—on my head. The signal. . . .

I kneel.

He helps me undo his fly. Stands, quiet and waiting, while I probe, gently despite my haste. Bring him forth into the hot-cold night. . . .

*Panic!*

A single, blinding instant of pure terror, when all the day and all the days are crystal-etched in montage on my retinas and explode within my brain. And then—the panic is gone.

My eyes melt. Fill with tears. Overflow.

The others wait, in a quiet line. Calm. Sure. Wait with a serene certainty as excitement grows, reaches its peak, dies. And begins again. Immediately.

The next figure advances, smiling. And the next. Each will have his turn.

# The 3rd House

*Short journeys, brethren, letters, studies, mental inclinations and abilities . . .*

*Forecast: Angie Valentine will put together her annual sumptuous Christmas Day feast, attended only by family and close friends—the guest of honor being, of course, the great Johnny Valentine, her rambling, swilling, swinging, one-time husband. In fact, maybe the secret reason she still holds the feast is to get Johnny to come marching home. But this year there'll be an outsider invading the inner circle, bringing with her a few surprises of her own.*

*Meanwhile, on the other side of the Christmas tree, the Dahlbergs never make a big deal out of holidays, birthdays, and such. Their inclination is competitive rather than co-operative.*

*And David Strauss, finding himself temporarily without a family, will take a Yuletide trip into Nowhereland.*

*As Venus, the planet of love, positions herself in Libra, her ruler and the planet of balance, we enter the Third House and the beginning of a whopping love affair—depending, of course, on how you wish to interpret love. . . .*

## Sandy Hallowell

"Buddy, what took you so long? We were worried. Hello! I'm Buddy's mother. I'm *so* glad you could come. Won't you let someone take your coat? Oh, you're not in uniform?

125

Were you just buying that, this morning, is that what took so long? It's very becoming. Yes. I thought perhaps you would still be wearing your little stewardess outfit. Buddy, take her coat! I've got to . . ."

Mrs. Valentine smiled again—a bright off-and-on—and left us, still issuing instructions. I glanced at Buddy from the corner of my eye and saw the tiniest little sag from one shoulder.

But it straightened right up again and he smiled at me.

"Welcome," he said, "to the Casa Valentino. That, in case you had any doubt, was my mother—the Castellana-and-Christmas cook. Here, I *will* take your coat. Just a minute . . ."

I handed it to him. It really was part of the stew suit; but the dress under it was strictly nonuniform type. Strictly Hallowell. Mrs. Valentine had been half right. The blouse was the one I had on hand, in my flight case, when we landed. But the skirt that went with it had looked just a shade too short—for a family Christmas invitation anyway. As she had suspected, I had bought the floor-length skirt on the fly, at the hotel's dress shop.

But, no apologies.

The Hallowell, whatever her other sterling qualities (and there are many, mah franz!) has also one peachy-keen sense of taste when it comes to clothing. Hoo-boy! It is a good thing I wasn't born rich, or didn't marry a rich husband. I could turn into some kind of a spend-crazy clotheshorse in about five seconds, from a standing start.

And the skirt was a prime example. Oh, no—I wasn't excited about Buddy Valentine, the well-known Capricorn. No, indeedy! Just two weeks' pay worth; two weeks' pay for a skirt to have Christmas dinner with him and his family. But the skirt *did* suit the blouse and my hair. And the little jade earrings that are just the exact color of my eyes. It did make me look a little taller, a little more confident, a little more gracious and poised.

It *did* make The Hallowell feel like a queen. (You see what I mean? Clothes *do* things to me!)

And it did get a quick little eye-widening and side-glance appreciation from Mr. Buddy Valentine, the Capricorn with the real laugh. So what better can a girl buy with two weeks' pay?

"Pardon me, ma'am," he said, "is your arm going my

way? If so, we will go and give a look at the loot." He led me out of the front of the house to a big room in the back. That is, the room would probably have *seemed* big if it hadn't been filled nearly to overflowing with Christmas things: a tree, of course (looking like something out of a department store window, the decoration was so slick and professional), and holiday trimmings on some of the furniture. But mostly, the room was full of packages.

Big ones. Small ones. Oblong ones. Tall ones. Some with strange shapes—and all, obviously, store-wrapped.

I thought about our Christmases at home, with the tree sort of lopsided under the weight of lights and ornaments that had been in the family for a million years or so, with a few very, very carefully selected presents for everyone piled under it, and the fun of running down at the crack of dawn on Christmas morning to open them.

"Dig it," Buddy said, quirking his head. "And that's just for openers, believe it! Last year, Dad heard that Ma wanted a mink—so instead of just buying her one, he had the head of Saks's fur department over—on Christmas Day, mind you—with two full racks of mink. For Ma to take her choice."

"You're *kidding!*"

"No *way*. No way, honey. Ma and the Old Man may not see eye to eye on a lot of stuff, but they both go for the big gesture. Sometimes just on the spur of the moment."

I didn't know what to say to that, so (for once) I kept still. And in a moment he went on.

"Christmas at the Valentine household," he said, "is an event surpassed in grandeur and sheer conspicuous consumption only by the effusiveness of the gratitude, from one and all. Just as long as you say 'Gee, thanks!' like you really meant it—*and don't go getting successful or giving expensive presents yourself*."

That was a stopper.

Well, what else would I have expected from a Capricorn? Knowing there must be a good deal more to Buddy Valentine than the bright-but-fumbling young man visible on the surface, I could still be startled when a big, bleeding chunk of the "more" popped out.

"What's that I smell?" I said, changing the subject again.

"Everything!" he answered, and the shadow that had been on his face dissolved into a wide smile. "I wouldn't even *try* to name the things, or describe them now. Wait until dinner and I'll fill you in, dish by dish. You're not Italian, by any chance, are you?"

"Not," I smiled back, "by any chance, or even on purpose. Most of my family's Scots, 'way back, so they tell me, except for gran'ma—my mother's mother—who was Polish-Jewish, and my great-great-great-something gran'pa. We don't talk about him around my house; family skeleton!"

"Far out!" Buddy laughed. "So tell me, and I'll black-mail you and the rest of your kinfolks with it. A man has got to have *something* to fall back on in his old age."

"Well—" I pretended reluctance, "that great-some-odd gran'pappy of mine was French-*Indian!* And a bastard, besides, to hear my dad tell it. I mean, his parents never got around to making it legal. The story is that his mother was a French girl who was captured during a raid a long time ago, and one of the bucks claimed her for a squaw. Later, when her people got around to rescuing her, she told them to mind their own business—seemed to like things just the way they were."

"Ah-*hah!*" Buddy nodded emphatically. "I *thought* so— a strong streak of sensual savagery. You can see it, around the mouth, there . . ." He pointed into a big wall mirror. I looked. And then he kissed me.

Well, sir, friends and neighbors, The Hallowell has been kissed before. And quite a few times by experts. What's more, I never really put much stock in kissing, anyway— blame it on this here wild young generation gap. If I mean business, I know better things to do with my time. If I don't, I'd just as soon play Scrabble. But that particular kiss was, in its way, a kind of revelation.

I think it surprised Buddy a bit, too. Because right in the middle of things, what had been intended, I think, as a casual gesture, mostly in the spirit of Christmas and general exuberant good spirits, turned into quite something else.

It was Buddy who finally broke away. "Uh—" he said, "uh—like I said, sensual and—uh—savage."

"Drives the men wild," I babbled. "I have been known to cause riots on the . . . hold it!" He had started to move toward me again, but enough of the glow had worn down (not off, just down) that I could remember exactly where and when we were. "Look—fun's fun, ol' buddy Buddy, but you—well—I just don't think . . ."

"Yeah," he nodded, his face entirely serious. "Like you said."

"Uh—yes. Indeedy."

And then we just stood there for a minute or two, looking at each other. Which was how his mother found us when she walked in.

"Buddy," she said, in a hurried but determinedly efficient tone, "haven't you made Miss Hallowell a drink yet?"

"Thank you," I said, "but I really don't . . ."

"Well, at least a cup of coffee, then. I'll get that. Buddy, you left your car in the middle of the driveway. Move it out of the way—you *know* your father likes to drive right up to the front door. Right now!" Buddy hesitated, maybe because he had something else to say to me, maybe for some other reason. "Let me see your teeth," Mrs. Valentine ordered. He bared them in a smile-rictus. "That one front tooth," she went on, "I still say you ought to do something about it. Get it capped. It's crooked."

"Ma . . ."

"Go on, now—he'll be here any minute!"

Reluctantly, but obedient as any child, he sauntered in the direction of the front door. His mother watched him go, then turned to me. "Please sit down, Miss Hallowell," she said. "May I call you Sandy? Good. I'll get your coffee. Turn on the radio or the hi-fi if you like."

She bustled out—leaning, I thought, just a bit to the left to compensate for the weight of what I had originally mistaken for a gaudy, oversized costume-jewelry cocktail ring on her right hand. The tiny flash when she turned had set me straight; Mrs. Valentine was fixing Christmas dinner while wearing the biggest and heaviest real emerald I had ever set eyes on—and I have seen a few, gripping the arms of first-class seats during hairy takeoffs and landings.

I turned my gaze on the Christmas presents. Loot. That's what Buddy had called them, too. I wondered how—and, for that matter, why—the Valentines managed to restrain their curiosity long enough to keep the packages untouched until Buddy's father arived in the afternoon. Funny, just yesterday he had been *Johnny Valentine* in my mind; now I could only think of him as Mrs. Valentine's ex-husband, Buddy's father.

Loot. And what a haul of loot it would have been, too, for some poor-but-deserving burglar, I couldn't help thinking. The family must have burglar alarms, or something, to keep larceny to a minimum on occasions like this. Otherwise, the place would be overrun with . . .

## Jack Dahlberg

". . . thieves! That's all people like that are—what else are they? Just thieves. Stealing credit, stealing profits, stealing the very blood of life from the Industry!"

Papa was in one of his oratorical moods.

I shut up and let him have at it.

To tell the truth, for once I was rather glad that he wanted to tell me (for the hundredth time; for the thousandth) how the unions and the independent producers were destroying the American film industry. And how the bankers were helping them do it. Not that I didn't pretty much agree with him, but I'd heard it all so often I'd have been almost bored, if it hadn't been for the fact that I was dead in my tracks anyway.

Between Clara and Papa—and David—last night had been a shambles right up through dawn. No sleep. Not even a nap or a doze. Merry Christmas! It is one hell of a note, I had told myself, when a man can't find a night's sleep in his own home.

And then I had given up and started in with the methedrine.

Great stuff, meth.

Tiny white tablets; take one and you're on a no-sleep and no-eat diet just as long as you want to be. Is your wife a drunken bitch who can't look at you without sneering? Is an old friend who could prove to be an embarrassment driving you nuts with crazy telephone calls in the middle of the night? Is your father-and-boss starting to suspect you might have some ideas of your own about the job he put you in to function as his personal yes-man-and-flunky-cum-mouthpiece?

Just take the little white pill and it'll be all right. . . .

I looked across the room at Clara. She was bright-eyed with the vodka, but at least she seemed under control. The straight-sided (two knocks for the price of one!) lowball glass was still in her hand, and I had seen her replenish it three times since Papa's arrival. But she was looking at him with every evidence of rapt attention, apparently hanging

130

on his every word. Hand it to her, that is one swell little actress. One great little trouper. One darling little girl.

With an effort, I forced my mind back to Papa and concentrated on the sound of his voice and the words. And just in time, too.

". . . seen your schedule," he was saying, "and some of the working titles—of course, that doesn't have to mean anything and I *haven't* seen a synopsis on most of them yet—but some of those titles, I'll tell you, they worry me, Jackie. They worry me!"

Now we were getting down to it.

The reason for the lecture—for the visit itself, maybe. Forget Christmas.

"Why?" I said. "What's wrong with them, Papa?"

"They're cheap, that's what's wrong with them. They sound trashy, some of them. They'd have been fine for stag movies a few years ago. That's not Monarch style, Jackie. We don't make stag movies. We make good movies; movies the whole family can like."

"Papa," I said, choosing my words with care to try to move into the speech I had been working up to for the past few months, "Papa, the business is changing. Everything about it is changing. A lot of the old rules . . ."

"Old rules, new rules—they're the same rules, Jackie. A motion picture is entertainment; if it's got some kind of message, something valid to say about the world, some ideas for people to turn over in their minds, so much the better—but only so long as you present it to the audience in good taste; only so long as you do the basic job, which is to provide entertainment."

"Papa," I started again, "that's exactly my point! Just what I've been saying all along, entertainment! In fact, that's the . . ."

"A Monarch picture," he continued, paying no attention, "is entertainment, like any other. But there is an added ingredient; something extra, something the theater audience can count on. Class, Jackie! Monarch makes big pictures; a man going to the theater, taking his family, he's going to spend ten, maybe twenty dollars for tickets today. Not like before World War II, when a neighborhood house charged a dime for adults, a nickel for kids; maybe, even, a family night where you could bring five kids, your wife, and yourself for a quarter."

"I know. But today, a family seldom . . ."

". . . so it's almost like an investment. An investment in the whole family's entertainment. And like anyone making an investment, this man wants some assurance that he won't be throwing his money away. He knows a Monarch picture is a big picture. He knows a Monarch picture is a Class picture. He knows because Monarch Pictures doesn't cheat him. It never has, all through the years. Always, a man's family could count on getting their money's worth if they knew it was a Monarch Picture they were going to see."

He closed his mouth, and gave me that steady, double-barreled stare while he took a deep puff on his cigar. How many times had he shut me up, doing just that? Ever since I was a kid. It was almost hypnotic; but I forced my mouth open and made sounds. Words. This once, just this once, I *had* to make him listen:

"The pictures I want to make, the ones on that schedule," I said, "*are* good pictures. They *are* entertainment. They have dimension and style; they are Class products because they deal with real problems faced by real people—exactly the kind of people and problems you've always said Monarch gave its audiences—but in the world as it is *today*. What's more, they are pictures that are not too expensive to film; they will recoup their negative cost early and be making profits for the company long before we have to start making foreign distribution and television deals."

That last point, I thought, should count heavily with Papa. His board of directors would smile, thinking of black ink. Black ink *now,* not next year or on the final off-release balance sheets. But it was wishful thinking; he hadn't come out here to argue or to discuss. And he hadn't come to see the schedule that I could have transmitted to him in New York weeks ago. Plus the fact that he had been lying about not having seen the synopses. Hadn't I found out a week ago that his spies on the Coast were getting the script outlines to him sometimes even before I saw them . . . ?

"These Class pictures with the dimension and style," he said, in the extra-quiet voice that always meant trouble, "they'll get a seal? From the Larabee Office, a seal, Jackie?"

I tried to dissemble. "A *rating,*" I said. "Like any picture

132

today, we'll send these over to the MPA for their people to check, and they'll give us a rating. It's not like the old days, Papa—they don't tell you whether or not you can release a picture. They just rate it."

"Oh—*ah!* Uh-huh," he nodded his head, the cigar clenched in the center teeth leaving a wide smoke arc as if to emphasize his point. "I'm getting old. Sure. They just *rate* the picture, I forgot. Let's see, now: PG, that's for pictures where the whole family can come, but the parents are supposed to be a little careful and decide for themselves if it's something their kids should see. The R rating now, that's for the kind of picture which is probably no good for kids—but they can still get in, as long as they've got an adult with them. And then the X rating: adults only; no kids, any time. That right, Jackie?"

"Well—pretty much. Sure"

"Uh-huh." *Pause. Puff. Stare.* "Uh-huh—so what kind of rating these pictures you want to make, the Class pictures with the dimension and style, what rating are they going to get, Jackie?"

Oh, Christ! It was a game with him.

Didn't I know it, before we started? Didn't I? Irving Dahlberg had played this game so often, so long, so well—with everybody who ever disagreed with him—what had made me think this would be different, this time? Because it was me? Because he had hired me, put me in charge of the studio, given me his old office? Because I was his son?

"I don't know, Papa. I told you, it's not like the old days when they could tell you, 'Take this out and that out and do this and do that and you get a seal.' Now they just . . ."

"They see the script. You send it to them before you start to shoot; you send them the corrections. They have an eye on the whole production, from synopsis to treatment to rough draft to finished script to the revisions under the camera. Anything they question, anything that could change the rating, you hear about it. This isn't so?"

"Yes, Papa."

"So what kind of a rating do these films—these Class pictures—what rating do they get, Jackie? Tell me."

"A couple get a PG."

"And the others?"

"A few will probably have an R."

133

"And . . . ?"

"All right, Papa. It's what you wanted me to say: X. The others all are pretty clearly slated for an X rating."

"Dirty pictures."

"*Not* dirty!" I had to fight to keep my voice down. From the corner of my eye I could see Clara, a little smile turning up one corner of her mouth, getting up to pour herself another drink. I forced myself to concentrate on what I was saying—one problem at a time. "Adult pictures, Papa; pictures for adults. Real pictures, about real people living the kind of lives people do live in the second half of the twentieth century in a society that has changed more in the past decade than it did in the whole nineteenth century. They are honest pictures. All right, they are not for the diaper set. But the audiences have changed, Papa. They won't watch *Love Laughs at Andy Hardy* these days."

"So? And what *will* they watch . . . *Kiss My Whip? Blow My Horn?* Class stuff like *that?*" He snorted. "Once upon a time it was courtroom scenes. One man made a picture with a courtroom scene; the picture made big money, suddenly everyone was making courtroom scenes. There was even a saying, no picture with a courtroom scene in it ever lost money! *Hah!* Then it was hospitals; every picture had to have an operating-room scene. The same old thing—one man does something new. It works. So do it a million times! Follow the leader—that's art. That's creativity! And now it's sex scenes. Follow the leader. Do it a million times. Is there just *one* of these Class pictures of yours doesn't have at least one sex scene?"

"They're legitimate, not dragged in by the heels. They play a vital part in the logical plot development . . ."

"Screwing on the screen; that's vital?"

". . . and besides," I added recklessly, "*Burn the First Card* begins with a sex scene. So it couldn't be all *that* bad. . . ."

I waited for him to shoot out at me, but to my amazement, no explosion was forthcoming.

"Okay," he said, shifting the cigar to the side of his mouth and leaning back in his chair. "You're executive vice-president. I still don't agree with you. About the audiences, I think you're wrong, particularly. But I'll look another time at the synopses. Now, about *Boarders Away!*"

*I couldn't believe it.* It was as though I had never mentioned *Card.* I glanced at Clara. She was sitting with the drink, the new drink, and apparently listening. But if she had noticed anything unusual, it didn't show.

". . . *cooperation.* It's vital, so we're justified, Jackie, in using any and all means at our disposal—*anything,* you understand—to obtain that cooperation from the navy."

"Uh—yes. Of course!" I made an effort to pull myself together. If Papa was in a mood to forgive my needling him about his cooz's sex scenes, by God I would meet him halfway! If *Boarders* needed help from the navy, then help it would get, by *any* and *all* means.

"You understand what I'm suggesting?"

I had obviously missed something.

"Uh—well, maybe not entirely."

"The *Stamp Fund,* Jackie! The Stamp Fund, it's still there. As always. Even the directors, they don't know about the Stamp Fund; we can use it, if that could help."

He meant it then. Around the studio, the Stamp Fund was a kind of ultra-in joke. I was supposed to be the only one who knew about it, of course. Papa assumed I was the only one, but he was wrong. Quite a few others did know; too many, by far, for it to be the secret he thought it was from the corporate board of directors. If they didn't bring it up, it was only because they didn't want to negate their right to charge him with misappropriation if anything ever went wrong.

An in joke the Stamp Fund might be; a laughing matter it was not.

*One million dollars.* That was the Stamp Fund; one semi-cool million in cash. Used bills. Not marked. Nothing smaller than a ten. Nothing bigger than a fifty.

Papa had started putting it together nearly thirty years ago, right after World War II. He was certain, at the time, that the country was in for another big depression after the war. A worse one, maybe, than the one back in the 1930's. He remembered the near panic that had swept the country then, and particularly the "Bank Holiday" that halted almost all business for days because nobody could cash a check or meet a payroll. Only those with ready cash at hand, bank notes or gold, had been able to turn the situation to advantage; to buy up whole companies for a song in some especially lucky instances, and continue normal operations at the very least.

135

So he had begun diverting money—as much, in each case, as he could expect to hide from auditors—from almost every part of the studio's operations, turning it into bills and hiding them in a special safe (one built into his private office john; not the "regular" one hidden behind the Vermeer that hung across from his desk in the office).

The big crash he'd feared had, of course, not materialized on schedule. But Papa had kept half-expecting it. And he had continued to pile up the Stamp Fund until it reached a million. That was where he decided to stop.

Finally, when the crash seemed indefinitely postponed, he realized that, for better or worse, he had a million dollars in unaccounted-for, and unsuspected cash at his disposal. He began to think of what could be done with it. And the answer he came up with was pure Irving Dahlberg.

Another man, one whose concentration on the movie business was less intense, might have seen it as a happy-hour kitty. Use it for the stray weekend on the Riveria; the odd yacht, the extra diamond bracelet, the wild weekend. But not Irving Dahlberg. For him, it became a secret source of power—grease, he told me once, for sticky wheels —in the Industry.

A major Monarch star, back in the old days when stars were under studio contract instead of producing their own independent pictures, drove down the main drag in Palm Springs, shooting out streetlights and shop windows. The word came at midnight; two hours later a Monarch press agent was paying off shopkeepers and police in untraceable currency for the damage to their property and for continued silence.

A female star, already six months into the shooting of a major-budget picture, found herself three months into the need for a competent, and mute, abortionist. There was only a weekend in which to handle the matter. But the abortionist was found, and paid in small used bills. The picture continued without interruption.

And there had been the dark day when insurgent stockholders, aroused by rumors of a breakdown in Monarch overseas production planning, had attempted a putsch—driving the stock down on the Board—to force Papa to unload; and then coming in secretly on the short side not only to make a whopping profit but in the end to gain control when his stock edge narrowed sufficiently. Papa had poured everything he could beg, borrow, or steal into the fight; it wasn't quite enough, until a "mysterious investor" suddenly turned up with a stray million he was willing to drop into the balance. And then it was just enough.

Every time, needless to say, the fund was painstakingly replenished after use until the standard level of one million was reached. I had never had occasion—or permission, for that matter—to make use of it in the time since Papa had moved up to the New York headquarters and I had taken over for him in Hollywood.

But now he had given permission. Hell, he had practically ordered me to bribe the Secretary of Defense! And, you had to admit, it would make a tidy little . . .

". . . care how you do it," he was saying, "or who you work through. Your friend, if he can help. Someone else, if not. The money, if it's needed—whatever else seems best. I don't care. I don't even want to *know*."

I was more than a little awed at the responsibility he was laying on me. Again I looked over at Clara for some sign that she was aware of what he was doing, but she continued to avoid my eye. I turned back to Papa.

"All right, Papa, We'll try."

"Try, hell! I didn't tell you to try. I told you to *handle* it, Jackie, and that's what I want. Results, not excuses. Results—they're . . ."

## Dolly Diamond

". . . the only things that count. Did you *tell* them yet?" He hesitated a moment, and I began to burn.

"Not yet," he said finally. "Not yet, baby, but don't worry about a thing. I'm seeing them, the family together, in just a few minutes, for Christmas dinner?"

"You'll chicken," I told him, the last haze of sleep and marijuana smoke finally clearing from my head. "You'll chicken, just like before, Johnny. You know you will!"

"Baby," he said, in that Velvet Voice, the big fixer way he has sometimes, "baby, *trust* me. You know I love you."

"I know you like to fuck me," I said, using the word because I knew it bugged hell out of him for me to say it on the phone (and particularly long distance) as much as it turned him on for me to say it when we were alone. "And I know you like it when I blow you, or when I let

137

you eat me. I know that. But about love—*love?* I know I love you. I know that. But how do I know *how* you feel about *me,* really?"

"Baby . . ."

"No, Johnny, tell me—how would I *know?* It's Christmas. But I'm here in the cold and you're out there, with your kid and your ex-wife and Sam, getting ready to have Christmas dinner all together . . ."

"But you know I always have . . ."

". . . and telling me about how much you love me, over three thousand miles of long-distance telephone wire."

He waited, but I waited, too. And finally he spoke up again. "Look, honey," he said, sounding smaller and older than before, "let's not do this. Fight. You know I want to be there with you."

"I *don't* know." I was beginning to enjoy myself. No matter what he said, he was sounding, and feeling, wronger and wronger every minute. It was a trick I'd learned almost as soon as I could talk, how to put other people (men, especially) in the wrong, on the defensive, in any conversation. And how to use the advantage. God knows I'd had to have *some* kind of weapon, just to keep from being trampled underfoot or forgotten. "I don't know—and I don't believe you, Johnny. You'll find some excuse, like always. . . ."

"Dolly," he was trying to be very sincere, I could tell, but it only made me angrier at him. "Just trust me. Only that. Trust me; I'll tell them."

"Tell them what?"

"That—I'm in love with you . . ."

"And?"

". . . and we're—going to get married."

"You *promise?*"

"Yeah, baby, I promise. I do. Really."

"Well . . ." I pretended to think it over before I sprang the *snapper* on him. "All right, then, Johnny. I believe you. But, Johnny . . ."

"Yeah, sugar?"

". . . I'll be waiting. For you to call me, and to tell that press flack of yours to give the story to the columns. And Johnny darling, this time you better keep your promise. Because if you don't, Johnny darling," I went on, "if you

138

don't, I'm gonna fix your wagon real good. Merry Christmas, Johnny darling!" And I slammed down the phone.

Now then, buster! I shoved the phone back onto the nightstand and rolled over and over across the bed, laughing like Judith Anderson playing *Lilith*.

As I had expected, it took about sixty seconds for him to call back. I lay still, listening to the ringing; counting the number of rings against the Venetian blind slats in the window. When I heard as many rings as there were slats, I told myself, I would lift the receiver off the hook and smother the whole damn thing under my pillow.

But it stopped when I still had maybe ten slats to go.

Good enough! Let the son of a bitch sweat a little. Dolly had done enough sweating in her life. Let someone else do a little for a change.

The phone began ringing again. I resumed the count on the blind slats. And then all the slats were gone and I rolled across the bed again, feeling absolutely *groovy,* and picked the receiver up. I started to stuff it under the pillow, as I had planned. But then I decided it might be even more fun just to hold it to my ear and *listen*. Hear him squirm.

". . . don't hang up. Please! I'm sorry I called so late last night." Oh, for Christ sake—David! God, wouldn't you think he'd have heard enough the last time, without calling back for more this morning? "But listen, Dolly, please. I have got to talk to you. Right *now!*"

"David, hang up!"

"Dolly—look, something happened. Last night. After I talked to you. Something real bad—the first time—first I *ever* actually—I mean, with strangers; people I didn't even—*please,* Dolly! I've got to see you."

I started to hang up, but stopped with the receiver an inch from its cradle. He really *did* sound desperate. Of course, he's an actor. He could be playing a scene, or just dramatizing himself, as usual. The last time I let him come up here, he was impossible. But he did sound bad.

Somehow that dope still knew how to get to me.

I put the phone to my ear again. "David," I said, making it as brisk and impersonal as I could, "it's Christmas morning, and I'm still half asleep. Have you been to bed at all?"

"No," he said. "I was—I was in—no. I haven't been to bed."

"Well, then, that's all you need. Some sleep."

"No, Dolly. I can't go to bed, not yet. Not without talking to you."

"Don't be ridiculous. What do you think, David, that I'm going to let you fall asleep in *my* bed? Not again, mister! Not ever! *Mommy* has resigned—permanently."

"Not, it's not that, Dolly. I swear to you. I just have to talk."

Oh, fuck. . . .

I thought back to the time I had met him, and how it had been between us then. He, the rising actor, the tall young pillar of strength with the brass balls. ("Does David Strauss *swing?*" The wardrobe mistress said when I asked her, "Honey, that man *clanks!*") And me, the little nothing with the little nowhere part in the off-Broadway play he was in, all pigeon-toes and bad makeup and Salvation Army clothes and inhibitions. He had smiled at me. (How old was I, sixteen? Well, I *told them* I was sixteen and when David found out I was underage he almost had a fit and we had to run down to Georgia right away, that same weekend when I mentioned it, and get married because everyone knew we'd been living together for months and it could have got him a twenty-year prison stretch for everything we'd been doing.) And when I saw that smile it was like suddenly being as tall and strong as he was, and right then I knew I had to have all that strength with me, trapped inside me, to make me strong, too.

Only it didn't work that way.

Even before we got married, I knew there was something wrong; something weak somewhere inside him. Something he tried to cover up with the Big Smooth Swinger act. And as soon as that Southern mushmouth judge made it legal— endsville! "Mommy," he started calling me. "Mommy" this and "Mommy" that, and going to sleep every night with my tit—my poor big-nipple, no-meat tit—in his mouth like a goddamn baby pacifier. Sex? *Forget* it! That last year, the whole last year we were married before Johnny came along, it practically took an act of God to get him to ball me. And at that, he always wanted me to be on top, do all the work while he just lay there, and half the time he lost it before we were done, before I was half ready.

Why couldn't he have been a man?

Why couldn't he, at least, have come right out and *told* me what he really wanted was to go back to blowing that horny little midget, Jack Dahlberg? Like he'd done when they were kids. Why let me find out in such a crummy way, saying his name—*Jackie!*—right in the middle of the first time I'd been able to get him *up* to ball me in three weeks. And then the crying and the slobbering and the "Mommy, help me; please, Mommy!" when I made him tell me all about it.

David had said something—I hadn't caught the words, and didn't give a damn—but now the phone was silent in my hand. Waiting. I closed my eyes and took a deep breath. Let it out.

"David," I said. "All right, David. Come over. But not right now. Later, make it later. About"—I rolled sidewise to look at the alarm clock, "—oh, five o'clock. Okay?"

"Okay, Dolly," he said, sounding so relieved it made me want to take back my invitation. "Five o'clock. I'll be there. And thanks, Dolly."

"Yeah," I said, anxious to be rid of his voice. "Yeah, okay. Later."

I hung up and rolled on my back.

The girl in the ceiling mirror looked rumpled and sour and used and naked. Not nude—naked. I hate to look naked. Her body wasn't pink and white with silver angel hair spread out under it on the black sheets, the way it had been last night. She was skinny, and her ribs showed and her hip bones stood out like antlers and her breasts actually turned *in* at the centers instead of out. And her face—for a clown. A clown Doll, not the baby Doll that should be looking back at me.

Well, fix that right now!

There were still plenty of papers, but I had to get up and cross the room to the crapper (that was one habit I'd learned as a kid—keep your stash where you can eat it or flush it quick) to get the weed. I took enough for about six joints and went back to the bed, lying on my stomach to keep from seeing the mirror girl.

Five minutes later, I rolled on my back again and smiled.

The baby Doll with the platinum hair glowed and beamed back at me, all happy and beautiful again. The Lover wasn't in the drawer where it should have been, but the mirror found it for me on the floor beside the bed. I got hold of it and wriggled to the middle of the bed.

David would be over at five. What a *bummer!* If there was anything I didn't need, it was another amateur therapy session with him. (I can *talk* to you, Dolly—you're the only one I could ever talk to!) All right, okay! So maybe I thought I owed him something. For what? God knows. I couldn't put it into words, really. But, come to think of it, he *had* helped me get my first Broadway part—since he was the one who had introduced me to Johnny. His friend, the big singing star, Johnny Valentine. Still, I wished he would be somewhere else at five. I wished he would walk in front of a . . . no! No, I don't wish that. No, I don't! I don't hate him. I don't want him dead. I don't even want him hurt, I just *don't want* him—especially over *here,* slobbering on . . .

*Huh?*

The tail end of an idea slipped past my mind. I grabbed for it. Missed. Waited for it to come by again.

*Aha-ha!*

Gotcha! Sure, of course! No problem, not today, on Christmas with nobody in New York doing much of anything. There was plenty of weed. Rafael would be coming around again tomorrow; I could score a whole new stash if we used mine up. Sure!

"A party, a party—gonna *have* a *lit*-tul *par*-ty . . ." The voice-that-launched-a-million-record-sales played tag with an old song as I picked up the phone again. I knew the numbers, all of them, by heart. Quick study, that's Dolly. Great little memory.

Greg answered on the second ring.

*"Hi, Gregs . . . Dolly! Yeah, having a Merry-Merry? You too, huh? Well, my freaky friend, that's why I called you, for sure! Yeah, little party; over here at my place . . . oh, about four; four-thirty or so. Yeah, uh-huh, and don't be late, kiddy—you'll miss out on all that crazy imported smog . . . right! Later!"*

I pressed the cutoff buttons on the cradle for an instant or two, let them snap up again, and dialed the second number.

The ringing took a little longer this time.

I winked—a big, phony one—at the mirror girl, and she spread her legs. Knees out, feet in. She was dry, and the

Lover had a little trouble making the scene. But it was all right by the time Dirk picked up his phone.

"*Hi, Superfreak . . . Dolly! Having a Merry-Merry . . . ?*"

I worked the Lover back and forth, getting rid of the dryness and keeping up my end of the conversation with Dirk. He was free, too, and four o'clock was fine. I hung up.

*Wrrrrrrrrr.*

The mirror girl arched upward, making a bridge from the top of her head to her feet, smiling a dreamy smile and beginning to vibrate in tune with the electric Lover. Once like this; once straight, and then make the rest of the calls about the big party at Dolly's place, and then get a little head start on the heads. I giggled at that, it was cute—a head start on the heads, and then at least one more *good* session with the vibrator.

A good slow, long, deep one with the Lover . . .

*Wrrrrrrrrr*

The mirror girl giggled again and tilted her head on her platinum-covered shoulder, seeming to make dimples that weren't really there while all the time arching higher and harder.

Would Johnny ever get a surprise if he could see Dolly *now!* Well, to hell with him. Daddy-Johnny, you're chicken. You went away on Christmas, and I *know* you won't have the guts to tell your family you're going to marry Dolly. I wish you *could* see me!

And would David ever get a surprise when he got over here at five o'clock and found out I wasn't alone. I giggled again, deliciously, thinking of how he was going to look . . .

*Wrrrrrrrrr.*

It was happening. It was *happening* . . . now . . . *now!* Oh, what a . . .


## Johnny Valentine

. . . kick in the head! Merry-Goddamn-Christmas to me; nothing to it, baby! No problem!

Just walk into Angie's house, say hello to the kids, tell old Angie she's looking great and sit down to dinner.

. . . and for dessert, just casually tell them you're going to marry a girl who's the right age for your son!

Nothing to it.


143

"Hey, Vanni—how's my breath?"

Sam leaned over against me and blew a big distillery exhaust in my face.

"Whatcha think? Angie gonna give me hell?"

I had to laugh. "What, should this year be different?" I shook my head at him, as much to dispel the gas balloon he had exhaled as anything else. "Five, six years anyhow you been coming to my place—*Angie's* place—for Christmas dinner, Sam. Angie ever miss laying it into you? Even once? Relax, Sam baby, it wouldn't be Christmas without she told you *next* year to turn up sober."

Sam grinned sheepishly. "Yeah," he said, "you're right, I guess . . ."

I sat back and watched the scenery unreel. That Sam! Toughest guy in his block, they say, back when he was growing up. And now, a big, tough, smart, powerful lawyer —you might be his best friend, pally, but you are sure as hell not his best, or biggest, client. That union connection of Sam's has got to set him up for a hundred fifty, two hundred thou every year, in addition to the big brass bollix he can swing when he wants to put union weight and Organization weight behind anything. Or against it.

Sam's the man who can say yes or no. And does that help him, does that get him one lousy *point* in a title go with old Angie? Does that keep him from worrying whether Angie is going to holler on him about having a little booze on his breath when he walks in?

About as much as anything ever helped *you*, when Angie decided to hassle you about something.

That Angie—yeah, Valentine, that *Angie*. And if Sam thinks *he's* going to have to listen to some home-style Italian hollering, wait till he hears what happens after I make *my* little announcement!

*Maybe I could wait.* Maybe.

Yeah. Sure, and maybe I could go take a long walk off a short pier; that crazy doll—Dolly, that ding; that truly *great* little talent. You think *she* was kidding? Never! She'll do something crazy!

From the first . . . five minutes after I met her at that nutty party Gino dragged me to, I asked her if she wanted to go to Billy's with me. (Some day, by God, I am going to

144

find *some* party, in *some* town, that Gino hasn't just left, isn't on his way to, or isn't at. What dedication!) And what does she say?

"I'd rather go in the bedroom right here. We can lock the door."

Ten years old, maybe, she looked like—with the long, white-blonde hair and the little-girl dress and the big slanty eyes and the no-tits. Ten years old and with a face of a Jewish angel; I thought she was kidding.

So to call her bluff I turn around and head for the bedroom—only where is *she?* What does *she* do?

Through the door—ahead of me.

And her hands on me, down with the zipper and open with the belt before I could even get that damn *door* locked, and then . . .

Jesus.

I never *did* get it locked.

But by then I didn't care; she was just so . . . Oh, brother! Look at you, Vanni baby. Look. Just look! Middle of the day; Christmas, it is; riding with Sam in his special chauffeured union limo, over to Angie's house for dinner— and look!

The heat in the middle. The virility salute that won't even let you get out of the car still looking like a gentleman-and-a-father.

And a stone-ache coming on!

What are you, Vanni baby; what are you, Valentino— some kind of a half-assed adolescent, getting all steamed up thinking about a dame? That's what you're acting like, baby. A kid. A lovesick kid. You'd kick Buddy right square in the ass if he acted like this, and here you . . .

"Hey, Vanni, what's the bit?"

Huh?

"We're here, baby. We're here! Wake up and come to dinner, kiddy. . . ."

"Oh—yeah. Sorry, Sam."

I climbed out of the limo just in time to see the door open and Angie waving a welcome to us.

"Hi, babe! How's my girl this bright and beautiful Christmas day?"

"Fine, just fine, Giovanni. My, but it's good to see you. Here, let me look at you." She held me at arm's length for a long moment; apparently I passed muster, 'cause then she turned toward Sam.

"Sam. You're losing weight! We can't have that!"

Sam grinned at her. "Ten pounds," he said, smug as hell, patting his paunch.

"Well, don't worry. I'm going to put it right back on you again. Wait till you see the *Pomodori Imbottiti!*"

Sam sighed and shrugged like a Palermo shopkeeper. "My downfall," he said. "Better than last year, it couldn't be. Tell me, Angie—this year, no Manicotti, eh? Twice, you wouldn't do that to old Sam."

" 'Fraid so!"

". . . and the *Conchiglie con salsa alle Vongole,* that too?"

"That, too."

"Uh—*Aragosta alla Diavola?*"

"Would it be Christmas at Casa Valentino without that?"

"*Cappelletti in Brodo? Scaloppine di Vitello? Agnello al Forno . . . ?*"

"Naturally."

"*Pollo Fritto? Zuppa Inglese . . . ?*"

"And *Gelato de Fragole!*" . .

Sam groaned in mock dejection, rolled his eyes to the ceiling and pretended to faint into the second biggest chair in the living room. "Already, I'm dying," he said. "And I suppose this year we also get some *Pane de Pasqua all 'Uovo?*"

Now it was Angie's turn to tease. "*Sam!*" she said in a stage whisper. "You *know* that's only for Easter. For Christmas, something simple—just *Grissini.* And *Melanzane con Olio e Aceto* with everything else on the antipasto tray, of course. . . ."

"Of course," Sam said, shaking his head. "What else would I expect? Just a *simple* little Italian meal you can whip up in a minute, if you happen to have a week to get it ready. Damn you, Vanni!"

"What did I do?"

"You married her before I could get a chance to taste her cooking. Jeez, how many real Italian girls are left who can cook like that? You got all the luck."

I glanced at Angie out of the corner of my eye and wondered if the whole menu conversation had been a deliberate setup between her and Sam. All to come down to that line about what a great Italian cook she is—meaning, of course, what a horse's can Vanni would be to marry some broad can't cook dago style. Someone, say, like Dolly.

Yeah. The crummy feeling I'd had on the plane, that something was up with the family over Dolly was right, like most of my strong hunches. There was one dinner course they hadn't mentioned among all the rest today.

*Everyone was going to get a big bite out of Vanni's butt.* Man, I needed a drink . . .

Sam got up. He knew we weren't staying in the parlor; nobody stays there in an Italian household. It's always the kitchen or, if you're real modern American, the den or rec room. I led the parade toward the back of the house, with the two of them trailing along behind and talking food all the way into the kitchen.

The bar was just where it was when I built the joint, and just as well stocked as Angie always keeps it when she knows I'm in town. I made a beeline for it, and had a stiff one half poured when I spotted the doll.

She'd been sitting in the room—in *my* chair, as it happens—but so quietly I really hadn't noticed her, with the bar and the bottle on my mind. She smiled at me.

"Hello, Mr. Valentine," she said.

She looked familiar. The type, anyway; you know—good gams and a build. But not the starlet face you'd figure to go with it. Damn it! I *knew* the face from somewhere. But where?

"Hi, baby," I said, playing it casual as hell, "get you a drink while I'm still sober?"

She smiled and shook her head. "Not yet. Buddy . . ."

But whatever she was going to say about Buddy didn't get said. Angie came in from the kitchen.

"Giovanni!" she said. The full old-country name. She was about the only one left who ever used it. "Come on out to the kitchen and taste the *Agnello*, maybe I got too much spice. Your stomach . . ."

Like always. Yeah. And like always, I went. To the kitchen, yeah; it's a hell of an odd thing—Vanni baby, the big, sophisticated swinger, on Christmas he can't resist sampling all the stuff that's cooking. Coming to dinner, here at Angie's, *that* might be a duty. This year even, the

the kind of duty I'd spend some time kicking around angles to avoid because Dolly was pissed about it and I kind of figured there might be some heat on this end, too.

But the kitchen, yeah! A pure joy. Hot. Smells. People moving around. *Yeah!*

Like it always was at my mother's house when I was a little boy. Okay, kid me about it sometime.

It's a riot. Vanni, a sucker for guinea cooking on Christmas.

But the first sip from the first pot, and I was a goner. All of it—the bit: family, friends, hustle in the house, dago smells. Nostalgia? Sure. But something else besides. Don't ask me what.

"You're looking great, Angie," I told her, and she was. The color of the dress suited her skin. Angie's a dark broad —lots of the black Sicilian blood—and those eyes . . .

Yeah, the eyes. Say what you want to, that Angie always got to me pretty good with the eyes. And they hadn't changed, no matter what else might be different. Dark and beautiful, those eyes. Black.

"Thanks," she said, and made a special, kind of phony motion with the hand to let me know she was wearing the big green rock I'd given her. I grinned to let her know I got the message, and she just beamed.

. . . And I began to realize that I wasn't going to be able to *do* it!

Okay, I'm a coward. Vanni the chicken. But right then, standing there in the kitchen, I knew for sure I was never going to be able to look around the table at these people and tell them, "By the way, Dolly Diamond and me, we're going to get married."

Not today, anyway. And, hell, maybe not *ever.*

The glass was still in my hand, untouched, so as not to spoil the taste of the cooking. Well, the cooking was great, but Vanni was not. I took it at one long open-throat guzzle and waited for the fire to hit bottom.

"Vanni, you're the opposite of Sam, you're putting *on* weight." Angie smiled at me. "I never thought I'd see the day!"

"Yeah." I laughed, glad the conversation was still on neutral ground. "Well, what the hell. You always said I ought to try to gain some, right?"

"On you," she nodded, "it looks good, Giovanni."

Suddenly I wanted to get out of that kitchen. In a hurry. I looked at my empty glass. *"Post time,"* I said, making the Joe E. Lewis gesture. "Someone swiped my booze. Who, I wonder?"

"Sure, run along, Giovanni, and pay some attention to that nice little stewardess girl of Buddy's, will you? Did he introduce you to Sandy? Oh, what am I thinking of? Of course? She was on the plane with *both* of you, wasn't she?"

She evidently wanted me to say something or other, but I didn't. To tell the truth, Vanni baby was sort of shook.

Now, of course, I tumbled—the girl in the den; no wonder I thought I knew her. That was the kooky doll on the 707. The one who wanted to know when I was born—yeah; the one *who'd turned me down when I tried to make a date.*

What in hell was she doing here?

But then I realized Angie'd laid it out for me. ". . . nice little stewardess girl of Buddy's . . .," That's what she'd said.

*Buddy?*

I went back to the bar to get the refill and gave the broad the once-over again, sideways, on my way. *Buddy's* girl? When she turned *me* down?

I just couldn't feature it; when the hell had she turned into my *kid's* girl? Before or *after* I'd put the pitch on her? Could my own bambino be cutting into the Old Man's action? Was that the date she'd had, as an excuse for not . . .

Then I wanted to laugh at myself.

Talk about showing your age—get a hinge at Vanni. Yeah, baby, this was a whole day full of gag lines. Well, anyway, her being there—didn't that kind of give Vanni baby an out; something to tell Dolly to explain why I hadn't busted the news to my family about her and me? Sure. Of course! Nobody could expect a guy to say something like that in front of strangers. Could she . . . ?

Well, anyhow, it was *something.*

"You're not drinking, Sandy," I said, putting a little extra into the name, to show I'd recognized her all along. "Scotch? Bourbon? Anything?"

"No. I thought I'd wait until after dinner, thanks."

"Whatever's right." I poured a double knock into my

149

glass, and the usual couple of cubes, and pretended to watch the melt-swirl when I moved the glass. The truth was, I was looking past the glass at this Sandy broad.

Say this for Buddy: the kid seemed to have good taste.

Not that I ever paid a hell of a lot of attention to the kind of dolls he ran around-with. That's Angie's business; raising the bambini. But this one looked okay, a nice enough kid. Yeah.

"I didn't know you and Bud knew each other before the flight," I said, to strike up a conversation (and check out a point at the same time).

"Oh, we didn't," she said. "It was just—oh, I know it sounds sort of funny, but you remember he sort of tripped and we both fell down, a little bit before we landed?"

I nodded; the memory was sort of vague, but something like that had happened, all right.

"Well, after we got up, he asked me to come to Christmas dinner with him. So . . ."

I made with the Johnny Valentine lip-and-eyebrow bit; the "Hey, how about that!" expression. "Hell of a technique," I nodded. "Gotta remember that—to make points with a stewardess, you knock her down and sit on her. *Swingin'!*"

"Just don't let the word get around," she smiled. "It's a secret of the profession; and besides, the other girls would probably sue me for their bruises."

Yeah, a nice kid.

But who needs nice. Right?

"By the way," I said, "where's Buddy, anyway? He's taking a hell of a chance, leaving you around loose. Someone else might trip . . . !"

She shrugged. "He went to change the music on the tape," she said. "I think your friend, Mr.—LoCicero . . . ?" I nodded ". . . went to find him."

"Oh, yeah. Sam the *padrino*. If they start talking I may have to go get both of them, and we never will get any music."

"*Padrino*," she said. "Buddy called him that, too. It's an Italian word, isn't it?"

"Uh-huh. Means 'godfather,' but—well, not exactly the way most people think of a godfather, see? More serious. I mean, us dagos have a kind of tradition about stuff like that. The godfather's a big deal. It's him is supposed to be the guy who really helps a kid along."

"But, all godfathers . . ."

"Yeah, sure. But with other people, it's just—oh, like you're a friend of the family and you hold the kid for christening and like that. But an Italian godfather, *padrino*, well—a man doesn't pick his own kid, his own flesh and blood, right? I mean, hell, a lot of the time he can't even be really sure it's *his* . . ."

She nodded, but still looked puzzled.

". . . but the *padrino*," I went on, "he took the kid on; he *volunteered*, kinda. Made the promises: see he gets raised right, gets the right slant on things, has someone he can talk to about things he'd be scared or maybe even ashamed to talk to his real Old Man about. That kind of stuff."

"It sounds like a big responsibility."

"It is. Of course, not every *padrino* takes it serious. He can slough it if he wants to; let it slide. But mostly, no. Sam, particularly, he's been a hell of a godfather for Buddy. They were always real tight."

She smiled, a big smile that did good things to her face. "Buddy was lucky, then," she said.

"Yeah," I said. "He was. It could have been real rough, I mean with me not being here all the time. He was pretty short in the pants when his ma and me went splitsville."

"Buddy says you were a swell father, though."

I shrugged. Crap like that always makes me nervous but I can tell you I didn't mind hearing her say it.

"A swell father, he's *there*. I wasn't. But Sam did a good job and so did Angie. Brought him up real good."

I drank the rest of my drink and got up from the arm of the big chair where I'd been sitting to fix a new one. While I was doing it, the music cut in on the concealed speakers behind the bar. One of mine. A Christmas album I cut a long time ago. I cocked an ear at it.

"A hair flat," I said. "But the voice was okay—*hey!* Listen to *that!*" The two speakers were far enough apart so I suddenly realized the song was in stereo; like that orchestra was on one side of the hall, and Vanni was on the other. Which was great, sure. But I hadn't cut it that way. That album had been done on the old monaural, and on 78s, at that.

151

"What the hell?" I wondered to nobody in particular. But the girl thought I meant her. She looked a question.

"That's in stereo," I said.

"Yes?"

"But I never cut the thing in stereo. I . . ."

"Oh! Buddy did that," she broke in. "He was telling me just before you arrived. He said it was nothing new; a lot of the old monaurals are being rerecorded in stereo."

"True," I said, still listening. "But mostly they do a kind of a crappy—hey, dig that, now!" And I held up my hand so she wouldn't say anything. The tones were real good. As good as I had ever been, or almost, in person. And that is pretty good. Yeah. But how in the hell had Buddy done that, working with just an old 78?

The record ended. Another one began.

"Look," I said, "uh—Sandy. Would you excuse me a moment? I got to—uh"—and I took off. Buddy's room was just down the hall. I came in to find him and Sam wearing stereophones. Sam's eyes were closed, but Buddy saw me. He waved a hand.

"Hi, dad," he said. "The *padrino* and I will be out in a minute. I wanted him to hear something I been tinkering with."

"Yeah," I said. "I noticed."

"Huh?" He jacked one of the phones up off his ear. "I'm sorry. What'd you say, Dad?"

"I said I heard it. In the den. *You* did the rerecording?"

He looked embarrassed. "Well, yeah," he said, "you know how I fool around with the stuff. Buddy the boy button bender. It's not as good as . . ."

"Hey, let's don't kid an old kidder, okay? It's great!" Christ, you'd of thought I pinned a medal on him!

"You liked it?" he said. "For true?"

"What's not to like?" I said. "You got the tones and you did something great—better, anyhow, than anything I've heard from the pro engineers; the orchestra really *was* on the other side of the stage the day we were cutting this one. And that's where it wound up in your version."

"Yeah, I know," he said. "That the orchestra was over on the left, I mean. And that you were on the booth mike."

I had to laugh. "My God, kid, you can't remember *that!* Why, you couldn't of been three years old when I made that record."

"I was there and I remember it," he said. "I hollered. And you told Ma to get me out of there. And then I cried. I remember."

That stopped me. Because, you know, he was right; now that he reminded me, that's just how it had been. Angie'd brought him to the studio—it couldn't have been much before the final bustup—and I was honked at her because I was afraid her being there was going to chill a thing I had going with a babe in the . . .

"What a kick!" I said, more to block my own memory than for any other reason. "Yeah, crazy. That's some memory you got, there. But what you did—the stereo from mono, I mean—could you do it twice?"

He shrugged, sort of diffidently, and snapped a button on the big console he had built into one wall. A battery of speakers, in a tricky arrangement around the room, cut in and I was surrounded by sound. It was another of the old monos, recut for stereo.

If I hadn't known better, I'd of sworn I made it that way in the first place. I closed my eyes and listened.

"I got quite a few," Buddy said.

I nodded, with the eyes still closed. Yeah. No crap, baby; old Vanni really did have it in those days. Yeah!

"Look," I said, "could you . . . ?"

Angie broke in, calling us to come and sit down, dinner was ready.

We went back down the hall, Sam trailing along in last place, and turned through the den to the dining room. "No crap, though, Bud," I said as we went, "why don't you come down and talk to a couple of the engineer guys at Lullaby. Maybe you really got something new there. . . ."

"What kind of a deal will you make?" Sam growled.

"Deal?"

"Deal, you know: *money*. For the rights to the B.V. Process."

I stopped and looked at Sam. "Hey, you got to lay off that juice, baby; it's breaking you up! We're partners, remember?"

Sam smiled blandly. "Uh-huh," he said. "And as your partner, I might try to pry the B.V. Process out of Buddy for free. But as his agent, I ain't gonna let me get away with anything like that, partner."

I had to laugh.

"Jee-*sus*," I said. "Sam the schizophrenic! You got to get a set of hats, one for every different job. That way everybody will know which Sam they're talking to. Including you!"

Sam just went on smiling.

"Aw, hell," Buddy said, and his face was bright red, "it's no big deal. I'll talk to the engineers if you want me to, you know that."

"He's right," I said. I reached over and messed up his hair. He really was a good kid, you know? "You listen to the *padrino*, Buddy," I told him. "And do like he says, especially when he's being your agent. Take it from me, kid; play it old Sam's way and you'll wind up with more pocket money than Irving Dahlberg keeps in his Stamp Fund!"

Sam grinned at both of us. "See, even your old man knows I'm right." He turned to me. "Hey, Vanni, funny you should mention the Stamp Fund. I wonder, has old Irving still got that?"

I shrugged. "Who knows," I said. "It's been a gag around town so long, maybe it's pure bullshit. You know how those stories get started."

"Yeah." Sam was serious now. Ruminating. "Yeah, sure, only I was thinking, Vanni. I wonder if the old fart ever declared that dough to the government? To the IRS, I mean."

"So what if he did or he didn't? You figuring to heist the joint, Sam? We're getting kind of old for that kind of crap, daddy. Besides, what's a lousy million between friends?"

"Heist, *schmeist*," Sam said, still serious. "What I was thinking—if he didn't, maybe it's an edge for us. On the TV deal, or whatever else we . . ."

"No," I said. "*No*, Sam. No *way!*"

"Vanni . . ."

"Forget it. I mean that, Sam. If we can rack the guy up, make him keep his part of the bargain or wish he had, some *legit* way, fine. You know I'm for that. But fuck the IRS! I wouldn't give those guys the sweat off my . . ."

"Okay!" Sam held his hands up, surrendering, with the baby-blue innocent stretch of the eyes. "Okay, awreddy. Only, if we want to move over to Priapus and he tries to make a court fight—to tie us up and queer the deal—a thing like that . . ."

"Sam," I said, "*Forget* it. Besides, I still haven't made up my mind about Priapus. It'd be a gasser, the way you tell it and all, but there's still a lot that worries me."

Sam started to reply, but never got the words out. Angie's face popped around the door of the dining room.

"Giovanni!" she said, still smiling, but meaning business this time. "Buddy—Sam—will you *please* . . ."

"Sure, baby," I said. "Sure. Right now."

I put one arm around Sam's shoulders, the other around Buddy's, and pulled them along. The table was all set, looking like a Palermo wedding banquet. I gave Angie a big grin, there at the foot of the table, and moved around to my chair. Buddy moved in beside the stewardess kid and Sam . . .

### Jack Dahlberg

. . . ducked around to the other side of the table.

"Lay one hand on me, you little motherfucker," Clara said, "and I swear to Christ I'll kick your balls off!"

I stood still and looked at her. I hadn't intended to hit her.

Clara, my wife. The girl I'd married and lived with for six years; the woman I'd wanted to have my children, back when she could have had them—a hard-eyed, nasty-mouthed lush standing across the still-littered table where we'd had Christmas dinner with Papa.

"What do you want from me, Clara?" I said, in as calm a voice as I could muster. "What do I have to do to make peace between us?"

"Nothing much, Shorty. Just give me a divorce settlement I can cuddle up with on cold nights. You know the kind of deal I'm talking about. So, give!"

I sighed. We'd been through this time and time again, and there was no way I could swing what she demanded to let go. And, so far, she wasn't listening to my compromise suggestions. At all.

"Clara, when you're willing to talk sense, that's when we'll talk about a divorce," I said. "You could . . ."

"I could have picked shit with the chickens for all you cared." She stood up straight, seeming much more sober than I knew her to be after knocking down all those drinks while Papa was here. "Four years—ever since you brought home that dose and gave it to me; that cute little disease you picked up from one of those 'talent school' sessions you used to like so much in your office after working hours. Ever since you gave it to me, and left me with my insides cut out like a *spayed bitch*."

*It wasn't true.*

I looked at her and wondered about everything. The whole business of living. *Four years.* Clara had been going around for four years, telling herself that lie.

Oh, I had caught a dose, all right. And fired the son of a bitch at the studio gym whose carelessness had let me in for it; he was supposed to run regular checks on those "starlet" kids. Make sure they were clean.

But I hadn't brought anything home. Clara'd just had a miscarriage. Her second. And this one was worse than the first because it was the result of a tube pregnancy. It had almost killed her; she let it go too far before she went to the doctor. He'd had to take both ovaries and tubes in order to save her life.

It wasn't until a month or so later she heard—studio gossip is a better communications network than NBC—about my little problem. It was cured by then. And I hadn't come within a mile of her all the time I had it.

But when I got home that night, she hit me with it. I was responsible for her being sterilized. I had given her a dose and the doctor was just covering up when he said it was the pregnancy. That was the first night I ever saw her drunk, so I didn't try to argue her out of it until the next morning. Then I had explained everything. Even got out a calendar; marked the days and reminded her that we hadn't made it during the whole time I was dosed.

She listened to it all. I thought I had put the point across. She'd never mentioned it again. Until now.

"Clara," I said. "That's not true. You know it's not."

"Oh, you little bastard," she said. "You little asshole! Do you think you could lie to me about something like that; make me *believe* it? I knew you were lying from the first; you and that doctor. But I couldn't tell you so. Oh, no! I had to wait, *wait* four years. Until I was ready. So don't try to shit me again, Shorty. Just *forget it!*"

"Clara—"

"To hell with you. You want to know what it's going to

cost you to get rid of me? Well, I'll tell you, Shorty. Plenty! Say, for example, a good hunk out of one million dollars, free and clear, no taxes; *plus* the alimony that I'd get in any normal divorce. Plus half of any community property."

I didn't know whether to laugh or cry.

"Clara, you've *got* to be nuts. If I had it, I wouldn't give it to you, and you know damn well I don't have it."

"Like hell you don't, Jack. Like hell!"

"In property, maybe. In stock, yes. You know that. But you know I can't sell much of either one and keep the money, or give it to anyone. The tax bite would be a gobble. Clara, if I *wanted* to lay hands on a that kind of cash, which I don't, there's no way on earth I could swing it. Oh, hell, look; you want a divorce and some dough and the rest, okay. I've told you you can have them. We'll talk tomorrow, all right? But huge sums, under the table—well, it's just plain silly. Sober up; then we'll talk."

And that got the biggest laugh of the day. She threw back her head and let fly. I stood there, completely nonplused. If there was a joke, even from a drunk's point of view, I just couldn't see it.

Finally, she stopped laughing and walked over to the liquor cabinet. She reached in and came out with the vodka bottle. I thought she was going to pour herself another knock. But instead she handed it to me.

"Take the cap off," she said. "Sniff. Taste."

"Clara—"

"*Sniff!*"

Okay, hell; humor her. I unscrewed the cap and sniffed. It was nothing. That was odd; vodka doesn't have much smell, but this wasn't even . . .

I sniffed again and then, as she'd suggested, tasted.

It was water.

"I was drunk this morning," she said quietly. "But I knocked it off before dawn. The rest of the day, I've been hitting straight water—and listening. To you and dear Papa."

"What for?"

"To make up my mind. About how to get what I want."

"So, big deal. We didn't say anything you haven't heard before. Just routine business. The production plans for next year." I was puzzled.

"Uh-huh. That's so." She nodded. "Just that, and one other little thing. Something I *did* know, as you say, but had almost forgotten."

"What?"

She smiled; the smile of a happy hunter squeezing off the kill shot. "The Stamp Fund, Jackie," she said. "The Stamp Fund."

I stood with my mouth open. She wasn't kidding. She really thought I could and would give it, or some part of it, to her, free and clear, to get rid of her. Somehow, she had decided Papa would go along with something like that, just to get me out of . . .

"You *are* psycho," I told her. "Really, Clara, look; no crap and all arguments aside, if you think Papa would use that money to square a beef like this, you need a head-shrinker. That, or a quick course in character analysis. Why, he'd see me in hell first, son or no . . ."

"Then don't tell him," she said in a flat voice.

"Don't . . . ?"

"Just take it! Give it to me. And don't tell him. He can't do a damn thing, legally; he can't complain about losing money nobody—except *us*—knows he's got."

"No. But he can fire my ass for me and make sure I never work again in pictures. That he could do, and that he would do. And where's your lifetime alimony-annuity then?"

Clara shrugged and did not reply.

"You couldn't spend that kind of under-the-table money," I pointed out, "unless you had the alimony coming in. Sooner or later, someone would want to know where your dough was coming from, and . . ."

"You wouldn't get fired," Clara interrupted.

"Like hell I wouldn't."

"Bullshit." It was one of her favorite words; I've always hated it. "You and dear old Margaret hold more Monarch stock than your father does. And she would back you up. If anyone threw anyone out, it would be your father who went . . ."

"You don't understand," I tried to explain. "Papa always votes her stock. He has a . . ."

"Proxy—which she can revoke at any time."

"But . . ."

"You know," she went on in a speculative tone, "I used to wonder why you and Margaret didn't kick the old bastard out, when it would be so easy and you've both got good reasons."

"Reasons?"

"Sure. Her because he treats her like some kind of servant, hiding her away down there in Miami Beach—his own wife. And you because of all the crap he makes you swallow all the time. You don't have to take it. Why do you, anyway?"

I started to answer, and then realized I couldn't. There was no answer. Things between us were just as they had always been, ever since I could remember. He was, well, he was just Irving Dahlberg. And Irving Dahlberg was the boss—always. The whole idea of actually fighting him outright for control of the studio . . .

Hell, I couldn't even imagine a thing like that. He was my father. I was his son. And he was the boss. That's how things were. How they always were.

"Clara," I said, "go to bed. I'm through talking for today, so you might as well. And forget the Stamp Fund, too; I'm not a thief. I don't steal money. And I don't steal studios. And I don't even *talk* about double-crossing my own father. So, drop it."

She stood looking at me for a long moment.

"Okay," she said finally, "you've had your say. And it was spoken like a real, red-blooded, hundred-percent-American boy scout, Shorty. But you get this: I don't give a good goddamn how you get the money, or who gets hurt. You've already heard the best offer you're ever going to get, and it's not going to be good forever. If you don't come through, I can make things awfully awkward around this town for you and your precious father who you'd *never* double-cross because that wouldn't be nice. Think it over, sonny. Cause that's how it's going to be!"

She turned—that swift, Loretta Young turn she'd learned in acting school—and swept offstage, toward the stairs.

I stood watching the space where she'd been.

Jesus! *Jesus Christ.* Now what in the . . .

## Irving Dahlberg

". . . hell do you expect me to do about it? Am I that imbecile's keeper?"

"No, Mr. Dahlberg. Certainly not!"

159

Even over three thousand miles of telephone wire, there was something oily and fawning about him; Quentin Burke was probably the best chief of public relations Monarch had ever had. But talking to him always made me want to wash my hands.

"But I thought you'd want to know," he went on. "Since you've taken such a special interest in the picture."

That burned me, too. What business was it of his how much interest I took in a production?

"All right," I said. "So now I know. What else?"

"Well, ah, I was wondering . . ."

"Come on, say it. Spit it out!"

"Well, would you like to authorize a—ah—*private investigator* to attempt to ascertain Mr. Strauss's whereabouts? I think, perhaps, the production insurance firm, the one that underwrote the policy on *Burn the First Card*, might be willing to share a portion of . . ."

"Goddamn it, Burke," I was almost yelling now, "since when do you ask *me* to authorize a minor item like that? Do it or don't do it. It's up to you."

I wondered, could the silly bastard be drunk?

"Ah, no sir," he said, "it's not."

"What?"

"Your order—the memo last month about reducing expenses. You said all nonbudgeted items must be cleared with you personally."

Oh, *Christ!*

"Jesus God, Burke," I said, "you of all people ought to know a memo to impress the directors from one that's on the level. Nothing is changed; that was just to convince those blithering numbskull comma pouncers we're cost-conscious. If you want a private snoop, hire him."

"Thank you, sir," Burke said. "That's a relief, believe me. We're really quite concerned about Strauss."

"Oh, hell, he's probably just shacked up somewhere."

"Perhaps, sir," he said. "Perhaps. But it seems he *had* an —ah—arrangement to meet a young lady Christmas Eve. He did not appear. It was the young lady who telephoned us; alerted us to the possible situation. And Mr. Strauss has not been seen elsewhere, either, so far as we can determine. So . . ."

"All right, all right," I said. "I think you got your bowels in an uproar for nothing. But use your own judgment."

"Thank you, sir."

"Oh, *Burke!*" I caught him before he could hang up. "One thing I did want to talk to you about . . ."

"Yes, sir?"

". . . your friend in the Defense Department. The ex-admiral. Did you talk to him about *Boarders Away!*"

He hesitated a moment. I had an immediate hunch whatever he said next would be a lie.

"Yes, sir, I—ah—did. And he was most enthusiastic. Yes! Very."

"But?"

"But—well, he *is* retired, as you know. He works there only in the capacity of civilian consultant."

"So?"

"The—ah, well, the matter is still being considered. It may take some time."

I was right. He was lying. The answer had been no. If the question had even been asked.

"All right then," I said, pretending to believe him. "I'll wait for whatever you can come up with. Keep at it."

And I hung up.

Ah, God, what a day! Christmas. Ah, God!

The cigar in my mouth had gone out and I relighted it, but it tasted like old rope wrapped in salvaged inner tubes. I threw it into an ashtray.

Politics. The whole damn thing with *Boarders Away!* was politics. My party was out of office; the opposition was in. And looked like it was going to stay in until hell froze over. Somehow, something was going to have to be worked; some angle found. Some gimmick.

And, as usual, it would be up to Irving Dahlberg. Well, he would find it. He always found it; every time, all these years. Nothing too big. Nothing that can't be handled. Irving Dahlberg always gets what he wants. *Always.*

I looked at the bedroom door and wondered if Gaby was still asleep. She had been when I walked in. Before the phone call. I felt a little sorry for her; Christmas Day, and how had she had to spend it? Cooped up in a hotel room. Alone. Maybe I should wake her up, take her out somewhere for dinner or something.

I took a step before I remembered. Christmas Day. What would be open on Christmas Day? What to *do?* What?

I snorted. Something that might have been a laugh.

In *this* town. *My* town—Hollywood. Irving Dahlberg alone and with nothing to do on Christmas night in Hollywood!

I took another step toward the bedroom, and all at once I was an old man. A very old man. And very tired. *Gaby*. Gaby. . . .

I tried to take hold of myself. Stand up straight; head erect, shoulders back. You're not tired; you're *not!* Irving Dahlberg is not like other men. He does not get old. He does not get tired. He is strong. He is young. He is loved. *Loved!*

I stood there a moment, trying to feel it; trying to make it true, as I always could in the old days. I tried, but it was no use.

From the other side of the door I heard a stirring. Sounds of footsteps. Gaby was awake. I turned, working to keep my own footsteps silent, and got away as fast as I could. Across the living room. Into the other bedroom, and across.

To the toilet. I went in. Sat down. And . . .

## David Strauss

. . . locked the door. It was quieter there in the john, and I had a chance to look at myself in the mirror.

*David Strauss, star of stage, screen, and ESP, invites all of you to take a piece of him home to the kiddies.*

Outside, in the living room and bedroom, I could hear the party in full swing. Not that it was much to hear. Some music; weird, soaring music that occasionally hit tones that set up a sort of sympathetic resonance in my head. A sitar, they called it.

I looked at my face. A dog's dinner would have been more photogenic.

Maybe, I thought, maybe I ought to go back out there and take one of those damn reefers. Better for you than the booze, so they say. Weed leaves no hangover. None at all. I looked down at the glass of Scotch I was holding.

And *that* stuff, I told myself distinctly, isn't helping at all. I took a deep breath and let it out.

All those people; why had Dolly invited them? I needed to be alone with her. To talk to her. I had managed to get through most of the day, looking forward to that; and when I arrived, there they all were. Dolly said they'd all been invited before I called.

*I wonder?*

Standing there looking at myself wasn't doing any good either. I tipped the glass and swallowed the rest of the drink and got out of there. The smoke in the room was denser than ever. I wondered if just breathing it could get me high.

Odd. I have tried just about everything, everything in this world. But not drugs, not even marijuana, not yet. Maybe I missed something? Yeah. Maybe.

A lot of people willing to give a lot of testimony on that side. An answer, they said; a different way to live and think and be. God knows I need something like that. But what was it Lenny Bruce said? *"I got enough shit flying around inside my head as it is. . . ."* Yeah, poor Lenny. He knew. And look how he wound up anyway.

*That makes two of us, Lenny. We both got enough.*

"David. Sit down, be friendly. . . ."

Familiar face. Unfamiliar beard. Who? Dyne the name was Dyne; the last name.

"Okay."

"You look like hell."

"Thanks."

"Don't get mad. Who looks good when they been working as hard as you worked the past year or so? Man, it should happen to me!"

"You really want . . . ?"

"Want to work? You bet your sweet sweetbreads I want to work. Don't tell me it's been so long—what, two years? No, not even two years yet. Don't tell me it's been too long for you to remember how it felt, waiting for the phone calls."

I shrugged, and couldn't resist looking over at Dolly. Yeah. She'd been picking up on our conversation. There was that cool, sneering look in her cat eyes; her Nefertiti eyes. Was that why she said come over? So she could put me down?

". . . do look bad, though," Dyne was saying when I tuned him back in. "You're shooting something now, aren't you? *Burn* . . . uh—something. I can't remember."

There was a joint passing around the circle of bodies on the floor. Dyne's turn came, he started to drag at the cigarette, but looked at me instead.

"You in?" he asked.

"No."

He pumped his eyebrows up and down, in no particular way, just to show it was nothing to him one way or another I guess, and closed his eyes while he took the mixed air-and-smoke lungful demanded by pot protocol. Then he handed the joint past me. It was about half finished. I looked back at Dolly.

*The blue-and-white Diamond.*

Blue, white—and pink. Yeah. If the general public could see her now; if they only could. Stripped to the waist, like all the other chicks here. And nothing but pants and shoes for the rest of the costume.

Wonder why the shoes?

Dyne had finished the breathing exercises. He looked back at me and his eyes were just a little bit glassier. I wanted to reach for my lowball, a gesture I have developed over the years to cover nervousness (as other people, I think, use cigarettes), but the glass had disappeared somewhere. I remembered emptying it, anyway, while I was in the john. So there was nothing I could do but look back at Dyne (what the *hell* was his first name?).

"Don't dig pot, huh?" he said.

I decided he was setting me up for a put-down. Okay. Fuck it. Let him.

"Just not my thing, baby," I said. I waited for the jab, wishing I was somewhere else, but he surprised me.

"Frankly," he said, "I'm not all that big for it, either. I just came because Dolly was giving this bash. To tell the truth, as far as weed goes, I'd just as soon stick to tobacco or to booze, like you, if I'm going for the *small* kick. . . ."

I looked surprised at him.

". . . but what the hell. I go with the group; if it's booze, booze. If it's pot, pot. And when I really want to turn on, then I do *my* own thing. It all works out."

*Vince!*

There was a little click in my head and the name finally popped out. "Sounds like you got it made, Vince," I said. "I wish I was there. . . ."

He looked at me soberly. "Really a rough time, huh?" he said. "You really feel whipped-out, all the work?"

"I've been in better shape."

"*Bummer,*" he nodded. "Stone bummer! I remember—

yeah, baby; I *do* remember how rough it was for my dad, back when he was hot in the business. How beat he always was when he'd get home. Not that he was ever as big, or as hot, as you are these days. But I know it can be rough."

"I'll get over it." See the great thespian? See how nobly he bears his burden? See how he condescends to the poor, unsuccessful acquaintance who has no great burden to bear? See the stupid, hammy son of a bitch being as phony as ever?

*Bullshit!* Have a little honesty, David. Have a little honesty for once in your miserable life! Thank you. Don't mind if I do. . . .

"Aw, hell, Vince," I said. "Don't let me kid you. I'm not just beat; not just tired from work and like that. Christ! Look, let's make a deal: I stop playing a phony prick named David Strauss, and you forget that last thing I said. Okay?"

"Huh?" His eyes focused. "What last thing?"

"Like I said, forget it. Listen, I'm a goddamn mess. My head is fucked up. I don't know whether I'm going or coming and the only reason I don't fog the whole thing up with grass is that I'm too chicken to try, because I never did it before. Now there, for once I said something honest."

He smiled at me; it was like the hairy bottom of his face breaking into two parts. I liked the smile. It at least *looked* like a real smile, not the careful production smiles I'd been getting from everyone—agents, writers, directors, producers, admen, fans, the whole phony world—for a year.

"Man," he said, nodding the beard smile, "you *are* wound up. Look, maybe you ought to go for a couple of joints. Forget the crap you've heard about it. It does lay a little happy time on you, and that you could use."

I shook my head. "No," I said. "If I'm on this honesty kick, I'll tell that straight, too. It's not just that I'm scared of grass; I need something else. Something that lasts, you know? A *little* happy time I can get, just from booze. I been doing that number and it's not enough anymore."

He didn't say anything, but went on looking at me.

"I came here to try to talk to Dolly." (Now I was really into the talk bit; hearing words come out that I hadn't planned, vomiting some of the sourness inside me all over this poor *schlunk* who had been incautious enough to act like a human being around David Strauss—and hating myself for what I was doing.) "I didn't know she'd already invited all of you. Wanted to maybe get my head a little straight. She used to do that for me back when we were married. But I should have known better."

"You want to *talk* to her?"

"I wanted to talk to her. I know it sounds weird; we been busted up since the guinea moved in. Hell, before that, even, if I'm going to tell the truth and it looks like I am. But sometimes—I don't know—sometimes, even with that guy on the scene and with all the work . . ."

Something was changing in his face. I couldn't be sure what.

". . . even then, sometimes, I could talk about things to her and it would—would be *all right* again for a while." I ran down. Out of words. "Aw, hell," I said, wishing to God I'd kept my mouth shut. "Aw, hell, erase that, huh? Forget everything I said. Forget I ever . . ."

I got a foot under me, ready to split for the door. But he reached out a hand and put it on my shoulder. I hesitated, just a second, and then sat down again. Across the circle, I could see Dolly giving us the double-oh; *oh yeah, her eyes were saying, oh yeah—the fag found a dear little buddy for himself. Oh yeah!* But I knew she was wrong for once. There was gentleness in this boy's touch. Compassion in his face. But nothing else; nothing of the I-know-*you*, nothing of the contact leer of the *young man on the make*. He was straight, and I knew it even if Dolly the blue-and-white Diamond didn't.

"Take it easy," he said. "You're among *friends*, friend."

And, by God! I suddenly felt I was.

We said nothing else for nearly a half hour. The party went its merry way. The smoke in the room got denser and one by one the reeking joints made their way around the circle. Vince took his regular turns, did not look at me or speak. I got up and filled a new glass with Scotch and water and ice (very little Scotch, very much ice and water) and sat down again. I sipped, but did not drink.

Something was coming. I knew that. Something was coming. Something good. Something that would help.

The time passed. . . .

"Okay," Vince said finally, when the crowd in the room was down to five or six, including us. "The time has come."

He uncoiled his legs—he had been sitting in the lotus position all that time—and stood up.

"Good people," he said in a low, melodious voice, "now that the diddlers and dabblers have gone—hear me. Be silent, and hear!"

And, for God's sake, they shut up!

"There is one among us," he continued when the only sound was that of his voice, "whose troubles are deep and many. He came seeking comfort. Seeking solace. But found none . . ."

Still not a sound.

". . . because his woes were too many and too strong for the battlements of booze or the prodigies of pot. He is still in need. And this is Christmas Day."

From the corner of my eye, I saw Dolly squirm. She moved her face to interrupt, to laugh maybe and break the spell of Vince's speech. But the sound died before she voiced it. She remained silent.

"His need," Vince continued, "is for insight, for a glimpse of truth; a telescope of clear lenses with which to see himself and the world. For a journey, a trip to truth. And this gift it is within our power to give him. How say you?"

Oh, God. I couldn't really believe any of this was happening. It wasn't real. Playacting—all of them were playacting; so mock-serious, so absorbed in the pompous and pretentious lines this—this *actor* was delivering. *Actors!* All of them; everyone in that room was an actor, playing a childish game for my benefit. I wanted to spit on myself. Get up and give this Vince punk *five,* right in his phony beard mouth, for putting me on this way. I wanted to scream and strangle him; strangle all of them. Especially Dolly.

But I just sat there.

"All right." It was Dolly, speaking with the same mock gravity as Vince. "So be it! If this—person is in such great need, then help him. Show him where truth lies."

"Let him *see* the world," said someone else.

"And let it be *now.*"

Vince turned to me, smiling again. *"Now,"* he nodded. "Yes, now! You came, looking for help, David. But are you willing to accept it?"

I wanted to throw my drink in his face; wanted to weep and curse and beat at them all for what they were doing

167

to me. But something stopped me. Held me. Forced me to play out the game with them.

"Yes," I heard myself saying. "I can. I will."

"Very well. Come!"

He pointed to a couch across the room. Like a man in a trance I got up and walked toward it. Dolly's head turned with me as I went. I could not read her expression.

"Lie there," Vince said, "and lift your head."

He took a piece of folded paper from his pocket, began to unwrap it. Inside was a white, oblong pill. He held the pill in his hand and smiled at me. "Your glass," he said. "The glass in your hand. Use that to swallow. It takes time to learn to get these down without water."

"It's not water. It's Scotch."

"All the better," he nodded. "All the better to *see* the world of truth. Take the pill, David. Swallow it."

*Damn* him! Damn all of them. Damn their game, and damn the hope I'd had. Children! And I was the most childish of the lot; they had an excuse, they were stoned on grass and happy enough maybe not to even know what a silly and pompous ass this Vince longface was. But I wasn't high and I wasn't even drunk anymore. No excuse for me. No excuse. So why—*why* was I playing along with them?

"What is it?" I said, looking at the pill. "What . . . ?"

"Truth."

"No, I mean what kind of pill. What do they call it?"

"Orange Sunshine!" He plucked the pill from his own palm, grasped my wrist, placed it in my hand, and closed my fingers over it. "There are several different kinds of pill," he said in an almost conversational voice, "called by that name. Some are just plain acid—LSD-25 in concentrated form. Some—well, some are bummers; ripoffs peddled around by thieves. But this is the real thing: *diethyltryptamine.*"

"What?"

"Diethyltryptamine," he repeated. "A new type; a hypnotic and psychedelic drug but greater, more consciousness-expanding, than anything discovered before."

"How can it help me?" I said, idiotically. "What can it do that any drug—I mean, I don't go the drug route, Vince. I never have. I've always been . . ."

"David," he stopped me. "Am I your friend?"

"I—I think . . ."

"Don't reply. You needn't make a judgment like that aloud, David. Just believe me. Believe this. I *am* your friend. All of us are. Yes, even your former wife, Dolly. It is no accident that I brought the Sunshine with me today. She asked me to. Yes, and I thought it was for her. But now I know. Always, she meant it for you, David. Because, in her way, Dolly still loves you."

I looked at Dolly. Her face was still, impassive, composed. Waiting. Again I had the impulse to leave. To get up and run. Something clear, logical and coherent in my mind told me this was all farce and that I was the patsy for a joke.

But it was the same part of my mind that had hurt me. Brought me to this place where I lived in terror. It was my enemy. It was the part I had tried to kill with liquor and with—with—

I couldn't think the rest. My mind ran away from the rest. Into the darkness of Central Park. I lay there, the glass in one hand, the pill in the other; lay there, watching and hearing the war inside me.

*David Strauss, star of stage, screen, and ESP, invites you to Armageddon. The final death of God, originally thought to be an exaggeration, has been confirmed. The crucifixion is scheduled for six o'clock. . . .*

I put the pill in my mouth. Swallowed it with a huge gulp of Scotch. Held my breath for a long moment.

And had an immediate impulse to stick my finger down my throat, to tickle the retch reflex that would bring the whole thing up before it got into my system. That logical part of my mind, that clear part of my head that kept hurting me, was hammering on my eyeballs and stamping on my thoughts to make me do that. But all the while, the part of me that was *me*—the part that lived and needed—was holding my hands, restraining my arms, and telling me over and over that . . .

## Buddy Valentine

". . . you're an ass if you do. That's all, pal. *You're a real ass if you do!*"

I didn't mean to hear that. Or the rest of the hassle between the Old Man and the *padrino.*

Dinner was over; Sandy and I had spent about an hour back in my room, talking and listening to some of the special tapes I had put together. She seemed to dig them. Not that she was real hip on electronics or sound engineering or any of that stuff. She was like most people that way,

She did listen, though, and hell, she could have been putting me on, sure, but I didn't think so. Seemed to enjoy the parts that were really far out. She even liked the demo tape I'd cut of the Kinfolk group. She had a sense of rhythm and an ear for tone, that much I knew for sure, and asked questions that showed her mind was attached to her mouth. In fact, in every way I could see, a really great chick.

No, I hadn't kissed her again. Or anything else. Don't ask me why; maybe for the same reason I'd landed in her lap and said "Ghoor!" the day before. Maybe just because of that. Anyhow, it didn't seem like the thing to do.

So there we sat, talking about some ideas I had of how a whole new kind of music was going to develop—a real art-form, as valid as the one begun by old J. S. Bach with his ear-ripping organ—from electronic instrumentation. We went from that to all kinds of other topics such as art and flying. I tried to be modest about mentioning my own few hundred hours of logged flight time and multiple ratings; she finally laughed at that, and so did I when I realized it wasn't a put-down. Then we discussed her family and my family and, finally, astrology.

The electronic piece "Switched-On Bach" was rolling on the tape when she sprang it on me by asking what time of day and where I had been born. It was just the way she'd asked, in the first place, what day it was.

I guess I looked blank again. "What's the bit?"

"No bit. Just me. You don't know, do you. I mean, off-hand?"

"Well, yeah. One thing: where I was born. Here in L.A. Over at Cedars."

"And what time?"

I shrugged. "Sorry," I said. "I couldn't be really sure. In fact I couldn't guess. My memory of the event has sort of slipped. Hell, it'd surprise me if *they* remembered. My folks, I mean."

*Oops!* That kind of slipped out in the wrong tone of

voice. And then, damn it, I could feel myself *blushing* again.

Sandy smiled. "You know, Buddy," she said, "you are a kind of a hell of a nice guy. You know that?"

I felt more like a fool than ever.

"Yeah," I said, clowning it up, "an easy blusher, that's Buddy-boy."

"You don't have to do that, you know," she said, and her face went serious and gentle. "Not for me. I like the person you are, Buddy, not the imitation of your father that you try to be."

I stopped with my mouth half-open. Oh, this chick was really something *else*. And she had old Buddy-boy down pat.

Okay. All *right!* So let's see what happens if just once, mind you, Buddy tells it like it really is.

"Thanks," I said. "You know, I hate being an imitation. But that's what I am. For sure. Maybe if I could stop that, a lot of things would change around here."

"Not just around here," she said, picking it up like it was the most natural thing in the world. "Start being exactly who you are, and the whole world changes. Believe me, I know."

And she did. I knew it; looking at Sandy and hearing her, I knew she wasn't pretending anything. And never would. It made me wish we were both someplace else; someplace with no one else around and all the time in the world. Just to talk. Not a big important dialogue or anything. Just talk. My God, I wanted to *talk* to this chick!

"You liked the Christmas presents?" I said.

She nodded and smiled. "It was awfully sweet of you," she answered. "Who was the pin for, really? Your mother?"

"Yeah. But she won't miss it."

"No, she won't." Sandy just looked at me for about ten seconds. "But you weren't asking about the present you gave me were you? You meant all those other presents, the tons of stuff that took more than an hour to open."

"Uh-huh," I said. "Those."

She closed her eyes and breathed in and out. "Beautiful," she said, opening her eyes again. "And terribly expensive. The furs. The jewelry. Even to a new car for your mother. Is it always like that at Christmas, Buddy?"

"Always," I said, wondering if she had seen anything else.

171

"And always," she went on, "it's ten presents for Mama and ten for Sam and the help and the business people and all the rest—and one or two for Buddy. Right?"

Yes. She'd seen.

"Good presents," I said, nodding at the special professional mix panel I'd already moved into my room from the den where I'd unwrapped it. "Expensive—very—and suited to things that interest me." I let a moment go by, choosing the words carefully. "It's not the price," I said, when I was sure, "and it's not the numbers, as such. Okay, Ma's car cost more than the panel and the specially wired jet flying suit put together. But it's not that—"

"No. It's not that."

"I'd take a Spiro Agnew watch," I said, "and a necktie that looked like an explosion in a paint factory if Dad had picked them out for me, himself. But as long as he doesn't, the comparisons get to me."

I stopped. It hurt and anyway, what the hell?

Like I say, this chick Sandy was something else. She knew what I was going to say. So, the hell with saying it. I looked at her, and I made the "So what else?" with the hands.

"They love you," she said.

"I guess so."

"They do. Not as much as you love them, no. But they do love you, Buddy."

"Yeah."

She gave me a quick so-let's-not-pick-at-the-sore-spot-anymore smile. "All rightee," she said. "Now then, go ask."

That went right past me.

"Ask what?"

"When you were born, Mister Capricorn. I want to know."

"Why?"

"To work out your natal chart. Come on, indulge me. Put it down to Sandy-is-outa-her-skull, if you've a mind, podnuh. But ask, huh?"

"Okay. Later."

"Now."

"But—"

"Please?"

What can you do? I made my bug-eyed ape face, and

she gave me back a perfect Groucho-Marx-in-heat eye roll. I laughed. She laughed. And I went to ask.

Which, for what it's worth, is how I happened to be coming through the kitchen door in time to hear what the *padrino* was saying, evidently in answer to something the Old Man had said. I don't think either one of them knew I had come in. Fact is, I'm sure of it. Because they went right on.

"She's a hell of a talent, gonna be a big star, baby. And she says she loves me, Sam."

The *padrino* made a face.

"Love," he said. "Love! What the fuck would she know? What is she, twenty years old? Twenty-two, tops? And been around the course since she was how old? Sixteen? Fourteen?"

"I love her, Sam. I really do."

Sam's face went hard and right then, without having to get close and smell his breath or anything, I knew he was drunk. Drunk the way only the *padrino* can get now and then; no wobbling or slurring of words but he won't remember anything about anything the next day.

"All right," he said. "So you say you love her. Big deal! *Love.* You know, Vanni baby, I take back what I said before. You're not an ass if you marry that cunt. You're an ass anyway. I mean it."

"Look, now, Sam . . ."

"Look—*shit!* If you love her, *love* her then, Vanni. Why the hell do you have to come to me or anyone else to talk about it, ask questions? Why do you need anyone to prove to yourself how you really feel? Love her? *Horse crap!*"

"Sam . . ."

"All right, Christ on a fucking crutch, all right, go on. Go on! Marry the *noffke*. Who the fuck cares?" Sam's eyes got narrow, suddenly, and his next words came out like buckshot rattling on steel. "Marry her and go fuck yourself. Skinny little slut—she's got no tits, she's got no ass—nothing but a mouth she's used on everybody in town . . ." And that was as far as he got. I saw the Old Man move—I saw the punch lifting, but I couldn't do a damn thing to stop it.

Then it was all like in slow motion. The punch connecting, solid, and with most of the Old Man behind it. The *padrino's* lip splitting, his feet going out from under him, him going down.

The action speeded up again when he hit the tiles.

He didn't say a word or make a sound. That's what was scariest—if you don't count the fact that any of this was happening at all—when he hit, the *padrino* just rolled. Back onto his shoulders and then, snap, a quick rock, just like I was taught in judo classes when I was a kid, that brought him back up with his feet under him and in a crouch.

The *padrino* took a step toward the Old Man, and it was like seeing someone I'd never met before. Everything good that was him, that made him the man who had practically weaned and raised me, was gone from his eyes. And anything in front of him was in trouble.

But nothing else happened. Between the two of them anyway. Because I wasn't the only one who had heard or seen anything; suddenly everybody was there, in the kitchen. Screaming.

I stood still and watched Ma, waving and flailing her arms while she shrieked what must have been words but didn't come across that way; she got between them and pushed at the Old Man, trying to move him backward. He didn't seem to realize she was there, but he didn't move forward either. She began telling the *padrino* to *please* and to *no,* and finally put her arms around him from the front, holding the *padrino's* arms tight to his side. He didn't move either. And for a while, both of them just stood there like that, looking at each other.

And then, right when I thought it was never going to happen, the *padrino* relaxed. He looked away from the Old Man, who went on staring at where he had been for a while, and said to Angie, "Okay, now. Sure. Don't worry; everything's fine."

She looked up at him and waited for him to say something else.

"Tell you what," he said. "I think it's time for old Sam to get in his car and go home, huh? And that's what I'm gonna do right now." And while we all stood there, still in shock, he lumbered out the door to his waiting limo. I watched as the chauffeur got him settled in the back seat, then drove off.

Ma had stopped screaming. She was crying instead. The

Old Man was still looking at where the *padrino* had been standing before everyone came trampling in.

"Okay," he said after a long while. "Okay, cool it, kid. It's over. Knock it off, huh?"

Ma cried all the louder.

"Look, Angie, will you *please*—aw, balls!" He started to turn away, but Ma was on him like a tiger. She grabbed both his arms and sank her fingers in until you couldn't see the painted nails anymore. "Vanni," she said. "Vanni, look at me!"

"Yeah?" You could tell the Old Man was surprised. And that he wanted to be somewhere else, right now.

"Vanni, you and Sam, our friend. Tell me the truth—what were you fighting about?"

"He's crocked, Angie," the Old Man said. "Loaded! Sam don't know when to . . ."

"It was about that Dolly Diamond, wasn't it, Vanni? Wasn't it?"

"Angie . . ."

"Vanni, *Vanni!*" Ma was crying again; big, loud, blubbery noises and watery marks of makeup down her face. "Vanni, *please!* Please, Vanni, you can't do this. You can't! It's wrong, Vanni. A sin! You can't do this to us; we love you. We always loved you. Think of your son, if you don't care about how *I* feel, Vanni. We always loved you. You can't, you *can't* marry her. This *child*, you can't . . ."

The Old Man didn't try to answer this time. He just stood there, trying to look—or maybe be—somewhere else, somewhere where Ma wasn't weeping and wailing at him.

"You can't, Vanni. Please—I can't, I *can't* stand it. Please! *You'll be punished.* Burn in hell; God will punish you if you do this thing. It's wrong. You'll be punished if you sin this way, Vanni! Oh, Blessed Virgin, don't let him do it! Don't let him do it! Oh, *Madonna mia,* don't let him! Oh, Blessed Virgin, don't let him. Oh, Blessed Virgin . . ."

"Buddy? . . ."

I jumped. Sandy was beside me and a little behind, sort of sideways as though she was about to peep around my shoulder. But not really *peeping* either, just standing as much out of the way as possible; trying to not be part of the scene. It seemed like a hell of a good idea to me, too, if you want to know.

"Come on, girl," I said, and moved both of us out of there; out of the room and as far as we could go out of earshot. Which was to the living room. It wasn't sound-proof, but at least what was happening in the kitchen was no more than a murmur sound, a rising and falling murmur in the ears.

"Sorry," I said to Sandy when we got there. "The Valentines aren't exactly models of decorum and classic poise under any circumstances, kid. But today, today we *really* outdid ourselves."

The kitchen murmur behind us had changed to a chant. It took me a minute to pick up on it; then I knew what it was. A rosary. Jesus *Christ,* a rosary! Ma was saying her beads.

"Buddy," Sandy was saying, "please, don't keep this inside you. A few minutes ago you were honest. Really honest, and it was good. I'm not an enemy. And by now, I'm not just an acquaintance, either. Don't turn it inside."

Her hands were soft against my face and, *God, I am such a child of a man sometimes—I really am—such a child,* I wanted to hold them against me and use them to cry into. I compromised, as much as I was able. I put my arms around her and held on. Thank God. She didn't say anything. She just stood there, and put her own arms in the right places. And held.

The bead chant from the kitchen got louder.

"I got to . . ." I started. And stopped. And clenched my teeth.

Sandy held me tighter.

I took a deep, shuddering breath and tried to relax. But it didn't do the work. Nothing was going to do the work now. Nothing but . . .

"I got to do something," I said. I don't know whether I was talking to her or just to myself. "I have got to do something. Got to fix this. Just this once, I have *got* to do something." And right then was when I decided to go ahead with the crazy plan I'd been kicking around for a while, when I saw clearly how to bring the Old Man . . .

## David Strauss

. . . back again to the place where all began; to the David Strauss of all the pieces, of all the broken glass who

176

is cold and alone. (See how the shimmering bits are alive, each one a living and laughing life mote of joy?) But I don't want to. I don't want to.

It is happy, being dead. Dead. Dead. Dead. . . .

". . . come out of it?"

"Couple hours. More, maybe. That was an eight-way hit."

"You shouldn't have given him so much."

"He needed it."

"Maybe. But a single, maybe a double hit. That would of been plenty, Vince."

"Think so? Look at him. See how-*ow-ow-ow-ow-ow* . . ."

Someone had set up an echo chamber here in the dead world. With a pipeline to the world of the unhappy ones, of the living ones. I could hear parts of their conversation sometimes when the singing of the big choir wasn't too loud. But parts of the words would get stuck in that echo chamber. And resound over and over and over, like a double echo only not getting any softer. I laughed for the joy of being dead and knew there was no pain that could reach me, no more trouble. No more trouble. No more trouble.

My body was gone—good! Good that my gone was body my body was gone was body my . . . *purple*. The sound of purple is new and frightening, but it didn't matter I knew that; it didn't matter because nothing can matter to the dead and I was safe and warm and the world was good around me being dead. My body was dead. My body was dead. My body body body body body body body dead dead dead dead dead dead dead dead dead how long long long long long . . .

I laughed. My body did not laugh because my body was dead, but the I-ness of me laughed and laughed. How long? How long?

I went on laughing because there was no time here in dead in debt in—oh, it was so *funny*—here in death. No time. How long had I had I had I hadI hadihadihadi . . . how long had-I had-to live by the face of the clock that measured what does not exist. Anywhere at all does not exist. Time is a lie, time is a lye-lye-lye? Lye. Yes my sister swallowed the lye-lye-lye and then she died-dye-dyed. She swallowed the lie and she died herself purple, and—ho-ho-

177

ha-ha, so *funny*—dyed because that is what people do who swallow a lye. The lie of time-im-im-immm . . .

". . . so wide. I can't tell if he's smiling or screaming or trying to bite."

"What bite? He's not going to bite."

"How the hell can you tell? Goddamn you, Dyne, giving him so much."

"You were there. Why didn't you stop him?'"

"Because I didn't know."

"Didn't *know!* You lying motherfucker, you sat right there and heard everything I said."

"I was high."

"Who the hell wasn't? I didn't know you were going to let the poor sad cat drop a whole eight-way hit. And of the D E T Sunshine at that. Wow! I mean, like *wow*, man!"

"He's okay. Look at him; happy as a clam."

"Happy. Yeah, now he's happy; wait till he really comes onto his head. It takes an hour or more. . . ."

"I tell you, it's cool, man. No sweat!"

"Maybe. I tell you, though, man—I'm splitting. Like, now! And anyone else who's got any smarts is going with me."

*Purple.* Masks and movements of purple around the world and voices of the live ones, unhappy ones, dead-alive ones. The only life only true life is dead. Is death. *I'm is only death-life I . . .*

Space.

Color. What color; a new one. They say there are no colors in the spectrum of vibrations perceptible to the human eye that mankind has not already seen and labeled, but this is a new no-color, an all-color, and that is proof. Proof I am truly dead for now it is true and now I know how true-rue-rue true it was. The wider world. The fuller spectrum. I perceive it all now, more color than color, more sound than sound-ound-ound, a wider universe, wider than I could ever have known in my living body. Body! Gone, my body and free my *me!*

All the colors of color. All the planets of suns. All the suns of the universe—mine all mine for mine for—joy! The shadows of the walls. The atoms of the air. The mosaics of dust and the musics of life, all—all tiny essences of joy.

My dead hand touches the fabric, and the dead nerves

178

transmit the sense of a million-billion tiny, indivisible, individual shards of joy. All of them alive. All of them thrilled to touch, wanting to be brushed and crushed and made more alive-dead for sheer joy. How can my dead body do these things?

I am not it. It is not me.

I am I. I. I-I-i-i-i—eye. My dead eye is dead is closed is blind is dead is my I.

But I see. My I sees—does not touch; sees the far and farther. Lye. Time-distance. Lye. Lie. Lye-eye-ye-eee. No distance. No time. Only me. I. Eye. The central. The center. The me—davidstrauss gone. David Strauss gone. Body dead. Broken to pieces, got small and smaller. Eaten. Their teeth, eaten. Eaten, eaten, eaten, eaten, eaten-n-n-n-nn.

Eye am free. No weight to drag me back to life-earth; free.

Free!

Up from the pits of hell from the realms of cold through the realms of fire through the circle of earth through the works of man, through the floors to where my dead-filth body lies chained by gravity to its couch, by lust to Dolly, by fear to work. Up past body. Past time.

Free!

And now, the stars—stars—ars-ars-ars-aaaaarrrrrsssssss!

*"Grab him!"*

"Jesus, it was so quick. He almost got to the fucking *window! . . ."*

Ho-ha-ha-ha—funny! So *funny.* Their hands go right through me. Their hands cannot touch the meeeeeee!

"Get—him—*down!"*

"Christ!"

". . . belt. Gimme your belt."

"Okay."

*"Quick,* damn it!"

"Here. Can you get it?"

"Yeah. Now! Over on his face. Get it—*tight."*

The million sounds of blackness. All the colors of dark, shot through, from the sides and from the center with heat. The choir, hear the choir. Heaven has a great choir, didn't I say that in some picture some role sometime, yes, what picture what time, I don't know, it wasn't this choir. Dead. All of us dead and nobody can touch my eye-ness while the music of the choir-oir-oir sings and all the sounds are solid like the steel holding me and more and more around me and around and downward I know. I know. I know—davidstrauss. No more davidstrausstrausstrausstraussss. But not pieces. Not a million davidstrausses, all screaming and moving and No! Just the David-Me! *The Me.*

Smaller and smaller.

Less and less.

Away.

*Nothing.* Now, nothing. No height, width, thickness. Not even position. Not even time. Just David Strauss. The center of the center of the center of my center.

Not even a dot.

Just the Me. Floating, endless as the endlessness around my endlessness. I was wrong. I am not dead. Not. There is no life there is no death there is nothing. Lies. Lyes; I swallowed the swallowed the swallowed the lyes like my sister swallowed the lies but now I *know.*

Now.

Eye.

Know . . .

# The 4th House

*Matters of the home and all domestic affairs, the father, property, the grave . . .*

*Forecast: All hell will break loose in the next few days. Burn the Last Card will find its bridges burned, Sandy Hallowell will wish she'd never met Buddy Valentine or taken up astrology, and Johnny Valentine and Dolly Diamond will do hassle with one another.*

*As we enter the Fourth House, Buddy Valentine will embark upon an adventure that will eventually gain the whole world's attention. But at what a price. . . .*

## Irving Dahlberg

"No," I told him, "there's nothing else to do. It's a blow and a disaster and a ruin, that's all."

There was a little wait on the line, and I could hear the wheels in Jackie's head turning over—the same way mine had been turning for two days. All right. Good! Let him carry part of the load for once.

"Well, all right, Papa," he said finally. "If you're sure, we'll file for the production insurance."

"There's nothing else," I said.

"You've seen him, talked to him? . . ."

"What *talk?*" Sometimes, trying to get an idea through to Jackie can be like pushing a banana into a piggy bank. "Who can talk to a madman, a *meshuggener?* On the set— you should have seen him yourself, only!"

"But what did he do?"

"My God, what did he *do!* Smiling, like he had gone to a doctor and had a stitch in each side of his mouth; not talking, not listening, just *smiling.*"

"Well, that doesn't sound *too* . . ."

"So they thought he was drunk. What else was to think? He had a shot scheduled for that day, but the director, Krugman, used his head—switched to something else they could make with almost the same setup; something he wasn't in. Then it really began."

"I *heard* he . . ."

"Whatever you heard, multiply by ten." Or a hundred; I couldn't get part of it out of my own mind, let alone into Jackie's. In a way, it was something you had to see to believe. "For the rehearsals, the run-throughs, he stays in his dressing room. Not a peep out of him. But when Krugman calls for a take—wham!"

"The way I heard it from Krugman, he . . ."

"Came out of the dressing room with a policeman's whistle in his mouth. Still smiling. They start rolling, it's going okay, and maybe five seconds from the end of the take, Strauss blows the whistle. The *whistle,* my God! Just once. Just enough to ruin the whole thing."

This time Jackie didn't interrupt. I got my breath and went on.

"So, okay, they still think he's drunk. They back up and everybody takes a minute and Krugman himself goes over and talks to Strauss. You know: fun's fun but this is costing us money so let's not make it tougher than it is, okay? Strauss just smiles."

"And the next time through?"

"He does it again, what else?" I closed my eyes. That was when Krugman called me; he knew something was wrong, so he called. Irving Dahlberg gets called because a director is having some problems. But I went. "The next time, they had taken the whistle away from him. He's still smiling but just standing there. But before they can even start rolling, into the shot he walks and picks up a flower—a flower that's been *established,* goddamn it, one lousy flower in a vase. He puts the flower under his nose and walks away."

"I can't believe it."

"Then one of the stagehands who's been standing there

talking to Gaby, he goes after Strauss; they're friends. He thinks it's all a joke; he tries to get the flower away from him."

"And that's when David hit him?"

"That's when. In the belly, in the chest, in the shoulder, it could have been—no problem. The punk can't hit worth a damn. But, no! In the *eye,* he has to hit the guy, and then in the *mouth.* The guy goes down. Strauss is still smiling. Still holding the flower under his nose and smiling."

"Well, Papa . . ."

"So, naturally, that day's shooting is done unless Krugman maybe wants to set up for a one-shot with Gaby. Which he's already got. They sent the other guy to the hospital and get a studio guard to take Strauss home."

"I see. But they didn't get there, isn't that right? Only as far as . . ."

"Columbus Circle. They're in a little bit of traffic—not too bad, it's still early afternoon—and suddenly, the guard says, Strauss is out of the cab and running toward Central Park. Still—goddamn him *still smiling!"*

"And that's when they arrested him for exposure?"

"That's when they arrested him for, my God! For opening up his fly, hauling out his *schvants,* and walking *backward* past the benches on that side of the park."

"Backward?"

"Backward!" It was too hot in the room. I was sweating like a horse. "All this time, mind you, Jackie—all this time, he hasn't spoken a word. Just smiling, but no talk. And what is the first word he speaks? What? To the cop who finally corrals him, and asks what the hell he thinks he's doing, he speaks. One word: *'Trolling!'* One word, one. *Trolling!"*

There was a strange sound on the other end of the wire. It took a minute to identify it. Then I knew: Jackie was laughing.

*"You imbecile!* You think that is so goddamn funny, get yourself a little giggle out of this: Now *Burn the First Card*'s closed down and off schedule and you're sitting on your skinny ass out there on the Coast not making a move to get *Boarders* or *Sadie* ready to go—and the directors will be meeting in two weeks, *two weeks!* I've got to tell them *something.* If those two big productions aren't sched-

uled by then I'll tell them this: that the studio has closed down all production activities. *All,* you hear that, *momser?* Everything! Including, by God, *your* office!"

This time the silence on the wire was a very long one. Long enough for Irving Dahlberg to get hold of himself; long enough to wipe his sweating face and sit down again in the chair behind the desk and cut the end off a cigar.

"All right, Papa," Jackie's voice was very quiet and soft when he spoke at last. "All right, we'll do what we can. I know you have problems. I'm sorry. I'm particularly sorry about David."

"Your *friend!*" I bit the word off hard, but I was in control again; the heat that had been in and around my head was gone. "Your friend David, that great talent, is through in pictures. I swear that to you. Even if they don't put him in a bughouse, and that's a good bet; I haven't even told you some of the things. How he seems to slide in and out of craziness. Sometimes laughing and saying words that aren't words, sometimes talking all right so you'd think he was normal. I haven't told you how he—ah, God! Who cares? He's *out!* The moment we have to file for production insurance because of him, right then, he's dead!"

"I know, Papa."

"Do you? Well, let me make it even plainer. So even *you* can understand. He'd be out probably anyway, because nobody could take a chance on casting him in a picture. They couldn't get production insurance with him in anything, and without production insurance, who would put up financing? But more than that. *Yes!* Men *have* survived that. They *have* managed to get back into pictures after something like this. But Strauss isn't going to."

"Papa . . ."

"No. Papa! Strauss is out and he's staying out because Irving Dahlberg is putting out the word—it's personal with me. Personal! Anyone who hires him, anyone, is Irving Dahlberg's personal enemy. From that moment on. You understand?"

Jackie sighed. "Yes," he said. "Yes, Papa."

"All right. Now get off your butt and get moving on that arrangement with the navy. Get working on the Dolly Diamond contract. And don't call me back, goddamn it, until you've got some progress to report!"

I snapped the switch to break the connection. Why in hell couldn't we have stuck to old-fashioned telephones, with earpieces or cradles and something heavy to make some noise when you cut off a call? Why all the gadgets? In the old days, a man could at least enjoy slamming down the receiver.

I could feel the heat, the pressure, rising in me again.

Closing in. They were closing in on the giant. All the midgets. A $6 million picture scrubbed off the schedule. Canceled, in the middle of shooting, because of an actor. *Actor*. Strauss, the mumbler; actor! Well he was through mumbling now, never doubt that.

Gaby. Screaming at me. Swinging with claws at me. Hysterical when I told her what we were going to have to do, as though it was Irving Dahlberg's fault.

Why can't anyone understand? Why can't anyone, just once, help me instead of making me drag them *every step of the way?*

That wife of Strauss's—ex-wife—Diamond. At least they're not still married. At least I don't have two headaches *married* to each other, at least Irving Dahlberg is spared that. A doper, that Dolly Diamond. I heard that. Uses marijuana. Who knows what all else? I wonder, did she learn it from that half-fag, dope-addict husband of hers? Or did he learn from her? Or were they both that way from the beginning? . . .

"*A bum trip*," the doctor called it. *Doctor!* Talks like some kind of walk-on from a Hell's Angels cheapie. "A bum trip—my guess would be acid, LSD. Or perhaps one other thing. They call it . . ."

What was it he said they called it? Orange—something. *Who cares?* Irving Dahlberg doesn't care. Alcohol on the set I can accept. Not as a steady thing, but it happens. You hear enough stories about someone, all right, you don't hire that someone for anything important. Maybe not for anything at all. But *dope!*

Well, he'll never work again, anyway. That's something. Never again, not in Hollywood, not in America. Not even in Europe; I'll make sure the word is put out there, too. Irving Dahlberg doesn't . . .

Got to stop thinking like that. Around and around in a circle. Crazy as that Strauss.

Call Gaby. See if she's a little quieter now. I snapped the switch and stuck the little plastic number-dialing card into the phone. All the modern . . .

No answer. All right. So maybe she's in there, lying in there sulking, not answering the telephone. My punishment, maybe. Punishment. That little bitch *punishing* the giant for having to be a giant. What else has it ever been? Giants are punished for being giants; midgets are petted for being midgets. Don't ask for justice. Don't remind them that all of them got where they are, that the Industry got where it is, because of giants like Irving Dahlberg.

*Don't!* Who needs any of them?

Dolly Diamond. That bitch, why can't somebody—*somebody*—do the job he's supposed to do? Get her to sign the contract. Get at least one, just *one,* worry off Irving Dahlberg's mind.

Who? Who can I put on it? That *klutz,* my son; a month he's been on it and what has he got? What?

Who, then? *You know who.*

Who else was it, ever? Who else doing the real work; who else pulling everyone's chestnuts out of the fire? *Who?*

Have the secretary—*no.* No!

Irving Dahlberg. Right from the first, a personal touch. A personal call. Personally placed by the giant, by Irving Dahlberg. To secretaries they say no, to Irving Dahlberg they say yes.

I fumbled through the dial-card file, but of course there was none for Diamond. I finally had to ring the secretary and have her get the number for me. From the private files.

Alone in my office I waited until the girl rang back with the number. I wrote it down. My face was hot and damp again, and I wiped it with the handkerchief and then threw the handkerchief away from me. Irving Dahlberg, sweating because he has to call up a baby, a pothead child who could be his granddaughter! It was humiliating, all right, but there was no other way.

I looked at my palms. Wet. Hot, wet face; cold, wet hands.

I looked at the telephone like it was an enemy; a living thing that could crush Irving Dahlberg. Make him a midget like other men. It seemed to get bigger, just sitting there on my desk. Bigger and more complicated, with dials like eyes. *No!*

I began to dial, carefully, my control and my will like steel now. Number-by-number. Checking the penciled note I had made. Waited . . .

The busy signal sounded loud in the empty, quiet office. I listened for ten seconds more before I could understand what I was hearing. Irving Dahlberg made a call. Himself. And the line . . .

## Dolly Diamond

". . . was busy. Look, let me call him tonight," I said. Johnny just sat there, looking at me. I couldn't tell what he was thinking. Somehow, he looked more—I don't know —*Italian* than I had ever noticed before.

"Keep trying," he said. "Every five minutes."

"All right."

At least he wasn't picking on me, screaming at me, the way he had when he first arrived.

He didn't move or change expression. I tried not to myself, but I couldn't help it. There were like tiny little worms moving around under my skin. I peeked over my shoulder at one of the mirrors and looked at us in it. Me, naked except for the hair. The long, beautiful blue-white hair that spread like wings.

Johnny could see it, too. On both sides. The way he was sitting, he could see the real me and see the reflection. But there was nothing in his face. I had never seen him like that before. Always, before . . .

"Try him again."

"But . . . !"

"Try him."

So I dialed David's number again.

All morning it had been like this. Ever since Johnny got there. When I saw him I was only half awake. I smiled and made a little noise and turned from my side to my back to push the covers away. I opened myself to him.

And he grabbed me by the hair!

"Where did David Strauss get the dose of acid?" That's what he said, holding me by my hair so I had to sit up and keep my face just an inch or two from his. He shook me when I didn't answer right away. *"Where-did-David-get-that-acid?"* Like that, he said it. Word by word. One word at a time.

What could I do? I told him. At least he should have seen I didn't try to lie or excuse myself or anything. At least he should have noticed that. I was honest. He had no right to be so mean to me. No right! But did he pay any attention? Oh, no.

Just one question after another, like a cop or something. One lousy question after another until I was crying, and then shaking me until I stopped, and then asking more questions.

I hadn't *done* anything.

David *was* here. At my apartment. On Christmas—of course he was, why not? Wasn't Johnny with his ex-wife? Where did he get off being so mad? So what if David was here?

It must of been the other that made him mad that way. The marijuana. I told him about that. I told the truth. Just that we were bored and there were a lot of people and someone had the stuff and we smoked a little bit of it. Nothing but that.

"Daddy . . . please don't be mad at me."

"Where did he get it?"

"I don't know."

He wound my hair a full turn around his hand, never letting go, and yanked my face back and forth until everything was blurred. I began to cry and I clawed at him but for all the difference it made I might just as well have tickled him with a feather.

"L-S-D," he said. "The acid. Where did he get it? Who gave it to him?"

"It was Vince," I said, finally. "Vince Dyne. You know, the actor with the beard. He did it. I didn't even . . ."

"Dyne was here?"

"Yes. But . . ."

"Who else? Who else was here?"

So I told him. All the names I could remember, anyway. The end part of the party was all blurry and I couldn't be sure of some of the people, but I told him all I could remember. And about how Vince had given David the stuff, the Orange Sunshine, to try to help him.

*"Help* him!"

"Yes. David was down, really down, and he wouldn't even try to pick up on the grass. So Vince thought he needed *something*."

He let go of my hair and dropped me back on the bed and sat down. For a long time, he just looked at me, in that real *Italian* sort of way, as though he'd never seen me before.

"We talked about the pot parties," he said after a while. "We agreed—no more of those."

"Daddy, I'm sorry. I'm real sorry. I won't do it again. Honest!"

"I thought I could trust you."

"*Daddy . . . !*"

That was when he handed me the phone and told me to call David. Get him over, so we could talk. All of us.

But David's line stayed busy.

I didn't understand why he wanted to talk to David anyway. He knew there wasn't anything between David and me anymore; not since 'way before we had started with each other. And neither of us owed David anything.

At first he wouldn't talk about it. Wouldn't explain. But in a while, when David's phone stayed so busy, he told me what it was about.

"The liars are always looking for something," he said. "Always. You know the kind of stuff they've been printing about you and me."

"I don't read it," I said, lying myself. "You told me not to read the columns or the fan magazines, so I don't."

"Yeah," he said. "Sure. But a lot of other people do. Not that anyone really believes half the crap in them, but you get enough people saying something and finally what's really true doesn't matter. It could be bad for you."

"I don't care."

"Well *I do!*" He steamed a little while, mad again, for some reason. And then went on, when the steam eased off. "I got some business deals right now," he said, "stuff I haven't told you about, things that could be kind of messed up by something like this."

I gave him the little-girl smile and the kiss-me look and said, "You can handle *anything*, though, Daddy."

It didn't work.

"Uh-huh," he said. "And that's how it's supposed to be, right? Every time I can't keep an eye right on you, I can figure to have to spend a while later squaring up something? Balls, baby, I mean, *balls!*"

He was really mad. Really. I hadn't seen him like this before. Gradually it was getting through to me that an awful lot of things might be in danger.

I began thinking like crazy. . . .

"Try the number again."

I picked the phone up and dialed without a word. But my mind wasn't on the phone. And while I was dialing, I got an idea that seemed like a good one. Maybe. At least, it seemed like it might get his mind off David and the little party I'd had.

"What did your family say when you told them about us, you and me, Christmas?" I asked him when the busy signal came again.

*A-hah!* That grabbed him; gave him something else to think about. He stopped looking so tough and big and started looking more like Johnny Valentine.

"You did tell them, didn't you?" I prodded him, knowing now that he hadn't.

"Well, in a way," he said.

"Did you or didn't you?"

"There was—some trouble."

"Did you or didn't you *tell* them?"

He took a big, deep breath and shrugged his shoulders. "Sam, you know, my lawyer—Sam and me got into it. In the kitchen, about you and me. There was a . . ."

"You *didn't* tell them, Daddy."

"They already knew. You know, that I was seeing you and all that. It would of been no real news to them, kid. Anyway there was this frammis with Sam . . ."

"You *promised!*"

"I . . ."

"You promised you'd tell your family we were getting married. You promised!"

"You promised no more grass, too!"

I turned on all the tear faucets, like I've been able to do ever since I was a little girl, and threw myself down across the bed. "You promised!" I sobbed. "You *promised!*"

And it worked, I guess partly 'cause I really was upset and wanting him to reassure me and hold me and love me. After a little while he was there, lying on the bed beside me and stroking my back and—well, anyhow, his mind was off of David and all that crap. I kept the tears up. But all the while my mind was going, figuring. Turning it over.

There had to be some way. Some way to get David off my back for good and get Johnny in front of a judge or a preacher or, hell, a rabbi for that matter. Somebody who could do the job.

I thought of two or three things and knew right away they wouldn't work. And I kept on thinking, trying to come up with a way, and looking up in that mirror over the bed while we were balling—as I had known we would be as soon as I could get him to start touching me—and I wrapped my legs as tight as I could around him. Tight! And raked my nails into his back so they left . . .

## David Strauss

. . . long, trailing streamers of blood. Everything that moves leaves a long trail when it hits me again. I know I'm crazy, those times. I know nobody sees the streamers but me. So I don't tell people about them.

But they're there.

I have to move, sometimes, to get out of the way because I don't want them to touch me.

When they do, the blood sticks. It burns and drips. . . .

"David? Are you still there, David?"

"I'm still here."

"You just stopped talking. I thought maybe something had happened."

"I'm still here."

"Well, what about it then? Will you let me try to help, David? It's very important, you know that."

"Yes. Important."

*"David!"*

She shouted my name, and it brought me back from the drift I had begun. I closed my eyes to shut out the blood trails but it was worse with them shut. That sent me back to hell, where I had been after the party where I . . .

"David, please! Try to hold yourself together and listen."

"All right. Okay, Gaby, I'm listening."

"David you *know* how much *Burn the First Card* means to me. It's my first picture—and if they suspend it, stop it the way they're saying they will, it could be the end of everything for my career."

191

"They've already scrapped it . . ."

"Not yet." There was something in her voice. A deep red. It reminded me of the blood trails, only the red in her voice was mixed with black and that was fear. It was wonderful, in a way, to be able to see the colors of voices.

". . . until the first of the year. They can't get all the release notices out, or file for the production insurance before then. Until that happens, there is still a chance."

"No. Dahlberg's made up his mind. They told me."

"Irving can change his mind, too." She said it as though she knew what she was talking about, and I guess she did. If Gaby duMain could get Dahlberg to put her in a major-budget picture without even a screen test—and she had—she could get the old boy to let the picture go on for a week or two. Sure, I believed that. The hell of it was, I couldn't seem to care one way or the other.

"I'll handle Irving," she said. "But I can't do a thing unless *you're* in shape to go on with it. And you won't be if you just . . ."

I lost the sound of her voice, looking at the window. From the couch where I was lying, I could only see part of it and that part should have showed me a few thousand acres of nothing but sky. It had ever since I moved in here, at the Towers.

But while I was watching, the sky filled and the shape of the window changed from square to no-shape; a dark-sided hole in the world looking into—*what?* There were *things* in that hole. Shapes and forms from somewhere else, riding and moving and coming closer. I couldn't look at them. But I couldn't close my eyes, either. A tiny, lost part of myself was screaming, trying to make me listen, saying that this was not real; that it was just the drug, the DET they had called it, asserting itself again and making me see things that were not real. They had warned me it would do that, from time to time, for a while—*flashes,* the people from the party called them; *recurrent delusions* induced by the poison, according to the doctors—but they couldn't tell me when it would stop.

And they couldn't *prove* to me it wasn't real.

How can anyone prove something like that?

You see a thing. Touch it, taste it, hear it, feel it—it's

real, you say. And it is. For you. Because you have that evidence of its reality. All right, but I saw, tasted, heard, felt all these things. I really did. So how to prove they are not . . .

". . . important to you as it is to me," Gaby's voice cut in again. "If you don't finish *Burn the First Card* you could be washed up in pictures forever. So you've got to let me help you."

"Gaby, that's nice of you . . ."

"*Nice!* Oh, you stupid *shit,* do you think I care about being *nice* at this point? Nice! I'm trying to save myself, David. *Save myself.* Do you understand that? I'm never going to get a chance like this again. Never! And I deserve it—God, do I deserve it!"

"Gaby . . ."

"You don't know—God, I couldn't tell you—what I've had to *do* to get a chance like this. And I'm not going to let you blow it for me. I won't!" There were new sounds, like crying. "You stay there. Where you are. I'm coming over now. Stay *there.* We'll get you straightened out. Now, do you hear me, David? Stay *there.*"

"I hear you."

"All right."

There was a click and she had hung up but I sat there with the receiver still in my hand. She couldn't help me. I knew she couldn't help me.

Help me what? Help me how? Sitting there and looking at the real world, full of the terrible things and the changing shapes I had learned, I wasn't even sure I wanted help. Better to see the real. Better to see the true. It put the other things into perspective; other things like davidstrauss, that poor fractured little man so self-important and so tiny, so—

The window turned black.

In the center, far away at first but then larger and larger, there came a single expanding point of light. It was a sound I had not heard before; all the sirens and bells and alarms of the world exploding and moving toward me at a speed that would blot me utterly from the consciousness of the earth. I sat and waited for it to strike me.

And then it was gone. Like the popping of a balloon it was all gone and I was just David Strauss again, sitting there in the living room of my own apartment, still holding a telephone receiver in my hand. I set it down, and it rang immediately.

Who? Gaby? No. She wouldn't be calling right back. She would be over, she said; she would be downstairs in the street, getting a cab and giving the driver my address right now. Not Gaby. Who? I didn't care. I got up from the couch and looked at myself.

There seemed to be less of me. And it didn't seem to matter. The phone went right on ringing and ringing and . . .

## Sandy Hallowell

. . . ringing. But Buddy didn't answer. No one answered. Which was peculiar, because he'd said last night that he'd call me about this time of day in New York. Well, I couldn't complain. Since I'd flown back to New York, we'd racked up quite a few hours on the telephone. I still had to smile when I thought of all that had happened in such a short time.

Not that it would have surprised me if I'd known in the beginning what was plain as day from the chart I'd worked out for Buddy. His signs crossed mine so *perfectly*—well, to a point, that is. Forget about *that*, Hallowell; you don't have to think about *that* yet. *So don't!*

Anyway, it had been wonderful. Not perfect. Who wants perfect? Not The Hallowell. Give me the rough stuff along with smooth; I go the reality route, friend. Lord knows that late-late show the Valentine clan put on, right in their own cozy little Bel Air cabin, had to count with the rough. Especially for Buddy; me, I was just a sort of nonpaying audience.

But it started something, oh yes! Funny the way things like that can work out. How long had we talked that night, after Buddy got us out of the house and away in his mama's car? Hours. Until dawn and after. About the whole *enchilada*. Everything. His family. The world. My family. What we were and what we wanted, what could frighten us and what made us happy.

Funny how little time it takes to know someone, really know them, when both of you want to take it absolutely straight instead of playing the kind of games everyone in the world tries to play. Games. Well, I've played them, haven't I? The Hallowell has had her own little share of personality gamesmanship; she is in no position to sit in heaven and hand down the judgments.

And that's even kind of lucky, in a way. Because if I hadn't been through all that, if I hadn't found out what the end of those games always seems to be—if I hadn't, how would I have had sense enough not to play some game like that with Buddy?

(Buddy. I still don't like that name; it's not his real one. His father hung it on him when he was too little to fight back. He doesn't even like it himself. But he won't try to change it. And we know why, don't we, Hallowell. Yes. We know why.)

I didn't, anyway. And thank God—or Buddy, or Mohammed or the Great Egg or whoever—for that, because by the time The Hallowell was ready for bed, it wasn't a lonely and solitary bed she was ready for. Buddy was so weird about that. Buddy Valentine; who would have imagined a guy like him could actually be shy with a woman? Or, anyhow, I guess he would have been if it hadn't been for that all-night session over the coffee cups. And even *then* . . .

A smile was aching the corners of my mouth, thinking about it. Never like that before. Never that way.

Sex? *Yessiree,* friend! The Hallowell digs sex. You betcha. But just sex—good sex, with someone you like and who likes you, which is really the only way to fly—just sex, while it's a hard routine to rap, is absolutely nothing like the kind that is more than sex and more than just liking.

Never before. Tender and together and warm and—what a strange thing—full of laughter and crazy games and no-time.

It was weird, the kind of weird I love that guy for. Oops!

Love. Damn that word, I knew it would come popping out. A label. My God, how I hate labels. Bad enough to label people. That's silly, because it messes up your thinking; makes you assume a person will always be the label way about everything, and they never are. But to label and stencil and define and set exact limits on an *emotion*—oh, Lordy!

All right. Okay. I know what I feel about Buddy

Valentine; I even think I know what he feels about me. Fine. But *love?* Why does the word have to be printed out and stuck on?

How long have we even known each other? A week. Not even that. So why does a big, fat label have to get stuck on there? You *lie,* Hallowell; you lie because it's forever and you couldn't know him better—he couldn't know you better —if it had been since the day you were born.

But my face was still hurting from the smile. And the phone was still ringing, with no takers at the other end. Which worried me, in spite of myself.

I hung it up and glanced at my watch (try again in five minutes) and then at the chart I had drawn for him. The natal chart, for Giovanni Valentine, Jr. Looking at it, I felt proud of myself. A professional, I ain't. A mathematics whiz, I ain't. The Hallowell is, in fact, not even an over-bright amateur so far as astrology goes; I have to go back and go back and check every single little point, every tiny little arithmetic problem, over and over. And even then I'm hardly ever sure I've got it right.

But this chart *couldn't* be wrong. Just couldn't. Because I hadn't cheated, hadn't pushed or shoved or hauled around at the math or the interpretations or the facts as I knew them—and it still fitted Buddy's life, so far at least, to a gnat's eyelash. Yessir, The Hallowell was proud of this chart, and more than a little anxious to show it to its subject.

That would be soon. I had a flight out to L.A. tonight. Not that he would believe the chart. Not Buddy; it was too new to him—the whole thing; me, astrology, everything —for him to buy the idea right off the bat. And, for that matter, not that I especially wanted him to.

Oh, sure, it would be nice. For him, I mean; nice if he could accept at least the possibility that there was something in it. A thing like this could be a help to him. He needed help. More, even, than I thought I might be able to give him; more than he would ever accept from me anyway. But at least he didn't have one of those closed-and-locked minds. And maybe this could be a start.

I walked to the phone again and barely restrained myself. I glanced at my watch. *One* minute had passed, not five. *Stick to the rules, Hallowell!*

I did another turn around my room and looked out the

window a minute and then, for no real reason I could put my finger on, it hit me.

His chart was by the phone where I'd left it. Of course, that didn't give me exactly what I needed to check out the sudden hunch. But it was there, all right. It was there. I checked my watch again, mentally ordered myself to come up for air and try the number in four more minutes, and sat down to work the problem out for *today*.

It was no snap. It gave me . . .

## Buddy Valentine

. . . plenty of trouble, sure. He didn't have to warn me about that. If you want to know, I had warned myself about it, in all-night insomnia sessions, ever since Christmas Day, when I decided to go ahead with the idea. On the surface, it was so wild. But the more I thought about it, the more it seemed like the only way I had left to go, even in spite of the appearance of a boss chick like Sandy on the scene.

"I know, Zeke," I said. "Like . . . I know the odds and I know what a bummer it could turn out to be. Both ways. Everything that could go wrong and all. I know . . ."

He didn't say anything, but standing there in the phone booth I could hear him still not liking it. Still trying to figure something else. That Zeke! Funny how you can be around some people for years—like, all your life, maybe— and never really *know* them, you dig? Never. And then some other dude, like Zeke, you know him . . . how long? Three months? Four? . . . Like that, anyway. Only, right from the first, it's as if you were raised together or something.

Take the way he turned me off flying helicopters. Oh, yeah! For sure. And that was money out of his pocket. Money he needed bad. There I was at Clover Field, all ready to pay him fifteen bones an hour to teach me to fly copters—and before we even get in the ship, what does he say? "Mr. Valentine, the best advice I can give you—as instructor—the best advice is to forget the whole thing!" How *about* that?

Naturally I wanted to know why. And he laid it on me: you don't interchange flying choppers and fixed-wing aircraft; one day one thing and one day the other. Not unless you're crazy or something. The controls are too different. You have to forget every reflex you programmed into yourself flying fixed-wing, have to put all of that out of your mind, because if you do anything like that with the controls of the chopper in your hands, you'll kill yourself.

Lots of people have both ratings, of course. Zeke, for one. But when the army switched him from fixed-wing to helicopter pilot, he made up his mind to *stay* switched. He said he just put a rubber band around all his fixed-wing logbooks and shipped them home and tried to forget he'd ever flown that kind of equipment.

"You're already rated, plenty of time and equipment proficiency, in fixed-wing," he said. "So . . . I'll take you on as a student, sure. But *only* on a solemn promise from you that you won't try to fly fixed-wing anymore after this. . . ."

And I thought that over and—what the hell, he was right—decided to give it a pass. Bought both of us some drinks instead. Talked. And all of a sudden, we'd known each other forever.

Him: trying to make enough dough as a copter pilot-instructor-mechanic to put together a nest-egg down payment on a ship of his own. *The Ezekiel Aerial Services Co.* Crop dusting for a starter; aerial survey, maybe, air taxi, whatever; build it up until he had one of the aerial crane biggies he'd heard Vertol had on the drawing board. Big money in that someday. Only . . . he'd been out of the army for three years already, and what with one thing and another he still wasn't even close to that nest egg. . . .

And Buddy-boy: sick of himself and bugged with his fam-damnily and uptight around his Old Man and looking for something only he's got no real clear idea what the hell it is. Yeah. Oh, for sure! Zeke and me, we knew each other *good* before the day was over.

So who the hell else would Buddy-boy lay the Idea on? Who else would help? Who else *could* help with a gig like this one? . . .

Only of course Zeke'd hated it from the start—really hated it. Come up with every one of the objections I'd already thought of and quite a few I hadn't. And now—even now when we'd figured angles to cover *all* those bases—still hating it. Still wanting me to forget it . . .

"Okay," he said finally. "Okay. All right. So you know. Fine. But . . . Bud, look: why don't you think it over a little more. Give it, say, a couple more days, anyway. Then if you—"

"Zeke," I cut him off there, "it's now. Right now. Tonight. Everything's ready; the ship's gassed and serviced, waiting for me. They know I'm going to be gone by morning."

"Sure. But that doesn't—"

"And *you're* ready, too." I made like I hadn't heard him. "It's all there. You said it was. . . ."

"Yeah. It's there . . ."

"Then—let's get it on, man."

There was another long silence. Weird, you know? The way he was holding back, I mean. Like, he stood to *make* on the deal, right? No fortune, maybe, but a little. The couple of thou he needed for that down-payment nest egg. And when it was done . . . who the hell knows? Maybe he would be such a hero or the *padrino* and the Old Man might be grateful enough—that the few bucks from me wouldn't even matter. I mean, there was no risk for him . . . and still he was worrying. How about a guy like that?

"What happens if I say no, Bud?"

That was a stopper.

For a fact, I hadn't even thought of that. Funny. But almost before the words registered, I knew the answer.

"I go anyway," I said. "The way it stands now, I *could* bring it off myself. The first part, anyway. And—well—I guess the second part would just have to take care of itself."

"Or not take care of itself."

"Yeah. Or that."

Another silence.

"I could blow the whistle on you. Right now."

"You could do that," I said, nodding into the mouthpiece. "And I could say you were out of your skull. You wouldn't have anything on your side. . . ."

". . . or I could wait until it's done," he went on. "And blow the whistle then."

I had to think a little about that. But not very long. "You wouldn't, Zeke," I told him. "You wouldn't do that."

"No." There was something different in his voice there. Something I couldn't quite pick up on. "No—I guess I wouldn't, at that. . . ."

"So?"

Another wait. But a shorter one this time. Much shorter. He'd made up his mind, now, and we both knew it.

"So . . . all right," he said. "Okay, then. You got the timing all set, right?"

"Right. And Zeke—no more calls after this. Not even from pay booths, like this time. The word is *go*. That's all."

"Okay. We go."

"For sure. Well . . . later, man."

"Yeah. *Later*. . . ."

And we both hung up and I let out a breath I didn't know I'd been holding. Okay. *Go*. Right! Suddenly it was plenty hot there in that booth. I was sweating.

I came out kind of slow. Checking—though I knew damn well it couldn't make a bit of difference—to make sure nobody had seen me in there.

And suddenly—*Jesus!* Suddenly, it was all unreal. . . . It couldn't really be happening. We couldn't be going through with it. I looked at the world. The sky and the sidewalk and the stores and the people and the cars and the smells and the air and the sound of my own footsteps. . . .

*Sandy*. Right then, right there at that moment, I wanted Sandy there. Not just to talk to or go to bed with or anything specific. Just . . . *there*. I wanted to be with her.

Oh, yeah. *Sure!* Go do that, Buddy-boy. Go do that. Spend a couple of hours lying in your teeth to the one person in the world you don't want to lie to. Go do that. Act like nothing is wrong when every single damn thing in the world is wrong and I am about to do something nutty. Something she wouldn't even *believe* if I laid it on her.

Sure, do that. And she'd have it out of me—the whole thing—in about five minutes. For sure! Some chick, that chick. No questions from her. Never. No prodding. No pressure. Only . . . every time, I wind up telling her what's on my mind, whether it's something I want to tell anyone or not.

*No*, Buddy-boy. No way! No Sandy for you today. . . .

Walking along the street—no particular goal, just killing time—I thought about the Old Man. I wondered where he was, what he was doing. How he would get the news. And would it all work the way I had it figured?

Hell, maybe he wouldn't even care.

It was a rotten thing to think. Especially right then. But it was one possibility, and so I had to think about it. Maybe he wouldn't. But how much difference could that make? Just for the sake of appearances—for the Image—he would have to show *some* reaction. Make a real Big Deal of it, right? And whatever he did, it would have to have the effect of shoving that Dolly Diamond action into the background.

Care or not, it would have to work that way. . . .

He'd have to split from wherever he was, with Dolly, and barrel-ass out to the coast and he would have to be *there*. With Ma. And that would mean no Dolly Diamond for him. For a while, anyway. And they would be together, Ma and him, worried about the same thing. Okay . . . so, maybe that won't put Humpty Dumpty together again—not really in the cards from anything I could see—but at least maybe they would, maybe they could . . . oh, hell. Could *what*?

How the hell would I know?

Face it, Buddy-boy: you can tell yourself it's for Ma and you can tell yourself it's for the Old Man and you can even tell yourself it's for Zeke (if you're really going to do a *professional* job of lying), or you can tell yourself any other kind of crapperoo you want. Any crummy, phony excuse. But face it—this one's really just for *you*. For you, baby. You and *nobody else*. . . .

*Sandy*. Oh, God, but I wished there was some way I could put her hip on the play. Let her know what was really happening so she wouldn't worry. Christ, what a rotten bastard of a thing to do to a chick that you love. . . .

That *word* . . .

We'd been real careful about that. Avoiding that Word. That big, bad, scary, can't-untie-it Word. Don't say it. Just be it. Just live and be happy and take what's there and what's real without a lot of crappy Words mussing up the scene and without a lot of stuff that really doesn't matter or figure into the play unless you say it does. And we had it good. Hell, we had it *great*. Great? That's the thing with words. They never say anything. Great? Suddenly I could feel the muscles of my face doing it again. Smiling. Without having me—outside, self-dialoguing, on-the-surface me—doing anything about it. That had been happening to me for a while, now. *Nutty*. Just thinking of

201

it had been, that first time—just *thinking*—I could feel it all again. I mean, it was *there,* man. *Right there!*

Hell *yes,* I'd made it with broads before. *Sure.* Balling, that's good. Just plain-old-hump—it's friendly and it's natural and it relieves a hell of a lot of pressure and, well, say this: it is better than going steady with your fist, right? Right.

But this thing with Sandy was as different from just balling around as . . . well . . . as flying a model airplane is from flying a jet airliner. It's not just that the jet is bigger. The thing that's different: the jet is *real!* Real. . . .

The difference between sensation in just *one* part of *your* body and sensation in *all* the parts.

Oh, *Christ*—the damn words again. The damn words. It sounds so impossible, so phony, so unreal, when you put the words to it. Like something out of some low-budget musical made in 1937 ("And *noooooow* the *twoooooo* of *ussss* are *onnnnnnnnne* . . .") or something. It sounds like a ripoff! Only, wow, you know stuff like this must of been happening even 'way back then to people, or how could some corny-crap songwriter have put it into a lyric, right? Right. Because it was true.

And it was no set piece. No number. No big buildup. Hell, it was the most natural thing in the world . . . Without even thinking, we were touching each other. Just with the tips of the fingers, like learning each other. Like making really sure the other one was there, and then it was more than touching and there was the minute when I could see the way the end of her back curved toward the two dimple-hollows and a fine, light down was really tiny, individual living entities—each reflecting light and making prism-rainbow colors, a whole beautiful and wonderful tiny world I'd never even suspected—and the scent of her was there. The scent of Sandy. Not perfume. Not sweat. Not musk. Sandy, herself. Her real self.

Suddenly she was *real* to me. Real in a way nobody else in the world, not even me, had ever been real. All the parts of Sandy, all the wholeness of Sandy, every single detail.

We had been pressed tight together, still learning each other, still teaching. Holding tighter and . . . suddenly the holding wasn't needed anymore. How do I explain it? How do I make someone understand: I could feel—*because*

202

*it was my own*—the response of her fingertips, of her toes, of her mouth and her breasts and her hips and even her eyes. I knew I could move her arm as easily as my own . . . and that she could move mine; that she knew all that I felt, too.

Just sex? Just very good sex? Sex was part of it in the same way that breathing was part of it, in the same way that taste was part of it, in the same way that the synchronized pumping of our hearts was part of it. But it was more than that. It was being really alive and whole and happy and sure and warm for the first time in my life.

Sensation was there. But not the same. Not what I'd thought was the most I could expect. What had happened to me before was a small, unsatisfying thing, like a thimbleful of water to a man dying of thirst. This was the full flow, the open faucet. The separate, yet whole, knowledge of joy and life—in every single nerve of *both our bodies and both our minds.*

God. Oh, God . . .

It had been that for us the first time. And it had been more the next. And still more the next, as though each new time we were together we began higher, climbing, and then beginning still higher the next time. . . .

*"Sandy!"*

I stopped in my tracks and wanted to put my hands over my mouth. Because that hadn't been just in my mind. That had come out of my mouth. I had shouted her name—just shouted it out, probably with that idiot smile on my face— walking down a public sidewalk.

Cautiously, I looked around to see if anyone had heard, had noticed. I started walking again. And making a good, strong try at putting Sandy out of my head. Completely. It was 'way past time for thinking. Especially about her. I had to stay *away* from this chick.

She would make too damn much sense when she talked. And think too clearly when she thought. And what she said and what she thought were suddenly pretty damn important to Buddy-boy all of a sudden.

What a yock.

I had turned around and was walking the other way, so naturally I passed the booth I'd used to phone Zeke and tell him the party was on for tonight. And I almost stopped. I almost did.

To phone . . . who?

No. Not Sandy. I had ruled Sandy out. And not Zeke, to tell him to scrub the whole deal; that was out, too. The word was Go. So who did I want to call?

The *padrino*. I just wished to hell I could pick up the phone and dial long distance and spend a few minutes laying the whole schmear on the *padrino*. Tell him the what. Tell him the why. Especially the *why*—because that was the main thing. The *padrino*, at least he would *listen*. Even to me. Even to Buddy-boy.

But . . . it was no go.

Not even worth thinking about. Because in the first place it was too late. I couldn't back out now. Even if I wanted to.

And in the second place . . .

Oh, screw the second place.

And the first.

Screw the whole thing. *Padrino*. Ma. Old Man. And *Buddy*-boy. Especially that prime jackass. It was Vee-One, on takeoff. *Vee-One*. The speed of Commitment. Once the indicator shows you've hit that speed, your alternatives are all used up. You got no more. You go. You are committed to fight.

Just like Buddy-boy Valentine. . . .

# The **5**th House

*Love affairs, speculations, emotions, and children . . .*

---

*Forecast: If cagey Sam LoCicero has speculated properly and if his calculations prove correct, he and Johnny Valentine are about to pin Irving Dahlberg right between the hammer and the anvil. But there are a couple of variables they may regret overlooking, namely, Jackie Dahlberg and Buddy Valentine.*

*As we enter the Fifth House, it shall be seen that children can come up with some strange and bizarre ways of getting their parents' attention. . . .*

---

### Johnny Valentine

"Well, it's what I want to do, Sam. I know it's going to be pretty hard to set up, but you can do it, can't you?"

"Well, Vanni . . ."

"Aw Sam, hell, you handled bigger beefs than this one. I remember the time . . ."

"Yeah, Vanni. Okay. Let's not waste your long-distance dough on auld lang syne. Maybe it can be handled. I say *maybe*. But you still ain't told me why you want it. What is this punk to you, anyway?"

"I owe him."

"For *what*, for Chrissake? Because you're making it with . . ."

He stopped, just in time to avoid getting back into the thing we'd both been talking around ever since Christmas night in Angie's kitchen. It burned me. Yeah, still it burned me, having to talk around it. We'd never had to talk around anything before, had we? But now there was this thing, and Sam couldn't just talk straight out on a lot of things because of it.

"I *owe* him, Sam. And besides, I want to do it."

"Okay. Leave it at that." He broke off for a minute and I waited. Sam doesn't stop talking with no reason; when he does that, it's because he's got an idea or something on his mind. So I waited. And finally he got back from wherever he'd been. "Yeah," he said, and his voice was different. "Hey, yeah, Vanni—maybe so. It could be there's a way to *use* this!"

"*Use* it?" Now there was a grabber. Use it? For what? "Hey, Sam, I miss a couple of bars there or something?"

"No. Look, there's been a couple developments here. I was meaning to call you anyway."

"Swinging," I said, wanting to keep him on the original subject until I was sure he was going to help, "but about Strauss, you'll set something up? To square it for him?"

"That's what I was going to tell you. Vanni, this could fit right in."

"In what?"

"The whole deal. Look, you made your mind up yet about the Priapus Pictures setup? Because if you . . ."

"Sam. No, I haven't. Stick to . . ."

"That *is* the point, Vanni. Because, look, it means we move, right? From Monarch to Priapus."

"Sure. But I haven't decided yet."

"Okay. All right. But Vanni, if we *do* move, see, then Monarch could bounce right back and use that TV production deal we had there, the one they're dragging their feet on now. They could use that to give us a real bad time, claiming nonperformance."

"Nonperformance! Sam, *they're* the ones who . . ."

"Yeah. Great! Try to prove it in court. And even if you could, it would still hold everything up; maybe even queer it for us. It's a matter of timing, you know."

"So . . . ?"

"So this: what if we use Strauss in a television production? A regular, running show idea, I mean. He's got a three-picture contract with Monarch. That could be converted into a TV deal; all we . . ."

"For Christ sake, Sam! Monarch won't touch him with *your* ten-foot pole. That's what the whole trouble is about."

"Yeah, yeah. I know."

"Well . . . ?"

"You wanted me to square the beef, right?"

"I—yeah. I wanted you to try, anyway. I promised I'd do it, and besides there's something you don't know about. If the deal gets too smelly, there could be a big rebound on . . ." I didn't finish because, there it was again. The big hole in the world. The stuff we couldn't talk about anymore. I felt the burn begin again. But Sam covered it, no sweat.

"I heard the talk, too. It was straight goods?"

"Yeah."

"Okay—so it could mess up a lot more than Strauss, and that's why we square it. By the way, Vanni, they're offering our price now, for Diamond in the lead for *Sadie*. Do we sign?"

"I don't know."

"Well, it's deciding time, because here's how it *could* work. We agree to signing her for the flick, on condition Strauss gets the break in the TV series. That takes Monarch off the hook for *Sadie* and gives them something to do with Strauss's contract besides pay him off and forget it. It also takes us off the hook there if we wanta go ahead on Priapus, and still leaves us the out with Dahlberg if he tries to squirm out of the Strauss deal or the TV deal or make any trouble at all. We can *still* screw him up on releasing *Sadie* when it's in the can."

"Okay." What else could I say? That Sam. All right, I was still plenty pissed at him, admit that. But when the guy goes to work figuring angles-inside-the-angles, you can't beat him. "Okay, Sam. Let 'em have it. I'll play."

"Attaboy! I'm tellin' you, Vanni, this'll work out for everybody. By the way, where's Strauss now?"

"Still here. But he'll be back there tonight. That's the other thing I called about, Sam. Maybe you can do something on that end, because it's a screwy bounce."

"What is?"

"He's flying back to the Coast, but he's not alone. The duMain bitch is with him."

207

"Dahlberg's cunt? She's with *Strauss?*"

"That's the scam. And don't ask me what the hell it means. I don't even know if old Dahlberg *knows* it."

"Hey, Vanni, you shoulda said something before."

"Why?"

"Well, hell, it could screw the whole arrangement. You know, if Dahlberg doesn't know; if Strauss is loony enough to take off with Dahlberg's broad—you *know* the guy'll never listen to reason if there's anything like that involved."

"Maybe there isn't."

"Yeah. Maybe." He thought for a minute. "Gimme the —uh—you got their flight? What airline and when it gets in here, I mean?"

"I can get it."

"Well, do that and call me back. If I'm not here, tell the office girl. I wanna meet them."

"Okay. Maybe you . . ."

"Oh, *crap!*"

"What?"

"Vanni, I forgot. I'm gonna be tied up tonight. Dinner. With Jack Dahlberg and his wife."

"So, maybe it fits in. Take them with you. A little quiet dinner. What's a better place to talk the whole thing over and see what kind of a reaction you get?"

"I don't know."

"What's to know? It's—hey, Sam! This isn't in public, is it, the dinner? I mean not at Scala or Chasen's or anything? It's going to be *private?*"

"Well, yeah. Private. Only . . ."

"Only what?"

"Private at—uh—at Angie's place, Vanni."

"*Angie's?* Well, I'm glad the two of you are friends again —but why at Angie's?"

"Well, I set it up sort of through the side door, like. Had Angie call the Dahlbergs and invite them without telling them I was gonna be . . ."

"Christ, Sam!"

"Look, it'll still work. I'll just call Angie and tell her we got two extra for dinner."

"She'll murder you."

"Not her. She digs this kind of action, you know?"

Yeah. That was the hell of it, I *did* know. Give this to old Angie. If she figured for a minute that anything she could do would be something that would shove her into anything where I was involved, she'd do it. Yeah. For just a moment, I felt like something in a trap; like the walls were made of iron and they were coming in on me.

Well, anyway, I wouldn't have to be there. And Dolly wouldn't have to know; at least no sweat on that score.

"Okay. Whatever's right, Sam. I'm counting on you."

"Always, baby. Did I ever let you down?"

"Nope. Okay, lemme know how it comes out."

"Right."

And that's how we left it.

It wasn't until I hung up that I realized just *how* lucky it was that I wasn't going to be there for Angie's little dinner party. Hey, like wow! Dig *that* action: Jack and Clara Dahlberg sitting across the table from Strauss, who had to be *numero uno* on the Monarch shit list—and duMain, who was Jack's daddy's current sleeping bag, on the outs with the old man because of the suspension of her first picture. Yeah!

I wondered if Sam had picked up on all the angles. Oh, sure. Trust Sam, he would have looked it over from every side. Still, I was glad as hell it was him, not me, headed for Casa Valentino. I thought a minute or two about the kid, Dahlberg. Kid? Christ, a man in his thirties; but everyone always thinks of him as a kid. Rough go. An old man like Dahlberg.

I wondered, could any deal *be* made? On Jack's say-so, that is? The word was yes-and-no. Yes, Jack could give you a solid nod on anything small; on day-to-day operations or low-budget deals. But he always had to make it a firm "maybe" if it was big, until he had a chance to check the action with his papa.

Kind of a rough go for Jack. Still, he must like it. He sure . . .

### Jack Dahlberg

. . . never made a move to get out. So where does it all leave me? Sitting here. In my office. Looking at one million cash dollars, and trying to think of some way I could get Clara off my back without stealing it for her.

I didn't bother to count the money. It was all there. Trust Papa for that; I knew (and had wondered from time to time just who else knew) that he counted it, at least to the extent of checking all the bundles, every time he came to the Coast. Including the last visit a week ago, at Christmas.

Looking at it, the money seemed like a lot more than it really was. In twenties and fifties, a million makes quite a stack. That was why the *"safe"* in my office was so elaborate. Irving Dahlberg had designed it and had it built when the office was his, and it was simplicity itself in a way —no really tough combinations, no heavy bank-type armor. A good safecracker could get through things like that.

Instead, Papa had simply arranged the whole thing to be invisible. The entire wall of the small, private toilet-washroom was set on swivels, to open at the touch of one particular button. A button was concealed (and this was the part that always somehow jolted me) inside the *nose* of the larger-than-life bronze bust of Papa, which dominated one whole corner of the desk. Radio control. I only changed the batteries from time to time.

Absently, I fingered another button—one of those set in the executive console on the desk top—and saw it flick on and off. That meant the concealed television camera in the wall had recorded these few seconds of Jack Dahlberg sitting in his office and looking off dreamily into the executive can. I didn't think that needed to be preserved for posterity so I pushed the other button, to erase it, and sat looking at the money again.

All week I had been stalling Clara, saying I had to think up something really *good* to tell Papa about what had happened to the cash if I removed any or all of it. Something he would believe. Not, as Clara said, that he could go to the police, or anyone else, when he found the safe empty. Papa would be the last man in the world to want to explain it to any outsider.

But he still could make things awfully rough on anyone inside the Industry who got his fingers on it. Or, I had an idea, anyone outside, if he could be sure who it was. That's what made me wonder whether or not I could really get away with handing it over to Clara.

The first—in fact, the only—idea I'd come up with was to carry it home, briefcase-full by briefcase-full, over several days. And when it was finally gone, and Clara had it well hidden, tell Papa someone had figured out the trick-wall setup and had burgled the place overnight.

The hell of it was, the whole thing sounded just a little too Hollywood. You can let them get away with something like that in a script. But in real life it is just too damn improbable for anyone, particularly a savvy guy like Irving Dahlberg, to swallow. He would smell a rat somewhere. All my life he'd always known when I was lying or unsure of my story. I had gone over the ground for hours, step by step, but in the end I still couldn't see myself telling the story to Papa and getting him to believe it.

No. It would have to be something else.

"Mr. Dahlberg?"

I jumped, my muscles overreacting to the sound of the girl's voice on the office intercom. I paused a moment for control, reminding myself that I hadn't been to the gym in more than a week and the body was starting to show it.

"Yes?" I said, pressing the button.

"Mr. Graham called. He asked if you had a minute."

Just for an instant, I wished that Saul Graham, my friend and adviser, was somewhere in darkest Tibet. Then the reality of the everyday world was back and I felt my mouth twist into a sour grin.

"Tell him to come in anytime he's ready," I said, and got up to stick a finger into Papa's nose and close the crapper crypt.

Saul walked in a few minutes later. He is older than me, in his middle fifties, and married to one of the richest and toughest society dames on the East Coast, whom he sees on the infrequent occasions he visits New York. That seems to be enough for him, and I guess anyone who ever spent much time with Gladys Graham could give you at least twenty good reasons why it should be that way.

He grinned at me with half his face, pulled out a fake cigarette—one of those pacifiers for people trying to break the smoking habit—and started chewing on it as he dropped into the big chair across the desk from me. That fake cigarette is an affectation with Saul. A nervous mannerism. Because I don't remember that he was ever a smoker.

"Our boy in Washington called back," he said. "And Happy New Year from the Party-in-Power."

"They said *no?*"

"They said go piss up a rope."

I shrugged my shoulders; it was only what I had expected. Papa could talk about "greasing the right palms" and "applying pressure in the proper places" until hell froze over. The head men in the party had long memories, and they wouldn't be quick to forget that Irving Dahlberg had made all those television ads at cost for the opposition last election time.

"All right. So where do we go from here?" I asked.

Saul sucked on the pacifier, looking at the window behind me as though something interesting were happening there.

"If you were Steve Pappas at Priapus," he said, "or The Eyedoctor over at Universal . . ."

"And if I had one arm and a slot I'd be working in Nevada," I said. "I repeat—where do we go?"

"Influence," Saul said. "Someone with real influence in the administration. Someone they owe a favor to, who owes us a favor."

I shrugged, a bit impatiently.

"Saul," I said, "we've been over that ground. Twice."

"And I still say . . ."

"Balls."

That ended all conversation for a while and I hoped he would get off the point. One man we had, with a production office right on the lot, who could ask favors of the current administration. One man who could claim a favor, even a really big favor. And get it. Why?

Because he had raised Christ-only-knows how many millions for the party campaign fund—the money that put this administration in office. And afterward they'd crapped on him. Sent a buddy of his around to say it was okay to be a friend of the candidate and even, later, a friend of the nominee. The Hollywood image had been swell during the election. But that for him to be a friend of the president was something else again, something the newly dignified winning contender could not afford.

It had gotten a snicker or two around town when the story came out. The big shot, the first-name-buddy-of-the-president, suddenly and publicly demoted to the stature actors have always had where the men of power are concerned: Please enter and depart by the rear door; kindly do not mingle with the guests.

A big yock for the guy's enemies, and he had a few. But

still a big unpaid debt for the administration. Weekends on the presidential yacht and intimate dinner parties with the first family might be out, but favor-for-favor political payoffs could still definitely be collected.

Oh, hell, yes! Johnny Valentine could claim a favor from the president. Even a pretty big favor, like the use of the Atlantic Fleet for a few weeks to make a movie. But asking him to do that *for* us, from *this* administration, wasn't even worth discussing. And Saul knew why, as well as I did.

"Look," Saul said, "face facts, Jack. If you want to make *Boarders Away!* the way the Old Man says it's got to be made, the Guinea's the only way we can go. Aside from him, no dice."

"He'd tell us the same thing they told our Washington connection."

"Not necessarily."

"Why not? You know what's going on, Saul; hell, you've even been handling the action most of the time. We've been stalling on the television deal we made with Valentine when he sold us the rights to *Sadie*. And by this time, they've got to see what's going on. So why the hell should he help us out on this?"

"You could make it personal."

"No way."

"Not even maybe somehow through the ex-wife, Angela? You know the scam, Jack—Valentine'll do anything the ex-wife asks him to do, except marry her again. Do you know her?"

"Angie? Sure. In fact, we're having dinner there tonight. But that's too remote. Forget it."

He shrugged. "Okay," he said. "Just a thought." He got up and stuck the pacifier back in his pocket. "I'll run it around the mill over the holiday," he said, "and see what else I get. Happy New Year."

And out he went, leaving me sitting there pondering about what leverage we could use to get Vanni to throw his weight around for us. My watch said it was getting late. Nearly six. Time for a quick shave and a change of shirt if I was going to look something like a human being at the Valentine house. I got up and marched, slow cadence, into the washroom.

The mirror showed me a bland-looking guy with blue

eyes that looked a little too pale for his tan and a bulging forehead with just the first traces of wrinkle-lines beginning to show. He was just a bit too short for the washstand. And the mirror because it had been built, like everything else in that room, for a larger person. A midget among the belongings of a giant?

No, not a giant, but a bigger man, all the same. Bigger, goddamn it, in more ways than you can measure with a ruler.

"Poor bastard," I said aloud to the face in the mirror. "Poor little . . ."


### Sandy Hallowell

. . . Buddy Valentine. The phone rang and rang. Now I was really worried. Where *was* he? I looked at the chart I had made up for Buddy, and beside it, the horoscope I'd worked out for today. I wanted—oh, *how* I wanted—to tell it all to the telephone company; to make them understand how important it was for me to contact Buddy.

I let out the deep, deep breath I found I had been holding, and put the phone down. My watch said I had exactly thirty minutes until check-in. All right, Hallowell. Come on! Charts are charts and the job is the job. Let's not let this get out of hand. So get cracking, girl. Go!

I picked up my bag and checked the mirror one final time. That's a habit they spare no effort to teach you in stew school; never leave for *anyplace* before you've checked to be sure you are our bright-and-beautiful hostess.

Okay. You look like one of those big-eyed paintings of children that got so popular a few years ago; not only are the eyes a little slanty today; they are also more than a shade oversize—probably because of what you turned up in the works for poor Buddy today, and because it seems you're not going to be able to warn him about it. Okay. *All right!*

But standing around here chewing your nails won't accomplish a thing.

Out the door, Hallowell. And that's just where I went, only to dash back in after a brief tussle with my key and the sticky lock, to grab up Buddy's chart and horoscope. No sense leaving them *here,* anyway. If you do reach him when you get to LAX, you can at least *read* him what you've found out. If it isn't too late.

It wasn't raining and I got a taxi downstairs with no trouble—for a wonder—and leaned back against the seat cushions, trying to relax and tune the mind down to a mild roar all the way to Kennedy.

*Buddy!* If *only* he weren't a Capricorn and if *only* . . . !

Oh, come on, Hallowell, come *on!* Buddy Valentine is a full-grown man and he has got along all these years (well, more or less, anyway) without *you* to warn him of every pitfall day-by-day, so what's the big rush, the big deal, about *today?* I told myself that. And it didn't work at all, of course. Because today *wasn't* just anytime. Not for Buddy. Not if my math was anything like correct, and I had checked it three times just to be sure.

Any long-considered plan put into action *today* would be sure to backfire. It absolutely *would not work!* Not today,

And I know, I was *certain,* that Buddy had something on his mind. Something he'd been toying with, for who knows how long. Something that made him leery of even making tentative *dates* to do anything after the first of the year. Yes. It *was* all there, in the chart.

I couldn't be sure just how bad the outcome would be. That was a little confusing. Something most peculiar going on in his Fourth and Tenth houses; something I couldn't quite interpret. There was a possible indication of a successful outcome in the long run. But I just couldn't see how that could square with the *very* bad . . .

*Stop* it, Hallowell. *Stop it!* There is nothing you can do—nothing at all, do you hear—between now and the time you get into LAX. If you were meant to, that would have shown up, too. And it didn't. So it isn't fated; it isn't a certainty.

*No. But nothing really is. It's not certain I can't help, either.* And if anything happens to Buddy! If . . .


### Buddy Valentine

". . . anything goes wrong, Zeke—well, then I'm *screwed,* that's all. For good and for sure."

He just looked over at me silently, as we walked along toward his jeep.

215

No particular way. He just looked; one thing about old Zeke, his face never tells you a damn thing. You never can look at him and have any idea what's really going on in there.

"In two days," I went on, finally, "in that length of time —sure—I could be in the wrong spot. I could even bitch up the approach and wash out the whole thing there and then. Or somebody could happen along, like, out of left field, and find me ten minutes after I ditch. . . ."

"Or be watching you the whole time."

I thought that over.

"I'll make sure no one does," I said. "Low and slow, looking around, before I really go . . ."

"You'll shit, too," Zeke said, still looking at me with plenty of nothing in his face, "if you eat reg'lar. The ocean is a big fuckin' place, Rich boy. Real big. Easy to miss something down there. . . ."

*Rich boy.*

Why in the hell did he have to call me that? He knew it bugged me, and most of the time he would call me Bud. But for some reason it was always *Rich boy* when something was eating him. I wondered what it was this time.

He'd handled his end of the deal, until now, strictly by the book. The survival gear—raft, food, dye marker, sea anchor, life vest, even a little inflatable water still in case the boat canteen wasn't enough—all of it here and all of it ready on the old Air Force practice-landing field at Northcutt, waiting for me, just the way we'd written the script.

Only one thing missing.

*No parachute.*

And goddamn it, I *wanted* one. Two, in fact. One for me and one for the raft and survival gear. We'd had a hell of an argument about that. But he had it his way in the end. . . .

My idea had been to hit the silk after pitching the gear out in its own chute and disabling the ship . . . or even setting it on autopilot to crash when the fuel was gone.

But Zeke wouldn't have it.

"That's why we're using a Cessna 310 instead of a Lear jet, Rich boy," he said, "so you can ditch nice and easy and soft, and pop out the top-hatch instead of trying to get through a side door."

"But the chutes . . ." I'd tried to argue.

"The chutes," he'd interrupted me, "are the biggest god-damn liability you could own up there. Number one: The skydivers are nuts. Jumpsacks are to use in emergencies only like if you lose a wing or the airplane is on fire—for anything else, your best odds are always staying with the ship. Number two: Even if both chutes worked, the time between when you pitch the gear out and when you go yourself could put you a mile or more—maybe a *lot* more —apart there in the big, wide open. And number three: A chute can float on the top of the water practically for-ever, sometimes, and they're easy as hell to spot from the air. You say you wanta be gone—missing—for anyway two days? Well, boy, the chances of that with two chutes float-ing nearby, or even just one, are pretty fucking remote. *No*, man. No way! You ditch, just the way I showed you. The way we practiced."

And that was the end of it.

So here we were. Ready to go. Only . . . Now I just wished to hell I knew him better.

Weird trip, huh?

I mean . . . not twenty-four hours ago I thought I knew old Zeke as well as I ever knew anyone on earth—ex-cept Sandy, of course—and, as we got into the jeep, it sud-denly smacked Buddy-boy right in the face that I didn't really know old Zeke at all. Not really.

There he was, nothing showing on his face and *"Rich boy"* coming out of his mouth, and I didn't know why and knew I couldn't find out. And this was the guy I was going to be trusting with my delicate, unique, irreplaceable ass from the moment I took off until . . . who knows when?

*With my life, man!*

Suddenly I wished I had a week, a month, a year to talk over all the details again and make sure old Zeke really was hip on them. That there wasn't going to be any mistake.

We'd figured everything, sure: ocean currents and speed, ditching procedure, how Zeke was to join the search and how he was to wait two days to do it while Buddy-boy's last radio contact (and the unclosed flight plan that would touch the whole operation off) would send everyone shag-ging around the Coastal Range and the San Joaquin Valley. And how he was to use his copter to search—on his own, maybe—along the *reciprocal* bearing of the position line being scouted by CAP and all the rest . . .

And, hell, I *knew* he was solid on the details. A good many of them were his, even. Things he'd come up with to make the whole thing as foolproof as possible. I *knew* he was with it. Sure. Only . . .

"*Rich boy.*"

Why the hell did he have to say that? Right now.

And why the hell did it bug me so much . . . ?

Why?

Why?

Oh . . . *bullshit!*

What's the use? I'm committed. I'm *in*. I've signed for the trip and all the worrying and thinking and wondering in the world isn't going to make a damn bit of difference now. The word is Go . . . *Go*.

Sandy.

Jesus, what a bummer for Sandy, you know? How long before she gets the word? Before someone tells her what happened? Will she have to get it all from the Boob Tube?

No. Not Sandy. Moment she picks up on it, she'll be on the phone with the private number I gave her, for Ma's place in Bel Air. She'll know the word will be quickest and greenest there. Sure.

And how'll Ma treat her?

Oh, for sure—that did bug me. Because, of course, I hadn't really clued Ma in about Sandy and me. But Ma's usually a pretty cool head where the chicks I'm seeing are concerned. Not real tight with any of them, you know. But nice. Polite and friendly.

Only . . . this'll be, to put it mildly, a kind of unusual situation. Jeez, you can't really tell how Ma'll act, a setup like that. If only I . . . if only . . .

*Forget it*, Valentine!

Forget it and pay attention to the Main Chance here. This is *survival*, Buddy-boy!

Survival . . .

Not that I really give so much of a damn if I don't make it. Not really. Unless . . .

. . . unless Sandy's right—some of that astrology number she's been doing for me as often as I'll let her. *Astrology*, for Chrissake! *Karmic debt*.

Ever since I've known her (oh, yeah . . . such a *long*

time, right? Right, Buddy-boy!) and she started coming on with the stars and the houses and the signs and all that—ever since then, it seems like everyone in the whole entertainment industry is getting turned onto that stuff. That, or I'm just noticing it more.

If she's right and the karma deal is for real, I guess then it *would* have to make a hell of a lot of difference what the Old Man—yeah, and the rest of the family, too—thinks about all this. The idea, the way Sandy tells it, is to play your own tune and learn your own lessons and cause as little grief as possible. So in that case—hell—next time God only knows what I'll come back as. A hydrocephalic pygmy, probably.

*And if I do make it?* Yeah. What then? Suppose everything goes like silk; everybody wins, nobody loses, and Buddy is returned to the loving bosom of family and friends, smiling and healthy, what will be changed? What will be different? And . . . for the better or for the worse?

Aw, hell. Who knows? You pays your money and you takes your choice, the way the *padrino* says. Yeah. That, too, the *padrino*. Uncle Sammy might talk a little bit rough and *Joisey* for a dude who's one of the most powerful lawyers in the world, but that doesn't mean he's a dummy. He didn't get what he's got or where he is by being a . . .

Yeah.

*For sure!*

What if the *padrino* . . . if *he* . . . !

Stop that!

Oh, my God, Valentine, stop that. The *padrino*. Sandy. Zeke. The Old Man. Ma. Astrology. Karma . . . *knock it off, man!* It's go, and Zeke's looking at you, wondering why you don't hit the button and . . .

*The watch.* Check it again. Okay. It's Go, too. Right! *The time is now* . . .

"Okay, Zeke—let's get it on."

"Rog."

And here I am, watching, like someone in the audience—not a participant at all—as Zeke starts the engine of his jeep, drives it to the other end of the old practice runway, and wings around to give me a little light on the strip and an aiming-point for takeoff.

Panel light on.

Throttles cracked. Switch on . . . starter . . . and here

we go. Here we go. Here we go . . . Number One engine.
Pitch, check. Go. Running . . . Number two . . . let 'em
run. Both sound sweet. Okay. Run up One. Hold it. Mag
check . . . and down. Number two, up. Hold it. Mag
check. Down. Brakes off. Turning right onto runway.
Lining up . . .

*The time is now.*

This is Go.

This is reality. This is the Real. Not the Dream. The . . .


### David Strauss

. . . real, sitting here at Angela Valentine's table with
Gaby duMain on my left and the fabulous Sam LoCicero
up at the head of the table, and Mrs. Valentine—the first
wife, the one they'd still call "Mrs. Valentine" no matter
if the Velvet Voice married fifty other women—down there
at the end.

*This is the real.* It's the other that's not; I have got to
hold onto that. I have got to hold onto this real and remember that it is. And just forget the people I can hear talking
(about *me?*) in the next room. The other people are not
there. Only the—how many? One, two, three, four of us,
only the four. No. More than four. How many?

But I counted myself. So that leaves—who? LoCicero,
Gaby, Mrs. Valentine, me—oh, God! Yes. And of course
I would try not to count him, wouldn't I? Yes, I would try
that. God, *God!* Nobody told me *he* would be here. I
couldn't have come with her, done what she said, if I'd
known he'd . . .

*"What?"* I hadn't been following the thread of the talk
too closely; too much noise from the other room. "I'm
sorry, I guess I'm kind of tired. Been up all . . ."

"I said you look okay, Dave."

"Thanks."

Yes. Oh, yes, thanks! Thanks and thanks and thanks till
time shall be no more. Thanks, *Jackie!* Thank you, Mr.
Jack I. Dahlberg. Thank you for your great kindness in
condescending to break bread with this your most unworthy
servant, Mr. Dahlberg, ruler and master of the world, sir.
And thank you for not having brought your mean-mouthed,
hating wife Clara along to dig at me with her cold, all-
seeing eyes. Or thank *her*, since she's the one who got sick

at the last minute—at least, so Jackie said—and decided to stay home. Anyway, thank whoever arranged for her not to be here to get on my back.

I look all right to you, do I? Well, that's very interesting and I certainly want to thank you for telling me, because you see I have been having this sort of trouble with mirrors of late. I am afraid to look into them because when I do, I see myself. My *real* self turned inside out, like someone had taken me by the tongue and given a hard, knowing jerk the way you do to a sock to get it right side out. Only *I'm* inside out, with all of my insides hanging around and all the blood over everything and the skin of me is hollow and I can see exactly what . . .

No. *Oh, please—no!* I won't think about any of that. It is not real. It will go away after a while and I'll be all right, just like I used to be.

Concentrate. Have a little concentration, David, darling. Thanks, I do mind if I don't . . .

". . . my chance! You understand, Jack, what I've *gone through* to get this one big break? It just can't end this way. It *can't!*" I didn't have to turn my head to know Gaby was in tears; they were right there in her voice.

". . . you've got to understand, too, Gaby. There is nothing that I can do, now. Nothing *anyone* can do. We've already announced the cancellation." Jackie's voice. I didn't look at him, either. But I knew how he would look anyway, like he always does when he's cornered. The head bent a little forward; the eyes darting occasional glances at you from under the brows, giving the impression he's either studying something closer to him than you are or that he's deep in thought and you're disturbing him or even—so help me, it *does* work—that he is looking *down* at you from a superior height.

Down! Jackie Dahlberg looking *down;* the only human being he could ever look *down* on was Alan Ladd. And they always had to get Laddie a two-step for his love scenes so he wouldn't be kissing the bitches right in the . . .

"You know that, don't you, David?"

*God.* I had lost the thread again. The best I could do was kind of nod in Jackie's direction and pretend to have my mouth full. Of what? I haven't been hungry since I started this . . . But it seems to be all right.

"You know the studio is only partly in control on a picture as big as the one with you and David, Gaby. Five million—that is just too much for us to carry without help. And the moneymen, the bankers, would never give us the go-ahead now. Never! If we tried to keep shooting, with David in the lead, after the kind of stories that have been—sorry, David; you know I don't believe it myself, but the point is the bankers *do*—the kind of stories we've heard about the past week, well, they'd cut our production insurance off in two seconds. And *nobody* makes a picture without that."

Gaby wasn't listening. She couldn't afford to listen.

Jackie knew that, and I knew it, but it didn't make anything easier for any of us. All right, she was fighting for her life, at least as far as her career in pictures was concerned. We all could understand that. But we all knew it was no damn use, too. I wished I could care about it as much as she did. I wished I could. It would have made sense, in a way.

The truth was that she might—just might—get another chance to make a motion picture. I wouldn't, I knew that. And for the moment, I just couldn't seem to make myself care.

*If only those damn people would shut up in the other . . . !*

The chandeliers were starting to open their mouths and reach for us by the time I realized what was happening and could give myself as firm an order as I was capable of issuing to turn them back into steel and brass and glass. When they were inanimate again, the lawyer, LoCicero, was talking.

". . . bad," he was saying, "but you know, Jack, there just *might* be some kind of answer for all of us. You, too, Miss duMain," he added, shooting a glance at Gaby, who had been staring down at her untouched plate ever since she stopped pleading.

The words should have meant something to me. They almost did, in fact. Almost. I took a firm hold on my knee, under the table where nobody could see, and tried to make the pain in my hand and the pain from my fingers digging in keep me anchored in the real. Gaby began looking at me very strangely and it worried me. What was I doing wrong?

"The picture's out—let's admit that right now, and see

222

where we can go from there. The studio won't lose much actual money closing down at this point, will it?"

"Well, there's the overhead and some . . ."

"But not much?"

"No."

"Okay, but unless I heard wrong, *Burn the First Card* was only the first picture of a three-flick deal you had with Dave, here, ain't that so?"

"Well, yes, but in view of the circumstances, we naturally . . ."

The lawyer grinned like a wolf at Jackie and flapped a hand at him *and the choir began a chorus of Hallelujah! Hallelujah! getting louder*—and I dug my fingers in harder and screwed my eyes shut.

". . . not be too natural too quick," LoCicero was saying. "You got that contract and, let's admit it, nobody is really going to just shake hands like *old buddies*." The lawyer's voice bore down on those two words, and there was a momentary flicker of his eyes between Jackie and me. Jackie didn't even twitch; I don't know what I did. "Dave's a corporation. He doesn't own all of himself. Other people—my client, G. V. Enterprises, included—own part of his action. For the sake of form, if nothing else, they'd have to sue you over the remaining two pictures. You know that, Jack."

Jackie gave him the under-the-eyebrows business, but didn't deny it.

"Now, at the same time, this client has a television production agreement with Monarch that hasn't been doing too well as far as performance is concerned. Right again, Jack?"

Jackie had stopped eating—Angela Valentine must have been ready to kill us for not doing justice to what looked like a really good meal—but nonetheless she wasn't about to interrupt.

"So here's what I was thinking: suppose we make us a movie . . ."

*"Nothing doing!"*

". . . for television," LoCicero went on as though he hadn't heard Jackie, "under the usual deal: it's for television release domestic, theater release foreign, and, of course, it's the pilot for a series. An hour show."

Jackie was looking at LoCicero like he had just landed

from outer space; Mrs. Valentine was doing a lot of staring, too. But Gaby was still looking at me. I hadn't noticed that for a minute, and when I did it startled me again. I guess I jumped; my nerves weren't in such great shape. Gaby gave me a quick smile followed by a quick, but surprisingly warm, squeeze on the under-the-table hand that was still clamping my leg, near the knee.

"But—that's the most *preposterous* . . . !" Jackie began when he finally convinced himself LoCicero was serious. "No network would even *consider* a cofinancing arrangement involving . . ."

"Who said anything about cofinancing?" LoCicero asked blandly. "We'd be footing the bill ourselves, and what possible loss could there be? If the flick sells to one of the nets —and they're always one or two short the way they mess around, you know—we probably get the negative cost back right there. Let alone if the show is picked up. And, of course, the foreign theater exhibition . . ."

But Jackie was shaking his head again. "We still couldn't get production insurance," he said.

"No problem," the lawyer countered, smooth as a Tenth Avenue pitchman, "we'd insure the deal ourselves. Alone. Anything goes wrong, it's our loss—and we still make out, because we are going to need a loss for next year."

Jackie sat perfectly still, walking around it and looking at the paint on the machine, trying to find the flaw. He couldn't.

"The contract with Dave," he said then, nodding in my direction, "calls for a *very* high price per picture. More than we could possibly commit to a television speculation. He also gets a percentage . . ."

"Details," LoCicero dismissed the objection. "Let's say Monarch's contribution might even be *limited to* contribution of the services of Mr. Strauss and Miss duMain. I— uh—guess you wouldn't be too mad about that, would you, young lady?"

I almost cracked up. Young *lady!* Oh, *Jeez!* Jeez. I glanced at Gaby to see how she reacted. Oh, yes indeed! *Yes,* Dear Heart, that lovely young lady was just as—as— *Strauss is a fairy and he's crazy, the people in the next room were saying; he's crazy-azy-azy-azy-azy* . . .

I relaxed. The strain was too much for me; I couldn't

keep up—which hell was the real and which was the un-real? How do you tell . . . ?

A black pit, shot with fire and radium streaks, opened just below my feet and I could feel myself sliding—slid-ing . . .

A hand gripped mine again, just as I was going over the edge. I held on. And the pit went away.

I looked my thanks at Gaby, and she gave me back another of those everything-will-be-all-right looks. I still couldn't figure it out. After all, I *knew* the girl. Hadn't I spent five shooting days in the kip with her? And even with old Irving D. running in every two seconds to grope me and make sure I was in no shape to make it with her for real, I'd have known if she had had any honest response in this world. And she hadn't.

Somewhere, somehow I had missed something. I knew that. But what . . . ?

". . . assume you'd be satisfied with a percentage of the television picture and, naturally, of the show itself if it should be sold, wouldn't you, Dave?"

Hell, I didn't know. But I nodded at him again, and as before he seemed satisfied. "Well, then," he said to Jackie, "what do you say, Mr. Executive Vice-President?"

That was really putting it on Jackie. I wondered if his Papa had ever given him that kind of authority. My mind had one of its momentary flashes of total clarity, and I could see the worms of doubt and insecurity eating at him, and I was glad. Let him feel some of it. Let *him* know what it was like in the worm world.

"I'm not sure . . ." he began.

"Like I say, I assume the deal's gonna work. Especially," LoCicero added, in an almost offhand manner, "since we're now prepared to sign Dolly Diamond for her original part in *Sadie*—at the price and percentage we discussed last week."

This left Jackie with his mouth wide open and nothing coming out. And come to think of it, I was pretty much the same way.

I shot a glance down to the foot of the table where Mrs. Valentine was sitting, also speechless thus far. If she felt anything in particular at the mention of La Diamond, it didn't show.

"You're kidding," Jackie finally got out.

"Nope," LoCicero said. "I never kid about sacred subjects—beggin' your pardon, Angie—and money is just that kind of a thing with me. Whadda you say?"

"B—b—but . . . !"

"Look, do you want Dolly Diamond for the flick or not?" the lawyer prompted. "It's a package, Jack: Dave, Miss duMain, the television picture, and Dolly. All or nothing. Take it or leave it."

"I'll *take* it!" Jackie had finally collected himself, and he shoved one of his small, powerful hands across the table to shake the lawyer's hairy paw. LoCicero grinned at him (that same wolf grin I had noticed earlier) and that was that.

David's future (not to mention Gaby's and quite a few other people's), all sewed up and officially settled in a few minutes' talk over a dinner table. I think I was pleased. I think so. But the trouble I was having getting objective reality to stay real seemed to be sloshing over and getting in the way of a proper appreciation of exactly what had happened. The whole incident had a dream quality, as though I were seeing all the people, myself included, through gauze and at a distance. I had the distinct impression that I had somehow missed a few very important moments of the conversation—minutes that held the key to all that had happened.

Evidently Jackie felt a little bit of that, too, for he sat staring at Sam LoCicero with a pleased but puzzled expression on his face.

"You're sure this is all right with Johnny?" he finally ventured, speaking to the lawyer. "I mean—it's *great*, don't get me wrong. Only I sort of had the feeling—well, that he was pretty unhappy with Monarch and . . ."

"He was." LoCicero's voice was calm and somehow almost disinterested as he went to work on the dinner with the first real gusto anyone had shown since we sat down. "But business is business, Jack. And this happens to be very good business for all of us."

"Yes. I see that . . ."

"For instance," LoCicero continued, "it's no secret—you don't mind me bringing this up, do you, Dave, Angie—that Vanni and Dave are two-thirds of a pretty rough personal situation."

I glanced at Mrs. Valentine; her eyes had suddenly gone a whole lot darker—they were plenty dark to begin with—and she wasn't looking at anyone around the table. You could almost *hear* the electric charges building up around her. But she kept her mouth shut.

"But Vanni's a businessman, too," LoCicero said, "and one of his companies, like I said before, has a piece of Dave's contract. So he has an interest in seeing that the guy goes on working as an actor. You just can't let personalities in, or everybody goes down the tube."

"I can see that," Jackie said. "But I wondered . . ."

"No." The lawyer shook his head. "This isn't exactly what we had in mind for everybody in the beginning. Frankly, Jack, we'd have been a hell of a lot happier just to negotiate on one point at a time and get the most out of each item."

"Then . . . ?"

"But if anyone's going to wind up with anything," LoCicero said, "it's a sure cinch Monarch has got to stay in the picture business, not turn into an oil-leasing outfit or a pure real-estate renting setup like Goldwyn or Fox or—hell—MGM has finally turned out to be. Now, you and your father are the ones who want to do it that way, right?"

"That's true."

"And there's a meeting coming up with the board of directors," LoCicero nodded soberly, a forkful of scallopini in midair, "where the word is there could be some heat."

Jackie shrugged, trying to look neutral and not quite making it. "There could be some dissent," he said. "But nothing really . . ."

"*Crap,*" said LoCicero, "begging your pardon, Angie. With a five mil flick suddenly going into the ash can and nothing really settled on getting *Sadie* rolling, we both know the crossfire could get pretty damn rough." He wolf-grinned at Jackie again, "In fact, some of the heat could even come from *our* direction. It's no secret we have a fistful of stock in one of the outfits represented on your board . . ."

Shock was visible momentarily in Jackie's eyes, but that was his only response. I wondered, fleetingly, if he *had* known that.

". . . so we'd have an investment to protect from that side of the fence, too. All right, then; we want *Sadie* made

—preferably with Dolly—and we want David Strauss working. So, add it up, what else could a halfway-savvy businessman do?"

Jackie blinked a couple of times, digesting all of it. There was still a question hidden behind his face (but maybe I was the only one who knew him well enough to see it there), that Sam LoCicero's easy explanation, logical as it was, hadn't answered. But it was plain to see he'd had all the explanation he was going to get for the moment.

"As you say, Sam," he agreed, willing to give up the probing for the time being, "it makes sense. I'll have our people get to work on the formal contracts after the start of the year. No, come to think of it, this is a pretty long weekend we're going to have here—three more days. I'll tell them to have the contracts ready for you Monday morning. Okay?"

"Fine by me, if you can do it that quick. Sure!"

"Good—by the way," Jackie had started to eat a little now, too, "do you have any particular vehicle in mind? For the TV pilot picture, I mean."

LoCicero's eyes narrowed just the tiniest bit, but his expression didn't really change. "Yeah, one thing," he said. "We'll kick it around with your guys after the contracts are signed. An hour show, it would be, something fairly light and simple. Modern dress and mostly interiors, cheap to shoot."

"That would be a big plus," Jackie nodded. "Have we had a look at it yet? Was it one of the shows you've already submitted, I mean?"

"No." LoCicero was definitely being a little bit evasive now, and I think Jackie sensed it, too. "But before we make any real firm commitment, maybe some of those should get a *real* check-out, Jack. Maybe—uh—you better have a look yourself. Okay?"

Jackie got the point. Even back East, I'd heard the Monarch TV department was body-blocking the Valentine production unit's projects. The lawyer was giving Jackie the not-too-subtle word: this time, no frammis with the deal. *This* time the projects get approved and the channels are greased, not blocked.

He nodded a tacit agreement on the point. "I'll go through them Monday," he promised. Then he brightened, and seemed to smile at everyone around the table. "Well," he said, "Angela, I'm awfully glad you invited me to dinner, and for more reasons than the food—which, let me quickly add, happens to be the best in town. In a way, you know, it's a pity you didn't go into the restaurant business. You'd have made a fortune!"

"I'm glad you like it." Mrs. Valentine finally managed to get a word into the table talk. "And that you're finally eating some of it."

She smiled and Jackie laughed; her words could have held a barbed hint that we all were being rude, talking business deals rather than eating, but they didn't come out that way. Instead, the remark cleared the air—allowed everyone to be graceful about admitting the dinner really *hadn't* been exactly a social occasion, and that the guests hadn't been selected by chance.

"You mean," Gaby piped up beside me, "you do your *own* cooking, Mrs. Valentine?"

"Please," Mrs. Valentine said, "Angela. 'Mrs. Valentine' is for strangers and the newspapers. Yes, I fixed this particular meal. But that was only because it's New Year's weekend and we gave the cook and maid the day off. Most of the time, they do the cooking," Mrs. Valentine went on, "but, believe me, they do it *my* way!"

*Suddenly, in a single instant, the voices were back.*

They had faded, little by little, all through the business discussion between Sam LoCicero and Jackie. I guess I had made the error of letting my guard down when I got interested in what was going on between them. But now I could hear an increasing babble—like seventeen separate cocktail parties all buzzing in the same room; only tiny snatches of the words were audible, but those words! I wanted to put my fingers in my . . .

. . . *got another chance but he'll blow it just like he blew those guys in* . . .

. . . *never could resist a handsome boy; sooner or later it's going to come across on the screen and when it does* . . .

. . . *no better than a pimp. After all, he sold his wife to Johnny Valentine to get a break in the movies and even* . . .

. . . *always was a drunk, maybe that's* . . .

. . . *wants a mama, that's all. Not a wife. Not a woman. A mama—he's not even* . . .

"Well, anyway," Sam LoCicero interjected, "it's a hell of a dinner, Angie. You know, I think I could lose fifty pounds if I stayed away from here for a year."

"You'd have to keep out of the Bistro, too," Mrs. Valentine said. "I've seen you in there, what few times I've been in myself, putting away lunches that would bloat a dock walloper."

LoCicero laughed.

"It's my office-away-from-home," he said, gesturing with his fork, "and if I didn't show up, nobody'd be able to get hold of me for business. Then where'd I be?"

Mrs. Valentine made a wry face at him. "That much," she said, "I'll give you. When I want to get hold of Sam LoCicero, I do know where to call to make sure the message gets delivered. Tell me, Sam, is it true you pay them a regular fee to be your special answering service?"

"Nothing in it," the lawyer scoffed. "They just do me a little favor now and then, take a message if someone calls when I'm not there. I don't even pay special for the phone they put in at my table."

"You have your *own* table at Le Bistro?" Gaby asked, obviously impressed.

"Well, I didn't *buy* it or anything like that."

"Sure, Sam," Mrs. Valentine said, needling him, "we know. But somehow or other nobody but you ever seems to be sitting there unless it's someone waiting for you or talking to you, or left sitting when you leave."

The sudden pop back into reality hadn't been a coordinated thing for me. Little pieces were still getting themselves reassembled; sensation returning in parts of my body that had gone numb while the world around me was changing shape. One of the last bits to return was the hand I had reached down to clamp my leg, and when it did, there was a little extra jolt in it for me.

The leg it had been squeezing under the table wasn't my own.

Awareness and action were almost simultaneous; I jerked the hand off Gaby's thigh as though it were red hot—and then froze, wondering if anyone else had noticed what was going on. Nobody had, apparently. I risked a glance at Gaby, to find her looking sidelong at me. There was the barest hint of amusement at the sides of her mouth.

*Now what in hell was she . . . ?*

Have a little grope, David, darling. Thank you, I don't mind if I do. Only—what if I meet Irving, coming around the other way?

I went on looking at Gaby, wondering. With my head clear for the moment, it occurred to me that nothing she had done today—or, for that matter, in the last couple of days—really made a hell of a lot of sense. If she was Irving Dahlberg's private cooz, what in God's world was she doing here in Hollywood? *With* me and *without* him? Somehow a last-ditch effort to save the picture—and her career—didn't seem to explain it all, despite what she said.

I wondered if Irving knew where she was.

If not, he was going to be just a shade miffed when he found out, and he *would* find out, too, with Jackie sitting there across the table. Besides, we hadn't exactly been wearing slouch hats and fake beards when we got on the plane for L.A. Several thousand people must have seen us, and if they couldn't place Gaby (since she'd never made a picture, though her face had been splashed around the fan mags for a few months), they would sure as Christ know me. Old Irving D. wasn't going to like that . . .

*David Strauss, star of stage, screen, and ESP, invites the world to witness his crucifixion; twelve noon, in the parking lot of Monarch Studio, Westwood. Dress: semiformal.*

Well, all right. Nothing I could do about it now. Hell with it . . .

". . . isn't that so, David?"

Jackie. Looking at me.

I hadn't heard anything he'd said until he got to my name.

"I'm—sorry," I said. "Guess my mind was wandering, or maybe I'm still a little flabbergasted by the idea of a reprieve, a TV series to do when I thought I was dead as an actor. It's quite a bit to absorb at one sitting, you know." I was babbling, trying to pick up the thread of the conversation . . .

*Bing-bong!*

Saved by the bell. I relaxed a little and made the courtesy motion of rising as Mrs. Valentine got up to answer the telephone.

Gaby had just started a cover-up rejoinder to my babbling remarks when her sentence was abruptly terminated by the sound of a scream coming from the next room.

"*Je-sus . . . !*" Sam LoCicero stood up, almost knocking his chair over backward, and his napkin fell to the floor as he rushed toward the sound. I found myself on my feet, too, and joined the others in rushing toward the noise. In the general shuffle, I ended up being last out of the dining room, and I halted in mid-stride when I came upon the chaotic tableau in the kitchen.

Mrs. Valentine was on the floor sitting where she had evidently fallen, with her back against a cabinet. Her eyes were closed and her mouth was open, and she was emitting a series of high-pitched shrieking sounds.

Sam LoCicero was hovering over her, trying to calm her with one hand and fumbling after the telephone receiver with the other.

He finally got hold of it, and while Jackie and Gaby took over soothing Mrs. Valentine, the lawyer stood up and put the instrument to his own ear.

"Who is this?" he said, urgently.

". . . Sam LoCicero," he said an instant later, evidently in reply to some question. "What's going on here—what the hell did you say to Mrs. . . . ?"

He stopped talking in mid-word, and his own mouth stayed open for an instant as the voice crackled back at him through the receiver. It was turned a degree or so away from LoCicero's ear and I could hear the sound, but could distinguish no words.

"You're sure?" LoCicero said, when the voice on the other end paused. "This is not a mistake or a gag or something?" There was a pause, then, "All right," the lawyer said, obviously trying to preserve his own control. "All right, yes. Here! We'll be right here. Call us back, please, the minute—no, goddamn it, we have no statement for the press!" He slammed down the phone.

"What is it?" Gaby whispered, and LoCicero turned his head to answer.

But there was no need.

Mrs. Valentine had recovered enough to scream in words, rather than mere inchoate syllables. "Buddy!" she wailed. "Buddy! My *Buddy,* my *baby!*"

"What . . . ?" Gaby repeated.

"My baby, where is my baby?" She was sobbing now.

"What happened?" Jackie, sober and quiet, looked at LoCicero.

"Not sure," the lawyer said, holding his voice steady. "He filed a flight plan for San Francisco and took off earlier today. Then the Frisco tower got part of a Mayday call, and they haven't been able to raise him since."

"My baby!" Mrs. Valentine was now rocking herself back and forth against the cabinet, tears streaming from her eyes. At intervals more words came.

"Buddy! Oh *Madonna mia* . . . Buddy! *Madonna mia!* Buddy! *Mi' bambino, Madonna mia,* my baby! Please find him! *Madonna, oh, Madonna! Please find him!* . . . *Buddy! My baby! My baby* . . . *!*"

"Sweet Jesus!" Gaby whispered.

*"My baby! Oh, my baby . . . !"*

# The **6**th
# House

*Illness, service, work, food, servants, employees and hygiene . . .*

---

*Forecast: As Buddy's plot thickens and the Valentine clan waits and worries, Irving Dahlberg zeroes in at last on a way to gain the upper hand over the man he has hated for so long.*

*And in the Sixth House, strains and stresses are looming large on the horizon although the New Year has barely begun. . . .*

---

### Sandy Hallowell

It was a rotten day for flying. Outside, on the other side of the window, the sky was invisible and only the streaks of rain on the glass gave a focal point. Sitting in the big chair, I reminded myself that LAX would probably be closed to landings and only allowing takeoffs on an irregular schedule.

Not that it mattered, as far as I was concerned. I had called the crew-scheduling office and had myself put on indefinite personal emergency leave as soon as I heard the news about Buddy.

Sitting in the den of the Valentine home, where I'd first seen him with the rest of his family barely more than a week ago, it seemed hard to believe so little time had gone by since Christmas. The Valentine Christmas tree was still up, drooping now and very dry. But it might as well have been a cactus for all it meant of holidays to the people in the room.

Mrs. Valentine was semibedridden; something about her heart, the doctor had said. I hadn't volunteered the information that The Hallowell was a registered nurse. For one thing, I wasn't too sure how much help I would have been trying to function as a nurse for the moment; Buddy sort of got between me and my usual bright, instantaneous response to the requirements of a job like that. And, more to the point, I had a peculiar feeling that a lot of the heart-clutching hysterics since I'd arrived were for audience consumption. Mrs. Valentine had impressed me (on our admittedly brief acquaintance) as a woman of parts, well able to deal even with the disappearance of her son—plus a miscellaneous Indian attack, if she had to.

Unjust of The Hallowell, you say? Maybe so. It just wasn't one of my generous days. And besides, there was still the little unsettled sliver of slitty-eyed suspicion I'd been carrying around, back in the part of the mind where I do my living, ever since I'd heard the news.

*That astrochart of his.* I wondered, for about the seven hundredth time in two days, whether the newspapers and television announcers wouldn't have had to dig up something else to honk about if I'd been able to get through to Buddy on the phone. It was all just a bit too pat. Buddy rents a small plane, takes off for San Francisco without telling anyone (including The Hallowell) where he is going, and some time later he sends a distress call that is cut off before he can give his location. Then, zilch.

Well, now, fellers, that could happen. Sure. Of course it could, and probably has sometime in the past. Anything is possible. But I had just a smidgin of trouble swallowing it in the here-and-now. The whole deal sounded too sudden, too unmotivated.

Most of all, though, the part that worried me was that darn chart.

No. What the chart showed was a project on his part—something in which he, not some outside force, played the role of prime mover. And the reason I'd tried to call him was that the various aspects of the day (Mars and Saturn in *his* sun sign. Hah!) all indicated a complete lack of success for any such enterprise—or at any rate that the action

236

he initiated would fail to achieve its intended result. I'd done my dead-level-damnedest to warn him.

I *had*. But going over all this in my mind wasn't getting anything accomplished, except to set The Hallowell right spang on the edge of a little demonstration of her own hysteria potential.

*God, if he were only here!* I looked at my hands and suddenly wanted to find a full-length mirror so I could give myself a total up-and-down raspberry.

The Hallowell, that bright-eyed pillar of strength, was huddling in a chair while twisting a damp hankie between her dear little hands. *Twisting a handkerchief!* If any of my brothers—let alone Dad—could have seen me, he'd have lost his lunch. After he got done laughing.

More to put a definite end to the handkerchief-twisting action than for any other reason, I got up and took a brief stroll in the direction of the kitchen, thinking that perhaps I might be of some use, stirring up something for dinner.

The sole occupant of the kitchen was Sam LoCicero— the big lawyer Buddy called his *padrino.*

"Give you a hand?" I offered, moving over to the stove to have a peek at the huge pot he seemed to be tending there. "What is it?"

"Stew," he replied.

"Stew?"

"Well, chicken soup, anyway, with enough hunks of other stuff milling around in it to make it easier to call it stew than soup. Hey—here, take a taste."

He loaded up about half a spoonful of yellowish liquid and, like the innocent I keep trying to convince people I am (because it's the truth!), I dutifully opened wide and let him pour it in—and almost let out a scream.

*"Umf!"* I said. It was the best I could do by way of complaint, short of the scream I had managed to stifle. "Umf—ooog, OW!"

I finally got the boiling broth down (and was able to note every inch of its progress down The Hallowell gullet; blisters are as good a means of broth tracking as you can find).

"Oh, Jeez—sorry!" he apologized. "I keep forgetting some people are left in the world who didn't get their burn buds seared when they were kids. Really—it was kinda hot, huh?"

"It," I said, measuring the words in terms of how much air was bearable on my incinerated tonsils, "was kinda hot. Yes."

The big man made a kind of ineffectual shrugging motion, and went on stirring. "How'd it taste, though?" he inquired.

"Don't ask me, brother. I may have to resign my membership in *Gastronomie International,* as it is."

He grinned crookedly at me. "Jewish penicillin," he said. "My old lady used to make it up by the gallon, and pour it into me like a keg. It's damn near the only thing I ever learned to cook. And at that, mine doesn't hold a blowtorch to hers." He chuckled. "When Ma made it," he went on, talking as much to himself as to me, "you *really* knew you'd had chicken soup. It could cure dandruff, burn out bellybutton lint, melt earwax, and dry up water on the knee. Some kosher cook, my old lady."

He was smiling reminiscently, and I heard myself saying, "But I thought you were Italian, Mr. LoCicero? . . ."

He smiled. "Call me Sam," he said. " 'Mr. LoCicero' is the name they cuss me by in the newspapers. And yeah, I'm a dago, for sure. Old Man was from Sicily—hell, so was most of the people in our block."

"But . . . ?"

"And I'm a Hebe, too." He stopped stirring, took a full spoonful taste himself, with no apparent discomfort, cocked his head a little to one side, and turned down the heat to simmer. "My old lady—she was Jewish. From some part of Poland. Or Russia. I never did get it straight."

"And that makes you *both?*"

He nodded. "Ask any rabbi," he said. " 'Your son, whose mother is a Jew, he is a Jew. Your son, whose mother is a stranger, he is a stranger.' Jewish law; they only go by the female side, if they're religious. And of course my old man's people, they only judged by the Papa's side of the family. So—both."

It was strange. He looked and talked like a character from a gangster movie most of the time. But now and then (and this was one of the times) he would seem to forget who and what he was supposed to be and let other people see just a tiny glimmer of something far different.

"You know Jewish religious law, then?" I said, consciously nudging him.

"Yeah," he said offhandedly, "I studied it some. My folks never had a fight, far as I can remember; I think they were about the only couple in the block that didn't. But she didn't always agree with him, either. So my old man, he saw to it I went to Sunday School and got to be an altar boy at St. Francis's—with the confirmation and all that, you know—while the old lady, makin' no fuss or anything, taught me Torah and to speak Hebrew (not just Yiddish, mind you; Temple Hebrew, for prayer) and how to observe Holy Days and all that."

He smiled again, remembering. "You know," he said, "almost from the time I could read, she made me make *Seder* and sing *Kol Nidre* at the right times. And I was circumcised, too. But I never was *Bar Mitzvah*."

"That's the coming-of-age thing, isn't it?" I said. "When you're thirteen?"

"Yeah." He nodded, the smile gone. "It hurt her bad, I think, that I wasn't *Bar Mitzvah*. But nothing she could do about it. No temple or synagogue in our neighborhood, you know? Anyway, it wouldn't of made much difference. I just ain't the religious type; never went back to St. Francis's, neither, after I got big enough to outrun Father Giuseppe."

"She must have been proud when you became a lawyer, though," I said. "I'll bet you were at the top of your class."

The last part of the smile vanished and it was like a cloud turning his face dark. "I was closer to the bottom," he said in a tight voice, "and she didn't know. Died a year before I even started in on that night law-school course."

"I'm sorry."

"Don't be. I'm sorry enough for both of us. . . ."

Suddenly, he made a quick, shuddering motion with his shoulders as though someone had dropped an ice cube down the back of his shirt. And as quickly as the unhappy look had come to his face, it was gone and the little smile was back on his mouth.

"And you," he said, "might have made a pretty good mouthpiece yourself, Sandy. Okay to call you that? Sandy?"

"Of course. I wouldn't, though. I had trouble making myself stick to two years of nursing school. It bored me."

"You a nurse?"

"Uh—yes." I kicked myself, mentally, for blabbing out

the very thing I wanted to keep to myself. "But I haven't worked at nursing for a long time. I left to be a secretary and then joined Union."

"Uh-huh."

Nothing else seemed to need doing in that kitchen, so we turned back toward the den. He paused to let me go through the door first, followed me in, and let himself down with a groan into the chair beside the one where I'd been sitting before.

"Gettin' old," he sighed. "Never get old, Sandy. It don't pay."

"I won't. My chart says I don't have much of a—" And that time I did manage to catch myself before *all* the words tumbled out.

The ones he'd heard had been enough for Sam, though. "Astrology chart?" he said, as though it were the most natural thing in the world. "Yeah, that's right; heard you and the kid talking about it before. I'm a hell of an eavesdropper, Sandy. I hope you don't mind." And I couldn't, with him smiling like an innocent shark. I could get to like this man, I realized; in a funny kind of a way, he was a lot like my father.

"So, the *chart* says you don't get old," he went on. "What's due to happen, does it say? Heart attack; stroke? Naw, you ain't built for either one of them." He looked me up and down with open appreciation.

"No," I said. "No stroke. No heart."

"What, then?"

"Accident. Before I'm thirty—which still gives me a good deal of time, believe it or not." It seemed the most natural thing in the world to tell Sam LoCicero things I had never told anyone else on earth. I could see why he was a successful lawyer. "Of course," I went on with it, "nothing's all that definite about the chart. No guarantee of success—or failure. Just a prediction of tendencies and probabilities, Sam."

He nodded thoughtfully. "Any particular way this accident's supposed to happen? Like, in a car—or maybe in the air, you being an airline stewardess."

I shook my head.

"Neither of those," I said. "Good strong signs against it. But water signs, those are bad for me. Very adverse."

He shrugged. "Stay off rich old men's yachts," he said,

"and you'll live to be a hunnerd. What about flying over water—that bad, too?"

"It could be. But I was careful when I picked the airline I wanted to work for. Union has no overwater routes. I know it's silly; most people think so—but, truth, I decided against TWA and Pan Am for just that reason."

Sam nodded. "Sounds reasonable as hell to me, kid," he said. "And I sure hope you *can* beat the rap. Because Buddy'd be one plenty messed-up guy if you went off and croaked before you was thirty."

I stared at him. He had said it so easily, so naturally, that I was almost tempted to accept the point and continue the conversation. But I couldn't.

*"Buddy? . . ."* I said.

"Buddy." And his voice was definite in a way that allowed no protest. "Don't tell me you don't go for him. I seen you two together, and it'd be a lie. And don't tell me he don't go for you, neither. The kid's kind of a jerk about a lot of things, but that dumb he ain't."

"Sam—you've only *seen* us. . . ."

"Once before. On Christmas. It was just one day—less, even—after he met you. And I was crocked, besides. Yeah. But don't let old Sammy kid you, Sandy. I was drunk, but I damn sure wasn't *blind* drunk."

I started to ask him something more, but decided to let it ride for the moment because there was something else that interested me more.

"Sam," I said, very carefully, "the way you're talking, you'd think Buddy was just in the other room, or late getting home from somewhere, instead of being lost, maybe cracked up, with everyone frightened to death. . . ."

The shark look didn't leave his face, but it was a somber shark now; a shark that had seen more things than it wanted to see.

"You and me," he said, "we can talk straight—right? About the kid, anyway. Stuff we might tell another way if there was anyone around to hear?"

"We can." I nodded. "Sometimes I just up and say things out when I don't mean to—embarrassing things, you know. But secrets are different. I'm no gossip, Sam."

"I know," he said. "Okay, then: I don't know exactly how come I feel this way, but I lay nine-to-one there's a grift—a joker—in this scam, somewhere."

"What makes you think so?"

He started to say something, but changed his mind and shook his head instead. "Nothing specific," he said. "Nothing you can put a finger on. But I know it's there. It's like when you're cross-examining some guy in court and he answers one of your questions exactly the way you thought he would, and he's saying what you really *think* is true—but right then, when he says it, a little bell goes off in the back of your mind and a voice tells you, 'The son of a bitch is lying.' That kind of a thing. . . ."

I nodded, very slowly. "Yes," I said, "I know what you mean. I don't hear bells, but I get the same feeling sometimes. For no reason at all. And so far, the feeling's always been proven right in the end."

"You don't buy the story either?"

"No. But not for that reason, Sam. Please don't laugh—no, you wouldn't, I needn't have said that—but I don't believe it mainly because it's not in Buddy's chart; his horoscope for that day, I mean."

For some reason, that surprised him a little. "You made a chart for the kid?"

"Yes."

"That's quite a bit of work, ain't it?"

"Not for everyone, really," I admitted. "But for me, yes, because I've never been on really friendly terms with mathematics and there's a whole lot of it in astrology. Just as there is in astronomy."

Sam nodded. "I know," he said. "There didn't use to be —in astrology, I mean, though. Not back in the old days— say in Arabia, where most of our own system started."

That stopped me. He had spoken offhandedly, as though he knew what he was talking about. But I couldn't imagine that he'd have an interest in astrology.

I wondered, abstractly, how many people had received a rude shock after dismissing him from consideration as an ignorant middle-aged lout. He was a smart man, Buddy's *padrino*. And *that* led me back to the prime subject.

"Sandy," he said, looking at me poker-faced, "Sandy, you were thinking one of those long, long thoughts. What about?"

"Oh, about Buddy," I said. "Wondering whether we could be right—about how much danger he's really in. And if we are, what would be the best thing to do for him when he gets home."

Sam nodded his head, a small and slow motion, never taking his eyes from mine. I had a momentary notion that he hadn't been fooled, that he knew I'd been speculating a bit about him. But if he thought so, he didn't seem to want to push the point. Instead, he accepted what I'd said at face value.

"Well, for one thing," he said, "just as a horseback guess, one of the best things for the kid might be you."

"Me?"

"You. You're a good-looking dame, all grown up and you got a good head on your shoulders. Yeah, I'd say that's just about what the kid *does* need. Christ knows he sure needs *something!*"

That irked me.

"Why," I said, "do you always call Buddy 'the kid,' and why do you say things like that about him, Sam?"

"What's better—I should just think them to myself, or maybe go around saying them behind his back? Look, Sandy, understand one thing: I'm on *his* side. And any time I criticize him, the truth is I'm kicking *myself.*"

I didn't follow. And it must have showed in my face.

"I'm his *padrino,*" he explained. "The godfather. That means—well, a sort of special relationship. Like, oh, Dutch uncle for some people, or sponsor for others. Only more so."

He grunted up on his feet, and lumbered over to the bar to fix himself a drink.

"If the kid's kinda confused about himself and what he's supposed to be doing—and for who, maybe—Sandy, it's my fault. Mine, and nobody else's. His pappy wasn't around when he was growing up, you know that. And his ma, well, Angie's okay. Damn good woman in a lot of ways, believe me. But there's things that come up that no dame can figure, or advise a man about, you see?"

"Buddy said his father would always take a phone call from him, no matter where he was. Or send him money any time he wanted it."

"Oh yeah, sure," Sam waved a paw, now folded around a swizzle stick, in the general direction of my comment. "Sure, Vanni did what he could. But he had a hell of an awful lot on his mind."

243

He turned around and came back to the chair with the drink, but did not sit down. "You know—a performer, trying to hold onto the top of the mountain. And slipping off, almost, the way Vanni did once, and then climbing back up. You don't get that done on a nine-to-five schedule, you know. Hell, almost *nothing* really gets done by nine-to-five guys. They're really just around for window dressing."

"I still don't see how that makes you responsible."

"Because I *said* I would be," Sam shrugged. "That's what the *padrino* is for. To be the pappy if the pappy ain't around, and to keep an eye on things even if he is. But if Vanni was busy with the career, so was I—with Vanni's career, and a few other performers' careers. And with my own, in the union."

"Yes," I said. "I can see how it might be, I suppose. It would take an awful lot of time."

"And it took more to *get* where I am than it does now to stay. Way things are today, I pretty much got it wired. One hand feeds the other. The union can provide financing for various entertainment and, oh, what you might call *leisure* projects, because the union is a hell of a lot richer than most banks. It's got money to spend and money to lend, and the top management of the union doesn't do either one without my say-so."

He paused to let me say something if I wanted to. But I didn't, and he went on.

"Being kinda in control of the union investment program," he said, "puts me in the position of being able to help my performers. And, playing it from the other side of the table, being the manager-lawyer-agent or whatever for some top performers makes it possible for me to do a favor to the union—or, anyway, for its investments—now and then. It took a while to get the setup together. But now, it's really a cinch."

"Only, while you were assembling it," I said, "Buddy was growing up and now you think you should have had more time for him, or made more time. Right?"

"That's pretty much how I see it. Bud's a good kid, Sandy. A real good kid. Only—this business aside, for the moment—I think he's heading in a direction that ain't right for him. Trouble is, I'm not sure what the right one would be. Or how I could help much, or get him to see it, if I did know for sure."

Sort of impulsively (or at least I wanted it to seem that way to him) I patted Sam on the cheek. "You're like a lot of people, Sam," I told him. "Like my dad, for one. Always feeling responsible for things they couldn't help. Anyhow, don't worry. As soon as we get Buddy back . . ."

But I never got a chance to tell Buddy's *padrino* what we were going to do as soon as we got Buddy back. The telephone rang. And everyone in the whole house not only stopped talking or making noise of any kind, but held their breath, too, They did that every time it rang, now.

Buddy's father picked up the call in the living room. I could hear him talking, but couldn't make out any of the words. And I didn't want to run to the parlor for fear of disturbing the call. So Sam and I stood still, straining our ears.

We didn't have to wait long, though. It seemed to me the call took a lot less than a minute, and when it was over, all hell broke loose.

Mr. Valentine slammed the phone down, said two or three words I'd just as soon not put on paper, and then started yelling.

"*Sam!*" he hollered, and I could hear him running toward the den. He came through the door looking as if he'd seen a ghost. "Sam! For Christ sake! That was some guy—he wouldn't say who or where he was calling from—who claims he's holding Buddy a prisoner! He says he was in the plane with Buddy and that he forced Buddy to land the thing, and he says if we don't pay up he's gonna take the plane back up *and push Buddy out of it.* Christ, Sam! What do we do?"

"Calm down, Vanni," Sam said. "What else did the guy say? How much money, and where do we deliver it?"

"Jesus, Sam, you think this is for real?" Mr. Valentine said, blinking rapidly. "You think they really got him somewhere?"

"I think we'd better not gamble that they *don't* have him," Sam said. "What did the guy *say,* Vanni?"

Mr. Valentine was looking stunned now. "He said two hundred and fifty thousand dollars. In cash. Small, unmarked bills, none bigger than a fifty. No bills in sequence. . . ."

Sam nodded, all business now. "Okay," he said. "No sweat about that. You're good for the dough—hell, you're good for twenty times that, or more. We can pick it up at the Federal Reserve or somewhere, Monday."

"No." Mr. Valentine said. "No, that's the thing, Sam. We don't have that long."

Sam looked puzzled. "Well, when, then?" he said. "And where in hell does he think we can lay hands on that kind of cash—in the size bills he wants—before . . ."

"*Tonight,*" Mr. Valentine said. "He wants it delivered by car in a part of the Nevada desert. It's got to be on time, and just the way . . ."

Sam was shaking his head violently. "He's nuts," he said. "We can't get it, and have it counted and all by that time. Besides, we'll have to bring the feds in on this now, and they should have time to mark it. Infrared or ultraviolet dyes; something like that. . . ."

"*Uh-huh.* And I bet that is exactly why the guy set the time limit," Mr. Valentine said. "Probably figures if he gives us time, we'd be able to bring off something cute that way. So he's deliberately nudging us."

Sam thought it over for the space of a minute while Mr. Valentine fidgeted. "Al Harlan," he said finally. Mr. Valentine nodded quickly, and Sam crossed the room and picked up the phone.

Sam talked for a few seconds, then slammed the phone down angrily.

"What'd he say?" Mr. Valentine asked.

"No soap."

"*What!*" Mr. Valentine couldn't believe it. "You gotta be kidding, Sam. Al knows we're good for the dough and he . . ."

". . . would probably be happy to do it for us," Sam cut him short. "Only Al's out of town. Some business thing that came up. Or something. You know how Al is. And nobody knows where to get hold of him."

"Christ."

"Him, neither," Sam said.

The two men stopped talking for a few moments, not looking at each other or at anything else, apparently. You could almost hear the sound of their minds working. And the time ticking by, toward the deadline.

I argued with myself. The call didn't really change a

thing. I still had the same reasons for doubting the whole situation; for wondering if someone was putting us all on. But somehow it *felt* different, now. Now there was a strange smell of *wrongness* about it all.

Maybe it was a gag, or some kind of confidence game on someone's part. But there was still the chance, no matter what anyone might think, that Buddy was in real danger— that he might actually be killed if we couldn't get it.

Something cold and damp seemed to spread over the center of my back.

And then the two silent men, Sam and Buddy's father, came to life.

Like twin puppets, moved by the same strings, they broke off their space staring, looked at each other—and said . . .

## Jack Dahlberg

. . . the *Stamp Fund*. One million, cash, just sitting there!

It was all I could think about, driving home from the studio that day. The Stamp Fund. The god-doubly-damned-in-spades *Stamp Fund!*

For an hour I had sat in my office, looking at it. And now, a mile away driving down the freeway, the sight of the money was still somewhere between the front of my eyes—which showed me the various turns and hazards of the road—and my brain.

The deal with LoCicero and the Valentine people for Dolly Diamond's appearance in *Sadie* had given me just the opportunity I needed to get my hands on the money. Or some of it, at least. After all, Papa himself had told me to use whatever I had to, to get her. Not to mention whatever the deal with the navy could cost. So whereas I had to keep a good chunk of it there just in case, at least I had an excuse for *some* of it to be missing. Not that Papa would be happy to see any of it go, God knows. Movie people are funny, the way they look at money. I had found that out very early, seeing and hearing some of the things I had as a kid around the studio.

Movie people can and will talk multimillion with perfect

aplomb, jabber about "collateralization" and "splitting the point—a mil each way, what's to argue?" They could be talking funny money—something out of a Monopoly game —as long as it's just figures in a corporate statement or a stock portfolio or an income-tax return made up by their business manager. But let the same people get their fingers on a real honest-to-God *dollar bill,* and it's Scrooge-Time-in-Tinseltown!

I have seen two big-name stars, each many times a millionaire in his own right, delay leaving a restaurant for as much as an hour while they tried to outfumble each other for the check.

I have seen one of the richest men in the industry order *real* mink to be used for a fur that was to be burned in a minor film sequence, instead of substituting a perfectly photogenic imitation—and then spend half the day crying to anyone who would listen because his gardener asked for a ten-dollar-a-week raise.

Irving Dahlberg was no different, really. And neither, I had suddenly discovered, was I . . . because I had gone to the studio with the idea of getting a start on the job of carting a chunk of the Stamp Fund away for Clara. I had opened the trick wall safe in the john, even started to pile some of the money into my attaché case.

But that was as far as I got. The thought of it momentarily overwhelmed me and I decided I'd wait just those few extra days until the *Sadie* contracts were signed. Because as I had begun putting the piles into my case, the Stamp Fund suddenly had become real money and I had gotten nervous. Clara would just have to wait a little longer for her payoff. Shoving everything back into the safe, I packed up my things and left.

I sat in the car a moment, the engine still running, before it registered that I was home and parked in the driveway. Waking up at last, I shut off the engine and headed for the door.

Clara was waiting for me.

And for a wonder, she didn't have a drink in her hand.

"It's about time you got here, Shorty," she greeted me, in her usual welcoming fashion. "Your father's been trying to get hold of you for twenty minutes. He's on his way here from New York and he . . ."

". . . wants me to come to the studio. Says it has to be in person. What about it. Sam? He'll be there in about an hour and a half; does that give us time?"

Sam glanced at his watch and thought for a minute.

"Well, yeah," he said, "I guess so. Depending on how long it takes you after that to get to the place in the desert where you're supposed to drop the dough. I'll line up a plane. . . ."

"Yeah," I said. "And a pilot—a good one who doesn't get lost or mess up using a small field to land in. A Lear would be the fastest way to get out there. But the hell of it is the nearest airport's too small for jets. It'll have to be something like a Beech or a Cessna. One of their two-engine jobs. And don't forget we need a car there, waiting when we arrive."

"Already got it. The FBI's lending us one. Already on the scene."

I didn't like that a hell of a lot.

"Why do they have to be in on it?" I wanted to know. "Look, they'll play along, won't they? No cute stuff with the guy who picks up the money. Because I won't take a chance on . . ."

"Yeah, yeah." Sam seemed a little edgy, though compared to me he was an iceberg. "They'll keep out, they said. But you can't ask them not to try to think of some way to spot whoever makes the pickup."

"The hell I can't! I told you . . ."

"Uh-huh. Only *nobody* tells the FBI—but nobody, Vanni."

"If that bastard sees someone spying on him, trying to tail him when he gets the dough," I said, trying not to do the shouting I wanted to do, "he'll think I double-crossed him. He'll . . ."

"Nobody's going to spot anybody. I got the top guy's personal word. They'll play that cool."

"What, then? . . ."

"I dunno. They'd of done the special-ink thing, I guess, if they had time. Maybe they're going to try to plant one of those electronic beepers. Or something like paint for the pickup car to get on its wheels so they can keep track of where it goes. You can't tell, and I can't do a hell of a lot of asking, you know."

I *didn't* know. "Why not?" I said. "If they're all straight-arrow with us, why shouldn't they tell us what they . . . ?"

"Because we ain't exactly straight-arrow with them. That's why," Sam said patiently. "The Stamp Fund, remember? Okay, so old Dahlberg does agree to lend you part of it when he gets out here. I figure he will, even if he wasn't too definite one way or the other on the phone. Just remember, either way, it's kind of a hell of a big risk for him. The money's in the hip pocket, you know?"

Sam glanced quickly, sideways, at the Hallowell girl when he said the last, trying to get the idea across to me without bringing her into the play. Okay. I could see why he wanted to be careful. No sense trusting a broad any further than you had to, and I saw what he was getting at.

Dahlberg had probably swindled that loot out of the company in a lot of ways he wouldn't want to discuss with the feds.

"What'd you tell the feds about where we were getting it, then?" I asked. "You know one of them'll be with me when I go out to Monarch. He's bound to see that's where I picked up the scratch."

"Yeah," Sam nodded. "But I covered that; told them ole Irving was such a buddy of ours—we're in business with him, you know, as far as the public is concerned—that he *borrowed* the money from friends of his back in New York and is flying it out here, personal."

"They buy that?"

Sam shrugged. "If they didn't, they did a good imitation. Just be sure the jerk who goes with you doesn't get to talk much to Dahlberg or see where the money comes from, there at the studio. I think you can ditch him in one office, or in the waiting room, while Irving *schleps* the dough from wherever he's got it stashed."

I took a deep breath. Christ on a crutch! What a lot of crap to go through to get money I could of raised just by selling a few shares of stock or making a quick loan on something light and movable if it had only been Monday instead of Saturday on a holiday weekend. Hell, even old Angie's jewelry would easily hock for enough to . . . *crap!* Suddenly I remembered.

"My God, Sam—I got to tell Angie! In all the frammis I forgot to fill her in; she's lying there in the . . ."

"Forget it," Sam said. "Sandy here gave her the scam."

I looked at the girl. "Hey, thanks, baby," I said. "It's a good thing you remembered. And it was nice of you to handle it; I guess Sam and me are sort of out of our tree today."

"That's not all you got to thank this girl for," Sam said. "She got a little phone call today. . . ."

"Phone call?"

Sam nodded. "Already somebody's giving out the number to the temporary line. So some asshole phoned and said he was someone in Sandy's family and could he talk to her."

"Yeah?"

"Yeah. Only when she answered, it was a lousy reporter from one of the scandal mags. And was this girl ever cool! Right away, she flags at me—all the time talking to the jerk, you know—and I get on an extension just in time to hear him offer to lay twenty-five gees on her, for an exclusive 'inside' story about how all of us acted during the hassle."

"Why, that . . . !"

"Twenty-five gees," Sam repeated. "And I think he'd of offered more if she'd haggled with him."

"What did you tell the guy?" I asked the girl.

"That if I ever met him in person," she said calmly, "I would take great pleasure in kicking his crotch up between his ears."

You know . . . I could see why my kid would dig this doll. "Sandy," I told her, "you're the greatest—I mean it. Not just for me, but for the whole family. I'll never forget it, either. Never! Hey, do you go for jewelry. Or maybe . . ."

She shook her head. I think she was actually kind of embarrassed Sam had brought it up. "No," she said in a very quiet voice. "I don't. Or anything. All I want, really, is just to get Buddy home."

Well, what the hell else could I say or do. Nothing. Believe it!

So I dropped the subject. But she was still one hell of a great little doll in my book. Why in the hell couldn't it be a dame like this for me, instead of . . .

"Hey, by the way, Sam," I said, "did we get any calls from Dolly while all this was going on? I been in and out, I mean, and . . ."

"No," Sam said. "No calls from Dolly."

"Okay. Good—I just . . ."

## Dolly Diamond

. . . wonder how long it will be before Johnny-Daddy decides to call me? I just wonder.

Okay, so something's happened to Buddy and he's worried about it. Sure. And probably rushing around making a lot of noise trying to get the kid back. But wouldn't you at least think he could find a minute to give me a call? After all, I'm going to be Buddy's stepmother. Right? If he ever gets around to *telling* them.

I looked at my watch and reminded myself it was time for me to be getting a cab to the theater. Only forty-five minutes until curtain. And it takes forever to get into the damn costume.

I threw on my poncho wrap, the one made of mink dyed to match my hair, and pinched the fire from the end of the cigarette. Then, as usual, I chewed the roach and swallowed it. That was all I could allow myself before a performance. Just one.

Not that I really needed a high before a show. I could still get excited—just like the first time it ever happened—thinking about the people out in the audience and the way they applauded my songs. The way they applauded my first entrance. The curtain calls after the third act.

Love, man! People love Dolly Diamond; the gorgeous, adored, desired girl in the mirror. I opened my eyes, very wide, at myself—at the image of the beautiful girl—and thought about love. The only real love. The only pure love. The love they give you when they know you're the best.

Yes. That could still give me a high, a bigger one than the happy time smoke, every single time. God, if they'd let me I would stand there, singing and listening to them love me for it, every hour of every day for the rest of my life.

If I could do that, I wouldn't need anyone. Not Johnny. Not Daddy. *Not anyone!* . . .

I looked at my watch again and five full minutes had

lost themselves somewhere, while I was looking in the mirror. Now it was *really* time to split. The door of the apartment banged behind me and I ran down the stairs instead of waiting for the elevator. But it was raining outside, and the doorman had trouble finding me a cab. Later. It was getting later and later . . .

"Here," I told the doorman. "Let *me* try."

He moved aside and I went as close as I dared to the curb, as close as I could without letting the rain get on my hair, and just *looked* at the passing cabs. With the eyes turned onto full power and the pathetic waif expression on my face.

It took me just six seconds—I was *counting*—to stop a cab with a fare already in the back seat. Some old guy, with white hair under his hat and a big belly taking up half his lap. "Please," he said, when he got the door open. "Won't you accept a ride to wherever you're headed, Miss Diamond?"

"Oh, *thank* you—you're so nice!" I threw a wink at the doorman as I turned to get in. Fuck Johnny. Fuck them all! You can get anything when they *love* you . . .

### David Strauss

. . . even when the world keeps turning into something out of the Arabian nights.

I rolled toward Gaby and took her breasts in my hands. An hour before, when I'd done that, they had turned into two volcanoes that erupted a purple ash of tiny spiders that grew larger and climbed onto my face. This time, they remained just breasts.

"My God," Gaby laughed, opening an eye and reaching for me, "don't you ever give up, David, darling?"

"You want me to?"

"No. I don't want you to. . . ."

Dahlberg's cabin at Malibu had some kind of electric heating, but it was off and we had broken in because Gaby didn't have a key—and of course she hadn't told Irving we were going to stay here. So we had had to build a fire in the living-room fireplace to keep from freezing, especially since Gaby insisted no one was to wear clothes inside the house.

The fire had burned down, now, and it was almost sundown. I thought for a moment it might be time to get some more wood from the big pile we'd found stacked in the garage, but it wasn't time to do that. Not right now. Gaby's hands on me, and my hands on her, knew it wasn't time to do anything like that.

The last red rays of sunset came through the window that took up the entire side of the room facing the sea. They set tiny points of color—twin messages from hell—in her eyes. I looked at the fires, fascinated, and she smiled, looking back.

Squeeze hard, she said. *Harder!* . . .

I did, thinking again of how strange but natural it had seemed to go with her, first to the hotel in the Marina and then here to the beach house, after last night at Angela Valentine's house. The night they'd found out about Buddy.

My memory of that night was not too good, of course. Not too good at all. In fact, my memory of anything—especially when the real and unreal kept getting mixed, as they continued to do on a pretty frequent schedule—wasn't too great these days.

"Harder," Gaby said again, pinching me under the thigh. *"Harder,* David. Bite me!"

I put the Valentine house out of my mind and turned from the fire points of her eyes, opening my mouth and drawing my lips back from my teeth.

*"Hallelujah!"*

Oh. God—that *choir.* The choir was back, and the noise in the next room; the noise of the party with its filthy voices and disgusting talk. I held my mind hard-closed against the sounds and brought my face against the softness of Gaby. I began to bite—and her breasts became two fat, squealing, fighting white rats who bit back at me and struggled to reach my throat. I bit more deeply, and the blood ran from their soft under-bellies, and . . .

*"David!"*

Suddenly the rats were gone, and the choir and the voices, and Gaby's voice was a high scream. I thought for a moment it was pain I heard, but I was wrong. In the faint remaining light I could see the teeth marks I had left on her nipples, a tiny break in the skin on one. But the scream had not been of pain.

"Hurt me!" she said, her voice octaves higher than it had been. "Hurt me, David. *Hurt* me!"

I closed my teeth on her again. Have another bite, David, darling . . .

"Hurt me, David, darling . . . *Hurt* me! There—there! *Hurt* me! . . ."

## Buddy Valentine

. . . hurt. Oh—*Jesus,* why in hell couldn't I have remembered to have Zeke throw some aspirin or something into the damn supplies?

Hey!

*Come on,* now, Buddy-boy. Try to act a little like a man, even if you're not one. *Hurt?* Crap! You got a little sprained wrist because, no matter how much instruction you've got on the subject, ditching an airplane in the open sea is one hell of a lot hairier than you'd expect, the first time you do it for real. So you popped the wrist. And it gave you a little trouble while you were getting out of the Cessna and getting the raft inflated and the supplies on board and then chopping holes in the ship to make sure it didn't float around for the next year or something—but, truth now, it really didn't hurt much at all until you had a lot of time to think . . . and a lot of ocean around you so there was nothing much to take your mind off it.

Chances are you wouldn't even notice it much if you were ashore. Right? Right.

So let's stop the nonsense and think about something else.

Right.

*What* else, damn it.

Time. Start with time. Check that watch again—right. My God, only *five minutes* since the last time I looked. Man, if I got to go on that way it's going to seem like the end of the century before the two days are up and old Zeke can buzz out here and be a hero by *schlepping* Buddy-boy's rosy little bod out of the drink.

Thirty more hours at least. Let's see: if I go on checking the watch every five minutes for thirty hours, that's . . . what . . . three-hundred and sixty more times I'm gonna be looking at it before then. *I'll go bananas!*

Five minutes.

I wonder—was it *really* just that long? Maybe the damn store lied to me about it being shockproof and waterproof.

255

After all, it was under salt water for a while when I missed my footing and went thrashing around in the sea before I managed to climb aboard the damn raft. And shock, too—it's on the wrist I popped. . . .

*Damn!*

There I go again, thinking about *that*. Aspirin. I sure wish to hell I'd . . . *no!* Got to think about something else. Something else. Something else. . . .

Radio. I wish I'd thought to take a radio with me. Just a little cheap-o pocket transistor, not a transceiver or anything like that. Too much temptation. Oh, for sure. You know it, man! If I had a transceiver I'd of been on it long ago, scrubbing the whole damn thing. Yelling for help.

Because—face it, Buddy-boy—I am scared right out of my tree. For sure!

Which is why I didn't bring one. That well, anyhow, I know myself. But I still wish I had a little pocket radio. Just to listen to some music, maybe, and pass the time that way. I could turn it to some station that had a news program. Find out if everything's going okay. If they're looking for Buddy-boy right on schedule the way Zeke and me planned it. I could do that, if I had a radio.

Sure. Oh, *sure*—and if the radio told me they *weren't* looking? Or if it told me *nothing?* What then, Buddy-boy. You *know* what then. Then, being a civilized, sophisticated, cultured, and fearless fellow like you are, you would exercise your reason. You would apply logic to the situation. You would meet it with those intellectual powers which differentiate man from the apes. In short, *you would fucking well panic!* And in about five seconds you would have the raft's oars out, and you would be burning up more energy than you can replenish from supplies on board, trying to paddle yourself ashore. That's what you'd be doing, baby. For sure!

For sure.

Yeah. . . .

. . . paddle. Paddle? *Paddle!*

Suddenly it was like I was lying on an anthill. I was scrabbling around with my hands. Around me. Under me. And around me again. I hurt the wrist even more—but hardly noticed it—before I could finally admit to myself something I hadn't even noticed until now.

*No paddles.*

Well, sir . . . that's a stopper. A real mind blower, man! Because it couldn't just be an oversight. Not that. And the paddles couldn't of been lost over the side while I was in the water or climbing aboard or tossing the survival gear out or anything. They're designed as part of the raft itself, designed so they're in sections and attached—inside the whole package—before it's inflated. And still attached afterward. They couldn't have been lost over the side.

So?

So . . . someone had to take them out. Remove them before the raft was packed into the whole survival kit. Leave the raft intact . . . but no oars. Nothing to go anywhere.

Zeke.

Sure—*Zeke!* Funny. He really *knew* Buddy-boy, that Zeke. Knew I might get spooked, get the bull horrors just the way I do have them right now, and try to paddle. And that if I did, I'd sure as hell get myself out of position. Off the drift line we'd figured so carefully from the current and drift charts before anything else. Be out of position, not where I'm supposed to be when he picks me up.

Sure. That's got to be it. Old Zeke—thinking every minute. Yeah.

Only . . . if that's the play, how come he didn't just *tell* me what he was going to do about the paddles? I'd of seen the point. He knew I would. Why the hell didn't old Zeke *tell* me?

And suddenly it was worry time again. Time to worry and sweat. Oh, for sure—sweat. Because that sun is hot, man! I remembered what Zeke had told me. How he'd warned me about that. Warned me that there'd be one hell of a temptation to respond to the heat by taking off all my clothes—and how, if I did, I would be dead before the end of the day from the combination of dehydration and sunburn, no matter what kind of burn cream and water I had brought with me.

Sure. Old Zeke—he knew. Old Zeke was my buddy. My *amigo*. What kind of crap was I trying to talk myself into, doubting the guy? Why would he have pounded so much survival knowledge into my head if he wasn't on *my* side? If he wasn't . . .

*Stop that!*

But . . . damn it . . . the sun is hotter than hell. Maybe

257

it's time for a little water. Yeah. Maybe so. Maybe. Only . . . it could get to be a long time between drinks before this is over. A *long* time, even with that solar still Zeke put into the kit.

So let's just keep a cool unit, Valentine.

Let's just tough it out, Buddy-boy.

No drink, not yet. Not until you *really* need it. And no more driving yourself nuts with worrying about stuff you can't control and that won't happen, anyway. And no more feeling sorry for yourself. It's that kind of crap got you into the soup in the first place.

No.

No way!

No more nothing. Just lie still. Just wait. Just lie here and stop thinking at all. About anything. Just relax. And close the eyes. And untense the muscles. And settle down. . . .

### Irving Dahlberg

. . . to wait.

That was all Irving Dahlberg had to do, now. Wait. The light was gone—days are short in winter, even in California —and I had not turned any lights on in Jackie's office. I was alone, in the silence, waiting for the detective to phone me.

*Ah, God!* This is the fate of a giant, never to be satisfied —not completely—with anything. No single day to let yourself rejoice. Not even on a day as successful as *this* one. And if ever a man had just cause to be pleased with the work of a few hours, it was Irving Dahlberg right now. Yes!

A pleasure was there, and a laughter, deep inside me. I could almost hear it in the silence, as I could still see the frustration and the anger in the face of the guinea. So clearly; the image dancing on the dark pane of my mind just as it had done hours earlier.

The great Johnny Valentine—humbled. Beaten, and willing to take orders again from Irving Dahlberg after all the years of telling the world what a Big Man Johnny Valentine is. Ah, God. *Yes.* Oh, yes . . . oh, yes.

A satisfaction. A satisfaction and a *mitzvah,* to see that

arrogant face of his pleading. Not even when he needed that one movie part to begin his career again, not even then would he plead.

Did he know, that time, that it was his wife who got him the part?

*Anne*. She was more than a woman, that one; a legend, even today—yes, even today. *More* than other women, and I wanted her. Irving Dahlberg wanted her, and she knew it. But she had married the guinea when he left his first wife and even when they fought and even when she was not true to him, she did not come to me.

But then he needed that part, and he knew it was a part that might have been written with him in mind. Perfect for him. Perfect to put him on top again. He offered to act the role for no money. Offered even to *pay us* to let him play that part.

I turned him down. Oh, yes—I *knew* he could do it. Too well I knew. But I wanted him to beg, and when he would not beg I turned him down. And then Anne Morgan came to Irving Dahlberg. And she did not beg; she *promised,* and I knew she did not lie.

She offered what I wanted in return for what her husband wanted. And I settled. Yes, I wanted Anne Morgan even more than I wanted to see the guinea beg me. And yes, what Anne gave me was value for value. Yes.

But always I was determined that one day I would see the guinea beg. And so it has happened. *A satisfaction.* . . .

I had been holding the cigar unlighted in my mouth, but now it seemed time to light and enjoy it as I waited for the call. The suddenness of the flame in the darkness made my eyes blind for a moment, and in the blindness I could see and hear it all again, just as it had been. . . .

"Irving, thanks—you'll never know. I appreciate what you're doing for us."

"Sure, Johnny. Sure! What's a quarter of a million cash to us?"

"A lot, when you haven't got it and it's the middle of a long weekend with everyone out of town, and you're running out of time."

"Ah . . . huh. Yes. *Time*. Well, time for us to get the money now, and count it."

I had touched the switch, in my bust, which still sat on

Jackie's desk, and the washstand wall moved aside. Valentine and I took the suitcase he had brought and went in to count out $250,000 of the money.

Having done so, we came back out into the office itself and I pushed the button again to close the panel, and we set the suitcase down on Jackie's desk. Then and only then did I permit myself to look at his face.

It was a worried face—the shortness of time was gnawing at him, forcing him to glance at his watch again and again —but there was no true humility there. He still thought the money was to be his for the asking; that Irving Dahlberg was his to command.

I spoke slowly, tasting the words and his reactions. "Now then, Johnny," I said, "I'm glad I could help you this way. I know how *important* your son is to you. But business is business. There are one or two little formalities. . . ."

He paid too little attention. His hands were already touching the suitcase, as if to close it and be gone. "Sure, Irving," he said. "I got a check. Already made out, dated as of Tuesday. That'll give me and Sam Monday to get the dough together. It won't be any trouble, then. . . ."

"Check?" I registered surprise with a gesture and an expression so hammy I could almost hear a director shouting to cut the action. But this was real, not on film, and I didn't care. "What *check?* Johnny, Johnny boy! Did Irving Dahlberg ask you for your *check?*"

"Well. But . . ."

"What—you thought this was a *loan?*"

That finally got through to him. He looked at me and his hands stopped the mindless playing with the fastenings of the suitcase.

"Well . . . *sure,*" he said. "I couldn't ask you to . . ."

"And you *didn't!* But Johnny—this money, it's a *gift.* A gesture, a token of my affection and respect for you. Personal. You and me, Johnny, we go back a long way. *Remember?*"

Yes. *Oh, yes!* He truly did remember—as I had never forgotten. Yes! And it was then that I saw at last the beginnings of the fear, of the begging, in his eyes. I smiled my blandest smile.

"What's a favor between old friends? What's a quarter of a million, *cash?* Eh, Johnny boy?"

"Uh—well, uh, thanks, Irving. I don't . . ."

"Johnny, *forget* it!" I waited a beat. Enjoying. And then

I sprang the trap. "Oh, sure, there's one little thing. A little favor you might do me, if you really feel obligated."

The fear in his eyes took solid form. His hands, no longer moving, curled around the lid of the suitcase and whitened as he gripped. There is no hate without fear—no, and so my gladness deepened as I saw the beginning of the hate.

"Johnny," I said, "you're a real big man with the current administration. *Big!* No, don't deny it; we both know you are. Who needs phony modesty? A very big man with the very big people in Washington, Johnny. Nothing you couldn't get from the president himself, if you asked. Nothing, even, you couldn't get for a good *friend.*"

Little by little, he was starting to see. Oh, yes . . . He stood silent, waiting for me to go on.

"But me, I'm out of luck. Wrong side of the political fence, eh? Backed the wrong horse last election. So when I need a favor—just a little *favor*—from the big men, I can't even *buy* it. For Johnny Valentine, *anything;* for Irving Dahlberg, *nothing.*"

"Irving," he glanced at his watch, and I could almost read the time in his face; the hours were minutes now, and they were ticking away. "Irving—please! What do you want?"

I went right on smiling. "Something small. Small for them, anyway; *big* for me, because it means the difference between making a very important picture, one I have wanted to do myself for a long time, and not making that picture. A small thing. . . ."

*"Please."* The word was not loud. Not arrogant. Not self-confident. The Johnny Valentine who had walked in owning the studio, owning Irving Dahlberg—that Johnny Valentine was gone. Now there was this small, middle-aged, fearful man. This *begging* man. . . .

"The navy," I said, when the moment had been thoroughly savored. "The navy . . . some of their ships; I need them for the picture. You know the one. *Boarders Away!* A good picture for *them,* good for their public relations; they come off a winner. They should jump at the chance. But do they? No. For Irving Dahlberg, who backed the wrong horse at election time, *no.* And I can't make that picture, the way it should be made, the way *I* make pictures, unless I can use some of their ships. In the Caribbean. . . ."

The hate and the fear were so solid in him now that

261

they turned his face gray-white; for a moment, I almost backed away.

But I went on: "A word from you, Johnny; a *word*. That would do it."

"Irving—that's crazy!" He had finally found his voice. "I can't just snap my fingers and tell the navy to give you ships to make a movie. They'd tell me to go fly a kite."

My smile stayed in place.

I could see the clock ticking in his brain and the money, the cash, turning fire-hot under his hands, and the pressure of the blood surging up against his neck where the muscles stood out in cords, keeping it from the too-white face. There was murder in him—hate enough for the murder. Oh, yes. But there was need, too. For Irving Dahlberg's money; for Irving Dahlberg's permission to close that suitcase and take the money away to buy back his son's life. And the need was too great, too strong for the hate. And so he begged.

"Irving—I can't. Please, there's no time now. We'll talk tomorrow. When I get back tonight, even. But not now; I can't. . . ."

"You can," I said, in a voice so quiet. So certain. So far beyond argument. I was not smiling anymore. I was not arguing. I did not bargain, and he knew I would not budge. Yes; he knew.

"*You can*, Johnny."

We looked at each other, silent, for one more moment. And then the tension of his shoulders and his arms and his back broke. The hate shriveled and soured back to a tiny thing, too small to be dangerous. And only the fear and the need were left.

"All right," he said. "You'll get your ships."

I said nothing.

"As many as you want," he said, "wherever you want them, whenever you say. All right? Do you want it in writing?"

"Writing? Between friends? *Johnny!* . . ."

"Why not? I could call Sam, tell him to draw up a contract. . . ."

I smiled, triumph surging in the center of me, and played out the last few lovely seconds of the game.

"From *you*, Johnny," I said, "what do I need with a

contract. I got your word. It's enough. Between *friends like us* . . ."

He looked at me one more moment; the single beat of a heart. And then the game was done. I stood still, already replaying the scene in my head while my eyes watched him snap the lid of the suitcase closed, fasten its straps, and turn to walk out of the office.

The door stopped him. It would not open.

I waited, just long enough to let him understand and look back at me over his shoulder, and then pressed the "privacy" button on the desk panel. There was an audible *click* as the lock was released.

He turned the handle slowly, still looking at me, and then he was gone, hurrying from the building to the parking lot where a limousine was waiting to take him to the airport.

And it was curious. . . . For just a moment, all my joy and my satisfaction were gone; I felt a stillness and almost an emptiness, standing alone in the room where I had won.

And it was all back with me again, filling me and expanding in Irving Dahlberg, the giant, who does not fear and does not lose and can never be beaten. *Irving Dahlberg!*

Soft laughter rose in my throat again, sitting there in Jackie's chair later and smoking the fine cigar as I waited for the detective to phone me. Johnny Valentine would not forget. He would hate me, but pride would make him do as he had promised. I would have the ships; I would make my picture. And the memory would burn like acid in the blood for Johnny Valentine each time he heard the name *Boarders Away!*

Forever! . . . Yes. Oh, yes.

The darkness was sweet and comforting, with the strong and reassuring presence of the studio—all the things that are the studio around me, silent and waiting to become a part of creation. Of the act which makes men more than beasts—the equal of God. *Power;* the greatest blandishment, the greatest temptress. Power to build. And power to destroy.

The telephone had rung three times before I heard it. Jackie had had the bell changed, tuned to the level of a faraway chime. But I knew I might have missed it even if it had been the knell of Big Ben. The power of God.

*The potency of God . . .* I picked up the receiver before the fourth ring.

"Mr. Dahlberg?"

"Yes. Is this Murphy?"

"Yes, sir—I understood I was to call you direct instead of forwarding my report to you."

"That's right." I took the cigar from my mouth and was surprised to notice that I needed to moisten my lips before speaking again. "Have you found her?" I said.

"Yes, sir. There was no trouble. . . ."

"Where is she?"

"At your beach house."

"*My* beach house?"

"The one at Malibu, sir. On the road below the . . ."

"I know where it is. I was just a little bit puzzled. I haven't been to the beach house for quite some time."

"Yes, sir." He paused and I wondered if he was waiting for me to give him a cue. But apparently he was only flipping through notes he had made. "She moved in there—ah—about two days ago, according to the police. They did not question this since they were aware that she was an, ah, an associate of yours, sir."

"Yes, go on."

"It was simple to find her. The luggage was delivered there by a handyman who worked at the hotel where she checked in shortly after arriving in the Los Angeles area."

"I see. Thank you." I drew in a deliberate mouthful of the cigar smoke. Let it out. "Is she there now?"

"I—think so, sir. I only left a few minutes ago."

"You didn't frighten her, let her see you or realize you were . . ."

"No, sir. I was careful. However, the man was out of the house when I arrived and he returned unexpectedly just after I had finished checking the premises. I do not believe he . . ."

"*Man? . . .*"

"Uh—yes, sir." My reaction had been too sudden, too little controlled. The snooper now knew I hadn't expected to find a man with Gaby. I made a mental note never to use this detective agency again. "He entered the house after passing me. The place where I was waiting. He did not knock."

"I see. Thank you."

"The light was not good, Mr. Dahlberg, but I'm certain I recognized him. It was Mr. David Strauss, sir. The actor . . ."

"Thank you."

I hung up the phone without waiting for him to say anything else. Already he had said too much. I took the cigar from my mouth and in the darkness, the dancing of the burning end—leaving a trail of light from each movement—told me that my hand was shaking. Yes. It was too . . .

## Buddy Valentine

. . . damn much. Or not enough. And I couldn't be sure just which it was. I wanted to ask one hell of a lot of questions, but something down inside me just didn't seem to think this was any time for them. This was, the something said, one hell of a good time to keep the Valentine mouth shut. . . .

"The raft—we *want* it?"

It was the crewman, the big beefy kid with Coast Guard and ASR patches sewn on his flight coveralls. But he was talking to the pilot of the copter. And the pilot shook his head, not even looking at me.

The crewman shrugged, burrowed into a locker on the starboard side of the helicopter's cabin, and came up with an air rifle. He aimed it almost offhandedly out the cargo hatch where Buddy-boy had recently made his somewhat undignified entrance, and popped off two shots—which I couldn't even hear over the ripping-leather sound of the blades.

*Good-bye, raft.*

Then he turned back, gave the pilot a nod, and the pilot shifted the pitch control. Five seconds later the drowning bit of rubberized fabric that had been my home for nearly two days had ceased even to be a smudged punctuation mark on the face of the sea as we climbed in a long curve toward what I guessed was the Monterey peninsula.

And then we had reached altitude and the pilot had time for me.

He grinned. "I'm Deac Hawkins," he said, "and that overgrown hoist jockey back there's Willie Wojinski. Welcome aboard!"

I squirmed around to shake hands with Wojinski, who had handled the crane hoist that lifted me from the raft and aboard the copter.

"Thanks," I said, meaning both of them. "I'm Buddy Valentine—and if you guys ever need anything, like a kidney or a heart for transplant or anything, just help yourself to mine! I figure I *owe* you. . . ."

He grinned again. "Commencing to get a little lonely down there, huh?" And then, just like the slapstick-comic stage gesture, he did a double take. "Buddy *Valentine?*"

Oh-oh.

That thing down inside was hitting the alarm buttons again. Only, I still didn't know why. Or how I should be playing the gig. Now—why the hell would he be *surprised?*

"Yeah," I nodded, pretending not to notice. "I'd just about given up the idea of anybody spotting me. Man, I guess I really screwed up good. Where was I, anyway?"

If he heard the question at all, it must not have registered.

"Buddy Valentine!" he repeated. And then, "Oh . . . Christ on a crutch! *Willie!*"

He leaned over his shoulder and yelled for the crew chief. "Yeah?"

"Willie—work the base, quick, on B channel, and cut me in. *Move,* damn it!"

Big Willie moved. A moment or two later, Deac Hawkins was talking to someone ashore. I didn't catch all of it because he was using his helmet mike and keeping his voice down a little to avoid blasting into it. But the words I did make out were enough. . . .

". . . Valentine," he was saying. "Ocean . . . miles off Point Lobos, vector 221 . . . raft . . ." There was a long pause; I couldn't hear what his base was telling him, but it seemed to make him impatient. "Negative, *negative!*" he said then. "Get on. . . . Immediate. . . . FBI. . . ."

FBI!

Oh . . . *wow!*

". . . affirmative. ETA Oh-Niner. . . ." And then he broke off suddenly to look at me, the long up-and-down. "You *look* okay," he said, yelling again but not into the

266

mike. "You in good shape? Any problems—base wants to know."

"Yeah," I said carefully. "A little thirsty and I could use a meal. Oh—yeah—I think I sprained my wrist a little when I ditched. Nothing serious."

He nodded, and told the base about that.

And then he was off the air and looking at me again.

"Hey, mister," he said. "I don't wanta seem nosy, but— did you say you *ditched* out there? Alone? I mean . . . nobody was with you when you put it down?"

The sky was clear, but the fog around Buddy-boy was getting thicker by the minute.

"*With* me?" I said, hedging. "I don't . . ."

I felt something nudging my side and looked around. It was Willie, leaning up from the cabin and poking a newspaper in my direction. I took it, and he just stood there, watching, while I unfolded the front page . . . it was the San Francisco *Chronicle*. . . .

"VALENTINE BEING HELD!"

Oh.

Sweet.

*Jesus . . . !*

For a moment, I couldn't seem to focus on the story that went with the two-inch headline. And when I did, the words didn't seem to make sense. Being held? *Being held!* But . . .

I looked up to find both Willie and Deac staring at me.

"But . . . I don't . . . Christ, who said I was *being held?*"

If they answered, though, I didn't hear them. Because the moment I said it, man, I *knew* who it had to be. Who else? The only other dude in the world who knew where I really was. The only one who could be sure I wouldn't turn up and blow the deal for him. . . .

*That damn Zeke!*

It fell into place, now. Why the timing was off: Zeke hadn't missed the rendezvous point, and I wasn't out of position the way I'd been scared I might be back there in the raft. That son of a bitch! He wasn't coming—ever! And that was why he'd been acting so weird just before I took off.

Why, that bastard . . . when I got ashore I'd . . . I'd . . .

*Nothing.*

I would *nothing;* nothing at all. Ever! Oh, for sure—the rotten bastard, he had me by the balls! Blow the whistle on Zeke? *Sure*—and let the whole world know Buddy-boy Valentine is a grandstanding phony who set up a cheap, lousy publicity stunt to grab off some attention he couldn't get any other way.

*That damn Zeke!*

And there wasn't one thing in the world I could do about it. Not a damn thing. . . .

"You—weren't out looking for me back there, were you," I said to Deac. But as a statement, not a question.

He shook his head, looking somber and thoughtful. "Routine patrol, Mr. Valentine," he said. "One we make over that sector about three times a week. They *were* looking for you—before the payoff thing turned up—but they were looking ashore. In the mountains and the valleys, Your flight plan. . . ."

I nodded slowly.

"Yeah," I said. "My flight plan. . . ."

And then I hesitated, just for a moment. I was going to lay it on him, now. I was going to Tell the Tale just the way I had rehearsed it—before the flight and while I was bobbing around down there in the raft—and once the words were out there would be no way, ever, to take them back. No way. Ever.

I looked at him out of the corner of my eye. He seemed like a decent guy. About my age, I guess; a Jay-Gee lieutenant in the Coast Guard. He'd picked my bod out of the ocean and now he was taking me ashore and he was a nice, average cat who was doing a job and probably having a pretty fair time at it and if I *really* rapped with him, I mean really laid the whole trip on him straight, he probably wouldn't understand it at all. He wouldn't be able to figure out *why* the hell I'd done it in the first place. Wouldn't dig it at all.

And why not? Because there was this one big difference between us: this guy, this Deac Hawkins, Lt. (jg) USCGR, he was a *man*. And this other guy, this Buddy Valentine, non-noted young singer, he *wasn't*.

Oh . . . God.

God!

And then I heard the words coming out of me. . . .

268

". . . got screwed up," I was saying, "in the dark; I guess I must of flown the reciprocal on the VOR. And when I finally missed my second checkpoint—well—I guess I kind of blew it or something. I wouldn't of really been in trouble, though—I could have made it okay—except when I tried to cross-feed the fuel the valve must of been stopped or airlocked or, like that, because both engines quit. I was low, almost on the water anyway, so I didn't have time to try to get them turning again. I just sent a Mayday and got ready to . . ."

*On and on and on and on and on.*

Weird trip. I was sitting there, doing the talking, with Deac nodding at me every now and then and seeming to believe it. And at the same time I was sitting 'way off somewhere, listening to myself and wanting to throw up.

Buddy-boy Valentine. . . .

Junior Birdman.

Senior bullshitter.

But why should it bother me now? Why? What was different? I'd been bullshitting and conning and all the rest for so long now, hell, I . . .


## Johnny Valentine

". . . could hardly tell the difference. Even with a whole line of stakeouts in the area," I said into the phone. "No one could make out any license numbers on that jeep. It whipped in beside the signal fire just a minute or two after I lighted it. And there was only one guy in it. He was covered up pretty well. Nobody got much of a look at him, even when he hopped out to snatch the bag. But he *did* say again that he'd get Buddy back to us in one piece. Now I guess we just have to wait and see if he's for real."

"Yeah, guess so. Listen, they weren't able to see where the jeep went after it left you?"

"Guess not—they weren't figuring on anything like that. A back-country crossroads, you know; they really thought someone was going to drive up in a car or something. So they didn't have anything to chase the jeep with, when it cut out cross country."

There was a wait, and I could almost hear Sam thinking.

"Okay, then," he said. "I guess you're right—there's nothing much to do but wait."

"Yeah, there is," I said.

"What's that?"

"Is old Steve Pappas spending the whole New Year's weekend in town?"

". . . Christ, Vanni, I don't know. Maybe."

"Well, early as you can, why don't you make a couple of calls and find out. And if he is, Sam, tell him I decided to go ahead."

*"Huh?"*

"The Priapus deal. I decided it's the thing to do if we—well, you, anyway—can get all the details worked out. In fact, I wanta get the show on the road just as quick as you can arrange it. He hasn't lined up anyone else, has he?"

There was another pause.

"You sober, Vanni?" Sam asked.

Now what the hell kind of a question was that? "Of course I'm sober," I said. "What do you think, I go around trying to rescue my kid while I'm bombed?"

"No," he said, "I don't think that. But—well, Vanni, ain't this all kind of sudden? And at sort of a funny time? I mean, screwing around with a *business* deal before we know if Buddy's gonna be safe?"

"Yeah, it's sudden. And yeah, the timing's way out and that's just why this is the time I picked to make up my mind. I'm straight, Sam. And nobody, but *nobody,* is kidding. In fact, the whole thing's tied up in a neat little parcel. You might say I got a little *help* making up my mind."

Sam still didn't understand, but I'd made my point. He knew I was for real.

"Well, all right, then. I'll call Celebrity Service and see if they know whether Mr. Stavros Pappadopoulos is here— or where we can get hold of him if he's not. I'll check anything with you, anything that puts a new angle in the deal, before we really commit ourselves, though."

"No, don't do that. Use your own judgment; I'll take your word for it that things are kosher. Just get it done, as fast as you can."

"Listen, Vanni . . ."

"What?"

He wanted to ask me a question. He wanted to know what all the hurry was about. He was short of information, and that was an unusual situation for Sam-baby. Well, let him wonder.

Maybe I'd clue him in later, when we could be private. And maybe not.

"Nothing," he said finally. "I'll get the ball rolling. You coming back here tonight or staying in Vegas?"

"Staying here. I'm bushed—they set up a room for me and another one for the fed, here at the hotel. And Sam—give Angie the word, huh? Everything's going to be okay."

"Yeah. I think so, too. I'll tell her, Vanni. . . ."

"Later."

I chopped the receiver back into its rack and got out of the booth. Okay, then. All right. Crazy . . .

There was still some action going on in the casino.

I didn't really feel tired; just—hell, I couldn't really be sure *how* I felt. Confused, maybe. More than anything else. Like I was being shoved, but couldn't be really sure who was doing the shoving. I had a little money with me, and I could always cash a check.

I started in, headed for the craps table. But I never made it. Talking about it to Sam (or avoiding the subject, really; just telling him what I wanted to do) and even before, when it was happening, I had thought I felt something big about what Dahlberg had made me go through for a lousy bag of money. I had been able to shift that part of my head into neutral. Let it hum along, idling, while the rest of the parts of me stayed at the party, pushing that crazy deadline out to the desert pickup spot; sweating out the contact, and worrying about whether it could all turn out to be for nothing. But now it hit me—really hit me. And, baby, I mean it was the worst.

Yeah, sure; I have known some true revolving sons of bitches in my day. There are even quite a few people wandering around loose in the world who hang that kind of a jacket on *me*. On Johnny-baby.

But now I knew. Now I had well and truly come face to face with the True Product; with the pure and uncut item. Absolute, cynical, self-propelled bastardy. Playing with my kid's life! Blackmailing me—setting me up where saying no to what he wanted meant my son would probably wind up dead.

Standing there, hearing him, the first thing that had popped up on the front of the bone-mounted computer was a card with the word "HIT" on it, in big black letters.

Hit. Contract. The *finger*. . . .

271

But that idea lasted only a second or two. Just arranging for old Irving to be taken suddenly dead—that wouldn't even the count. No way! By God, I wanted the time to *enjoy* him.

Somewhere along the way I had a stray thought about dropping the whole thing and telling Irving to take a flying leap. He couldn't *make* me keep the promise. But of course the old bastard had me there, and he knew it. Because it *was* a promise, and he knew damned well I'd have to keep it. If I didn't, I'd lose something that makes me tick. And if that happened, the old bastard would have won anyway.

It had taken me ten minutes, not much more, on the ride out to the desert, to come up with something that would let my feelings off the hook. I walked around it, sniffing and trying to find some real flaw, the rest of the afternoon and evening. But I couldn't come up with much of anything.

So this was how it was going to be: the kiss-off for Irving Dahlberg, the movie mogul from Monarch. The kiss-off. The whiz. The long goodbye. Starting with (a) the trouble Sam had suggested, holding up release of *Sadie* when the flick was finished; and going on to (b) moving production on the television projects to some other studio, with as much fanfare as I could arrange, to be sure nobody missed the nature of the insult to Monarch; (c) making the deal—as quickly and quietly as possible—with old Pappas, to get into the Priapus action; and (d) edging around at the same time to see how much trouble a minority stockholder—like me, for instance—can make for a big public corporation like Monarch Pictures, Inc.

For the moment, I couldn't really tell you just how the thing could be worked—how any of those angles could give Dahlberg any permanent grief.

But I been around a hell of a long time now; more years than I want to remember, you know. And if there is one thing I have noticed, it is that the further you get into a particular situation, the more information you pick up. And the more information you pick up, the better chance you've got to really shake the nowhere tree on someone.

Ohhhhhhhh—*yeah!* The money stayed in my pocket and I turned around and walked out of there; out of the casino and out of the hotel and out to the highway. There weren't too many cars buzzing by, that time of morning. I got a little time to walk—and glance up, now and then.

It was a cool night. Almost cold. I didn't meet anyone I knew. And I had a hell of a lot of minutes, all strung together like beads—minutes and hours—to do a lot of serious thinking.

# The 7th House

*Partnerships, contracts, marriage, unions,*
*lawsuits, open enmities,*
*dealings with other persons . . .*

---

*Forecast: Dolly Diamond will stop at nothing to make
sure that Johnny Valentine is bound to her by legal contract. Gaby du Main will again trade partners, keeping it
all in the family. And Irving Dahlberg, now basking in
the glow of victory, has not yet begun to suspect what that
sweet vengeance will end up costing him.*

*In the Seventh House, many lives will change drastically,
and keep on changing. . . .*

---

### Sandy Hallowell

I must have fallen asleep finally, in the big chair, sometime before dawn.

The dream—naturally there was a dream—was the same
one I keep having when too many people want too many
things in too little time. The insecurity thing, with me running down the street and people tearing various bits of
clothing off me until I am, as our British cousins so aptly
have it, starko.

Only this time the snatching-and-subtraction didn't end
with the last of my clothing. Cold, moist hands kept reaching
out for me. I could feel the wetness and the soft slimy touch
as they plucked at my skin and I began to scream. . . .

"*Sandy—wake up!*"

I wanted to. I tried to. But I just couldn't seem . . .

"He's *home!*"

It was Mrs. Valentine's voice, and she was shaking me. The words finally got through. I think I hit the floor running. . . .

Buddy was still just inside the front door.

Maybe a careful analysis of a tape recording of the general babble that followed would yield a coherent version of each individual's words. And maybe not. To me, even though sleep was as close as an eye-blink of memory, it was like the sound made by the sea or the jumble of comment in a store at Christmastime. Only the emotion really comes through. And the emotion was clean, good, and honest—just about the first of its kind I'd come across for a long time.

I stood on the periphery, watching but really not seeing much of anything but Buddy's face.

He was smiling. He was whiskery. He looked sunburned, and very tired.

The family seemed to be competing for parts of him.

His father was in the middle, of course. He had the biggest part—a bear hug locked around Buddy's torso. Buddy was returning the hug as best he could, but his mother was everywhere at once. Mostly she seemed to be alternating between long kisses on his forehead and cheeks and shorter ones on other assorted bits of his face. Buddy blinked when necessary and bent his head in her direction—less by choice than because she had a lock around his neck and was pulling him toward her. Even Sam LoCicero was in close, occasionally mussing Buddy's hair and grinning his wide-mouthed grin. If he had reservations about the entire matter —and I knew he'd had them once—they were evidently in storage for the moment.

Of those present, only a man in what looked a bit like a police uniform (only it was blue-gray) and a rumpled, bald man in a business suit, whom I recognized as one of the FBI agents detailed to the house, stood as much as a fraction of an inch apart.

I could feel myself grinning, and I remember being just a little bit surprised at my face acting that way without letting me in on its intention.

"Hey . . . *Sandy!*"

Buddy had an eye open, momentarily—his mother was

kissing some other part of him—and he was looking across his father's shoulder at me. "Hi!"

"Hi, Buddy."

"You been here all the . . . I mean . . ."

"All the time."

"Great! Uh . . . I . . . " But it was no time for conversation or explanations or anything of the kind. I saw one hand which must have been his poking out of the general clasp of arms and bodies, and I took it and held on. It was cold, that hand. And wet. Not like Buddy's hand at all—more like the ones that had clawed at me in the dream —and for a fraction of a moment I wondered if I were holding hands with someone else.

But the clasp tightened and—did you ever notice how easy it is to identify another person just by their hand in yours, if you really know them? I hadn't, really, until then. But it's true. . . .

"Well . . ."

I don't know who said it. In fact I don't even know how long all the body clutching and general exclaiming—or the hand holding on my part—had gone on. But of course it had to end sometime. And the word was a sort of prelude signal. Gradually everyone began to sort themselves out of the huddle. Buddy was, for a second or two, unclutched and unsupported—except for my hand, which he continued to hold. He dragged me closer to him and I moved in the indicated direction.

"Hi . . . hon."

Whoa. That stopped me. Caught me up short. Because there was something just a little bit . . . *wrong* . . . with the way he said it. Or maybe with the words themselves.

See, we weren't at the "hon" or the "dear" or the "darling" or any of the later accustomed-word stages. Does that make any kind of sense? I don't know. It's always seemed to me that there are times and points in knowing each other that people reach by degrees, sort of one-degree-at-a-time. It's part of getting acquainted; getting to know each other. The words come, then, sort of naturally—or maybe you even make up a word or two along the way. Your own words. Just for the two of you.

Anyway, it wasn't "hon" yet, between Buddy and The Hallowell.

But he had said it, and he still had hold of my hand, and

I came toward him and his arms went around me and kissing him, then, seemed the most natural—and, somehow, unnatural—thing in the world.

It wasn't a big production-model kiss.

And it wasn't—more important—the kind of kiss it had been, between us, the first time there in that house. The Christmas Day kiss that had surprised both of us. In fact, the kiss turned out all wrong.

But we went through the motions. And if Buddy sensed that there was anything wrong it didn't show on his face a moment later when all the babble and the movement started again.

"Hey—Sam," Mr. Valentine was shouting over our heads, "those reporters camped out front . . . go talk to them for us, huh?".

"Okay," Sam said. "But they'll want pictures."

"They shoulda got them when he came in. The hell with them . . . he's inside now, and here he stays."

"Well—all right. I'll tell 'em later."

"Tell 'em go piss up a rope. . . ."

Buddy was smiling at his father and smiling at Sam, but I could see an occasional quirk of the eyes in my direction. There was color rising in his face. Almost a blush.

"Are you hungry? Did you eat? You *didn't* eat! . . ."

Mrs. Valentine, now being the indomitable mother instead of the hysterical invalid, was tugging Buddy in the direction of the kitchen. I went along.

"Buddy, are you hurt? Show me where you're hurt—is the doctor coming? Somebody call the doctor . . ."

"Ma, I'm not hurt."

"The doctor—how soon can he get here? Sam, Johnny—*somebody*—somebody call the—"

"I'm okay, Ma."

"Sit down. Do you want some milk? Do you want some breakfast?"

"I'm okay. But I *could* . . ."

"Someone, get out the eggs. Get the bacon."

"Coffee. I could use a . . ."

"Get the coffee. Sandy—would *you* get the coffee?"

"Yes. Of course."

"Is somebody calling the *doctor?*"

Half of Buddy's face kept the smile, but on the other side it was slipping. His eyes jumped back and forth from each

278

one of us to the other, like a man watching a tennis match. He was looking at his father when the jumping finally stopped.

"Dad," he said. "Look—I'm . . ."

"Okay. Yeah, I know. For your mother, though—do it, okay? Let the croaker look you over."

"All I need is a shave."

"Yeah. Okay."

"Vanni, won't *you* call the . . ."

"Sure. Sure, Angie. . . ."

Mr. Valentine made a move to go out of the room, and then turned back to grab Buddy by the head. He kissed him, hard, on the forehead and hugged his head against his chest, and then grinned at Mrs. Valentine and went out to use the telephone in the den.

"Mr. Valentine?"

For a moment I thought it was someone talking to Buddy's father, but the rumpled FBI man had been standing in the kitchen with the rest of us and he was looking at Buddy.

"Uh . . . yeah?" Buddy looked at him blankly.

"I'm Haggarson, FBI," the man identified himself. "I know you're busy right now. But as soon as possible . . ."

"Right now he's going to eat," Mrs. Valentine broke in. "And be checked over by a doctor. Nothing else, until he eats and . . ."

". . . we'd like to talk to you. Get a full statement on the crash . . . and the other developments."

*"He doesn't talk to anyone until he gets something to eat."*

The FBI man looked at Mrs. Valentine, and apparently he knew when he was outweighed. He smiled thinly at her. "As you say." He nodded. "But . . . when you think you can, Mr. Valentine. . . ."

"Yeah. Sure . . . of course."

The FBI man nodded again and sort of wandered out of the room. Mr. Valentine passed him, coming back in. "The doctor's on his way," he said. He looked at Buddy. "You are okay, aren't you? I mean, you didn't—?"

"No, Dad." Buddy smiled, like a five-year-old looking up at an adult. "I'm fine. Except for a sort of swollen wrist I got in the landing. . . ."

"Your wrist!"

Mrs. Valentine stopped doing whatever it was she was doing at the stove and moved over to grab his hands. He was wearing a sweater and it was only now, when she pushed the sleeve back, that I could see the red swelling around the wrist.

I identified it mentally as a bad sprain complicated by deep bruises. It looked painful—but not dangerous. So much for the R.N. training . . . I decided not to go into shock.

"Buddy . . . it *did* hurt you. Oh, Buddy!"

"Ma, it's okay. Nothing's wrong with me at all, really. . . ."

"Get some ointment."

"Yes, Ma. . . ."

"I don't need any . . . *please,* Ma!"

"And some bandages."

"Ma. . . ."

"You're going to be all right. You're going to be fine; just as soon as the doctor gets here . . ."

I watched it all, feeling peculiarly detached. I mean, whether the plane crash was legitimate or just something Buddy had dreamed up for some reason, I know I should have been concerned. Especially since he did have that sprained wrist. But I couldn't seem to feel a thing. I looked at Mrs. Valentine. She was still fluttering around, probably adding to Buddy's discomfort more than she alleviated it.

Somehow or other, it reminded me of something Dad had told me once; about how the worst fate imaginable for an Indian brave, back in the good ole days, was to be captured alive by an enemy tribe. Because if that happened, they might turn him over to . . .

### Jack Dahlberg

. . . their women.

Funny thing—when I was in my twenties I really thought I knew how to handle women. There never seemed to be a problem. Or if there was I guess I didn't know about it.

But the older I get, the less I seem to be able to figure.

I had expected at the very least a week of argument about the money, with a constant background score of screams and smashed glasses and bottles and the whole number. Postponing the payoff to Clara was going to be a panic-button deal.

Instead . . . nothing. She heard me out and agreed to wait until the contracts were signed and we were set to go on *Sadie,* so if Papa found part of the Fund missing I could tell him I'd had to use it to grease the tracks. Maybe by next week I'd be on my way to being a free man—or at least, free of Clara.

Driving to the studio early that morning (don't ask me why; I don't know why I went in—the place was shut down, none of my staff would be working. There was nothing I could do in there that I couldn't do better, quicker and easier right at home. But I went. I don't know why) I wondered if maybe I should have pressed a little, myself, tried to get something like an argument—call it an explanation—out of her. But, let's admit a fact, I am pure chickenshit when it comes to things like that. Roaring and fighting I do not like; sue me, I don't go for it. It really turns me off. So when it looked like a chance for some quiet instead of some loud—I just naturally took it as manna from Above, and shut up.

Papa, however, was an entirely different matter. Still, I kept telling myself, I would handle Papa when the time came. I would simply stand up to him. I would look poker-faced (the way *he* does, himself, when he is holding a hand that may or may not be good enough) at anything he said or threatened, and wait for him to remember I was the only human being in this wide, wide world he could trust; the only one he could be sure was on *his* side.

But the oftener I said that to myself, the thinner it sounded.

Passing the Beverly Hills Hotel, I had a momentary impulse to forget about the studio and stop in there for a drink. The Polo Lounge would be open. And probably not crowded right now except perhaps with types feeling as antisocial and generally outside-the-gates as I was myself. But I changed my mind before my foot ever got to the brake pedal.

No way. Because if the Lounge was empty when Jack Dahlberg walked in, you could bet your sweet ass it wouldn't be empty for long afterward. (How the hell do they do it? Is it some kind of tremendously high frequency radio? Is it radar? Have the bastards bribed half the hotel personnel to let them know who is where doing what?) Within a single sip of the first Tall Mary, someone—an agent, a producer, a director, an actor, a moneyman; *someone* with the greatest idea you ever heard—would be sitting down beside me.

Just by chance, of course.

But what a hell of a lucky break, Jack, finding *you* here! . . .

Oh, hell yes.

And even if not—even if, just this one day out of the 365, the goddamned jungle telegraph wasn't working—there would be Sandra Moore. She would be there, on the tennis court, and if I would not come out to knock the balls back and forth with her, she would come inside and sit and talk to me.

And that, for some reason, almost decided me to turn the car around and drive back to the hotel.

Because it would be an act of mercy. And a guy with a ledger in no better shape than mine could use a few extra points on the plus side of that big book in the sky.

*Christ, poor Sandra. . . .*

Which would give a lot of people in this world one hell of a laugh, I guess; how can you call a woman "poor Sandra" when she's still a pretty terrific-looking dame—a dame who still doesn't need too much diffuser or jowl pinning to walk into a tight close-up—at fifty or so? Especially when she's had a twenty-year career as an actress at the very top of the heap, and had smart, gimlet-eyed business managers and tax lawyers to keep the dough intact and growing for her despite all odds, including an ox-stupid husband with a satyr complex who must have cost her a real bundle to dump. And who, even now, with the career on the downhill side, could command a very healthy bit of change for starring in a daytime soap opera? How can you call a dame like this "poor"?

*Easy, mister—very easy!*

Because what else could you call a dame who is just too rich to get fucked?

Sure. Figure it. She's always got to wonder: Does he want her bod . . . or her dough?

Pussy . . . or a career boost?

Figure it any way you like . . . she can't afford to be

282

seen with damn near anyone, at any time. She can't trust anyone enough to get herself laid.

So?

So the poor bitch takes it out on the tennis court; three hours a day, four hours, five. Six, even. Good exercise. *Yeah!* Keeps her in beautiful condition. *Yeah!* And—combined with the cold showers and maybe a course of shots your friendly neighborhood pill-roller can recommend—it keeps the sex urge down at least to the point where she doesn't spend every night tearing the plaster off the walls with her fingernails! . . .

My God, I am probably one of the few men in this world Sandra *dares* to talk to.

And if she knew me, really *knew* me, I'd be off the list, too.

No.

No drink with Sandra at the Polo Lounge.

Not today.

What, then? My mind snapped suddenly back into the here-and-now as I realized I was driving in the front gate at Monarch.

If old Barry, there guarding the gate as he had done since I sold magazines on the lot, was surprised to see me so early in the morning on a holiday, he didn't show it. Or stop me. Who *made* the rule, All Cars Must Stop at the Security Gate?

I did.

Who *violates* the rule every single time he thinks no one is looking?

Guess. . . .

I pulled into my own stall in front of the Admin building, and almost switched off the ignition before the semi-sensitive nerves leading from my ear to my brain warned me to let the motor run—and the radio play—a little longer.

I had to switch the head to full attention, though, before I understood why. . . .

All the way from the house to the studio I'd had the radio on, listening, like nine out of ten motorists, to background music. Commercial Muzak; sounds to pay no attention to. But now the music had stopped, and an announcer—someone obviously not accustomed to such work—was reading a news bulletin:

283

, . . had paid $250,000 in cash for the return of his son. Police and FBI men refused to comment on the progress of their investigation of the crime, but an authoritative source reported the law-enforcement agencies as yet have no definite clues to the identity of the extortionist. Young Valentine, who had spent almost three days in a rubber raft after his small plane went down at sea lost, was unable to give any lead to the possible identity of the man who collected the payment.

I snapped it off then.

Of course I should have felt a lift, knowing the kid was okay. The first thing I ought to've done when I got into my office was to have the switchboard girl get through to the Valentines on the private line—to let them know I was happy for them. And I *was* happy, really. So why no lift and relief? What was I—some kind of freak, some kind of psycho? Had I finally lost all fellow feeling for the non-me portion of the human race? Or what? But by the time I was in my office I knew the answer.

No lift because no fear; no relief because no strain . . . and no strain because, by God, there was something about the whole plane-crash charade that had never tasted right. My mind did a swift but detailed replay of the events of the night just before Angela Valentine got the news her son was missing—the dinner invitation, the unexpected presence of David and Gaby duMain, Sam LoCicero's quietly logical proposals (yes, Jackie-baby; *yes,* you *had* better get on the horn to the Valentines. After all, you will be working with them, at least in a financial way, for a good long time to come,) and my acceptance of the proposition. Followed by the call with the plane-crash news— which put a flat final end to any thought or discussion of anything else.

*Well?* . . .

So what if it had? Was there something else to be thought, something else to wonder about that? Not really. No. Those proposals were just the kind you might expect from one of the sharpest and most successful lawyer-negotiators in the industry.

*So why did the whole thing make me uneasy? Where was the joker?*

I looked across the desk at the bust of Papa, which stared blandly back at me and offered no answers. That was Papa, all right; never any answers for Jackie-boy. Just questions. And, when I couldn't answer them, the careful kindergarten teacher walk-through of each point until I could snap back the answer myself . . . whether I understood it or not.

Suddenly, for no reason on God's green earth, I felt the rush and fullness and burn of tears—not potential, not maybe, but *right now,* in the space behind my eyes.

Suddenly, for no reason on God's green earth, I knew I wanted to get up and run around to that damned cold statue and throw my arms around it and cling to it and tell it that the world was empty and I was alone and I was hollow inside and I was frightened and . . . please . . . kiss it and make it all well.

The realization of the impulse turned me colder still.

Time for pep talk number 2684-J—You Are a Man Now, Jackie, So Act Like One, Hey.

I did not love the statue.

I did not slobber over it—or over myself.

In fact, I did not do anything at all for what must have been several minutes; until I could be sure I was back under control and able to be Jack Dahlberg, executive vice-president, again. Until I could relax my jaws . . . and wonder whether I had knocked loose the caps on my back teeth.

*Jeezus God, what a morning!* . . .

What I did, finally, to keep from screaming was play tick-tack-toe with the buttons on my desk top.

Funny thing—you know, I had been wanting to do that ever since I first moved in; before I had the button console expanded to its present atomic-weapons-deployment-and-control size. No reason. No object in mind, really; just poke away at the buttons and hear in the third-floor silence a buzzer announce itself in a faraway office (you know I had never heard that before?) or the automatic doorlock go clickety-click or the nasty-looking little .38 terrier snap out of the concealed panel in the desk and snap back out of sight ten seconds after the button was released, or the window drapes start to close themselves and then open again, or the television set turn itself on and then turn itself. . . .

Only I didn't *quite* stab the turnoff button for that TV.

I meant to. It was chance and nothing else. Maybe if it had been a regular working day, I would have had too many other things on my mind already to pay any attention to the tape even after accidentally setting it in motion.

What matters is that I *did* start the playback. And I did *not* shut it off . . . because the first thing I saw, in beautiful sharp focus and with the sound turned up just a little too high, was Irving Dahlberg sitting in my chair behind the desk. And the second thing, when he moved into range, was Johnny Valentine's back. And the third thing was the reversed face of the plexiglas calendar clock on my desk, plainly showing the date and the time the tape had been made.

I sat through it, the first showing anyway, with my finger still frozen above the cutoff button.

And when the screen finally went blank it took me quite a few seconds, maybe even a full minute, to move my finger to Rewind. I played it over again. And rewound. And played it another time. And another. . . .

Even then, I had to make absolutely sure. . . .

Actually, the count was almost unnecessary.

I had sat enough hours in the past week, looking at that stack of soiled paper, to know at once that a large portion of its substance was missing.

But there was something *required* about making an actual count. And about recounting it when I had completed the first tally. And about searching—with extra light from my butane lighter, even—the deepest cracks and recesses of the safe. Just to make sure it really was $250,000 short.

*Which it was. . . .*

I closed up the safe after stacking the remainder of the money in place and started to return to my desk, but detoured—a real Laurel-and-Hardy turnabout—back to the tube. I reached into the tape receptacle and retrieved the cassette, and then went back and sat down with it in my hand.

If there had been any laughter, any laughter at all, left in me I would have laughed then. At the walls of the office. At the bust of the great Irving Dahlberg. At the crapper. At the safe. At the money. At Clara. At the world. And most of all at myself; at Jackie-boy, the *schmuck* who spends half his time worrying about things that are simply not going to happen. Not to him.

Because this was *it*, mister! Eye-Tee: *it!*

There in my hand, its plastic shininess glinting back the morning light of the windows, was the Seven Cities of Cibola. The Hanging Gardens of Babylon. King Solomon's Mines. The Golden Fleece. The Grail. The Browsing Permit for Fort Knox and the Key to the Executive John. . . .

Let's see: start with the money itself: *undeclared assets,* according to the tax people both federal and state; *embezzled moneys,* from the viewpoint of the stockholders; *skim,* in the jargon of the labor mobster; *unpaid wages,* from where our employees would stand; *slush fund,* in terms of the general business community. The mere existence of the Stamp Fund was the smallest part of it—in *that* respect, I was as guilty as Papa. Sure.

But from Valentine's angle, the tape could be more dynamite.

After all, Papa hadn't *loaned* him the money; he had *paid* it to him—in return for a political favor.

Thinking about that aspect, I found my breath coming even shorter . . . for the fact that he could peddle Washington muscle—Administration muscle; White House muscle —was a point that could hardly go unremarked and uncommented on if any of the story ever came to light. Valentine was *supposed* to be fresh out of friends in the White House; the President's refusal to stay at his home in Scottsdale had drawn a nation-wide chorus of gasps and whistles from the press when it was disclosed.

Hell—just turning it over in my mind, minute by minute, it finally came home to me that, far from having just Papa or Johnny Valentine by the ying-yangs, there was one damn swell chance that, depending on future events, I had a fairly viable grip on the presidential sweetbreads as well.

How long did I sit there, staring at the shiny plastic weapon? Don't ask me, mister—I do not know and I do not care; it was a happy time . . .

*"Miss duMain to see you, Mr. Dahlberg."*

The words that broke in on my reverie were so crazily well timed—so madly apropos—that I almost laughed into the speaker on my desk. It was rigged, of course, to function both as speaker and microphone and to be hooked up with the downstairs guard's desk at times when there was no one else around to keep the weirdos off me.

But I didn't laugh.

Instead, I just sat there like a lump, wondering if I had somehow managed to stumble into the wrong world by mistake; somehow awakened today in a mad universe almost but not quite like the world I usually lived in.

*"Mr. Dahlberg? . . ."* the speaker prompted.

"Send her up," I said then, snapping back to life.

And the waiting hum of the system clicked off to silence. I opened the middle drawer of the desk, slipped the video cassette into it, and had it locked long before Gaby's knuckles tapped at the door. I hesitated (as a matter of policy) just the barest moment before touching the lock-opening button to open the door.

"Hello, Gaby," I said. "Come on in."

She smiled, walked about a pace inside the room, and then reached a hand just behind her—keeping the eyes steadily fixed on me—to close the door. She did not speak, and she did not take her eyes off me.

"I was just wondering about you," I lied. "You and David will still be here in town tomorrow, won't you?"

Her eyes changed a little at that. But she didn't reply.

"Because we'll be wanting to settle details of the television deal—and other things that will require both of you. . . ." I trailed off to soundlessness. Because there was something in her eyes I didn't quite understand. Something. . . .

"David? . . ."

She said it as a question.

"Uh—yes. I understood . . . uh . . . I mean, you and David . . ."

"What about David and me?"

"Well—you know, now that you and . . . uh . . . my father are . . . well, no longer . . ."

That sentence wasn't getting anywhere, either, so I just stopped it and let it lie there. Frankly, the whole scene was beginning to get on my nerves. And it occurred to me, quite suddenly, that I really didn't have the slightest notion what the situation between her and Papa might be now. I didn't even know if he—Papa, I mean—knew where she was.

And I was beginning to have some real doubts about whether I knew where I was, too. . . .

Gaby went on looking at me for a moment, and then seemed to relax in some subtle manner. She looked away,

288

glancing curiously around the office, and walked slowly toward me. She did not stop at the usual place or take one of the chairs across the desk, as I had expected. In fact she did not pause in any of the expected places. Instead, she just kept coming—around the desk to my side, and right up to my chair—where she stopped for a brief moment, looking down at me.

I hate that. Having people look down at me. It reminds me of the fact that there are damn few people in this world I don't have to bend backward to look at—even when I'm standing up.

So I didn't keep my eyes on her.

I just sat there, looking straight ahead.

Which may sound kind of silly, as explanations go. But it's the only reason I can give for the fact that it came as a complete surprise to me when she reached over without a word, unzipped my fly, and . . .

## Dolly Diamond

. . . started fumbling around inside.

But all of a sudden it was a lonely, impossible business and I was just me—just Dolly the blue-and-white Diamond —sitting there in my own empty room with my own empty hand down in my crotch again after, oh God, how many years, and I stopped. And pulled my hand away. And started to cry.

I thought of things, even while I was crying.

Things I could do to make myself less alone. Raphael had made his usual call yesterday and I knew the bedside table was full and I could try the brand-new papers he had left ("All full of mango taste, honey; and these others, they taste like coffee!"), or I could get out the Lover, or I could go shopping and spend more money than I had in the bank account, or I could call up Irma and Freddie and meet them somewhere, or get hold of Bertha and have her send over one of the Very Special Tricky boys (the ones who piss on you or shit on you or anything else you want; don't ask me why, I dig that Golden Shower routine sometimes, it's a kind of a kink and who does it hurt? I mean it's not lonely, and they're getting paid so they can keep their mouths shut, for sure!) or . . .

The crying stopped finally, but not because of anything I'd been thinking. It just did. And I was still there, in that room, alone.

Oh . . . *damn* Johnny!

I looked at myself in the mirror and I was a mess. I mean a real total and complete mess; the pink and blue and white doll was all red and wrinkly and somehow I looked *old*—I mean, really, *old*—and that was the worst thing of all. Because no one wants you when you're old.

*But who wanted me now, even when I was young?*

That was a thought I had to stop—*had* to—before it got out of hand. I looked around the room, and there was nothing else to do but snap on the television set. I drummed my fingers on it while it took its own damn time warming up and then it was nothing but daytime television crap— a cooking show and a rerun of a prime-time show that had been canceled last year and a talk show and an old movie (would you believe *Flash Gordon and the Space Creatures* with Buster Crabbe?) and I almost turned the damn thing off before I realized what the announcer doing the short news spot had said.

. . . entirely unharmed. His father, actor-singer Johnny Valentine, refused to talk to reporters or to comment on his son's rescue, but a spokesman for the Valentine family said $250,000 in cash had been paid. No clues to the identity of the extortionist were immediately reported, but an FBI spokesman said the investigation had been intensified now that the young singer was home and safe. . . .

Then he went on to something else.

I waited a minute or two for him to get back to the story about Buddy, but instead a commercial came on and then it was all over and they were starting to show a cartoon.

*Why hadn't he called me?*

I mean—sure—I was glad Johnny's son was safe, all right. Of course I was glad. But the main thing, the part I was trying to get straight in my own head, was what Johnny was doing, now.

Like . . . why hadn't he called *me?*

There he was, out there in Hollywood, with that fat-assed ex-wife of his and the rest of that weirdo collection he keeps around, and the boy was back and he was safe and

290

all that and how the hell come I had to find out about it over a goddamned television set?

Suddenly I was so mad at Johnny.

*So damn mad!*

I could just see him—there in that old bag's house—doing the loving father bit with the son and all the people and everyone smiling the Big Smiles at him and telling each other what a wonderful father he was and all, paying that money to get the kid back and how wonderful everything was . . . and who would be thinking about Dolly?

*Who?*

Would Johnny be thinking about me—would he be on the phone to me, would he be telling me all about it and saying when he would be coming back? Would I know about it before every motherfucking newspaper reporter and television announcer and radio bastard in the world? Or would I find out by the time it was in the fan-mags? . . .

I looked at the girl in the mirror again.

I kept on looking. What could I do to make him sorry he'd left me all alone, sorry he hadn't called to tell me Buddy was back and he was coming home to me? What could I do that would make him realize just how much he'd hurt me?

I looked down at my hand and gave myself a little surprise. A little shock. Without noticing, without even thinking about it, I had taken a large pair of scissors from the drawer and they were there, in my hand, half-open. For a moment—just a moment—I had an impulse to turn them point first and push them into some part of me. Into the chest. Or stomach. . . .

I looked at the scissors.

And then the idea came—partly from them, I guess. Partly from who knows where. But it didn't matter and I didn't waste any time thinking about its source.

The venetian blinds were closed. I snapped them open and looked out—down, at first, and then over the edge of the window. I only half-remembered it, but I thought there was a ledge out there. A wide ledge just above the window of the floor below; I could see how easy it would be. . . .

*Snow?*

*Ice?*

No. I looked carefully and there didn't seem to be much

291

of either out there. I leaned back and looked around the apartment. It would be cold outside; I wanted something on besides what I was wearing, which was pretty nearly nothing, you might say. Something both warm and dramatic; this had to look right. . . .

And then I hesitated. Part of me wanted to get it on, right then; go right ahead and *do* it. Part of me wanted to forget the whole thing and sit back and wait for the phone to ring. For Johnny to call. I stood real still, real quiet, making up my mind.

And then I threw off my nightgown and walked naked to the closet. Grabbing the stupid mink Johnny had given me—which I wouldn't be caught dead in (hah! very funny, under the circumstances)—I tossed it over my shoulders and headed for the window. Christ, it was cold out there! I buttoned the coat up to my chin, then stepped out onto the ledge and stood there in plain sight of the doorman across the street. It seemed like ages before the idiot finally looked up and saw me and went scurrying off. I waited for something to happen. The wind was a lot more than I'd bargained for. Even through the fur it got to me. I pulled the coat tighter around me and shivered.

"Please, Miss Dolly—*please* come in!"

Jenny, my maid, was leaning out the window, looking at me with her eyes as wide as they would go. They looked like white holes in a coffee-colored blanket and I kind of felt sorry. Jenny's a nice kid and I've had her since before the show clicked. But there wasn't anything I could do.

"Go 'way, Jenny," I called to her. *"Go back or I'll jump."*

Ten floors below I could see the people. All stopped. All looking up at me. Looking at Dolly the blue-and-white Diamond. As it should be . . . what else do you *do* to a star? You look up. . . .

"Miss Dolly—*please!*"

Jenny was back at the window, but not so far out of it this time. She was crying. Some reason or other, it bugged me, her crying like that; shit, if anyone should of been crying it should of been me. After all, it was my ass if I fell, wasn't it? . . .

"Why'd you go out there, Miss Dolly . . . *why?*"

I stared back at her.

There was about five feet of empty space between us, not to mention, of course, the ten stories of empty space below the ledge; the ten stories I'd fly past if my foot happened to slip. I'd been wrong, looking out, before, about there being no ice or snow. There was ice. I had to be damn careful.

"Nobody loves me," I told her. "Nobody loves me—and I can't stand being alone anymore. All anyone ever wanted from me was my voice anyway—"

"Miss *Dolly!*"

". . . I'm sorry I can't leave my precious voice. But you got the records. So it's okay. You all got what you want. . . ."

"Miss *Dolly!*"

Oh, for Chrissake . . . why in the hell did they have to get Jenny up here anyway? This wasn't the way I'd planned it. I wanted them to have to call Johnny, get *him* back here to talk to me. And they hadn't even said anything about that. . . . Oh, shit, those motherfuckin' TV newsmen! How'd they get here so quickly?

"Leave me alone. I'm going to *do* it!"

Jenny screamed and ducked back through the window and I teetered a little, to keep the show going. Christ, but it was getting cold. A lot colder, it seemed to me.

"Miss Diamond!"

A man's face, this time.

"Miss Diamond—I'm Sergeant Drayco. Can I talk to you?"

"*No!*"

"Please, now—Miss Diamond; there's plenty of time for us to talk. No rush, is there?"

"*Don't come near me.*"

"I won't. I'm just going to . . . *uh!* . . . climb out and sit on this window ledge. See? Just to be comfortable while we talk. . . ."

"*Stay away!*"

I pretended to be frightened of him and made as if to edge away, but I didn't move my feet.

The sergeant was a fat man, wearing a police uniform. He didn't have his cap or his gun. Not even a coat. Sitting out there must have been cold for him, I thought. But, looking closer, I saw I was wrong; Sergeant Drayco didn't appear to be cold at all. In fact, there was a little drop of sweat hanging from the end of his nose.

"Tell me, Miss Diamond—by the way, I'm quite a fan

of yours, you know; so's my wife, we saw your show three times. We both loved it. Everybody loved it, Miss Diamond —may I call you Dolly?"

I looked at him as though I didn't quite understand what he was saying. Then I nodded my head a little.

"Well, Dolly," he went on, talking faster now. "Like I say, we loved your show, like everybody did. Everybody loves you, Dolly. See all those people down there? They're all worried and scared right now, because they all love you and want to see you safe back inside here."

I looked down at the people milling around. Love me? In the theater they love me, but what about now, when I need them? I heard a buzz of noise from below, even heard someone yelling my name. I strained to listen. *And then I heard it!* I almost leaned forward to hear better. They couldn't be yelling that! *They couldn't!*

The sergeant was still babbling on about love, but the only voice I could hear now was the one down there, the one that kept yelling "Jump, Dolly, jump!" Jesus! There was love all right.

For a minute I almost wanted to jump, right down on that bastard's head. Then I got really mad at those creeps down there. They wanted a show, for Chrissake—all right, by God, they'd get a show!

Balancing precariously, I wriggled out of first one sleeve and then the other until I was holding the mink coat in my hand. The wind was Christ-awful cold on my bare skin, and I could feel my tits puckering up like prunes. But I was still more angry than cold.

*"Here, you bastards,"* I screamed. And I balled the mink up in my hands and let it fly, right down at the gaping faces. *"Take that, you creeps!"*

I looked back at the sergeant, and, sure enough, his eyes were bugging halfway out of his . . .

### Jack Dahlberg

. . . head, bobbing up and down in my lap. "Christ," I breathed, half in amazement and half in ecstasy. No wonder my father had been wrapped around this girl's little pinkie! And then it was over, and Gaby smiled up at me. On her knees, there between my legs, she looked almost innocent— and about ten years old.

"If you don't know what's happening by now," she said, "I don't think I could possibly explain, could I, Jackie?"

"Well, maybe not," I said, zipping myself up as she sat back on her haunches and continued to regard me with a level look. "But you could give it a try. What about Papa, for starters?"

"What about him?"

"What did he say when you told him you were leaving? I mean, it was my impression that the two of you . . ."

Her eyelids covered her eyes, though I knew she hadn't really closed them. It was just a device women use when they don't want you to see their expression. "I *didn't* tell him," she said softly. "I didn't say a thing. When he said they weren't going to go on with the picture, I just phoned David . . . and left."

"Oh, God."

She looked up at me, now, the eyes all innocence; a damned hard thing to pull off, believe me, when you've just finished blowing a man. Face it: this chick had real acting talent . . . yeah. Real talent, all right.

"Did I do wrong?" she said.

I looked at her and shook my head. I couldn't believe what I was hearing. I didn't want to believe it.

"He . . . knows now, though," I managed to say. "He does know now, right?"

Her face didn't tell me a thing.

She shrugged her shoulders lightly but her expression didn't change; still sweet innocence.

The bust of Papa faced me, across the desk.

The expression on *its* face didn't tell me much, either.

I sighed. "Okay," I said, doing my best to keep a cool unit. "Okay, girl . . . give. Tell me about it."

"About what?"

"The whole number—the whole bit. You. Papa. David. *Me!* You're no dummy; I know you're no dummy, so let's not kid around. What's it all about? If you walked out on . . . my father . . . without saying good-bye or telling him where you were going, you had something in mind. So: tell!"

Then she smiled, and I could see something. Little red points. Fire tips. At the back of her eyes.

"Let's say . . . well, let's say I was bored."

"Bullshit."

"That's my story, anyway. I'm not property; I'm not married and I don't owe a nickel in this world . . . to anyone. Why shouldn't I go when and where—and with whom—I damn well please?"

"Because," I said, quietly and carefully, "that . . . what you just said . . . isn't true."

"Not true?"

"Not true." She waited for me to go on. "In the first place, girl, you *are* property. And nobody knows it better than you do. First of all, you're Irving Dahlberg's private tail—his openly avowed and publicly recognized mistress, if you don't mind my using an old-fashioned but highly accurate term. And you know a man in Papa's position can't afford to let anyone get the idea that one of his women can just walk out on him. Hell, he can't even admit a thing like that to *himself!*"

She smiled a little at that.

"And in the second place, there's the small matter of a contract; that makes you property in a legal sense as well. I know how it reads. I have to draw up plenty just like it, or approve them, anyway, every day of the year. It's the nearest a citizen can come to giving up all her rights under the Constitution and the Bill of Rights . . . and you signed it of your own free will."

"Did I?"

"You did. And finally, let me remind you that you *do* owe money—to Monarch, if to no one else, and I strongly suspect there might be another debt or two, here and there, that I haven't heard about yet."

"So?"

"So, you can drop the crap about being free, white, and twenty-one, and . . ."

And that's where she laughed.

Not just a giggle or a stage-effect laugh. It came from deep down and bubbled up out of her. I waited to hear what had caused such merriment. I didn't have to wait long. She grew serious as she said, "You're right." Her voice became low. "Anyway, you're two-thirds right. *White,* yes; I'm white. And free . . . freer than you think."

She paused a moment, drawing breath.

"Because, Jackie, I am not twenty-one. In fact . . . I'm not twenty. Or nineteen. Or . . . eighteen, either."

She stopped there, to let it sink in on me. To let me mull it over.

*Not eighteen?*

My God, I told myself, an old campaigner like Papa—he'd *never* miss checking a point like that. The angle was too old; too hoary, too much of a cliché. Never on this earth would Irving Dahlberg get himself mixed up with anything under the age of consent.

Or, anyway, I told myself, at least he wouldn't fool around with jailbait in any *public* way. . . .

I thought of a quick way of testing her out.

"Quick, now, Gaby: *what year were you born?*"

She laughed at that. "Jackie," she said, "you told me you don't think I'm stupid, right? You don't think you'd trip me up that easily if I were lying, do you? Which I'm not. Here, I'll prove it to you."

Her purse was on the floor beside her and she opened it, fumbled for a second, and then handed me a piece of paper. It was a photocopy, duly certified, of a birth certificate.

The person named was one Goretta Aaronberg . . . and the date would make her still just under eighteen, right now.

I shrugged and handed it back, but she didn't seem to want to take it. "That's for you, Jackie," she said. "You'll want to have someone check it out for you."

"Why would I do that? I don't know anyone named Goretta Aaronberg."

"You do now, Jackie."

I thought it over.

"You can't *prove* you're—"

"You can hardly see it, on that copy," she said, "but I have the original and it has a very clear footprint. It checks out with mine, if you ever want to nail that down. And there's a fingerprint record, too."

"Fingerprint?"

"Uh-huh. Right there in that same New York State courthouse where the birth certificate was issued; where the official copy's filed. When my mother died, I got sent to a state home—and they always take your prints. . . ."

It had to be a lie; Jesus . . . it just *had* to!

But, looking at her, I knew it wasn't.

297

"Okay, then," I said carefully. "Okay, so where does that leave us? I still don't know why you left Papa without telling him, or why you went with David or, for that matter, why you're here with me."

"I don't have a lot of education," she said in a tone that was as calm and reasonable as any lawyer's, "but, growing up the way I did, you either learn survival . . . or you die."

I didn't say anything.

"Irving Dahlberg's got plenty of power, and I got him to use it, to give me the break I needed in a big-budget picture. That was fine. It was worth the payoff . . . and besides, I actually kind of liked him."

"Then . . . ?"

"After the picture was canceled, I brought David out here with me in the hope that I could show you, or someone, that he would be all right. Irving would never have let me do that and besides, I had to convince David that he was okay with me."

"But it didn't work. And now . . ."

"And now it's set up a different way. It'll be harder to make it to the big money, sure. But I'll still make it. Only by the time you made the deal with that lawyer guy, Sam what's-his-name, I'd already screwed myself up with your father. But that's all right, he'd never have put me in anything that big again. He's too scared of his board of directors to do it now."

"I *still* don't—"

"Irving's going to be mad," she said, "about me. And David. He could even try to back out of the television deal because of it. Or something—I don't know—but I know he could come up with something cute. But as soon as he gets a look at this little birth certificate, he ought not to want to make any trouble—about the picture, or about us."

"*About us!* Where do you get *that?*"

I couldn't believe what I was hearing.

"I thought everything over after dinner at Angie Valentine's the other night," she replied thoughtfully. "And I realized that it wasn't *David* I should have been with—it was *you!*"

"Whoa, slow down," I countered, when I had absorbed that bit of information. "I'm not saying it's an all-wet idea, mind you." It had its points, from more than one angle. "But why *not* David?" I got a special kick out of the idea of David being my immediate predecessor in that luscious pink mouth—even more than the rather nervous thrill I got out of the thought of taking up with Papa's ex-mistress. It was all very intriguing, I had to admit.

"Well, he's sweet and all, but he's no one to lean on; no one in an important position, who can get things *done,* like you. He's a baby—and besides, David's too likely to end up in a loony bin somewhere, an . . ."

### Buddy Valentine

"*. . . attempted suicide!*"

The Old Man's voice, filtering in from the den, cut me off in mid-sentence just as I was telling Sandy, trying to tell her, anyway, how great she looked and how glad I was that she'd been at the house when I got back. The hell of it was, that wasn't what I really *wanted* to say to her, you know?

What I found myself wanting to tell her was the truth. Like, the *truth,* dig? That the whole plane-crash number was a phony; that I was sorry as hell about having scared her and everyone else, but how it was just absolutely something I had to do.

I wanted to lay it all on her . . . how I got the idea for the crash, how I'd been stewing for years about the way love was passed out in my family, but hadn't been able to come up with any surefire way to handle things until I'd started fooling around with small planes and got to know Zeke, the pilot with the far-out mind. (Boy! Just *how* far out Zeke's thinking was I didn't know—imagine that creep screwing my Old Man for all that loot on a phony payoff deal. Pure brass gonads!)

And yeah, sure, I was sorry about the worry for everyone and all, what else? But I was glad I'd done it, all the same, because . . . well, look how it had worked. Right?

I mean—here were the Old Man and Ma, back together and acting like they were still married or something, without all the hay and horseshit with the Diamond broad and without all the praying and screaming and rosary-clicking.

299

It was a bummer, maybe, that I'd had to do it. But at least when I finally made up my mind I had brought the whole crazy thing off—and it had worked!

Only . . . I couldn't say a damn word about it.

No way.

So there I was, more or less alone with Sandy for the first time since I walked in the door and with a clear field to tell her how I had missed her and all that, all of it, and the best I could do was a lot of yittity-yittity-yittity about how good she looked and how good it was to see her, like she was some kind of old buddy I just hadn't bumped into for a few months or something.

That's one trouble about doing something phony. To cover it up you got to be three times as phony in everything else you do and always know exactly what you're going to say before you say it and never—but *never*—tell anyone exactly what you're thinking or exactly why you did something or exactly how you feel.

Every word I said to her was phony, and I knew it.

And hated it.

And couldn't think of any way to stop. . . .

Worse, I could see something wrong in Sandy's face. She was smiling, and the smile was just as big and just as room-lighting and just as sincere as always (this was one girl who would never have to be careful not to come on phony; she couldn't if she tried!) but it didn't warm me as it had. When she talked, the words were just as real and the sense of fun was just as strong . . . but I couldn't accept them as I had before.

And there was a strangeness, almost a guardedness, in her eyes; not that the curtains were all the way down or anything. But, I don't know, it was just that I could sense she wasn't entirely buying anything about me right now. That something had her worried; that somehow she didn't entirely trust me. . . .

All of which, no doubt, was just guilt on the part of Buddy-boy, that well-known phony.

God . . . all I wanted to do was put my arms around her and melt into her and be warm.

And I couldn't lift a finger.

Which may have been why I didn't hear part of what the Old Man said. He was only a room away and, unless he's really trying to be hush-hush, he has the kind of voice you can hear even through a closed door. It was only when he came to the last two words of that sentence that I finally picked up . . .

". . . *attempted suicide!*"

Yeah, baby.

*Right on!* I picked up on that, for sure, and of course so did just about everyone else in the house. There had been a kind of buzz-buzz going on, general conversations involving everybody and everything but those words stopped them all.

In silence, we listened to the rest.

". . . windowsill. Yes . . . but, how long did she . . . oh, Jesus! Oh, my God. What in the hell did . . . uh-huh; sure. Yeah, sure . . . listen, she's okay now? Yeah. Great. But, Christ! What? Oh—oh, uh . . . yeah. Yeah, you know it. Listen, I'll be on the next plane I can charter or buy or lease. Tell her that. Tell her cool it—you know . . . and I'll be there!"

The middle of me—heart, lungs, belly, bowels, and balls —suddenly wasn't there anymore. With no warning at all— they were all gone.

It wasn't that they went cold. Or sour. Or nervous. Or anything like that; no way! They weren't even numb. It was just that—with no warning at all—they were gone.

I knew what the call had to be, of course.

Oh, yeah. I knew.

And I turned to stone, standing right there; turned to stone with my eyes focused on the middle distance and my head pointed in no one's direction. I was glad I wasn't really pointed at anyone. I didn't want to see Ma's face. I didn't want to see the *padrino's*, either.

I didn't want to be in that room. But I didn't have a choice. . . .

"*Sam!*" The way he said it let me know he was off the phone. "Sam, gimme your car keys!"

"Vanni? . . ."

"The keys. The fucking *keys!*"

"But why—"

"The car phone—it works?"

"Yeah."

"Same call letters as always?"

"*Sure,* but. . . ."

"Okay, so listen, already: I'm heading for L.A. International. Get me a jet, a charter, the fastest you can hire. A whole airliner if you got to. But it's gotta be fast and it's gotta be ready for takeoff when I get there. You can tell me where to go by telephone, quick as you got it locked in, right?"

"*Vanni. . . .*"

"For Christ sake, Sam. Don't hassle me, just *go!*"

The *padrino* started to say something else. He had been holding onto one end of his car keys, with the Old Man on the other, and his mouth was open to argue. But he closed it without anymore words. It didn't make any difference.

He knew as well as I did, as well as everyone *else* in that room did, where the Old Man was going and what the hurry had to be. Anything else would have been just details and mouth flapping. Nobody and nothing could of stopped him. Say that for the *padrino*, he doesn't fight fights he knows he can't win. . . .

"*Giovanni!*"

Here it came.

Oh, yeah, for sure, here it came. Ma was standing between the Old Man and the door, and there was no way he was going to get by her.

"*Giovanni*—give Sam back his keys."

Just like that.

An *order*.

If there had been a chance—just the slightest little chance—of turning him off the idea of splitting for New York, there wasn't any after that. No way.

The Old Man didn't seem to hear, or maybe he just wanted it to seem that way. He headed for the door, aiming right for her.

"Where are you going, Vanni?"

"New York. Look. Angie . . ."

"Why?"

"Angie . . ."

"*Why.* Tell me why!"

The Old Man waited just long enough for you to hear your heart give one beat. Then his face went as hard as Ma's.

"Because I want to go there," he said in a tone you could slice ice with.

"It's her." Ma tried to say it flat and cool, but her voice wobbled on the second word, and her face started to fall apart. "It's her—*her!* That white-haired little bitch. Her!"

"Angie . . ."

"Your son—your only son—your *son,* he's home a few minutes after nearly being killed. You're here, with us, with people who love you. All of us . . ."

"For God's sake!" He pushed toward her, tried to squeeze through to the door, but she shoved back. Short of actually hitting her, he was blocked.

"Don't go! Vanni . . . don't go to her! *Don't!*"

"Angie—she's in the hospital." He backed off and looked at Ma and, for maybe the first time in my life, I heard him almost pleading. Almost. "She tried to kill herself. I got to go. . . ."

"Don't. Vanni, you *can't!*"

"I *got* to!"

"Vanni! . . ." It was a wail, from a low and solid note riding right up the scale to a screech, and Ma's eyes closed and the tears came and she wobbled, her knees going crooked, and she sat down hard right on the floor in front of him and the wailing went on and her mascara ran and I stood there trying not to look, and the *padrino* was looking with his eyes hooded under his skull and the Old Man looked—at all of us and said, "Aw . . . *shit.*"

And turned on his heel and walked right out of the house through the side door from the den and to the car and a moment or two later I could hear the sound of the car's engine, starting . . . and moving away at high speed.

And that was that.

The *padrino* came to life first. He looked, a quick glance, at Ma and then away. He moved into the den, and I could hear him pick up the phone. He dialed and, though he kept his voice low, I knew he was setting up the plane charter.

Ma wasn't screeching anymore. But she was sobbing quietly and she had her beads out and the sobs finally took on a regular cadence as she said the rosary.

And Sandy . . . looked at me.

I tried to play it fairly cool. I tried to just look back at her and not let it show. I tried—*Jesus,* but I tried—and of course I wasn't anymore successful at that than I have been at anything else in my whole, entire, complete, summed-up life. I looked at her face and I looked at her eyes and I thought of all I'd done—all I'd tried to do—

and all the lies I'd said to her face and her eyes and how I was probably never going to be able to be honest or sincere or clean with her again, or with anyone again, and I couldn't stop it . . . the tears, the wet and hot child-tears came squirting out and I could feel myself splitting, right down the middle into two screaming parts, and . . .

*Oh, God.*

"It didn't work," I said; the first honest words I'd uttered since I walked in the door. "Sandy—Sandy! God, Sandy . . ."

She touched me, her hand soft against my face, and she came close to me and I put my arms around her and the words were blurred and garbled because my throat was squeezed shut by an iron garrote of pain and self-disgust. *"Forgive me. Sandy. It . . . didn't . . . work. . . ."*

# The 8th House

*Legacies, astral experiences, money and goods
of others, death and all matters
concerned with the dead . . .*

---

*Forecast: Sam LoCicero is plotting and planting his
garden of greenies. If the weather conditions are right, he'll
produce a crop of hardy perennials that will harvest itself automatically for the rest of his life  not to mention
Johnny's.*

*To Sam, in the Eighth House, money is life; to David
Strauss, money is death. . . .*

---

### Irving Dahlberg

Five times I had played it over. *Five times*—and still I
could not believe. . . .

*Steve Pappas.*

His voice, yes. No chance of a mistake, no chance of
someone fooling Irving Dahlberg.

But still I could not believe.

Steve Pappas. *Stavros Pappadopoulos.* How many deaths
has he died, knowing some of us know the name he was
born with? And how much worse would it be if he knew I
don't know the one that I was born with! Old Steve . . .
talking to that guinea-Jew bastard LoCicero; talking about
a deal to sell Priapus!

I looked at the little machine in front of me.

Tape recorders Irving Dahlberg has got. How many of

305

them? And how many more, of what wonderful powers, could I have for the asking? Right here in the office, here in New York, there are two—one for the stereo and one for monaural—connected to the buttons on my desk. But the little machine . . . I had to use the little machine to play this tape.

Because *who knows* what those other buttons do, now? Do they just play the tape for me to hear, like they're supposed to do? Or do they play it for me—and also for someone else, like the ones old Steve Pappas has on his desk there at Priapus. Is *my* office a sound trap, a snoop bin with an enemy listening, like his?

I pushed the button back and rewound the tape.

For twenty seconds, maybe, it rewound and then clicked to a stop. I couldn't resist listening again.

The earphones were lying there, on my desk. Privacy; that's what earphones could give you. Privacy. No way of bugging the earphones if the machine itself isn't plugged or bugged, and I checked the machine every day to make sure it couldn't be.

No one was going to bug Irving Dahlberg. *No one!*

I put the earphones on my head, blanking out the soft *sssssssssss* of the air conditioning and all other outside sound (why can't the air conditioning be silent, for what we're paying to use these damn offices?). I pushed the playback and there was a crackle while the tape leader ran through the head and then. . . .

STEVE PAPPAS'S VOICE: Sam, I'm glad you could come. Sit down, Sam. You want a cigar, or a—

SAM LoCICERO'S VOICE: Thanks. No, Steve. Nothing. What's all the excitement? You said on the phone—

STEVE: Sam, I wanted to say this to you, personally, to your face, otherwise I'd be a coward and I never been a coward. Sam I can't do it, I can't go through with the deal. I'm sorry, Sam.

SAM: You . . . you *what!*

STEVE: Don't be mad.

SAM: *Mad?* What the fuck do you mean, don't be mad? Steve, what in the hell are you talking about, can't go . . .

STEVE: I knew it. I knew you'd be mad.

[*Pause*]

SAM: Okay. [*Pause*] Okay, Steve, listen, I ain't mad. Okay? Now I ain't mad. I wasn't mad in the first place, only—Steve—I don't understand. I got to tell you that, Steve. I don't understand it. Okay?

STEVE: Sam, can we talk? Can we talk, now, huh?

SAM: We talk.

STEVE: Good.

SAM: Yeah. So, what do we talk about, Steve? I'm listening. . . .

STEVE: I want to explain. Sam, listen, you know I want to go through with it, don't you? You know I want to go through with our deal.

SAM: I thought so. Until about five seconds ago.

STEVE: Only, Sam, last night I got to thinking. You know how it is, Sam. You can't sleep, so you get up. You got the whole night and you're all alone and you can't sleep and so you think . . .

SAM: I know.

STEVE: So, here's what I got to thinking, Sam. If we went through with the deal, I would have a partner. Right?

SAM: Yeah. That's right. But—

STEVE: Sam, you know how long it's been since I had a partner in this studio? Any partner at all?

[*Pause*]

SAM: Well . . . yeah. I guess I do. As far as I know, it was just after the war. When your brother died. But even then he wasn't really a partner, not *your* partner, anymore than your other brother was when he was alive. Because both of them—

STEVE: Right! That's *it*, Sam. Both of my brothers were my partners. But both of them were older than me and they got out of the active business a long time ago. I had it all my way, Sam.

SAM: So? . . .

STEVE: Sam, those men were my brothers. We didn't always agree. While they were active, we decided by vote—two to one—right? That way, sometimes I won, sometimes I lost. Okay. But . . . no knife in the back.

SAM: Right. I guess everyone in town knew—

STEVE: Only . . . if I went through with the merger

307

deal, with you and Valentine, I would have a partner *again,* Sam. . . .

SAM: Yeah? . . .

STEVE: And Sam, this time, it wouldn't be one of my brothers . . .

[*Pause*]

SAM: Oh, *shit,* Steve! You don't—?

STEVE: Listen, Sam, you don't understand what it is —how it can be—for an old man like me. Sam, I been in the driver's seat a long time.

SAM: Steve. *Steve!* Read the contract again, Steve, *read* it! Where in there does it say Steve Pappas isn't running the show, *his way,* because he took in the record company?

STEVE: Nowhere. But—

SAM: Johnny Valentine, or his nominees, run the record company, yeah, sure; we run the record company to suit ourselves. But the studio management stays just like . . .

STEVE: I know that.

SAM: So what's the crap about not being your own boss anymore, Steve? You think *Vanni's* going to give you a hard time? *Listen,* Vanni—

STEVE: No! No, Sam, not Johnny. *Vanni.* Not Johnny Valentine. I know him; I like him. He likes me. And you and me, Sam, we get along . . .

SAM: Well, then? . . .

STEVE: But Sam, who says it would *be* just you and Johnny?

[*Pause*]

SAM: Huh?

STEVE: That's what worries me, Sam. That's why I can't go through with it.

SAM: Jesus. *Jesus,* Steve, I just don't get you! *What* are you afraid of? *Who?*

STEVE: That Johnny'll *sell!* Him, I can trust. You, I can trust. Well, hell, I can trust the two of you as much as anyone in this town can trust anyone else —but, you know, how can I be sure I could trust someone you might decide to *sell* your interest to? *How?* No, Sam, no! I can't take the—

SAM: Good, sweet, holy *Christ!*

308

STEVE: What?

SAM: Is *that* what's bugging you? For Christ sake, who we might *sell* to?

STEVE: Yes. It does, Sam; I can't help it. Sam, I got to have peace of mind; that much peace, anyway. I got to. I'm getting old. I can't go to sleep every night wondering, is *this* the time—this day coming—is *this* the day I get a partner who comes from behind with the knife!

[*Pause*]

SAM: Shit.

[*Pause*]

STEVE: I'm sorry, Sam. I wish—

SAM: Aw, hell, Steve. I thought . . . Jesus, I thought it was something *serious!* My God, what a fucking relief!

[*Pause*]

STEVE: Sam?

SAM: Yeah?

STEVE: It *is* serious, Sam. I ain't going through with the deal. It's *that* serious. I'm sorry.

SAM: And you're not going through with it because you're scared we'd sell and you'd wind up with a partner you didn't want; someone who'd give you a bad time, right?

STEVE: I'm sorry, Sam.

SAM: Sorry? What's to be sorry? Listen—when Vanni *got married* this time, to the *Diamond* cooz, that worried you a minute or two, *right?*

STEVE: Yes, but . . .

SAM: . . . but we got around it, no problem, the way *any* business does. We got insurance. Anything happens to Vanni—or me, because I'm in for my little hunk of action, too—you don't wind up with our heirs, wives or whatever, on your back because the contract says the insurance pays off to buy up their share of the company, current market price. They don't lose, they got the dough, and you don't lose by having them as partners. That was okay?

STEVE: Sure. Yes, sure, you *know*—

SAM: Okay, then! *Okay,* goddamn it! Steve, how

would you like to be able to say yes or no to *any* deal either Vanni or me might make to sell our part of the company?

STEVE: *What?* You mean? . . .

SAM: I mean that right now, before I leave the lot, I will go out there and get any secretary you say—someone you trust, I'll take your word—and dictate an agreement to become part of the main merger contract that guarantees Steve Pappas two things: first, that any time either of us wants to sell, Steve Pappas gets first refusal! You get the chance to buy back our interest yourself if you wanta; that makes sure you can keep us from selling to a guy you don't like.

STEVE: But, what if—?

SAM: *Lemme finish!* That's the *first* thing we guarantee. The *second,* if you don't want to buy it yourself or can't get the financing at just that moment, you get to accept or refuse—or *refuse,* Steve—to allow us to sell to anyone!

[*Pause*]

STEVE: Sam . . . you can really put *that* in a contract?

SAM: You're fucking well *told* I can!

[*Pause*]

STEVE: Let me get this straight: You'll make it part of the contract, I can either buy your shares and Johnny's, or if I don't want to I can *still* tell you, no, I don't want to let you sell, to anyone I wouldn't want as a partner of mine. *Anyone at all.*

SAM: That's right.

STEVE: My God. [*Pause*] My *God,* Sam, you'd do a thing like that for me?

SAM: Get the secretary; call her in and sit there and listen. Then phone your own lawyers and let them check it over, word by word, and tell you what it means, exactly, without telling them, first, what you want. If they don't like the wording, they can change it to suit you. However you or your lawyers want it, that's how it will be. Would that satisfy you?

310

[*Pause*]

STEVE: Sam . . . I can't tell you . . .

SAM: What?

STEVE: I can't tell you, Sam, what this *means* to me. What a *load* it is, off of my mind.

SAM: Steve, don't even think about it. Hell, it's nothing to us—I tell you, it doesn't even *matter*. Vanni and I, we're not going to sell. So what do we care?

[*Pause*]

STEVE: Okay. That's what we'll do. Sam, thank you. I just. . . .

SAM: Don't mention it.

STEVE: The office next door, it's not being used right now. Would you do it in there? I'll send a girl.

SAM: Next door? Okay. But—Steve, just make damn sure the girl, whoever it is, is someone can keep her mouth closed. You know we don't want *anyone* hearing about this before we're ready to announce it.

STEVE: Sure. Oh, sure, believe me, the people here can be trusted. Especially the girl I'll send. She's handled all the work on the deal to now—and you know how close we've kept it.

SAM: Okay. [*Pause*] Oh, Steve . . .

STEVE: Yes?

SAM: Steve, one other thing before we go ahead, now. You know the doctrine of *equity?*

STEVE: Equity?

SAM: Legal thing. Basically, it's a matter of "Do unto others as you would have them"—you know, Steve?

STEVE: Uh . . . sure, Sam. Okay.

SAM: So it'll be okay, then? We set it up both ways?

[*Pause*]

STEVE: I . . . uh, Sam, I don't quite . . .

SAM: I mean, we give *you* the deal where you get first refusal right to buy and the right to approve or disapprove any other buyer . . .

STEVE: Yes. *Right!*

SAM: . . . So of course, you'll give *us* the same deal, wouldn't you? I mean: equity. It works *both* ways.

STEVE: God! *Sure*, Sam! Of course. Certainly. Why *not?* We're going to be partners, and we're already friends. Sure!

SAM: Good! Good, Steve. Just wanted to be sure you understood! . . .

STEVE: Good. Sam—I should have known. Always, you had the brains; every single time. How come I can't hire a lawyer like you, Sam?

[*Pause*]

SAM: *Hell,* Steve, what you want with a punched-up old bad-mouther like me? For Steve Pappas . . . class! Lawyers from Harvard. From Yale. From Princeton. Class! You got the real class lawyers . . . you know that. Everyone knows that. Hell, they'll probably have a circus, later, rewriting Ol' Sam's bad phrasing and clumsy law. Lawyers like Sam, you don't need.

STEVE: But guys with Sam's brains I do. . . .

SAM: [*A big laugh*] Yeah, sure! Okay, then, Steve . . . I'll let you have a look, just to make sure it's all like you want it, before I leave. Okay, Steve?

STEVE: Okay, Sam.

SAM: Right! [*Sound of door opening. Sound of door closing.*]

[*Long pause*]

STEVE'S VOICE: Sam. [*Pause*] And Valentine. [*Pause*] My *partners!* . . . God, but it'll be good.

The tape went on after that, but I stopped it right there and wound it back again.

*That old fool Pappas!*

I sat there, looking at the machine, with the earphones still on my head. *That old fool!* Piece by piece, hour by hour, I ran the whole thing around and around in my head—and still I couldn't get it to make sense.

Valentine and LoCicero were in business *with me!*

With *Irving Dahlberg!*

Okay, all right, maybe it was my idiot adopted son Jackie who had made the deal. All right. He made the deal, but he couldn't have made it work without my okay; not without Irving Dahlberg sitting back and nodding the head at him. Yes!

Valentine. *Was* his wife or was his wife *not* almost fin-

312

ished making a big picture—an Irving Dahlberg picture—
for Monarch studios, in Hollywood? And was that picture,
or was it not, going to make Dolly Diamond the biggest
star in the world, all in one single swoop?

*Sadie.*

It would be the Big Picture this year. It would win all
the awards. I had the word from everyone on the Coast
that it was a sure winner. Not just a best actress for the
Diamond bitch; best director awards, it would win; best
camera, best story, best song, best score, best set design,
best—*everything!*

If it didn't, then black was white and Irving Dahlberg
knew nothing about the movie business.

*All right, then.*

And besides that: was Valentine's own television production company, or was it not, shooting new episodes
*right now* for that goddamned *Stop, Thief!* series, for that
goddamned David Strauss? And did that series, or did it
not, have a clear-and-firm green light from ABS—and in
a good time-slot, too—to begin the season, this fall?

*All right, then.*

And more—*much* more—had Irving Dahlberg even
stayed his hand? Hadn't I gone so far as to let that no-good,
two-timing underage bitch Gaby duMain go ahead and
make Jackie's TV pilot and star in the series segments
when I could have made sure she sank without a trace,
never mind that she was jailbait. (Jesus, isn't it like Ruth's
*nebbish* son to pick up the giant's cast-off women?)

*All right, then.*

The only thing that stinking guinea had in this *world*
that wasn't tied up, firm, in something where Irving Dahlberg could call the tune was his stinking record company
. . . and what would that be worth if it didn't have *him*
out front, piping in the talent?

*Nothing.*

Nothing, that's what!

*All right, then.* So why was he cuddling up to old Steve
Pappas? Why was he making deals with Steve? Mergers,
even, with Steve?

*What did they have to gain, either of them?*

Money? No. Both losing money, I heard; the studio was
messed up since Steve's son-in-law was fired and the television thing had fallen on its keister. The guinea's record

313

company was losing, too. No records selling much—not even his own.

Combined loss? Maybe. But how good a reason was that—how good, if Steve Pappas was willing to take a partner in the studio—for the first time in his life let anyone not named Pappas have a piece of Priapus? No, it just couldn't be that.

*He was doing it to get at Irving Dahlberg!*

Yes!

All these years; giants competing against each other all these years! And now it comes out. Now he thinks he's taking it right from under Irving Dahlberg's nose!

*Yes!*

I took a deep breath and let a sigh out into the air of the office, and looked at the tape machine again, and smiled a little.

All right, then.

*All right!*

So, let the old fool. He could have them—all of them—he could have them and to hell with them and when it all came down around his ears, who would laugh? Irving Dahlberg would laugh. Irving Dahlberg . . . *yes!*

I ripped off the earphones and snatched the cassette of recording tape from inside the machine and put it in my pocket and pushed the machine away from me across the desk and picked up the telephone.

"*Yes, Mr. Dahlberg?*"

Hand it to the girls on the switchboard; they were on the ball today. No waiting for them to answer.

"The direct line," I said. "I want to talk to Jack Dahlberg."

"*Yes, Mr. Dahlberg.*"

That Jackie; I wished I could be around somewhere, hidden, maybe, to see his face when the news broke on the Coast. The news that his great and glorious deal with his old friend, David Strauss, and his new friends, the Valentines, had turned out to be nothing but a blind that Sam LoCicero had figured out to keep everyone guessing while he worked out a stab-in-the-back with old Steve Pappas!

I wished I could be there. . . .

And I wished there was some way I could tell him how and why that guinea, that wop bastard, had used his influence to get the navy to let us use their ships . . . no . . . don't even *think* about that. I wondered if he ever wondered how come the navy all of a sudden got so nice and cozy and cooperative about *Boarders Away!* when he couldn't get to first base before? Jackie? No, of course he didn't wonder. He didn't have that much brains.

*Brains!*

*Guts!*

That's what it took to be a real giant. A giant like Irving Dahlberg. People like Jackie—midgets. Always. Even the midget's wife—ex-wife—Clara. Even *she c*ould take him for alimony that would kill a horse; just to get rid of a woman he would pay that kind of money. Agree to it, even. Through his lawyers. So the Reno divorce (Reno—how cheap, how common can you get? Not even Las Vegas; not even Tahoe!) would go through quick. But at least she didn't get as much as she wanted.

Women.

Like streetcars: miss one, another comes along in five minutes. Ten. Twenty. *Thirty;* at the most thirty minutes between women. But could Jackie ever see that? Ever understand it?

No.

Everything he needed—everything—he had, right there at the studio. I arranged it, didn't I? Before I left there, didn't Irving Dahlberg have the world's greatest recruiting system, the Monarch Pictures Talent School, set up and operating right on the premises?

Reports on the Talent, even.

*Reports!*

True age, marital status, physical condition (checked twice a week for clap), and sexual status. Muscularity and probable sex interests; emotional hang-ups, size and condition of genitalia . . . you name it! The special gym-massage setup hooked in with the Talent School can give you a concise picture of *everything* you might want to know . . . fresh and factual, on your desk every morning.

What a recruiting setup!

And does that stupid kid use it?

*He does not.* One time he gets the clap—and never again. Who doesn't get a dose once?

That damn Jackie . . .

315

Fool about women, fool about pictures, fool about business and—God help us both—that's the boy I had to adopt for my son!

I stabbed a forefinger at the telephone cutoff button. "Yes, Mr. Dahlberg?"

"What the hell's taking so long on the call?"

"I'm sorry, sir. We're having a little trouble getting through, sir. There seems to . . ."

She stopped talking finally, and there was some static on the line. And then Jackie's voice, saying . . .

## Jack Dahlberg

". . . Hello, Papa! How's the weather back there?"

I hoped my voice didn't sound as phony to him as it did to me. What a *hell* of a time for a call. My eyes flicked to the two other faces visible to me in the office. They didn't show a thing. I did my best to match their impassiveness—but it wasn't easy. Every now and then, I could feel the corners of my mouth wanting to turn up in a smile . . .

"It's lousy, the weather, but I didn't call you up to talk about it. Listen, Jackie—do you have the release agreement signed yet, for *Sadie?*"

I took a deep breath; the first one I'd allowed myself since the call came. "No, sir," I said. "Not yet. But there shouldn't be any trouble. The Valentine people want to make money just as much as we do. And you can't make a dime on a picture that hasn't been released. Besides, Dolly Diamond's in it."

"So. What does *that* mean?"

"Well . . . after all, Papa . . . well, *you* know."

"What do I know?"

"Why . . . Dolly and Valentine. He couldn't hold us up long. She'd raise too much hell with him. It's her first picture."

There was a long wait.

God, if *only* he'd called maybe ten, fifteen minutes *later!* I leaned back as far as I dared in the chair and did my best to control my breathing. But it wasn't easy.

I wished to hell I could *see* Papa right then. I wished I could see what he was doing . . . *without* his seeing what I was doing. Somehow, I had the funny feeling he wasn't really talking about the release on *Sadie*. That he'd had some other reason . . .

"Sure," he said, when he finished whatever it was he was doing on the other end of the wire. "All right. Keep me informed, then. I want to know when they do sign the okay and I want you to check with them *today!*"

"Today. *Right!*" I caught myself actually nodding—and leaning forward again—as though Papa's voice had eyes or something.

"And another thing, Jackie," he said. "About *Boarders Away!* Are we firm with the navy on those dates now?"

"Uh . . . just one . . ." I let my voice trail off, rooting around in the side drawer of the desk until I found the typed schedule Saul had handed me during the morning conference. I snapped it down in front of me, doing my best to keep my attention on it.

"Yeah," I said. "Yes. It's here. We have firm dates."

"When?"

"Uh—let's see—the crews arrive (oh, *Jesus*, why couldn't he have called later!) in New Orleans February one . . . the complete shore-side installation is due for completion . . . uh . . . right on the base of course, on . . ."

"Never mind that." His voice was like a static crackle on the line. "I don't want a whole day-by-day rundown. Just the sea sequences. Is *that* firm?"

"Yes, sir!"

"Give it to me."

(Oh, Papa, if you knew what! . . .)

I forced myself to look halfway down the list and isolate the proper dates. "Camera ship," I said, steadying my voice with an effort, "to be on the base and ready for it March twelve. Navy people estimate two full days for dismounting that ship's guns and setting out cameras in the vacant mounts. . . ."

"Did you get O'Riorden?"

The name was a null for me. I clapped my hand to the mouthpiece and looked at the other two. "O'Riorden? Cameraman?"

"Specialist." Saul's face came to life and he snapped the words at me shorthand-style. "Old geezer. Boss camera. Expert. Marine sequences. *Mutiny* and *Captains* and *Caine* and *Bedford* and, fuck, you-name-it. . . ."

"We got him, Saul?"

"Oh . . . yeah!"

I uncorked the phone and felt myself falling back in the chair once again. The muscles in my thighs and my butt were beginning to twitch a little. I fought them. "We have O'Riorden locked in," I said. "He'll shoot all the stuff afloat, and of course, most of that will be done concurrently with footage taken ashore; two units working . . ."

"Yes." He seemed to have dropped the matter, mentally, before I was done talking. "What are they giving us for a camera ship, Jackie?"

"You'll be pleased with this," I said. "It's one of the navy's brand-new gunships—kind of a minidestroyer that can do forty knots. Combination jet and diesel power. No problem keeping up with a subject, or like that . . ."

"Good. *Fine!* At least I get one piece of good news for the day." And he really did sound pleased. "Which gunship is it?"

"The *Olathe,*" I said.

"Never heard of it—not that it matters."

"I can get a rundown on it if you want," I said. "The ship's history. A breakdown on her skipper and crew. . . ."

He hesitated. Thinking it over, maybe.

"No," he said. "Not now, anyway. Later . . . we'll see. I always like to take care of the guys, though, in a setup like that. You know—a present for the ship, stuff for the crew. Or a tour of the studio, later, if they want it. Or—hell—*something.* . . ."

I didn't need the word "something" interpreted.

"Sure, Papa," I said. (Damn, I wish I could get over calling him that every time I'm a little off guard!) "We'll see to it. Anything else?"

Another pause. (I noticed, in the silence, I was breathing a little faster than I should have been; I concentrated on bringing that under control.)

"No, I guess not. Daily financial reports on the telex?"

"Yes, sir."

"All right, then . . . call me if anything comes up . . ." (Oh, *Papa!*)

And he was off the line before I could answer.

I sat there a moment like a dummy, still leaning back. I realized a silly little smile was on my face and the phone

318

was still in my hand. But if Saul or Morrie noticed, they made no sign.

"Okay," I said, finally. "All right . . . he's off. . . ."

They relaxed. I leaned forward and picked up a pencil.

"Problems?" Saul was the first to speak.

"Nothing much. Only, Saul, maybe we better hit the Valentine people today about that permission to release the Diamond picture. . . ."

He shrugged. "Jackie," he said, "I don't think so."

I doodled on a piece of paper in front of me and didn't reply. He went on after a momentary hesitation.

"After all," he said, "we're not really through shooting, even. Not yet. And we don't know ourselves exactly when we want to release it, because there could be a problem or two on cutting. . . ."

"Problem?"

"Well . . . you know. A musical. Always *something* on a musical. . . ."

"On *this* one," Morrie came to life, "there better *not* be. I mean it, fellas . . . there better *not* be!"

We both looked at him.

"Says . . . which?"

Morrie's face is a kind of featureless moon. A blandness ringed by jowls and eye bags, surrounded by fat. It never has much expression. Neither does his voice. But as close to passion as he could come, that close he came now.

"I say, first, we all know this picture has *got* to be released before the end of the year. *Got to!* I don't care whether anyone likes the cutting job, I don't care what else is wrong—*we have got to release it before the first day of January.*"

He hesitated again, waiting for someone to interrupt him. (God, man, go *on*. Go on—distract my mind a minute, or . . . ) But no one did; we just sat waiting.

"Because," he said, "we've already committed a hell of a lot of money to the publicity program. The major magazine spreads and the side features and all the rest, and to advertising. And to take full advantage you got to cop some Oscars next year. And *that* means you got to release it *this year*."

"All right," I said. "So who's arguing? What else?"

"Second," he said, "what with the tough money situation right now we are up to our ass, *to our ass,* in this.

319

Every day we got to delay release is costing—*believe* me—damn near $4,000! And I mean *interest alone*. Am I getting on your wavelength, bubbi?"

He was. I almost forgot what else was happening while he talked.

"And to make the cheese more binding," he paused to smile at what I swear to God he must of thought was a brand-new turn of phrase, "we got the other problem. What I call the *pack-rat problem*, with La Diamond. . . ."

I could almost hear myself groan inside.

There, anyway, Morrie was on firm, familiar ground—stories about that were already too well known and too numerous to be kept an inside joke at the studio. They were beginning to show up regularly in gossip columns. Even in throwaway material for comedians.

"She's a menace!" Morrie said, and his fat baby face seemed about to weep. "Who *knows* what she'll want next? She's taking everything off the set that doesn't have roots."

I looked up from my doodle. It was a strange one; a long thing, like a sausage, with what might have been a smoke ring around it; it reminded me of the hood ornament they had on Buicks, more than twenty years ago. The one the bluenoses finally made them take off. "How near are we to wrapping it all up?" I asked.

"Five days, I think," Saul said.

"You *think?*"

"Well . . . we got a definite maybe."

I thought it over. The thing should have been wrapped —been in the can and ready for final cut—by now.

"How much really has to be done?" I said, aiming directly at Saul this time.

He hesitated. "I could call," he said slowly. "Get a day-by-day sched if you really . . ."

"I do." I looked up from the doodle. "In particular, I want to know how much of what's left is essential and . . . uh . . . (Oh, Jesus, I had lost the thread. Damn it, why couldn't everything have been fifteen minutes *later?*) . . . and, uh, how much involves Diamond herself. *Herself,* understand?"

"You mean how much loop and how much footage in which she must personally cooperate?"

"Yup."

He smiled. "I thought you'd *never* ask," he said. "And the answer is: Zero. *Zilch!* What we got left is odds and ends and she doesn't even have to be *alive* for them!"

I nodded, still looking at him.

"Okay," I said. "And we have no future commitments where she's involved. Right?"

"Right."

"Then—fuck her," I said quietly.

"Huh?"

"Fuck her. Anything that bitch pack rat hasn't *schlepped* off the lot as of *now*—stays *there*. Get me?"

"I surer'n hell do!"

"Good."

I looked at them, individually, waiting for some new subject to be introduced, but none was. So they knew the conference was over. Morrie got up without another word and slouched out. Saul started to follow. But by the door he hesitated, and then turned back toward me.

"Jack. . . ." he said.

"Yeah?"

"Listen, just tell me if it's none of my business but . . . you *okay?*"

*Oh-oh!*

"Sure. Of course I'm okay. What makes you ask? . . ."

"Nothing . . . I guess." He really wanted to leave. But he was really curious, too. And in the end the curiosity won. "It's just you . . . seemed kind of nervous," he said. "Jumpy, like. And—you were smiling, all morning—like for nothing at all. . . ."

I smiled at him again—a big one; a big lie (God but I wanted him *out* of there!)—and shook my head.

"Everything's fine," I said. "No pain, no strain."

He nodded, still not convinced. But he got out of there anyway, and that's all I wanted. I hit the cutoff button, the one that locked the office door and made the rest of the desk panel inoperative—including intercom—until I wanted to turn the world on again.

Then I leaned all the way back, closed my eyes . . . and let myself go. . . .

*Oh. Jesus. Christ.* Oh . . . *jesus*god . . . *jesus*god . . . *jesusjesusjesus* jesus . . . I wonder what the poor people are doing . . . *jesusgodjesusgodjesusGOD!*

And then it was over.

I just sat there until my pulse had slowed down and my breathing was back to normal.

Then I moved back from the desk.

Gaby turned those fire-pit eyes of hers up at me. She grinned. *"Gobble,"* she said. "Gobble-gobble-gobble!"

I laughed and waited for her to put my newly limp manhood back into my pants, and zip the fly. Then she crawled out from under the kneehole, stood up, and ran the tips of her fingers along the side of my face.

"I always wondered," she said, "why they built desks that way, with the front side completely paneled so no one can see what's going on underneath."

"And now," I replied. "You know. . . ."

"If those two had only known what was going on while the *big conference* was in progress!"

I chuckled. "They'd of wanted to cut themselves in for part of the action," I told her. "And as for my *father!* . . ."

That got a reciprocal laugh out of her.

"If your father knew," she said, "if *he* knew what was happening while you were on the phone with him . . ."

### David Strauss

*". . . he'd have a fucking heart attack!"*

I listened.

I listened, yes; but I couldn't believe what she was telling me. It just couldn't be true.

"Under the *desk,*" I said. "You got to be *kidding!*"

"Like hell."

I just sat, staring at her. She had to be lying, of course. She *had* to be. Ethel Davidson was a nothing on the Monarch lot; a little nothing whose sole claim to employment, for the moment, anyway, was the coincidence of being exactly the same height as Gaby duMain. That meant she had steady work—just so long as she didn't become a nuisance, and she knew that.

So why take a chance like this?

Even in *bed!* . . .

"She *told* you a thing like that?"

"Fucking-A," Ethel said, rolling sideways in a position that shoved one of her overdeveloped mammaries almost into my armpit. "Fucking well told she told me that. Hell, for all I know she's told everyone on the lot! God knows *we're* not all that tight."

My mind was doing a series of double takes.

But the chick had to be giving it to me straight-arrow; I knew that. No advantage—to her or anyone else—in playing it any other way. That, anyway, explained why I'd had such a lot of trouble talking to Gaby since that first couple of days . . . when she disappeared from old Dahlberg's beach house, and I'd split to the Château Marmont . . .

I clenched my mind against remembering. It was over. It was done. It was in the past.

*Have another memory, David.*

No, thank you, I don't need that one; I didn't want it in the first place.

*Have another mental image, David, darling!* Go ahead: build it up piece by piece from all the little things you know about both of them. Think how it must look . . . Jackie, there on the phone. Leaning way back in the big chair, but with the bottom half of his body still well concealed under the desk.

And Gaby, kneeling out of sight, giving him the super special knob job. Would that . . . No!

It was all getting to be too much. I had to get out of there; to get very far away from the room and from Ethel and from my memories.

"What's the matter, baby—tired? I can fix that."

It was a second or two before I could connect the voice with Ethel. And Ethel with what was happening, down below. Her hand. On me. Moving and manipulating while her tongue . . .

*No!*

I sat up suddenly, almost knocking her away from me.

*"Hey!"* she said. "Hey, hold on, there."

But I wasn't listening.

I was outside, blinking in the freshly smogged brightness of the famed southern California sun, before I realized I hadn't stopped to put much of anything on. I was wearing a brief Japanese-type robe, and I cinched it around me with its belt, but I could still feel a rather pleasant breeze across my *cojones* as I walked.

Gaby. Gaby . . . and Jackie.

Why hadn't I gone to Jackie when I found out he was splitsville with his wife? Why hadn't I told him again how

I felt; how much I missed and needed him. Why had I waited for *him* to come to *me?* He never would.

And why did it have to be Gabrielle—*Gaby*—with him *now!*

I had been walking at a fairly brisk pace, and if you'd asked me point-blank, I'd have said I had no definite destination. I was just walking; trying to substitute movement for action.

But of course I wasn't just walking. The back end of my mind had aimed me where I wanted to be. I snapped back into the present at the door of the studio administration building and some kind of emotional momentum carried me through it.

I stopped, facing the lobby guard.

He looked up and half-smiled at me. "Yes, Mr. Strauss?"

I didn't smile back. And I couldn't speak, for a moment. "Mr. . . . Dahlberg," I said finally, when the silence became too much. "Mr. Jack Dahlberg. Is he in?"

The guard blinked. I think he had been half hypnotized by our mutual paralysis.

"You got . . . an appointment, Mr. Strauss?"

"No."

IIis mouth opened again and I think he was on the point of telling me outright that I looked weird and was acting weird and that he wouldn't let me in even if I did have an appointment.

But instead, he picked up the phone and said something into it. He waited, nodded, and then held the receiver in my direction.

I took it, held it to my ear, and said hello.

"*Just a minute,*" said a female voice I didn't recognize. There was a soft click. And then: "Yes, David?"

Jackie.

Fine. Only . . . what the hell could I say, standing there with the guard's ears flapping in the breeze, and the secretary probably getting an earful, too.

"Jackie," I said. "I'm downstairs. You busy? Right now, I mean?"

No answer for a moment.

No answer. So for just that long, I thought I might be wrong. I thought my subconscious might have steered me right for once. I thought he might . . .

"Well . . . yeah, David. I am, kind of."

"Oh."

Another pause.

"Was it anything important?"

"No."

Another pause.

"Well, then," he said. And I knew him so *well*. I knew the false briskness in his voice when he wanted to come on like a big exec playing Mr. Nice Guy. I knew the next words he would say and I lip-synched them, with him. . . .

"Look, I'm tied up for the moment," we said, together, him out loud. "Let's make it soon, though. Lunch? I'll call you."

I took a deep breath.

"Sure, man," I said. "Right on," I said. "Later," I said.

I wondered if he was lip-synching with me.

It was a thing—a kind of code we'd had, years ago. To talk to each other with; to talk and be understood without actually saying the real words when other people were around. "It's terribly original," I could say to him, and he'd know I thought it was nowhere. "You're reading it with a really new dimension; it's awfully intriguing," he would say—and I knew he meant it was zilch.

I handed the phone back to the guard.

The undertalk was over. And the message was clear: *We've had the course, baby.* Jackie-boy was off the bicycle and running a straight center. . . .

*So where did that leave good old David-darling?*

I turned around and got out of there.

Have a little rejection, David-darling.

Have a . . . *Oh. My. God!*

. . . the choir was starting to sing again; it was the first time in nearly two months and I had thought it was over forever but now the choir was singing again and this time I could distinguish more words than the *Hallelujahs*. This time the words were distinct . . . and they were filth. *Filth!* The choir was singing a Hymn of Hell, and I . . .

*David Strauss, star of stage, screen, television, and ESP, invites you to come and go mad with him!*

I could feel my lungs inflating—a breath they would expel as a scream and a plea for help when there could be no help—and I tried to stifle it, but it was coming and I could hear the far-off laughter from the cocktail crowd; they were back, too, and the lungs were full to bursting; I could not hold it back anymore.

*"Hi, David—I think they're ready for us."*

I stood, a living statue of inflated stone, but—the scream did not come. And as suddenly as it had begun, the choir's singing ended. And the cocktail-crowd voices began to mumble and blur, and mercifully the whole scene began to do an old-fashioned . . .

## Buddy Valentine

". . . fade out." The *padrino* looked down at the plate of cherrystones and decided it was really done; no more clams. And he sighed. "That's what everyone—everyone—in the fucking town seems to want: a good finale scene with a clinch and a walk into the sunset, with the words The End and closing titles. Only—the assholes—*they want that in real life!*"

I had been only half listening. But something about the way he said that snapped me back to full attention. And to remembering that his table here at Le Bistro in Beverly Hills was his own, private little office-away-from-the-office.

A lot of people used the place that way, of course.

Sid Korshak, for instance. Aside from the *padrino,* he's the only guy big enough to have a specific table always reserved for him in the place, and his own private phone there, but just about everyone else in town makes the scene at the Bistro sooner or later. And one hell of a lot of business gets done over the noon hour . . . or later.

Which made me suddenly very conscious that my *padrino* had been pretty insistent about me meeting him.

And I hadn't wanted to. I mean—no way! Because, like, I'd had a lot of other things to spend my time on. The kind of things I'd been doing ever since the big Homecoming Scene. Things like booze. And broads. And—you know— all that crap.

Yeah.

So of course I tried to talk the *padrino* out of it; said I had a date to see a guy about maybe some recordings (only, hell, I ought to of known that was going to be lead-balloons-ville, right? Because the *padrino,* he knows who's thinking about me for anything), and then I told him I was sick, and then, like you'd have to know, of course I told him sure. Right! Twelve noon. Sharp!

"Look at 'em," the *padrino* said, nicking his head sideways at the rest of the people in the place. "Look: all of them. The beautiful People."

I looked.

"The *beautiful* people," the *padrino* was saying again. "Envied. Copied. Applauded. Listen to them crap each other, sometimes, when they talk about how they hate to be recognized on the street. Oh, *yeah!* They *hate it!* And the first time they're not recognized, the butler—or the maid, or the keeper, or whoever's hired to hang around them—had to hide the sleeping pills and all sharp objects! The *beautiful* people! . . ."

He looked up as another plate of clams arrived.

Two, in fact. One for him, and one for me.

"*Beautiful People,*" he said, taking a deep breath after swallowing a clam, "*all they want is love.* They're entitled —right? Right! They're entitled to *L-O-V-E* just because they're the Beautiful People. And they're entitled three hunnerd-and-sixty-five days of the year!"

The *padrino* nodded, not looking at me but with his eyes roving back and forth around the room.

"The Beautiful People know that love is the Great American Dream! It's the *reward.* It's what you get if you're good and finish your prunes. It's the answer to all problems."

I swear to God . . . I knew all this to be leading somewhere; the *padrino* does not go in for long, aimless lectures. But damned if I could see where this one was going.

"Sure," he said. "Sure! Of course they told themselves that's the way it works—or, anyway, the Beautiful People who came before they did in this business, they started the whole cruddy romp. *They* said so. They said it not just once, but over and over and over again. Right from the first. From the time a moving picture stopped being just a back-room novelty that could draw a crowd by letting them see a steam engine running toward them; from the time that just the fact that a picture could move would sell a ticket—from *then*—the people who turned out flicks that had a story made damn sure that the story always had the same message: if you're the hero, you get love. If you're the heroine, you get love. Right! And who the hell was ever anything but the hero—the good guy—in a story he made up about himself?"

Okay. All right. I took a deep (and silent) breath. Maybe that was all the *padrino* wanted to say. Hell, for all I knew he was right. Profound even, maybe. I was willing to let it go at that, if that was what he'd summoned me here to hear.

But it wasn't, of course. . . .

"So—if you grow up hearing a thing like that, and you spend most of your life telling the same crap to other people —Christ, you get to believe it the same way you believe the world is round and the sun is hot." The *padrino* put down his clam fork and looked away from the other tables, back to me. His eyes were like the barrels of a shotgun. "Some people," he said, "Especially if they read fan magazines and listen to gossip, think that sex is the big deal in Hollywood. It's an easy mistake to make. And they get the idea that the Beautiful People of the movies are all superstuds and nymphomaniacs. *Bullshit!* Sex is a side issue; a by-product. Nymphomaniacs—no! *Lovomaniacs*—you bet your ass! But don't bother to look it up, it ain't in Webster's.

"Funny," he went on, "but a lot of people, people who don't know the score, think a nympho is the way she is because she gets too much out of sex; because she digs it the most! Not true. A nympho is a nympho because she's got a hang-up—one kind or another—that keeps her from getting what she thinks she ought to out of sex. It's never a whole thing for her. Never complete. So she has to run after that final thing, whatever she thinks it is, that *final thing*. Forever. More and more sex. All the time. Looking for the big action. Only, for her, it's never going to be there . . . sad, huh?"

This time he nodded, like he wanted me to agree with him.

Okay, I nodded. This whole deal was getting weird . . .

"Well then, see, a lovomaniac is the same way," the *padrino* said. "All these Beautiful People in here. All of them, lovomaniacs. More and more they need. Poor Beautiful People."

Oh, wow!

Now it was really getting foggy.

"Especially," the *padrino* continued, "if you're a performer, it's that way. Kid, you ever wonder how come performers have such a hell of a time trying to stay married? How come the divorce lawyers do such a hell of a business around here?

"You know how it goes? It goes like this: Start with the idea that you get love if you're the good guy. And you get more love if you're the best guy. So, naturally, if you make it to the top—if you're a star—you get more love than anyone else! You deserve it. It's the *reward*. Right?

"So, if you're a star, everyone in the whole world's gotta love you!"

The *padrino* nodded, and pitched into his order of clams again. Mine was still sitting in front of me, untouched.

"Only, how come a nymphomaniac can't get the sex ride she's after? Easy: she can't because she can't give anything back; she's frigid. She's not concerned with giving; she's too wound up with getting.

"All right; so why does a star, a topnotcher, become a star? What does it take? *Everything!* That's what it takes. You got to want to make it worse than, say, you want to breathe! Oh, sure, sometimes there's an accident, someone makes it to the top just by being in the right place at the right time. Like your Old Man did . . . in the beginning. Yeah! Face it, Buddy boy: Johnny Valentine was nothing special in the way of singers to begin with. He just happened to be in the right family, with the right mother and the right *padrino* with the right connections to push him—and a little bit of voice and a little bit of talent. Not near as much as a lot of other people who never got there at all. An accident—at first!"

No one had ever said that, right out, before. Not around me, anyway. And for sure not the *padrino; he* hadn't said it.

"So, naturally, it didn't last." The *padrino* shrugged. "You weren't old enough to remember, I guess. But you know the story. Vanni, he was washed up, for a while there. Because you don't stay on top for a lifetime by accident. No way! And he came back for just one reason: because he wanted it more than anything in the world, and he was willing to do anything—and everything—to get what he wanted.

"Lovomaniac? You bet your butt! One woman, Angie, your ma, how could she be enough for Vanni? She wanted love back. From him, even! How could that work? A lovomaniac can only *take,* not give. Not give love, anyway. The nearest to it that this kind of guy can come is what he gives in a performance—a really good performance—to the audience that sees and hears him. And kid, I don't have to tell you what your Old Man can give, sometimes, in a performance. . . ."

No.

He didn't have to tell me.

"See, that's the only love that can last, the only kind that can be real for a lovomaniac. Like Vanni. Like any of them—the poor beautiful People. The kind you get from an audience; that kind, it's the big love orgasm. Why? Because it's the only time a lovomaniac can really be involved; the only time he can give something back. The performance, see? *The performance,* that's the love he can return . . . the only kind of love he can give in return for the love he gets! And, hell, it would be okay, too, if a guy could be content with just that. Only, no one can. . . ."

Yeah. The *padrino* was getting at something, all right. He had something on his mind, and this was his way of clearing his throat to say it.

"So what happens? To love he gets from the audience, the big love orgasm, he tries to tie it down; tries to turn it into something else. He wants to get all that from just *one chick*. And when he thinks he has found a chick who can give him that, a broad who loves him in the total and pure and never critical way an audience can—taking what he has to give and never asking for more—why, then, she's The Dame, right? The Dame! Her, he's gotta have, no matter what else—because she's gonna give him that."

He nodded, his mouth full of clam, and stopped for a moment.

But he wasn't through, of course.

"Only, naturally," he said, swallowing, "that's bullshit. He's bullshitting himself because there are no broads like that, it's something he's been taught to believe and he wants to believe it. It never works out for him, and then he's all disillusioned and depressed and, if he's real lucky, he can go back to the true love . . . back to the audience. You get the idea, kid?"

Hooray! For once I knew what the *padrino* wanted—and was ready. I nodded.

And the *padrino* nodded back.

"Sometimes," he went on, not looking around now, but

with his eyes on me, "sometimes that can happen over and over again. And that is sad. Also kind of expensive. But, hell, it's part of the trade, I suppose, anyway, it seems like it always has been. For the Beautiful People. The poor, unfortunate slobs." He nodded again, looking through me for a moment, and then focusing once more on Buddy-boy's face. "It's also pretty hard on the people who get involved with a lovomaniac, like wives and kids. For instance," he said, "you take Jack Dahlberg, now. There's a sad case if ever I saw one."

I guess the surprise registered in my face.

"Jack Dahlberg," the *padrino* said, "would sell his soul —hell, maybe he already has sold it—for just one belch in his direction, an honest belch and from the heart, *just one pat on the head*—from old Irving. Yeah! He's driving himself crazy and fucking up his life, trying to get love from his father. . . ."

Oh, shit. *Oh, shit!* I could see it plain now; see it coming. And there I sat. Stuck to the chair. Letting him hit me with it because I didn't know what else to do.

". . . from his father," the *padrino* repeated. "Just like you, Buddy-boy. *Just like you!*"

Well, what the hell do you say? I elected to say nothing.

"What do you think, kid," the *padrino* said softly, "I'm blind? I see the way you been going, the past few months. Ever since you got back. Ever since your old man rushed off to New York to marry that skinny little cooz instead of sticking around to let you know he was glad to get you back. Ever since then. Months. That's what it's been. You turning down what nightclub dates and anything else I could get for you. Sitting around town, half-bombed every night. Making the scene with every two-bit cunt—every hustler—you could find. You think I didn't see? Vanni won't pay any attention, so little Buddy's going to show him. Oh, yeah!"

All right.

Fuck that.

Enough of that. . . .

I was about to let it rip; tell him, you know: Drop it. Knock it off. Only I held my breath about a second too long, and before I could make the first sound, he was off and running again.

"Tell me, kid," he said. "Tell me, how long's it been since you saw the chick? How long?"

"What chick?" I asked, stalling.

"Cut the crap." His voice was flat and hard. "How long since you saw Sandy?"

I had a big impulse, then; a big urge just to walk the hell out of there and not come back. Only I didn't do it. Oh, I'm great that way. Resolute, you know? Yeah. . . .

"A couple weeks," I said. "Maybe a little longer."

"Lie to me," the *padrino* said in a very soft voice. "Lie to me just one more time, Buddy boy—just once more—and we are gonna give the slobs in this beanery a real treat. They're gonna have the fun of watching me get up from eating clams to beat the living shit out of my *figliastro*. . . ."

He meant it.

"Okay," I said, still doing what passes for my best. "Okay. All right, already—more like three months."

"Uh-huh." He nodded. "Why?"

I knew he'd follow up with a question like that; didn't I know it? Yeah. And I knew I wouldn't have an answer, too. And, by God, I didn't. Not one I wanted to come out and tell the *padrino,* anyway. So I just sat there and didn't look at him and kept my damn mouth shut—like some kind of a baby—waiting for him to *pounce* me.

Only, he didn't.

Instead, he asked, "You been doing any work, since then? Any work at all."

Another no-answer question.

But not quite as no-answer as the last, so I had a hack at it. I looked at him with as much innocence as I can get into a face like mine, and said, "Well, yeah—a little, anyway. Not singing myself. But kind of—like—a directing job, see?"

The *padrino* nodded.

"With the Kinfolk," he said.

The Friendly United Christian Kinfolk.

The group I had been pushing for so long.

"Yeah," I said. "That's right. The Kinfolk."

The *padrino* speared the final clam on his plate.

And swallowed it.

And sighed.

And then looked—not just straight at me—but right through the fronts of my eyes and into the middle of my head, the way he's always been able to do since I was just a little kid.

"How's it coming?" he asked.

"What . . . the Kinfolk? Okay, I guess. They're working . . ."

"In shithouses, yeah. Like always. I mean the job *you're* supposed to be doing for them, Buddy. The rock opera—how's *that* coming?"

Oh, man.

I could feel my sphincter tighten up. Sure as hell. Sure as hell, the *padrino* could see inside my head, and—

*"I said, how's it coming?"*

"Okay." Even from inside, where I sit, the voice sounded weak and nothing. But the *padrino's* expression didn't change. "We're making some progress. See, the way we're—"

"You're a liar."

He didn't shout it. He just said the three words in a quiet, conversational tone, still looking inside me.

"Okay," I said. "I'm a liar. It stinks, what little we've actually got done in the past month or two, and if we keep on this way it'll never get finished at all."

The *padrino* nodded. "So," he said, "what's it going to take to get this . . . what do you call it, the thing you're working on?"

*"Moses-Ten."*

*Moses-Ten,* yeah. Well, how much you got to do before you got at least a completed score?"

"We got one."

That, at least, seemed to be news to him. One eyebrow bounced maybe half an inch and the corner of his mouth quirked up. "So what are you doing now?"

"Parts of it aren't right," I said. "They don't exactly fit and they don't seem to go together right with the rest of the work. We're changing these—anyway Joe is, he's the real composer in the group—and meanwhile Pete and I are orchestrating and—"

"Uh-huh," the *padrino* cut in. "So when that's done, what?"

"Well, then we're ready to record—"

"Record? For who?"

"Well . . ."

And, Christ, of course I didn't have an answer for him because that was a question I'd been having to duck with increasing regularity around the Kinfolk for the past few weeks. And I didn't have anymore answer for the *padrino* than I did for them.

The *padrino* waited for me to say something else. And then, when I didn't, he just nodded. "So," he said, "you'll cut a demo tape of it, maybe here, with your own equipment, and then try shopping it around. *Right?*"

I shrugged. "Something like that."

"Uh-huh."

The *padrino* leaned back in his chair and sighed. "They sure do a great job on the clams here," he said, patting his stomach. "Too bad your appetite ain't better today, kid. Try one. You can't just leave them there on the plate. If you do, ol' Sam will just start snitching them . . . and that's bad because I'm way over my diet already. Listen—fuck the demo tape. When you're ready . . . go for the whole enchilada. Hire the people, check with me and I'll tap the right studio, put it together—professional— and then bring it over to Lullaby. That way . . ."

I couldn't believe it.

"Look," I said, "we *can't* just . . ."

". . . that way," the *padrino* went right on, paying me no attention, "you're selling the package instead of just the idea and the group. It makes all the difference in the kind of contract we sign for you."

"But—where . . ."

"Where what?"

"*Padrino*—hiring people, getting the studio, making a master that's really release-quality, Christ! That's going to run into real *money!* Who's going to . . ."

And, right then, I knew I had said too much.

Asked the wrong question.

Walked into the semantic trap the *padrino* had been building for me all through the meal. I had said what he'd brought me there to say. I had asked the question that gave him an opening to say . . .

"Why . . . you are, Buddy. Who else?"

Okay.

All *right,* already—wasn't I expecting it? Sooner or later? For sure! So why was my belly suddenly so cold?

I couldn't answer him.

It was like my jaw muscles locked. . . .

"All that stuff," the *padrino's* tone was as casual as if he'd been telling me it was three o'clock, "it's expensive, yeah. But, kid, *it just couldn't cost a whole quarter of a million dollars.*"

And suddenly, you know, I couldn't seem to feel much of anything.

The depression. The sense of something bad in my head, the bummer I'd been on ever since I tumbled to what Zeke had done—yeah, and the ball-freezing suspicion that had been smeared all over the disordered, unkempt landscape of Buddy-boy's mind since I walked in here—all of that was gone.

*The padrino was hep.*

I knew it; not the details, no, but I *knew* . . .

So . . . all right.

So . . . *nothing!* Somewhere inside, I realized I had finally lost the ability to give a damn. If I felt anything, I guess it was just kind of relieved. Almost—*Jesus*—almost happy!

"All right," I said with all the nothing I felt right there in my voice, "okay, *Padrino*—you got something to say. So say it. . . ."

The *padrino* played it very cool.

"*What?*" he said, registering innocence. "All I said's that stuff couldn't cost a quarter-mil. Something funny about that?"

"*Padrino*," I said, "you been playing games. Word games. With me. Ever since I walked in here. In fact, in a kind of a way, I just realized maybe it's been word games with us ever since I can remember. So now—no more. You got something to say. Say it."

The *padrino* nodded. And—weird trip—I almost thought I saw something like approval, far back in his eyes.

"Okay, Bud," he said. "No more games." But he didn't go right ahead. Instead, he kind of hesitated. And then, damn it, he *smiled*—that big, all-across-the-face crooked smile of his that I remembered from when I was a little kid. "You know," he said, "you know, Bud, for a while lately I been wondering if we was *ever* gonna get you raised. Well. We'll see. . . ."

I wasn't going to reply to that.

I just sat there and waited for him to spit it out.

"So now," he went on when he saw I would wait him out, "no more games. Fair enough! And for an opener, I'll

335

level with you. We didn't get the whole two-fifty back from your pal Zeke. . . ."

"*Huh?*" I couldn't help saying.

"Fair's fair." The *padrino* shrugged. "You gotta give a guy at least walking-around money, right? Especially after all he did. And especially since he's going all the way to South America. And especially since we're not giving the dough back or anything. . . ."

Oh, wow!

I'd figured this for heavy action, sure.

But . . . what the *hell?* . . .

"Oh, yeah," the *padrino* went on, "and for keeping his kisser shut, too. That's worth money. So we laid twenty big ones on him. Whatcha say, keed? That fair?"

Okay.

Enough!

"*Padrino,*" I said, and I kept my voice steady. But just barely. "*Padrino*—I think you better take it from the top."

He seemed surprised.

"Yeah?" he said. "Well—okay. If you say so. Start with this—I *never* bought the crap about you getting lost, having engine trouble, ditching in the sea. Not from the very first. Oh, sure . . . there was a chance it was on the level. So I had to play it that way—help lay on a search and all that. But, for true, Buddy boy, I didn't really buy it . . . not a damn bit more than I ever bought the payoff gimmick. Follow me so far?"

"Yeah. So far."

"So all right. If you'd been picked up a little earlier than you were—just a few hours, maybe even less—we'd all have been in the soup for sure. Because they'd have been able to nail your buddy there in the desert, when he picked up the money. He'd have spilled his guts. And it would've made the papers. And there'd have been hell to pay from all angles. As it was, you were found just *minutes* after the pickup. And he was away, with the dough, before the word got around."

"So?. . ."

"So—you came back. And everynone played it real big. And—hell—what with all the slobber, the money gig almost got lost in the shuffle. Would have been, maybe. Only I'd had my boys—the union investigators—on the job from the very first. And, Bud, they *really* got to work after they had a chance to interview the copter crew that pulled you outa the drink."

It didn't register.

What did the copter people have to do with it? Was one of them in on the deal with Zeke? I was about to ask that —but the *padrino* was still talking. . . .

"Kid, in some ways, your idea wasn't too bad. And you brought it off as well as any amateur. Only—like an amateur—you did slip up on some pretty important points. Count 'em off:

"One—you were in a life raft. But where'd you get it? The guy who rented you the plane didn't put it aboard. It's not part of the normal equipment of the airplane. So, where? Simple . . . you brought it yourself. But for *why?* That flight plan of yours didn't have an overwater leg!

"Two—you were a shade slow in reacting when you heard the copter engine. I think, there, the timing was off. Zeke was supposed to come either earlier or later, and you hesitated to throw what—water, food, whatever overboard. You didn't want to dump it if it was a stray ship and they didn't see you. Right? No . . ." he held up a hand, "no, don't tell me. It doesn't matter. What matters is, you waited so long that the copter pilot spotted some of the stuff—half-empty water jug, maybe, or cans or something—before it sank. And he remembered it for my boys.

"Three—Buddy, you're just too good a pilot to pull a dumb stunt like that. Maybe I ain't the best *padrino* a kid ever had. But I still know a hell of a lot about you, boy. And that wasn't in the cards. Okay. With me so far?"

I nodded at him, but didn't speak.

"Okay, then . . . so with all that, I *knew* the crash had to be a hustle. But Zeke's bit with the dough, now that was something else. I couldn't see you going for a play like that anymore than I could buy the idea of you getting lost and crashing at sea.

"On the other hand, whoever got the money *had* to be in on *your* play. And he had to be someone you trusted— trusted enough to believe he'd come for you and find you —so that kinda narrowed the field. The survival gear, of course, that was the icing on the cake. Saved the boys maybe two, three days. They had the store where it was bought just three hours after they talked to the guy who found you. Had Zeke's name twenty minutes after that . . . and had *him* before the day was over. Questions?"

God.

Questions? I had maybe a million. But one of them seemed more important than the rest. . . .

"You could have blown the whole thing," I said, "brought Zeke in, turned the money back to Dad. You're his partner, *padrino*. Part of the money was really from your own pocket. Why didn't you?

The *padrino* smiled. Just a little smile that went away in a hurry. And shook his head. "That question," he said, "is one we let you answer. Go ahead. . . ."

He was right. I knew. . . .

"If Zeke was busted," I said slowly, "and came to trial, he would have to tell it all, sooner or later. Worst he could get is an extortion rap—while I'd come off a phony, and the Old Man wouldn't look too good either. . . ."

"So far," the *padrino* nodded, "you're doing okay. Keep going. . . ."

Going where?

As far as I knew, that was all of it. I looked at the *padrino* and tried to think of something else. But I couldn't.

"Okay, then," he said finally, when he saw I was out of gas, "there was *me*, too. The *padrino*. Your godfather—see, kid, old Sam, he's kinda on the hook for this one."

I couldn't follow that.

But he laid it out for me.

"Buddy," he said, and his voice was almost gentle, "you weren't in on the money deal. No. But why *any* of this? Why should you pull a caper that could easily get you killed? What would be worth it to you?"

I looked away.

"Maybe I just wanted some publicity," I said. "Face it, my career is going nowhere. Maybe I needed something, a gimmick, to get Buddy Valentine into the public eye. Into—"

*"Bullshit!"*

I still couldn't look at him.

"What, then?" I said.

"Not what," the *padrino* said, "*who*. It was for Vanni, kid. For him. For your Old Man. You wanted him to love you; you wanted him to notice you were around, like.

You wanted him worried, so he'd knock it off with that skinny little bitch he was screwing around with—hell, maybe you even figured it would put it together again, between him and your Ma—"

"Padrino—"

"*Non mi da il padrino!*" He was still smiling a little, but his voice had gone hard. Not louder, he was still almost whispering. Just a lot harder. *Padrino!*" he snorted. "Some *padrino* you got, boy. I'm supposed to be the one you come to when the Old Man's not around, when he can't help, when it's something you can't talk to him about. So how well did I do *my* job? I knew how things were going for you—yeah, and how the deal with your Ma and your Daddy was hurting you—all this time. And what did I do about it? Nothing. See, kid, the *padrino*'s not clean on this one, either."

"Aw . . ."

"Aw *nothing!*" He sighed and took a breath. "Look— your 'buddy' Zeke tried to get you killed, kid. Figure it: he had the dough. Was he going to pick you up, the way he agreed, out of the ocean? When you were the only guy on earth could tag him with the ripoff stunt? No *way!* Only, he does come off with this much credit . . . He could've screwed up that inflatable raft of yours. You'd never've known it was no good to you until it was too late. He could've done that, only he didn't. Why? Because nobody is all bastard, that's why. He could decide not to come back for you, pick up the dough, and be ready to hide. But he couldn't go for outright murder . . . which is why he's free and starting a helicopter service in South America."

I waited for him to go on.

"In case you're wondering—and you should be, by the way—the answer to one question you shoulda asked me is no. Your Old Man don't know about any of this. He's not even hep that the crash at sea was a phony. And he'll never hear it from me or my boys. And—sonny—he better not hear it from you, either. *Kapeesh?*"

I just nodded.

"So," he went on, "that leaves just one little item. Just one. *You.*"

I shrugged and wanted to look away and couldn't. "Me?" I said. "What *about* me? You gonna work me over, *pa-*

*drino?* Like you used to whomp me when I was a kid, and needed it."

The *padrino* snorted again.

"That'd be easy," he said. "It would, wouldn't it? Bet your ass! Take us all off the hook. You get to stop feeling like a guilty asshole. I get to tell myself I did my job again. Except that's gotta be a lie. It wouldn't really solve a thing. For anyone. Any other ideas, kid?"

No.

Not a one.

"Okay, then," he said, "so try this on for size: you got obligations, boy, and so have I. Also, we got something over two hunnerd gee to start paying them off with."

*"Huh?"*

The *padrino* gave a little laugh.

"What the hell, kid," he said, "you figure me for a thief? Think I was going to just keep the dough? Look, I told you, I got a little egg on my face in this one, too. So we do it this way . . . Bud, from here on in, you start acting like a man."

"That's easier to say than . . ." I began.

"Shuddap!" he cut me off. "A man pays his markers—he respects obligations. You got one to the group, as you call them. The Friendly United Christian Kinfolk. They think you can help them. They think you know what you're doing —that you could be a director. Okay. So we find out if they're right or wrong. I'll handle the money angle. You can't just walk into a bank with a quarter of a million in small bills and make a deposit. I'm already running the dough through a Swiss bank. I deposited it, I'll get a loan against the deposit, make the whole deal look kosher. That's not your worry. What is your worry is making a good master with those guys . . . so do it."

I didn't know what to say to that.

It sounded good.

But I'd been wrong so damn often. . . .

"But most of all," he went on, "the big job is paying your marker to yourself. Listen, boy, you took your best shot where Vanni's concerned. Face a fact—he's never gonna give you what you want. You or your Ma either. Hell, he can't even give *himself* what he wants. But you still owe *you.*"

That, I didn't get.

Not at all. And I guess it must've showed in my face. . . .

"Buddy," the *padrino* said, "what the fuck are you really after—a standing round of applause from the world? *Forget it.* You'll never get that. What are you, one of the beautiful unfortunates? The lovomaniacs? A prime jerk, like them? Or are you a man? Love? Maybe it's not there —for you—not anywhere. Not even the phony, addictive kind your Old Man has got to have. But maybe you're one of the lucky ones. Maybe you can have the kind that's real. I don't know. And neither do you, now. Because until you know you're a man—until you're sure of that—how the hell can you love yourself? And how the hell can anyone, ever, love a guy who doesn't love himself?"

He shook his head a little, and grinned. At himself, I think.

"Anyway," he said, closing the subject for good, "I'm still the *padrino.* The godfather. But this is the last time, boy. From here on, I can't help. From here on, it's your own show . . . you're buying the tickets. I dunno if you'll hack it or not. But you got the best chance, right now, that you'll ever get. And, Buddy, I'm betting on you."

And then, I guess, he was through talking.

And so was I. Because I didn't have anything to say, anyway. What the hell *could* I have said?

Besides, I had work to do.

And things to think about.

And—*yes,* by God! And . . .


## Sandy Hallowell

. . . a telephone call to make.

Face it, my feller Amurkuns—The Hallowell was trying to play by the rules, but a girl can get awfully damned lonesome playing by the rules, sometimes. *That darn Buddy!*

I had a good half-hour before flight time.

And about five dollars' worth of small change.

One absolutely great thing about Kennedy International, when they built the place they didn't forget to put in the right number of pay telephone booths. You can always find an empty. At that, though, I stalled around—telling myself this and that—for a good (bad?) five minutes before I finally walked into a booth and spread out the change and dialed the number.

There was the usual holdup.

And the operator's voice telling me how much for the first three minutes (which was *wow,* because, after all, it was the middle of the day and the middle of the week) and then the change going clank . . . and then the wait for the number to ring. In Los Angeles. . . .

All of which gave me time (too much, maybe?) to think.

Okay, friends, so it's all right for me to *know.* To have the understanding. And to trust. That's fine, and I do. I really do. But face it, there is a great big difference between natal and horary astrology, right?

Right. *Right,* my friends and feller Amurkuns. And, gee whiz—I was letting it *all* ride on that number this time, and I defy anyone to feel really comfortable doing that.

Because, damn it, I really *did* miss that darn Buddy!

As soon as I was sure—sure inside myself—that he was the Capricorn I'd found in the Fifth House of my natal chart, The Hallowell had started casting horary charts to determine the when and how of things. And of course I'd known there would be the setback sometime, even known part of the reasons for it.

Don't get me wrong.

People sometimes have the notion that things you find in your chart are inescapable; that there is some kind of outright good or bad that you just can't escape. And that is rarely true. Almost never, in fact, well, at least if you admit the inevitability of such things as death and the sun rising and breathing and the absolute need for food, shelter, air, and suchlike.

You are *not* going to defy reality.

That's for children. . . .

But, admitting things like that, if you look deeply enough into anything that happens, you'll notice there is no unrelieved black or white in there; no absolute good or bad— even if you see something unpleasant coming and either can't or won't do anything to avoid it. Look, don't get me going on that. I'll be talking the rest of the day. . . .

Anyway, I knew there'd be a little trouble. And I also knew this was the time it could all be repaired. Today.

Now.

The best thing to do, maybe, would have been to just lie doggo—"set small in the weeds" the way my Dad always said—and let it happen. Let Buddy come to me. Sure.

Only, there was this schedule foul-up, see?

*See?*

And, well, if he *did* call, right on schedule, the phone would ring in my apartment and I wouldn't be there to answer it. And it might be a day, or two . . . or more, even . . . before we made contact, and—

*Damn* it, I *missed* that guy!

I really . . .

Now the phone was ringing on the other end. In Los Angeles. At his mother's place. Of course, there was no guarantee he would be there. In fact, seeing the time difference and all, it was a pretty good shot he wouldn't.

But maybe *she* . . .

"Hello?"

*Mrs. Valentine?*

"This is Sandy Hallowell. I was trying to get in touch with Buddy. Is he there? . . .

"Oh—yes. I mean, *no.* Buddy isn't here—but I can give you a number where you might reach him. Are you here in town, Sandy?"

"No. I'm in New York. But I'll be on a plane for Los Angeles in a few minutes, and I . . ."

"Of course. I'm—uh—afraid we don't see as much of Buddy as we should, since he got his own place . . ."

She sort of trailed off and I could hear the phone being set down on something hard, I guess while she looked for the number. His own place, huh? Sounded like Buddy was making the break at last.

# The 9th House

*Dreams, visions, long journeys, psychic
experiences, education, intuition . . .*

*Forecast: There'll be some wild shenanigans at a sump-
tuous Malibu party, and fangs will be bared. But for
Jackie Dahlberg and David Strauss, the worst is yet to
come.*

*In the Ninth House Sam LoCicero has a dream, Sandy
Hallowell has an intuition, the Valentines have a divorce,
and several long journeys are about to begin. . . .*

## Jack Dahlberg

Why can't I have just a minute or two of peace.
Just that?

The question had been going through my mind ever
since I got to the studio that morning. And all through
the day. And now, with the day behind me, it was bigger
and more urgent and more unanswerable than ever.

It had been, all things considered, one hell of a day.

Papa's call had been waiting for me when I got in, and
of late, those calls were never just exactly the greatest
things that could happen.

I wished he could be out here.

Or that I could get back there.

Somehow I had the idea—a wrong idea, probably, but
it seemed like a kind of final hope to me—that if I could
see Papa in person, we could work things out. On the

345

phone was different. Even if he could set up that person-to-person television hookup he'd been talking about, it wouldn't be the same.

Anyway, he was on the phone when I got in and of course I had to answer at once. And again, as usual, he was all business. Just as he had been ever since the day he found out about me and Gaby.

All right! I knew he wasn't exactly going to jump for joy.

That I couldn't expect.

I mean—how many guys do you know who wind up with their father's ex-mistress?

How many?

So, all right. But if he'd been here or I could get back to New York, I *knew* I could talk it out with him. I *knew* it. But it was out of question, really. Too much going on right here on the West Coast even for an overnighter back there. Besides, I had just the tiniest little suspicion that Papa might refuse to see me even if I did hie myself to New York. And I didn't want the door closed that firmly between us.

So I took the call and told him what he wanted to know.

That, at least, wasn't the worst thing in the world. Not for the first few minutes, anyway, because everything—well, *almost* everything—was going pretty well at the studio.

So far, for the whole year, not a single one of the productions I had set up, and that I was keeping a firm tab on from day to day, had run over budget. And two or three had actually come in under their original estimates. By God, he couldn't beef or fault me on that score.

And, whether he knew it or not, I had taken a page from his book and set up a little spy system of my own back in *his* office—so I knew the daily gross reports from the pictures now in release (pictures in my own program, that is) were nothing but terrific. Naturally, I didn't ask Papa about those figures. I could see where he could get kind of touchy about something like that, especially since he'd been so dead set against the whole thing in the beginning. Not that he would want any part of Monarch's program to be falling on its face.

Of course not.

After all, any kind of win record at all could only make

him look good and it sure as hell wasn't what you could call common Industry gossip that he'd been against the skin-flix program I'd set up for the studio on this end. He could take a report like that to the directors with a smile on his face, and that was a pretty important kind of thing. Because it was getting to be annual meeting time again.

Still, I knew it would be a hell of a sore point for me to bear down on. At least for the moment. Because the only part of Monarch's production plan for the year that wasn't working out worth a damn was the part he'd handled personally. The part on which he'd exerted the famous Dahlberg touch.

*Sadie* was the point where we were in trouble.

And it was getting more and more serious every day. Worse still, it was becoming increasingly evident that no one, Irving Dahlberg specifically included, had the smallest damn idea of what to do about it. Because the truth was we had absolutely no leverage with the Valentine people. No leverage at all.

And without a lever . . .

*"You talk to that fucking guinea kike?"*

That was Papa's way of asking me if I'd managed to set up the conference he'd requested with Sam LoCicero and the rest of the Valentine people for the end of the week.

And I had to tell him I hadn't.

Oh, I could talk to them all right. Sure! All I had to do was phone Priapus Studios. They would "relay my message to Mr. LoCicero" or "contact Mr. Valentine" and, more often than not, I'd get a personal call back from one of them. All of which would come to absolutely nothing when adding-up time rolled around, because that was exactly what you could get out of either one of them. Nothing.

A lot of words.

But in substance, nothing.

"The usual, Mr. Dahlberg?"

It was Emil, the downstairs bartender at The Flower Club.

Coming here had become pretty much of a routine for me recently. What with living in a rented place in Stone Canyon—I'd turned over my house to Clara in the divorce —and both Gaby and me working our heads off, we'd taken to meeting, usually here at the Club, Gaby and I, when we were done for the day. It wasn't as fancy as The Candy Store or The Daisy or Factory and that's why I liked it. Just an anonymous joint to toss down a few drinks and unwind in.

Anyway, we'd got into the habit of meeting here.

"The usual, Emil," I said. "And, hell, make it a double."

"Yes, sir."

Say this for old Emil; the guy never cracks. If he thought anything, one way or the other, about my starting off the evening with a double, you'd never know it from his face.

I wondered what he'd think, really think, if he knew it wasn't my first double for the day. Or my second.

Not even my first double in the past half hour.

But by God, *I deserved it!*

"Jack, I'm *warning* you." That's what the great Irving Dahlberg—my father, mind you—that's what he'd said to me on the phone just to give my day the right start. "I'm warning you, we've got real trouble with the directors— maybe with the stockholders themselves, even—unless we can show them some kind of action on *Sadie.*"

"Papa—you know I'm doing my best."

*"It's not good enough, Jackie."*

Now, I ask you, what the hell do you say to that?

"Papa," I began. And caught myself just in time. I mean, believe it, *just in time.* Because what had been on the tip of my tongue was the one thing I couldn't say, couldn't even hint at, in any conversation. That I knew why Valentine and his people were so adamant about not letting us release *Sadie.* That they had it in but good for Papa since the payoff.

Papa still didn't know about the tape that had recorded the deal he'd made with Johnny Valentine.

I was holding that.

A real zinger.

Holding that in reserve, a final card to play if the strokes got too short.

*What a hell of a way to have to deal with your own father!*

"A double, sir."

Emil handed it to me, and I nodded to him (he had the trick, known only to really good waiters, of managing to seem shorter than even his shortest customers; hell of a man, Emil) and walked it up the stairs to the poolroom on the second floor.

A poolroom?

Yes. Don't ask me why a poolroom, in what once passed for the most exclusive club (it was fading and drooping a little now, The Flower; that happens eventually to any club, private or public) in town. It was just one of the things the owners set up as a "something different" attraction when they opened the place.

Funny. I'd never played a game of pool in my life before the place opened. A little billiards once, yes. Back in the days when we all lived together, Papa had somehow got hold of the idea that real class involved having a billiard room in the house, so naturally we had one built (I think he said once that that room had cost him maybe a hundred grand, not counting the money he lost to various people playing billiards in it) and I even had a tutor in billiards for a while, would you believe it? True!

But that phase had passed and it had been maybe ten years since I'd even seen a flat table, sticks, and the rolling balls—and I'd still never encountered a pocket table anywhere except on a movie set—when The Flower opened.

Still starting several miles behind just about anyone in the club, it only took me four months to become the club champion.

"Game?" I said to Max Benson, the comic, who was upstairs getting himself stiff—as usual—when I walked in.

"Not with you, Mr. Mosconi," he said, giving me the world-famous Benson leer. "Tell me, Jackie—do *your* balls move as fast as those on the table?"

I grinned at him and wished I had a writer around to slip me a good comeback line. Not that it would've done me any good. Nobody, *but nobody*, comes off ahead trading lines with Benson. Drunk or sober, he's the quickest tongue in the West when it comes to stand-up comedy.

There was no one else around, so I racked the balls and began a game against myself.

Or, anyway, I did after sending a waiter down for another double.

And the place was quiet—even the balls didn't seem to click so loudly—for the next half hour.

It was good, being there.

And it was good to concentrate on the game.

And on those doubles.

The thought crossed my mind that it was probably for the best, after all, that the game for The Flower was pool. Having to work at it, instead of winning with hardly any effort the way I can at, say, ping-pong, was the perfect anodyne for too much Thinking About the Studio. Can't think about the studio—or anything else—and really do a good job at pool. Or drinking.

I hardly noticed the time go by. But occasionally, between shots, I did stop long enough to wonder what in hell was making Gaby . . .

### Johnny Valentine

". . . so goddamned late!"

She looked up, tossing the crazy-colored knit poncho she'd been wearing across a table and paying no attention when it slipped off, onto the floor.

"So I'm your wife," she said, turning those baby-blues on me with that nutty wide-innocent look she can do without even trying, "and I'm late getting home—so what?"

We been starting an awful lot of conversations that way lately, Dolly and me.

Only, tonight, I just wasn't in the mood.

"Okay," I told her. "So I don't want to know where you were. No questions-and-answers tonight. Come over here—"

She looked at me. still wide innocence, but like at a stranger.

"What for?" she said, not moving.

And suddenly I just couldn't swallow anymore of anything. Or, what was worse, understand it. Talk about a generation gap, for Chrissake . . . it's bad enough when you got one of those with your kids, but having one with your wife!

"What is it, kid?" I asked her.

"What's what?"

"Between us. I don't get it. We've been married now— how long—just a few months. Yeah, not even a year—"

I let the sentence trail off because, suddenly, I knew it was leading to a place I didn't want to go. Dolly was just standing there still, looking, and there was something about her, the way she looked or stood or something, that told me she would give me a straight answer if I asked the question I had half-formed in my mind. And if she did, I wasn't going to think a hell of a lot of the answer.

She was still one gorgeous broad.

If you go for the type, anyway. And I do.

Okay, like Sam said that time (and I couldn't get that time out of my mind, either, though I hoped old Sam had) talking about her, no tits and no ass! Right! Standing side-wise, Dolly Diamond needed the famous mane of hair just to let you know she was around. She couldn't have been six inches in width, turned sidewise.

So what was it about her?

*The face.*

Yeah . . . the face; still like an angel. Born with it, I guess. Maybe that's what tore me up so bad when she turned bitchy. The long hair always sort of reminded me of angel's wings.

"You were saying something to me," she spoke up finally. "You were asking some kind of a dumb question."

I shook my head.

"Forget it."

"Let's not."

She came a little closer and then I smelled it. Funny thing, you know, a year ago I wouldn't have known what I was smelling. That sweetish-pungent smell. The hay-shakers, guys who been around farms and like that when they were kids, they claim it smells like a haystack burning. I wouldn't know. Never smelled a burning haystack.

But I knew the smell I smelled on her now.

"How many?" I said. And right away, I could've torn my tongue out; I'd made up my mind before—no question-and-answer games tonight. Tonight a little snatch-grab-and-tickle. Right! Only, smelling that, the words had just popped out, kind of.

"Six," she said. "Or seven. Who counts?"

Say this for the kid: she doesn't try to con me about it these days.

"Why?"

She shrugged, just a tiny twitch of the thin shoulders. "Why not?" she said.

I couldn't help it:

*"You fucking well know why not!"*

Dolly looked down her eyes at me, those wide angel eyes of hers, and didn't seem to see me at all.

"I know you *told* me not to. I know that. Is that what you mean . . . Daddy . . . that you *told* me not to?"

"I mean we agreed! . . ."

"The fuck we did." She stood there, her voice flat and kind of older than it usually was, and said the words without putting much of anything into them. "We didn't agree—Daddy. We didn't even discuss it, if you remember. What happened—Daddy gave an order. An *order,* man!"

"All I said—"

"All you *said* was—if I remember, and I remember for sure—that it was too dangerous for people in your position. Too dangerous because if I got busted, you'd be smeared, too. So I wasn't to do it again."

"Well. Isn't it true?"

"It's true."

"So? . . ."

"So, what? I'm me. Me, Daddy! And if I want to smoke a whole key—a whole fucking key, not just a joint or two—I'll do it. Just exactly the same way I expect you'll finish a bottle of your precious booze tonight if you want to. What's the big deal?"

I knew I should stop right there.

*I knew it.*

But I couldn't; she was right about one thing. I already had more than a couple of belts in me. And the way things were coming on right now, I knew there were going to be quite a few more before the night was over. So, hell, maybe it was a little bit the Old Bejoyful talking. But mostly it was just me.

"The big deal," I said, "is that something like that can screw your career before it ever gets off the ground. Look at what happened to that faggy ex-husband of yours. . . ."

"Oh, great!" Now, at last, there was a little animation in her face. She turned her eyes upward and closed them a minute and made some kind of gesture, meaning *what* I wouldn't know, in the air. "Great! Start in on that again. David blew it because he was on drugs, right? David smoked grass and that led him to become an addict, right? Jesus Christ . . . Daddy . . . Jesus *Christ,* what a lot of middle-aged crap!"

"David *didn't* blow it?" I said.

"Oh, yes, Daddy."

"He *wasn't* high on something?"

"Oh, yes, Daddy."

"Well then, why all the smart-ass chatter, huh? What's the middle-aged crap bit?"

"Because that's just what it is."

She turned around, started to walk out of the room, I think, but changed her mind and flopped down on the couch.

"David never smoked grass in his whole fucking life," she said. "Never! You dig—Daddy? *Never!* David Strauss, my faggy ex-husband as you seem to get a big thrill out of calling him, David Strauss never did any grass and never did any pills and never did *anything* as far as I know except juice, except the booze."

"And sucked a few cocks," I said. "Dont forget that."

"I wouldn't know. I wasn't there."

"You weren't?"

"I wasn't."

"Then," (oh, shit-no! my mind was yelling at me even as I said the words; oh, shit-no! but I couldn't help it) "where'd you learn the trade so good, kid? Tell me that."

It was like she'd turned to ice.

"You—really want to know?" she said.

No. My God, no, of course I didn't. But what could I say, after that? What the hell could I say? So I didn't say anything. And she laid it on me.

"Okay," she said. "Let's see—start with the beginning. The first guy I blew—I was all of twelve at the time—that was old Sebastian. You know: the screwy composer? He took me up to his room and, at twelve, I knew all about screwing and all that from watching Mama doing it with every 'Uncle' she brought home ever since I could remember. But I hadn't ever screwed anyone myself, not yet, and I wondered why she liked it so much so I let him take me up to his room. But he didn't want to screw me. No way! All he wanted was to convince me what he had between his legs was a popsicle . . ."

I wanted to shut her up.

I wanted to scream at her or stick a pillow over her mouth— anything to stop her from telling me these things.

But I couldn't.

All I could do was just sit there.

"And then when he'd taught me all he could, he started handing me around to his friends. It was a big joke—the best little blow job in town and, look, fellas! Look! She's only twelve and she gobbles it like a pro! So after a while it got to be kind of a party thing, you know? I'd come to the party and someone—whoever was paying the freight for the moment—someone would point to someone, and say, 'Do him!' And man—I would *do* him!"

Well, I told myself, it wasn't exactly a bolt from the blue. After all, how had *I* met her?

And it was a long time ago, anyway. A long time ago and when she was only twelve and, hell, how can you hold something against a kid only twelve years old, right?

But she wasn't through.

"And that's how I finally got the first little part in the first play. The first one—the one where I met David—I got that part by blowing the producer and having a friend take a picture of it and offering to show it to the law. Because I'd been the best blow job in town for three years then—for three years, Daddy—but I was still underage and I still looked it."

Jesus.

*Jesus,* if she'd only stop.

"So then there was David and—what do you know, Daddy—David, my faggy husband, *David was the first man who ever screwed me. The first!* How about that? Faggy. You call *him* faggy? Like I told you, Daddy, I don't know how faggy he was because I wasn't ever there when he made it with a boy and I don't give a good goddamn. *But he was the first one of you dirty bastards who was ever man enough to fuck me!*"

"Dolly," I finally managed to say. "Dolly—look—"

"No look! *You* look—Daddy—you look. At yourself! Count up sometime, don't take my word for it, count up sometime how many times since we been married, *married,* Daddy, have you actually thrown a *fuck* into me? How many? Don't tell me the answer. I *know* the answer because I keep score, for your information. And then count up how many times you couldn't get it up so I just had the fun of licking that thing."

My mouth opened, but no sound came out.

"And while we're about it—Daddy—let's take this little truth session a step further. You bet your withered old ass I was smoking a few joints today. And, truth, there were a

354

hell of a lot more than five or six or seven or eight that I smoked. You want to know why, huh? You want to know *why*—Daddy?"

I didn't. But—Christ help me—I couldn't seem to make enough noise to *say* so.

"Because I was trying to keep from making a phone call. Yes, Daddy, a phone call. To an old friend. Because I was so bored with all you old sonsabitches I wanted, real bad, to call my friend and have him get me in touch with a friend of his, you probably know her, a bulldagger here in town who runs a call-boy service. You know the kind of call boys I mean?"

I didn't.

No.

And I didn't want to.

"I don't mean cuntsuckers or other specialists like that. I mean the Golden Shower kiddies. You dig Golden Shower kiddies? You know about them? Do you, Daddy?"

Oh—God.

"Well, just in case you never heard of them, they piss on you and shit on you and do anything else you think you need. Anything else you think you need to get down to the level people live on in this *stinking, lousy, rotten shithouse of a town!*"

She was out of breath at last, Thank God.

But she wasn't done.

Oh, no.

She was not done.

"And why," she said, when she had a little breath back. "Why all of that? You really don't know, Daddy? You really don't know?"

Dolly had been facing me all through the time she was shouting, but now she seemed to have gotten rid of something inside her and she didn't need to face me anymore. So she had dropped back, limp, on the cushions of the couch and she was just talking in a conversational sort of tone, looking at the ceiling. . . .

"Because you don't give me what I need, Daddy."

I didn't speak.

If she wanted me to carry the ball part of the time in this conversation—if that's what you could call it—she was out of luck. Just like I was out of words.

"You spent today," she went on, "doing a little work. Seeing some people. Doing your own thing, right? Well, you know what I spent the day doing? I spent the day blowing a few joints and wishing it was something bigger, because it seems to be the only way I can get the things I want. The things I need. The things I'm into. . . ."

Very quietly, very deliberately, she reached into her handbag and brought out a homemade cigarette. A pink one. And set fire to it. I didn't have to inhale to know it wasn't tobacco.

"I never particularly wanted a career. You know that? I never really did. But, if you can't take care of me and be good to me the way I thought you would be; if you can't do that, I've got to have one. Only, the way you've got me tied up, I can't even have a career. You sit and sit and sit on the release for my first-and-only picture. *Sit* on it! Why, Daddy? Why? Just to make sure you keep me under your thumb? That's it, isn't it? . . ."

"No." I managed to say. "No. That's *not* it, kid. Look, we been over this before. I got reasons—good reasons, business reasons—you wouldn't—"

"Thats right," she cut me off. "That's right. I'm some kind of moron and I wouldn't understand Daddy's big and important reasons he won't let the public see my picture."

"It's not that. It's just—look, let's don't—"

*"Let's do!"*

She sat up now, taking a deep one off the reefer and holding the smoke down inside a long time and then letting it out, looking hard and straight at me, not wide-eyed anymore, just straight and, hell, a way I'd never really noticed before. Not from her.

"Let's *do* talk about it, Daddy. Because that's where it's at right now. I want you to let the picture loose, Johnny. I want you to let it loose *right now.*"

"I . . . can't tell you why, not all the—"

"I don't want to know any reasons. I wouldn't listen if you told me. I wouldn't believe you if you swore on something you believe in. And I don't give a shit. *You let that picture go.* I need it. I need it—out and with people looking at it—and I need the records that go with it released by Lullaby and I need to cut some new ones and if you don't . . . if you don't . . . I'm going to find me a lawyer who can make you tell the world, not just me but the whole

356

world, exactly *why* you won't, because I am going to sue your fucking-daddy *ass!* . . ."

I stood up.

"Don't threaten me, kid," I told her. "Don't order me and don't threaten me. I told you before. *Suggest. Suggest* . . . but *don't order!* And don't . . ."

"Fuck you."

She said the words calmly and she meant them and . . . in a funny way, you know . . . that was that.

Between us, I mean.

That was that, right there and then.

My arm twitched a minute or two. It wanted to belt her one, right in the choppers. Only it didn't move from my side. She just sat and looked at me—I kind of think she *expected* me to sock her—and waited to see what I was going to do. And finally it got through to me there was *nothing* for me to do. Nothing at all. Nothing in this world . . . except get out of there.

So I did.

I put the glass down and I turned around and looked for my hat, only it was where I'd tossed it, in the bedroom, and I didn't want to go all the way in there because she might say something else and if she did that, I might . . .

"Go on," she said.

"Go on what?"

"Whatever you were going to do—you *were* going to do something—do it, Daddy."

"I'm doing it."

And I turned around and headed for the door.

"If you're stuck for a place to sleep tonight," she said as I touched the knob with my hand, "you can come back here in an hour or two. I won't be here. I got other things to do."

"Be my guest."

I got the hell through that door and closed it behind me, not slamming it but making sure it locked so I would have to get out my keys or something to go back in, and I went down the stairs—went down them fast—and got in my own car and thanked God she hadn't parked behind me to block the drive as usual because I knew I was in no shape to be back there and in the same room with that stoned adolescent who was—God! how had it happened?—my wife—and I had to get away. I had to get away . . .

. . . in a big hurry.

Tell it like it is, my friends and feller Amurkuns, Mr. Buddy Valentine was in a hurry when he came through the door of our apartment . . . and, for sure, The Hallowell does dearly love to see her man in that much of a sweat to be with her.

*For sure!*

Of course, I suppose some girls might like a little more finesse. I mean—ever since Buddy and I moved in together, I've been sort of expecting him to cool down—or *slow* down —or something. But it hasn't happened yet . . . and now and then I think I'd cut his ever-lovin' throat if it did.

*"Hey, babe! . . ."*

That's the standard greeting. That, and the swift grab for whatever portion of The Hallowell happens to be handiest at the moment (over the weeks, I have gradually developed the habit of trying to make *that* part something of a relatively insensitive nature. A forlorn effort. More and more, I notice just about every part of me has grown sensitive. *To him,* anyway) and then . . . up, up, and *awaaaaaay!*

You see what I mean?

No finesse.

None at all.

And a quick thumbing of the nose at the kind of girls who think of finesse as a necessity. . . .

About—oh, say—half an hour to an hour later, we were resting. Together. On the bed. With the ashtray covering his navel and darn little else. (Finesse—*phooey!*)

"Hey, babe . . ." he said again.

And I started to roll in his direction. But about the time I had moved into the half-roll configuration, sanity had asserted itself. At least to some degree.

"Oh . . . *no!*" I said.

"Huh?" he said.

"The *party*," I said. "And don't tell me the hell with it, Mr. Valentine, sir."

"Aw, hell. . . ."

"Aw, hell, nothing! And I do mean *nothing* . . . !" He made a pretty determined grab in my direction, but we Hallowells are pure murder on evasive technique and broken-field running (as a couple of schools in the Big Ten discovered when they hired my brothers for their amateur football teams) and I made it to the bathroom and had the door locked before he was even on his feet.

"Hey . . . Sandy," I could hear him complaining outside the door as I made a tentative stab at the shower and jumped back to avoid lethal burns. "The hell with the party and the hell with the people who're going to be at it. What do we want with the party, anyway?"

"What we want," I hollered back at him, "is that your *padrino* said it was one you should attend. And you—you dope, you—let *me* find out about it. So . . . attend we do."

"Sandy! . . ."

"Later, man! Later!"

And he shut up—at least long enough for The Hallowell to do the quick-rinse bit and the quick-comb bit. (Look, that is one perfectly *great* thing about not being the most beautiful thing that ever walked on two legs; you can keep the hair and the rest of the face in fairly efficient fashion and be in and out of a bathroom in less that five and a half hours, right? Boy—believe it—that can be one hell of a saving, too. Some of the girls in this town have to spend as much as a *whole day* getting ready for a party, in order to come out all sweet, clean, and wholesome-looking with the hair tied back and plenty of no-makeup on the face.)

Buddy, that bum, hadn't even made a good *start* at getting ready.

"Move it, sport," I told him. "Make with the shoes and socks and such. *Speed*. O Lout. . . ."

He just sort of grinned at me.

"Sandy," he said.

*"No!"*

"No . . . I mean . . . *okay,* all right. We go. To the party I mean. But—look—I been thinking . . ."

"My God! Thinking, yet!" I nabbed his shoes and trotted them over to where he was sitting on the edge of the bed. "Did it *hoit* you, *bubbi?*"

He made a face. "Very funny," he said. *"Very* funny. But—for real, babe—I been meaning to ask you for a long time: Sandy, how come you made it all so easy for me? . . ."

Oh, wow!

Now what kind of a question was this? Especially with

less than half an hour to get out of here and get something to eat before we were due for a fashionably late entrance at Len and Nora's place in Malibu. For just a moment, I thought it might be some kind of a *maneuver,* you know? But, looking close at his face, I realized he was asking for real. So I had to answer. . . .

"Made it easy?" I said, wanting to make sure I had the question straight. "How you mean, chum?"

"You *know* what I mean."

And, yeah, I did.

Buddy and I hadn't seen each other for God-it-seemed-forever until, well, say about forty-eight hours before we moved into this place and, looking at it objectively, I guess it did seem kind of weird.

It wasn't, though.

Not to me, anyway, and not (or so I had assumed) to him, either.

After that phone call to his mother's house shortly before takeoff in New York, I'd tried the number she gave me for his new apartment, but I hadn't connected, and I was even beginning to have a doubt or two about the accuracy of the chart I'd drawn for the day by the time I landed in LAX.

All doubt disappeared, though, about five minutes after landing when the gate steward handed me a note as I followed the passengers from the plane. It said "Please call Buddy. Urgent!" And gave a number . . . the same one.

And so I did. . . .

"I didn't really make it easy, Buddy," I told him, "*You* did. By calling. And by the things you said . . ."

He shook his head.

"You'd have been perfectly justified," he said, "in making me sit up and beg, like the dog I am."

I shrugged. "For why?" I said. "Hey, man . . . you're no game player. Not really. You tried to be one once, as I remember. But it was a total washout because, Buddy, darling, you are just not built for that kind of a course." I kissed him—a quick one on the end of the nose to avert the kind of developments that make people from an hour to five hours late for parties—and then, because he looked sort of puzzled still, I added, "And that, O slowpoke, is one of the things I dig most about you. Now, damn it . . . will you put on your *shoes!*"

But he still just sat there.

"That," he said slowly, "isn't quite what I mean. At least, I don't think it is. Sandy . . . tell me something for true, now . . . did you have any idea—any inkling at all—that I was going to call you? That day, I mean; that day in particular?"

*Oh, well, gee whiz!* . . .

A question like that, mah fraanz, gives you two choices: *lie,* or spend an *hour* telling the exact truth. No in-betweens. . . .

"Buddy," I said, "lookit . . . I make you a deal: put on the shoes . . ."

"Aw, babe. . . ."

"Put on the shoes, honey—and the rest of the clothes—and while you're doing it, I'll answer the questions the best way I know how."

He thought it over.

"Look, couldn't we just—"

"No, we couldn't! Now, *damn it!* . . ."

"Okay, okay, awreddy." He got up and went hunting around, one shoe off and one shoe on, for something or other. "Where the cottonpickin' is my . . . oh, here it is. All right, now—I'm getting ready—so? . . ."

"So all right. Actually, you know part already," I said, moving over to let him hook the back of my bra. (All right, *sure,* I can hook it myself; but who the heck *wants* to?) "About what I think. About astrology, I mean. . . ."

He hooked the bra, and started in a little stroking program I wisely (and with considerable strain on the character; I absolutely love to be stroked!) moved away from.

"I know," he said, when I was out of reach, "that the star-stuff is your bag. Your thing. Sure. But . . ."

"*But* . . . And that's why I don't often try to tell any-body anything about it. That sounds too much like I'm selling something. And I'm not."

"Uh-huh. So what's that got to do with—?"

"Everything," I said. "And nothing. You asked me if I *knew* you were going to call on *that* day."

"No, I didn't. I asked if you had—well—some *idea* I would . . . on just that day."

"Same thing. And same answer. Buddy . . . yes, I *thought* we were going to get back together. I thought so from the first. And, yes, I thought it would be that day, too. So—that way the answer is yes."

"And some other way the answer is no?"

I pulled the pantyhose up tight and let them snap shut on me. Somehow or other, there is a kind of security connected with a good hearty *snap*. Makes you feel like you can handle . . . things.

"Well, not exactly no," I said. "But a definite maybe, if you follow me."

"I don't."

"Well, look at it this way, Buddy . . . an awful lot of people have some pretty weird ideas about what astrology is, you know?"

"Yeah," he said. "And more and more, girl, I am getting to be one of them."

"Uh-huh. That's what I mean. Because—Buddy—astrology is *not* a matter of deciding in advance exactly what is or is not going to happen. It doesn't work that way."

"Okay . . . so teach me. How *does* it work?"

"Well, sometime I'll give you the whole course—the way the law of probability works and the rest. But for now, think of it this way: your natal chart, or the chart for the place and time and event if you're doing horary astrology (I'll come to that later, maybe) shows what natural forces —planetary and other zodiacal forces—are at work. Like the law of probabilities. These astral forces, determined in your case and everybody else's case at the moment of birth, indicate such things as the kind of person you'll be, inside and out; your personality, character, physical condition, weaknesses . . . the whole works. But they still leave you plenty of choice—plenty of room to work out your own life. . . ."

He nodded, really thinking about it. "Okay," he said. "I don't necessarily buy that bit about the 'astral forces.' But accepting that, just for the sake of argument, you're saying they don't give you an absolute answer about what's gonna happen. Not every single time?"

"Not only not every single time, love—not even *once*," I said. "You are your own man. You make your own destiny, your own answers. Every time. All the natal chart —all that astrology itself—can do is give you some idea of the kind of obstacles that may turn up in your path; the kind of hurdles you may have to clear along the way . . . and, best part of all, the kind of *equipment* you have to do the job with. . . ."

362

He nodded again, still thinking. but—bless his habitual little bones—still changing clothes at the same time.

". . . and one more thing, Buddy: the chart can also tell you *about yourself*. It can give you a chance to know yourself; the opportunity of seeing yourself as you actually are, rather than in the way you've learned—or been taught—to see yourself."

It was a stopper of a thought. Anyway, it had been to me, when I first came across it. And, sure enough, it stopped ol' buddy-Buddy . . . right in his tracks.

"That's . . . that's what you did. *Wasn't* it, Sandy?"

Well, okay, he didn't say it as a question; count that as progress, I *think*. Not as a question. He was *telling* me. Not *asking*. So . . .

"Guilty," I said, "as charged."

"Not just yourself, I mean," he went on. "You know, one of the best things about you, doll, is the way you're, well, kind of *together* . . ."

"Thank you, sir."

" . . . and, from what little I ever understood about people, I always kind of figured it was because you knew yourself pretty good. Right? Right! Only—you didn't stop with that. *Did* you? You went right ahead; first yourself. Then other people. . . ."

I stood perfectly still, waiting for him to say it.

". . . like me!" he finished.

*Well, okay then.*

That was true; sure it was true. But, well as I think I know my man, I have got to admit I stood there with a little bit of a skip in the heartbeat. The Hallowell had taken herself one hell of a big chance, saying what she'd said. And she was just a *leetle* bit finger-chewy about how it was going to come out. Because you just *can't* be sure how anyone is going to take the news that you think you know more about them than maybe they do themselves.

For all of which . . . thank *God* for Buddy.

Because it *didn't* turn him off. No way! Maybe, at least from what I'd seen on the natal chart I'd worked out for him when I finally had the times and places and what-all nailed down, if it had been anyone but The Hallowell saying those things to him, it might have been different.

But, as long as it was me— that was cool by him.

Maybe even *groovy,* even! . . .

"Hey. babe," he said.

"Hey, yourself."

"Hey, babe . . . you know sump'n? You are really sump'n else! . . ."

I grinned back at him, with more relief than I had any intention in this world of letting him know about. Grinned. And hugged. And . . . then ran like hell!

Because a thing like that is habit-forming.

*For sure!*

And I'd practically promised the *padrino* on the sacred relics that I would deliver Mr. Buddy Valentine safe, sound, sober, and sane . . .


## Dolly Diamond

. . . to the party.

I hadn't intended to go, before. Oh, I was invited, all right. Sure. In fact, in a funny way, I was invited twice. Once as Mrs. Johnny Valentine, and once as Dolly Diamond . . . potential superstar.

Only—what the hell—I had better things to do with my time, the way I saw it, than go poking around some gunky beach house with a lot of people who would probably turn out to be straight-arrow Hollywood bores and old enough to be my grandparents.

But after Johnny went crashing out of the pad I changed my mind. Dolly the blue-and-white Diamond has got better things to do than mope around the kind of up-holstered mausoleum the great Johnny Valentine would pick to live in.

The hell of it was . . . yeah . . . the hell of it was I didn't want to go alone. In fact, to tell the truth, I wanted to go with someone who would be just a little bit of a surprise to one and all. From what I'd heard, a couple of the Hollywood column types were due to be there. I wanted to show up with someone who would give them an item; someone who would just blow the mind of the great Johnny Valentine.

Only, goddamn it, *who?*

I couldn't come up with a name.

Oh, sure—sure—I could come up with plenty of *names*. I toyed for a moment with my mental list of Hollywood fagboys; a lot of them are in the big star and superstar

category and would make column items. And it would be
an in joke, something that would bug Johnny, for me to
make the scene with one of them. For one thing, there
would be the idea that I went out with a fairy in the first
place. And for another, it was a pretty safe bet *he* wasn't
going to show up there, not considering the kind of mood
he was in when he left. So if I turned up, without him, and
on the arm of a . . .

*Oh, shit!*

I was on my feet, worrying back and forth across the
carpet, when it struck me. If I went with a fag, I'd be
pulling the same thing his first wife—that nowhere bitch
Angela—had been pulling ever since they split up. Hell, it
was a standing gag around town that Angela never went to
a Hollywood function alone . . . and never went with a
man, either.

*What the hell is it with these Catholic chicks?* Angela
and Johnny have been busted up—*divorced, for Chrissake*—
all these years. And they're divorced because Johnny had the
rep for being the Golden Superstud of Hollywood, for loving
everything he could get his hands on. So all right . . . but
does Angela give him the business right back, the same
way, like any really smart chick would do? She does like
hell! Oh, no—no—Angela Valentine's got a rep in town for
never having laid any man but her ex-husband because the
way that mackerel-snapper brain of hers works, she's still
married to *him*. So instead of making it with studs, she's
never seen with any guy who doesn't have a lavender rep;
never with any guy who can get it up for a chick. . . .

Wait a minute. I know who! Perfect! Guaranteed to set
them all back on their heels and *especially* guaranteed and
*certified!*—to fix Johnny's wagon. Oh, yeah! Not that it
needed much fixing right about now. In fact, from the looks
of him when he barreled out of that door, one little shove
would put him . . .

## Jack Dahlberg

. . . right over the edge and down my gullet. Nice stuff
in that double. I motioned with the glass to the waiter for
a refill. Something in the back of my mind was still bugging
me. What was it?

Maybe it was Gaby.

Where the fucking hell was Gaby!

I looked at my watch—that big, beautiful, tells-the-time-of-day and times-the-time-of-day and does-everything-but-press-your-pants watch of mine. But it didn't tell me much of anything right now. Because the dial was out of focus for some reason and . . .

*"Get back in focus, you bastard!"*

That made me blink. Because I think I must have said it right out loud. Bad sign, talking to yourself out loud. Very bad sign. Ask anyone—*very* bad sign. I blinked again and noticed I was letting my cue stick slip and tightened my hand around it. Just in time, too. I had the damn cue stick by its thin end. Almost dropped it.

Almost. . . .

*What the hell was I forgetting?*

Gaby.

*Something about Gaby.*

Something I was supposed to remember. Well, screw Gaby, too. She was supposed to *be here*. At The Flower. We always meet here at The Flower and where the fuck was she and it was all her fault if I was drinking too damn many of these doubles because I wouldn't of had so many if she'd been on time, and what the hell time *was* it anyway? . . .

I squinted hard at the watch—very hard at the watch—but it just wouldn't focus the way it was supposed to do and besides the light up here in the poolroom was bad and besides . . . fuck the watch; it would by God get back into focus or I would throw the motherfucker right out in the . . .

I stepped back, to get a better view of the watch.

But it wouldn't get into focus even with me stepping back and what the hell kind of way is that for a watch to act? Especially an expensive one—a really good one—like this one was supposed to be.

*"Motherfucker!"* I said.

And realized I had said it out loud, again.

"Hey . . . *watch* it, will you?"

Well . . .

It took me a minute or so—or, anyhow, it seemed like a minute though it could've been shorter or longer—to sort that out. I had said the first thing. But the second thing . . . I *hadn't* said that.

Well, then, who the hell had?

*Someone behind me.*

Oh. . . .

I pulled myself to my full dignity, as befits the executive vice-president of a major studio, and looked around over my shoulder. Just turning my head. Very carefully. So it wouldn't fall off or anything.

Some guy there.

Some guy . . .

"You . . . speak?" I said.

"Yeah. I said *watch* it—and now, how about getting offa my foot?"

That took a little assimilation time, too.

He was right, I guess.

I sent a sensation probe down my legs and found that the end of one of them, the right one, I think, was indeed tilted at a funny angle to the toes. Yes, indeed. Probably he was right. The executive vice-president of Monarch Studios was standing on that man's foot.

Well, screw his foot.

And screw him.

I took it off—but not before giving just a little extra shove, with my whole weight—down on the arch of the foot that was under my heel.

Love it, citizen. *Love* it! This town is full of people who would kiss ass for a chance to get Jackie Dahlberg to stand on their feet. So *love* it. . . .

I moved back in the direction of the table.

"Boy . . . you take some awful chances."

It was the voice from behind me again. The voice that belonged to the foot I'd just impressed with a sense of due respect for Jackie Dahlberg. Only the voice was *not* respectful.

He needed a lesson. . . .

"You talking t'me?" I said, turning around to give him the full benefit of the Jack Dahlberg under-the-eyebrows stare. Only it wasn't so effective in this instance; I tripped —over my own feet, I think—getting turned around. And then he turned out to be pretty large for that kind of treatment. Somehow I had forgotten that I wasn't sitting down at my desk, and . . .

"Yeah," he said. "I'm talking to you, *Shrimp*. Like, keep offa my feet."

367

The new double I'd ordered was in my hand—I don't remember just how or when it got there—and I sucked a little on it, sizing the character up.

He was a big, beefy one, all right.

Wearing one of those crappy aloha shirts all tourists, and even some people here in Hollywood, seem to think are just the thing. I'd never worn one, myself. They make me look too . . .

*That's how long it had taken.*

How long it had taken me to get the words he'd said firmly into my mind. It occurred to me, abstractly and as if from some other time or some other place, that I might be getting just the smallest bit over-the-edge on the booze. But it was too late, now, to change the script. The whole thing was already in production. . . .

He had called me *"Shrimp"!*

That tore it. He would pay for that.

"Tell ya what, Shrimp," the man went on, compounding his original error, "you been lapping up a little heavy on the stumpblower, don'cha think? I mean—watching you try to play pool—just about anybody could see you're practically out of it. So why don'cha let someone call you a . . ."

He did not finish.

I finished the sentence for him.

Both my hands were full; the left one with the double in it, the right still clutching the small end of the pool cue. Now, if there is one thing in this world I've learned, it is this: if you're going to really go for someone . . . you've got to do it without much warning.

So I didn't say another word, or do anything else to give this imbecile the edge.

All I did. I just dropped the drink that had been in my left hand—and used that hand to add to the strength of the right, which was by that time raising the pool cue into position. With both hands firmly on the cue, and while already in motion, I measured the strikeout zone near Aloha Shirt's head and shoulders . . . and *swung for the fences . . . !*

Only—well—call that strike one.

On Jackie.

Because, for the first time in many long years, Jackie's timing was just a tiny bit off and it seemed like Aloha Shirt knew what was going to happen a long time before anything did. So by the time the heavy end of the cue reached the spot where his head should have been, it wasn't there anymore—and, the force of that swing being what it was—I sort of lost hold of the cue (maybe my hands were a bit slippery) and away it went, flying out of my grasp and sailing through the air to smash a lamp on the other side of the room.

Aloha Shirt suddenly popped up again . . . maybe two or three feet to the right of where I'd last seen him.

"*Easy*, Shrimp," he said, and he was kind of smiling, now, as far as I could see. "Just take it a shade easy . . . you'll last longer."

Strange. For a moment or two I couldn't believe I'd missed.

And then I realized it was high time I got myself into some kind of attitude of defense; a man seldom fails to retaliate when someone has just swung a pool cue at him . . . whether it connected, or not.

But Aloha Shirt didn't seem to be preparing any attack. He just stood there, still looking faintly amused (and, I thought, just a bit wary—as though he wasn't sure how many friends he really had in that room) and doing absolutely nothing.

"*Cool!*" he said. "Cool—come on, now—the big cool, right? No sweat, nobody's mad. Just take it . . ."

*Too much! No!*

It was all just absolutely too much for a man to bear; I can take almost anything—from anybody—except condescension; don't fucking *patronize* me! From my father, maybe I have to take that kind of crap. *But not from anyone else on the face of this earth!* . . .

"You wanna have it out *here*," I said, "or outside?"

The big man didn't seem to understand.

Well . . . perhaps he was entitled. I realized my pronunciation was suffering from the effects of all those doubles. (But that was Gaby's fault; where the hell was she? *And what the hell was I supposed to remember about tonight? . . .*)

"Have it out?" the big man was saying. "Wha'cha mean, *have it out?*"

"I mean," I said, being very careful about the words and saying them slowly so as to be sure he would understand, "that I take no crap off you or anyone else . . . so do you want your ears beaten off right here, in fronna God 'n everybody (the tongue was slipping again, a little; I ordered myself to correct that, and was obeyed) or do you wanna go somewhere else, where there won't be so many witnesses."

And then he laughed.

Oh, god*damn* him!

He laughed! . . .

Goddamn him. And goddamn his aloha shirt. And goddamn his size. And goddamn Gaby. And goddamn Emil. And goddamn Papa. And goddamn all the rest—all the rest of the people in the world who are so fucking much bigger than Jack Dahlberg and who think they have some kind of secret laugh on Jack Dahlberg because they're taller than he is and who think they're so much smarter than Jack Dahlberg because they're taller than he is and goddamn them, damn them, *damnthem!* . . .

I think I made some kind of noise.

I'm sure of it, really.

But it wasn't a word or a phrase or anything else—just the sound of something breaking loose inside my head, or anyway that's what it felt like. And I made the sound as I went for the man in the aloha shirt.

My first swing was wild; he stepped away from it easily.

But the second surprised the hell out of him. And out of me, too, because with that very first swing I had suddenly realized just how badly my reactions had suffered. I was bombed. Really bombed. But, for a miracle, the second punch I threw *connected*. As he came toward me, I noticed I had—by pure accident—opened a tiny cut over his eye. I guess because I'm not tall, he had been guarding low, and the second wild punch went right over his guard and into the eye. Not a good, scoring punch for a regular boxing match. But pretty fair for the kind of fight we were in.

But now—with the drinks dying on me and what looked like the back of a camera truck, clad in an aloha shirt, coming at me—I had damn little time to do much of anything but sidestep. And not quite get out of the way.

Aloha Shirt missed his punch, but his rush carried him into me . . . and knocked me sideways.

Which could have been disastrous.

But it wasn't, because it took Aloha Shirt a moment or two to recover . . . and gave me time to line up on him.

Boxing—or fighting, which was what *we* were doing—is mostly a matter of counterpunching. I let him set himself. And, whatever else he may have been, he was no boxer. Because even though he moved well, right on his toes and apparently in fairly good condition, he telegraphed badly.

When he started to throw a combination, I evaded it easily—well, fairly easily—and hit him twice, with most of my weight in the punch, right in the solar plexus.

The activity had kept me keyed up, but being held by several people and not trying to get free from them gave my pulses a chance to slow down . . . and that was fatal. Endsville.

All the doubles I'd had since before sundown suddenly rose up to confront me. And I kind of lost track of things for a while.

The next thing I can recall is being downstairs—still inside The Flower—and sitting at a table while someone or other discussed telephoning for a taxi.

"Don' need a cab," I said. "Got my car. And my girl's meeting me."

I smiled brightly, and leaned back again . . . and it was at *that* moment it suddenly came to me. All evening—ever since I got to the club, in fact—I'd had a nagging suspicion I was forgetting something. Something that had to do with Gaby, and why she was so late getting here.

Now it came back to me.

The day had been so lousy and so full of confusion I'd completely forgotten . . . she'd accepted an invitation, for both of us, to attend a party at Malibu. Somebody's beach house.

*Who?* . . .

Yes! My God, it was Len. Len and Nora; they were throwing a hell of a bash at their place. *And I was supposed to be meeting her there!*

"Oh, good Jesus! . . .

"Telephone," I said. "Gotta make important call."

My head was clearing a little as I went to find a phone. My first call was to the studio—to get the number at Len's Malibu house—and then, getting myself together a bit more, I had them patch the line through the board so they could dial for me.

The phone must've rung ten or twelve times before someone finally answered.

"H'llo? . . ." A drunken, slurring voice spoke to me and I could hear voice-and-music sound effects in the background.

"Hi," I said. "This is Jack Dahlberg—my girl there?"

*"Who?"*

"Dahlberg," I said. "Jack Dahlberg . . . !"

*"Ain't here,"* the drunk said.

"Okay," I said, doing my best with the materials at hand. "Is his girl, Gaby, there, then? . . ."

"Who?"

Now I was getting a little hot; why in the hell can't people who give parties delegate *someone*—a waiter or something—to stay sober and answer phones and deal with emergencies.

*"Gaby. Gaby duMain!"*

*"DuMain?"* The voice gave a drunken chuckle; a chuckle with a leer in it. "Like, *forget* it, man—that cooz is *took!"*

I stood a moment in complete silence.

"Who is this?" I asked, when I had myself in hand again. I made the question pleasant and casual-sounding. I wanted the name. Badly.

"Ne'mine," the drunk said. "Ne'mine, pally. But . . . look, now; you're a *guy*, right? I mean—you ain't just a bulldagger with a deep voice?"

*"What? . . ."*

"I mean—if you're a *dyke,* well, okay! Like, different strokes for different folks; I got no prejudice. . . ."

"Listen—*what the hell do you . . ."*

"But, if you're a *guy*—forget it! The cunt may be AC-DC an' all that; I guess she *is,* an' I guess she can fake it pretty good—anyway, she musta for Jackie-boy Dahlberg and for his old man before that, what I hear—but if you're looking for her tonight, baby. . . ."

*"Why, you dirty son of a . . . !"*

". . . like, go find some other kinda trouble t'get into. Because this is *for sure* li'l Gaby's night for *girls!* Man, you oughta *see* it! Her an' . . ."

There was a sudden clatter and I could hear the drunken voice protesting, and then more clattering and the drunk faded away. Another moment, and someone saying something muffled. And then Nora's voice—clear, calm and sober:

*"Hello?"*

I started to reply. But didn't. "*Hello!* I'm really *terribly* sorry—I didn't hear the phone ring and one of my guests got hold of it. I hope you weren't annoyed? . . ."

I still didn't answer.

"Hello? . . ."

I just stood there.

"Hello! Please—who *is* this? . . ."

I hung the receiver up, very quietly and very definitely, and moved away from the phone.

*Gaby?* . . .

Oh, for Chrissake. *Gaby.* It was bullshit. It *had* to be bullshit. *Had* to be. I mean . . . say what you will, I'm no kid. And I been a couple of extra routes myself. All in the past, now; nothing like that for years and years. Not since David, really. But what kind of a jerk would I have to *be,* not to be able to spot? . . .

Suddenly I needed another drink.

A big drink.

Very badly.

But not here, after that mess upstairs.

I headed for the door, concentrating on walking straight and ignoring the stares . . .


## Buddy Valentine

. . . of all the celebrity gawkers at the party.

"Some party," the *padrino* said, looking at the milling throng in the downstairs part of the beach house. "Man, you don't hardly never see 'em like this anymore, do you?"

"I never *did,*" I admitted.

The *padrino* turned to grin on me. And on Sandy.

"Ya know," he said, "you two really missed something—not being around in the old days. . . ."

I grinned back at him. "Tell me, *padrino,*" I said, "tell me how it was, way back before the invention of the wheel." I nudged Sandy. "Did you know," I said to her, "that if the *padrino,* here, hadn't kept after Edison to work out the electric light idea of his . . . we'd all be watching television by candlelight?"

One thing about Sandy; that girl always laughs at my jokes. Even ones like that. And so did the *padrino;* it was that kind of a party—so far, at any rate. I hoped I could find out why he'd been so insistent about my being here, and get it over with, in time before the usual brawl or loud arguments developed.

"Okay," he said, "okay, young'uns. Laugh if you wanta. But parties these days . . ." he gestured at the assorted couples with glasses in their hands ". . . they're just not *in* it with the kind they used to throw in this town."

Okay. So—I tossed him the line: "What's so different?" I said.

"Whole *thing*." The *padrino* nodded at the room, partially cleared of chairs to make more space. "Len and Nora," he said, "probably did whatever arranging there was to do themselves. Oh, sure, they got a caterer and all to come in and bring the food and handle the drinks. And the caterer brought a coupla waiters and such. But in the old days— why, do you know there were two or three guys made a living, and a damn good one, just planning parties? Not catering, though they'd handle it if you wanted them to. Not serving the booze or even hiring a combo to make music. They charged whopping fees for just *planning* the evening. And did they plan some beauts."

"I used to hear about things like that," Sandy piped up. "But I never really believed them. Is it true that . . ."

"Honey," the *padrino* interrupted her, "*whatever* you were going to ask, I can tell you without hearing it—it's true. Listen: every party used to have some kind of theme; some special-effect kind of things, planned by the party planner. Hell, I remember one in the afternoon. It had been planned for outdoors, only it rained. But did that stump the planner? Oh, no! The guy just set his tent up *indoors*, draped it with blue cloth, and then *back-projected* clouds to float all over his sky!"

Sandy let out a peal of laughter. I think the drink was getting to her a little. "You've *got* to be kidding!"

The *padrino* shook his head.

"Sometimes," he admitted, "I have a little trouble believing it myself. But I was *at* that one."

Sandy finished off the last of her drink and handed it to me. "Please," she said, "I want to hear more about this . . . but it's nose-powdering time for The Hallowell. Save it till I get back?"

"With pleasure!" The *padrino* made an exaggerated courtly bow and hand gesture to her. "It is so seldom I can corral an audience for my stories. Everyone else—including our young genius here—has heard 'em before."

Sandy made a face, and turned toward the stairs.

"Hey, Junior," the *padrino* said, tapping me on the shoulder.

"Huh?"

"You and me got things to talk about, and I think maybe we better do it before your chick gets back."

"Sandy can keep her mouth shut, *padrino*."

"I know." He took a small sip from his glass and, from the way he did it, I suddenly realized it was ice water instead of gin or vodka on rocks. Okay: all right. That made it official. When the *padrino* goes to a party and only pretends to be drinking, something *really* serious has to be going down. . . .

"Shoot, *padrino*." I said.

"First thing," he nodded, checking our vicinity to make sure we couldn't be overheard, "how's the new album coming with the Kinfolk?"

"Oh, great! Nothing like *Mover-Ten*. That's kind of a one-of-a-kind thing, I guess. But this one'll go. I'm sure of it."

He nodded again. "Good," he said. "I was afraid that after the rock-opera thing went so well with you doing the arranging *and* directing, you might not be too sold on the idea of sending in an arranger for the next album. You and this Shepherd guy—you get along okay?"

I shrugged. "What's *not* to get along with? The guy's a pro. You ought to know, *padrino* . . . Shepherd's been around quite a few years. Check his credits: composer-director-arranger-performer; a track record like that's pretty rough to beat!"

"Good again," the *padrino* said. "You're going to direct this album, though. Not him?"

"Yeah," I said. "Unless you got some other kind of plan . . . and I hope you don't. Shepherd could do it, I guess. But his experience in directing albums is kind of limited. It's a different kind of thing—more different, really, than movie directing is from stage directing. . . ."

"I know. You know, kid, you've confirmed something I kinda thought was true all along . . . or, anyway, I hoped it was."

"What's that?"

"You got sense." The *padrino* nodded at me, with that calculating look he gets sometimes. "Not just ordinary sense; enough to get along, hold some kind of job that's figured out for you beforehand, like most of the world. But *sense*. All you needed was a start, you know? Just a start. The rest you did yourself. You—yeah—and maybe that girl of yours, too. Hey, that reminds me; something I wanted to say to you kinda off the subject—kid, your ma, she knows about you and Sandy. Living together, I mean."

I looked squarely at him and said it: "So?"

"So."

For a moment I wanted to look away; to drop the eyes and scrape the foot like some kind of kid caught with his hand in the cookie jar. Old habits, right? Hard to break.

But I didn't do that.

"It's our lives," I told him, saying it quietly and firmly. "If Ma's sore or worried or—hell—even ashamed or something, well, I'm sorry. I really am, *padrino*. I don't want to hurt her or anyone else so if I have, it's rough, and I really am sorry."

"But? . . ."

*"But.* Like I said. It's our lives."

The *padrino* hesitated a long moment, looking at me, and then nodded his head slowly. "Okay," he said. "No argument. Or maybe just one . . . and it ain't got nothing to do with Angie. Kid, is this deal, living together, I mean, is it just your idea or is it hers too?"

Hearing him say that was kind of a shock.

From what he'd said earlier, I guess I had somehow got the impression the *padrino* was beginning to believe I had some brains. But—a question like that! . . .

*"For God's sake,"* I said, suddenly madder than I'd realized. "For God's sake. . . . You really do think I'm a horse's ass, don't you?"

I don't know; maybe I said it a little hotter and madder than I meant. Or maybe it was just the words themselves. But it surprised the *padrino*.

"Well," he said. "Well, now, look . . ."

"You look! You think I'm such a fool that I don't know what I've stumbled into here? If it was up to me, she'd be Mrs. Valentine right now. I been proposing to her every goddamn day for the past month—and I'm going to go

376

right on proposing, and meaning it every time, until I get an answer I like. *Listen, damn it,* I'm no Einstein . . . but I'm not an idiot, either. Christ knows I have seen every kind of a bad marriage in this town—yeah, and I mean my Ma and my Old Man just for openers—and I know every single way it goes rotten and sour and winds up twisting people inside out until they're nothing. I know all of that and, face it, in my whole life I'm not really sure I ever saw a *good* marriage . . . one that was working. So? So maybe, like an awful lot of people, it would be pretty logical for me to say the hell with marriage and all that kind of crap—let's just live together as long as we feel like it and then just split with no hard feelings. Because marriage, as an institution, is used by people for every kind of a damn silly thing but the one thing it was intended for. Well—all right. Every bit of that is true. But I still say: *Balls!* Balls to that. I want that girl and I want her to be my wife; I want to be her husband. Now . . . is that clear enough?"

The *padrino* blinked.

"It's clear," he said slowly. "So what's the problem?"

"*Problem!* Damn it, what do you think the problem is? *She* won't marry *me*—that's the problem. What . . . that's some kind of unique? It never happened before? I'm the first guy ever proposed to a chick and got turned down? . . ."

"Maybe," the *padrino* said, still putting the words out slowly, "maybe—you're just not asking her right?"

"Name a way. I've tried all of them."

"I . . . don't get it."

"Neither do I."

And there the whole thing dropped. I glanced out on the patio and there she was, my gorgeous broad, happy as a clam playing with Len and Nora's two kids. Some Hollywood chick she'd make. When a waiter came by, I finished my drink in a hurry and nabbed another off his tray before he could get away. I tell you—there is just no one in the world can poke a finger at the sore spot the way the *padrino* can sometimes.

"Okay," he said finally, "leave it for the moment."

"Leave it for good," I said. "Listen, *padrino*—Sam— listen, *Sam* . . . on that subject, no more talk. *Ka-peesh?*"

His face registered shock, and then anger, and then, finally one of the biggest smiles I'd ever had from him.

"Kid," he said quietly, still smiling, "what you said a minute ago—about not growing up—I think you can stop worrying."

"Huh?"

"Didn't you notice?"

"Notice what?"

"Kid . . . that's the first time in your life, *the first time,* that you ever called me by my first name! . . ."

And you know, by God, it was at that!

I thought that over. Of course it wasn't as big a deal, really, as the *padrino* . . . as Sam . . . was making it. But, in a way, I guess maybe it was, too. Yeah. Maybe so.

"Like I said," he went on then, "all of that just makes me more sure than before—you're the man I been needing."

"Oh?" I said. "For what?"

"A big thing." He nodded solemnly. "Very big. Kid, one of the things I always kinda figured about you, when you were a kid, even then, with all the bullshit there was still a lot of things about you that weren't bullshit. Like the music. And the way you look at it. Not the way your Old Man always did; Vanni comes on pro in a lot of ways . . . but he's still got the attitude of an amateur. He knows—but he don't know *why* he knows; with him it's guesswork, instinct kinda, always. So he's wrong a lot oftener than he'd have to be . . ."

I just stood there and let him talk. I still couldn't see what it was all leading up to.

"But you—you're something else. You *think.* You got instincts like your father, yeah. Real good ones. About music and about other things. But you don't just play it by ear. *You,* you're the kinda guy has got to take the clock apart to see what makes it tick. And a lot of time when a guy does that, he sees a way to put it back together again a different way. A better way. Like with the Kinfolk, that nutty folk-rock group of yours."

"The Kinfolk?"

"Yeah. Okay—so it started a pretty screwy way; maybe you really *didn't* care about anything except getting *them* to help *you* get into something you thought you wanted to do. All right. But at the same time, you really did know that this idea of theirs, the folk-rock opera thing, had some good stuff about it. And you saw where you could fit into the setup."

378

"Oh, maybe. Maybe. But it was *you*—"

"We been over that. Yeah. *Maybe*. All right. But—when the heat was on, you didn't fold. You know how good that album is going, kid. You really know."

"Yes," I said. "I do know."

"*Right!*" Sam nodded again. "You know, because you been checking the sales and return figures every day. I heard about it. You know something? Even for his *own* records, your old man never checked a sales report in his life. Hell, I ain't even sure he could figure one out. And that's the difference between the two of you."

I'd started nibbling on my new drink. But all at once I stopped. Because suddenly it got through to me that Sam hadn't brought me and Sandy to this party for anything small. And that I'd better keep a very cool unit for whatever was coming up.

"Now it was *you*," he went on, "not Joe or the other guys of the Kinfolk who came up with the idea of actually producing the *Moses-Ten* thing on Broadway. And making a movie of it. Listen . . . the record, okay; maybe that was a kind of lucky break and something just anybody with a little knowledge could have come up with. But the bigger plan—that was something more. And here's how good it is, Buddy: it's the only project Priapus Studios has been able to get financed for this coming year. *The only one!* You know what that means?"

My God. Yes; *yes*, I *did* know!

And I could hardly believe it. . . .

"Sam," I said slowly, "the way I been getting it, the studio lost dough the last couple of years and that's how come old Steve Pappas was willing to let you and the old man in there as partners. But the plans, the production plans, for next year—they were supposed to pull the whole thing out of the fire. *Without that* . . ."

Sam's eyes were actually kind of sparking at me, and the muscles of his face were almost trembling with the effort of holding back a laugh. "Too right, sonny boy," he said. "*Too right!* Ever since before Steve took Lullaby in on the merger deal, his people—with him making the decisions every step of the way—been putting together that big program; *Priapus's New Plan* they been calling it in the crap his press agents been planting in the trades and in the financial sheets. The 'Today' plan. The 'Now Generation

Approach.' It was going to be to movies what the New Sound was to pop music. *Yeah! . . ."*

"They finished it," I almost whispered. "Put the whole package together, and . . ."

". . . and fell flat on their faces when they took it back to New York. *The Wall Street people won't play.* One tiny fraction—a single entity—they *schlepped* out of the whole deal; one piece they said they'd back. One picture: *Moses-Ten*. Aside from that, *nothing!* And, kid, there is only just one way in this world you can read them, the bankers. One way only; kid, *they don't trust old Steve no more*. And, kid . . . they want him *out!"*

It was coming on too fast.

Hell, even growing up in town the way I did, I'm no movie historian. But, *Steve Pappas!* He's been the man at Priapus from the beginning; even when his brothers were alive and were his partners it had been *him* who called the shots. Everyone knew that. His was the first studio to go into major sound production—the first to pay a really big price for screen rights to a major novel; the first to go for the big production musicals. They spotted the gangster-and-prison film trend of the thirties before it *was* a trend, and led the parade. They were the first major studio to move into television in the fifties; first to spot the changes in financial structure and how they'd affect the old studio system; *first . . . first . . . first and in the lead* all the way! And always it had been Steve Pappas who made the decisions; Steve Pappas who showed everyone the way. His judgment—his foresight—was practically Holy Writ. It was Priapus's single most valuable asset.

But if the bankers wouldn't go along with him anymore; if they didn't think he knew what he was doing . . . didn't trust his judgment! . . .

"Uh-huh." Sam still was wearing a poker face. But his eyes were reading me; inside my head, like always. "That's right, Buddy. Those bankers don't own a *share* of Priapus stock, most of them. And Steve's still in full control, even with the Lullaby merger, so far as actual corporate structure is concerned. *But the bankers can call the turn.* No financing, no production; no production . . . *no studio!* Without the Wall Street people squirting the money-oil in there, the whole machine comes to a sudden halt and the studio's just another piece of distressed real estate."

*"But . . . !"*

"That's the word Steve used: *but*. He couldn't believe it either, at first. And almost nobody else knows how things stand, for the time being, anyway. Just Vanni and me—because we're major partners—and one other group, I'll tell you about them in a minute. And now . . . you."

Right. And now Buddy.

Right.

But—why Buddy? *Why?* The *padrino* . . . Sam . . . was no talker; no loose mouth to blab things around just to show how "in" he was and how much he knew. If he was telling me all this . . .

"Okay, Sam," I said. "Okay. So . . . where do I fit in?"

He smiled, now, at last.

"Kid," he said, "you're growing up real fast."

"Uh-huh. So? . . ."

"So, this other group I said I'd tell you about: never mind the name of the outfit. It's an oil company, or was in the beginning. Now it's a conglomerate; Christ, they got pieces of trucking lines and airlines and a pipeline and some mines and a steel mill and a car factory back in Detroit and—hell—I'm not sure even I know what-all else. And I oughta; I'm a major stockholder . . . or, anyway, I *represent* a big bloc of stock. Some of it's really mine. Some of it belongs to one of the unions I represent. Some of it—well, hell, never mind about all that. Here's the point. Buddy: this outfit, the conglomerate, has a tax setup that makes them have to expand every year—or drop a hell of a chunk to Uncle. So they're always looking for new properties. They look for one of two things . . . either a company that's making a lot of dough or, for the tax loss, one that's losing a lot of dough. Still with me, kid?"

I shook my head. "Not really, Sam," I said. "I see what you mean about a conglomerate; I'm no business genius, but just listening to you and Dad sometimes I picked up a little bit. Only, you were supposed to be telling me where . . ."

". . . Where *you* fit in. Right. Like I said, a conglomerate wants a business that's either making or losing *big*. But even if the loss is the attraction, they'd rather be able to see some kind of future for the business; some indication that it can be turned around and moved into the profit column. And that's where you come in, kid . . . because the Kinfolk and

381

that rock opera *you* backed are the only winners Priapus has got in its stable right now. And I figure there's some pretty good reasons to think that *your* judgment is the asset that's needed."

"Oh, *for* . . . !"

"No; no, now!" He held up a hand to stop me. "This is no smoke-blowing session. I'm not talking about you assuming open control of the studio or even appearing on the list as a director. Not yet, anyway; you're still pretty much of an unknown as far as the business in concerned. And for the moment, that's a plus. Hell, your name doesn't even appear on the label or in the ASCAP listing for *Moses-Ten*. And that's a good way for it to be, at least for now. What we need is not Buddy Valentine, son of Johnny, fronting a deal for us. What we need is Buddy Valentine—his own man—calling the creative shots. Exercising judgment . . . and getting listened to."

I turned that one around and looked at it from two or three sides. I tell you . . . I didn't really know what to make of it. Still, Sam seemed to be serious. "Well, hell, then," I said, "okay—so all this does happen. *Where do I make?*"

And now Sam did laugh. And raise the ice-water glass in my direction. "That's m'boy! The right question! Where do you make? Well . . . I tell you: for openers, you invest every nickel you can, right now, in Priapus stock. The price is down, but it'll jump pretty good when, and if—though there's not a hell of a lot of question in my mind—the sale to my other clients is announced. And then you make us a deal: take your payoffs on everything mostly in stock from here until I tell you different. Buddy . . . that way, between us, we can wind up in absolute control before many more years go by. Not just control because the conglomerate people want it that way. But *control.* . . ."

I took a big gulp of the drink.

It tasted brassy.

My mouth was kind of dry.

"Okay," I said. "Okay, Sam. I buy all that. But we're still just talking. Guessing. Because we don't really know *who* Steve'll sell to. You can't be sure he hasn't got someone else lined up. . . ."

Sam shrugged, and his mouth quirked in a way I knew meant he couldn't care less.

"He could have fifty buyers," Sam said. "Or a hundred. And it wouldn't mean a damn thing, Buddy. Not a damn thing. Because there's a clause in the merger agreement, a codicil, that gives Steve—and your Dad and me—equal right of first-refusal *and of approval* if either of us wants to sell out." Sam nodded, his eyes remote. "Steve Pappas wanted it that way. He even *demanded* it, in order to go into the merger deal with us. It was his idea; he can't complain now if the situation is the reverse of what he thought it might be. He's the one who made the deal . . . so now, *we're* in a position to keep him from selling, from getting out of the spot he's in by selling, to anyone but the people we pick. And what's more, it's gonna cost Steve quite a few extra millions to get us to agree even to *that. . . .*"

"Huh?" I couldn't help voicing the question. "Why?"

"Because Steve selling doesn't mean we're selling. We'll get our own price; sure, we *are* selling, too. But we're going to need really big dough—*in cash*—for what's next on our agenda. On Vanni's and mine. . . ."

I waited for him to go on.

But he didn't.

He just looked at me—with all the shades pulled down in his eyes again. And his face saying absolutely nothing. Like I said, the *padrino* . . . Sam . . . is no loose mouth.

When I was sure he'd said all he was going to say—and that I'd asked all the questions I was going to get answered that night—I began looking around the room, making sure Sandy still seemed to be all right. (She did.)

Passing the time, still standing with Sam, I looked over the crowd.

The house, there in Malibu, was really something. I'll say that—really something. Just *what*, I couldn't have told you. The word was that it had set Len and Nora back $500,000 and that Len had designed it himself and then furnished and decorated it. It figured. Beautiful display of Contemporary Tasteless. But big, you know?

There were about two hundred guests, all gathered by this time into little knots of conversation—one superstar per knot; superstars are rationed, please do not exceed your quota—and a few of the heavy juicers at the long bar that started *Here* and ended *There*. . . .

Occasionally the door would open, at the back of the

place, away from the ocean, and someone would drift in. Or out.

Earlier, I'd seen my Ma and said hello. She'd asked Sam to bring her, but Ma's got more sense than to hang on his arm through the night. She's known Sam a long time, and he doesn't go to parties—especially not parties like this one —for fun.

Ma was out of sight, missing, by now. So I looked around for more familiar faces. Funny—I'd half expected to see the Old Man. Nobody would give a bash in this town without inviting the great Johnny Valentine, whether they thought he'd come or not. But he wasn't around, so far as I could see, and neither was my new stepmother (oy, veh!) the blue-and-white Diamond.

I didn't see Jack Dahlberg, either. Which, I suddenly realized, spotting a couple of women with their arms around each other, standing on the ledge leading from the entranceway to the sunken living room, was just as well.

Because one of the women was Gaby duMain.

And the other was Jeannie Lynton, one of the most beautiful and most notorious lezzies in town. And they didn't seem to be making any secret of their attraction for one another.

All we needed now was Jack, or David Strauss, or Dolly the blue-and-white Diamond. And that, so help me, was really and honest-to-God what I was thinking at the *very moment* the door opened . . . and in came Dolly.

*Dolly. The blue-and-white Diamond.*

Christ! I almost exploded my drink all over Sam's front. He noticed it. Looked where I was looking. And froze. His eyes went narrow for a minute (come to think, probably mine did, too) and he watched her as she smiled and nodded. But she wasn't with the Old Man. Oh, no. My darling stepmother had chosen for her escort this evening the one man who I knew the Old Man had expressly *forbidden* her to see: none other than her erstwhile husband, David Strauss, looking, I noticed, very much like he'd rather be almost anywhere else in town, or in the world. Especially when he took in the Gaby and Jeannie tableau. But Dolly was unfazed by the stir they'd created. She seemed to be grooving on it, despite the fact that she wasn't exactly dressed for the spotlight. She was wearing a freak-type knitted poncho over what looked like some kind of grubby muu muu. Her hair was tangled and looked dirty. No makeup, of course. Which, somehow, made you all the more aware of her eyes.

And that was point number two. Because Dolly's eyes said she was *stoned.*

Look, I admit I am not the world's greatest authority on the current drug scene. I know a little bit, like most people. But I've never even been much for grass, myself. It's just not for me. Still, I've lived enough years and known enough people in this town, including freaks, to know when someone's full of the true and original superfreak mindfuck.

*And Dolly was.*

I did a little breath holding. But everything went like glass. Dolly glanced just once at Gaby, while David made a point of looking away from her and Jeannie. Nora appeared, like magic, said hello and led the two of them off toward the bar—and then I kind of lost track. Because here came Sandy in from the patio.

It's nutty.

I mean—I live with that chick, right? I see her all the time, as many hours as I can manage, every time she's in town. And it's been going on that way for quite a while now.

And still, every time she's been away for more than a few minutes, I get that kind of shock—an electric kind of a thing—seeing her come toward me. Which I did this time, too. . . .

"Hey, babe," I said.

But I didn't get any further.

Looking at Sandy had distracted me, for sure, and the last I'd seen, Dolly and David were moving away toward the bar. With Nora. But now Dolly was back in my range of vision.

She and David had come up to the entranceway level from the sunken part of the room—behind Gaby and Jeannie Lynton—and they were both standing there, looking kind of uncertain about which group to join, when the door opened and I saw a bloodied and disheveled figure stagger in.

It took me a long moment to recognize the figure as Jack Dahlberg and by the time I did he had focused on Gaby and Jeannie and was heading toward them, bellowing like an enraged bull. At this, David broke away from Dolly and ran to head off Jackie, catching him in his arms and clasping him tightly to his chest. I had a fleeting impression of Dolly glaring pure contempt at the two of them before she turned on her heel and walked out of the party. Just as I was reaching for Sandy's hand and thinking. "What next" Jackie began to sob, then sank to the floor. David crouched over him, crooning and rocking him back and forth and kissing his face and whispering to him. I looked away, embarrassed.

People began to move about again, and Nora ushered a frightened-looking Gaby and Jeannie out of the room, When Jackie began showing signs of life, David, with the help of Len, lifted him from the floor and half-carried, half-dragged him outside to a car someone had pulled up to the door.

Sam came over to where we were standing. "I've had it with this freak show," he said. "Thank God Vanni wasn't here for that little number. *And* that Dolly scrammed before Angie ran smack into her, speaking of which, let me grab Angie and let's the four of us get outa here. Whattaya say?"

What I said was yes. And we got.

# The 10th House

*Profession, occupation, honor, fame, promotion;*
*relations with one's employer and standing*
*before the world; affairs of the nation or*
*of the national government . . .*

*Forecast: Johnny Valentine's naval "favor" to Irving*
*Dahlberg may sweep them both into turbulent international*
*waters, with others, like Jackie Dahlberg, getting caught*
*in the wake.*

*And as Sandy Hallowell and Buddy Valentine enter the*
*Tenth House, the time of destiny for all concerned draws*
*near. . . .*

### Johnny Valentine

The ringing of the telephone cut through the blackness of the Chivas Regal doze that I try to call sleep, and jerked me back into bed.

I held my breath and prayed for it to have been a dream. But it rang again. . . . Christ.

I reached out for the damn thing. But it wasn't where it was supposed to be. That's been happening a lot lately—stuff keeps moving around.

Another ring.

What the hell was wrong with the hotel desk? They had strict orders never to call me before—and then I remembered. I wasn't in the hotel. I was in Scottsdale. Came

387

down late last night. *Someone stirred and made a noise, close to me in the darkness.* Yeah. With a broad . . .

The fourth ring did it, finally. I sat up, took a deep one, and remembered that the phone was on the other side of the bed. God, it's awful getting old! (Old, who's old? *Me?*) I thought I could actually hear my bones creak as I went around the foot of the bed to get it before it rang again.

" 'Hlo . . ."

"Vanni?"

"Sam."

"Yeah, Sam—who the fuck you expect?"

A pause.

"I wake you?"

"Yeah, you woke me. What the hell time is it anyway?"

"Ten, here, Vanni; that means—aw, hell, I'm sorry—I can never get my hours straight when I go flying around on jets. Wish the things had never been invented. It's seven there, I guess."

I yawned. "Yeah. Okay—so, what?"

"You hear the news yet?"

"News? . . ."

"On the radio. And TV, too, by now—Vanni, the fucking Cubans, they snatched one of our navy ships!"

I sat there and tried to let it sink in; tried to make it mean something to me. But damn if it did. I shook my head and tried again, but it was still no good. "I'm sorry, Sam," I said. "Real sorry. But what's *that* mean—like, did we go to war with them or something?"

"Vanni—Jeez, I shouldn'a called so early. And of course you don't know the whole bit. But, Vanni, it means we could be in some trouble. Look: how many people—not politicians, I mean; *people*—know you set that navy deal up for Irving Dahlberg?"

God. How the hell would I know? I wanted a drink. I wanted some coffee. I wanted to go back to sleep.

"Vanni?"

"I'm still here—lemme think: *you* know, of course. And Irving. And I set it up through Jim; remember, you said it was the best way to handle it. Send the word through him, and . . ."

"Right. He's a *politico.* He can't talk because he's in it up to his eyes himself. You never told Dolly, did you?"

"Fuck, no!"

"Good. Nor Buddy or Angie, or . . ."

"No one else, Sam. I'm sure of it."

"Okay then, swell. Hell, maybe we're in the clear." I still couldn't get the two things together in my mind.

"Sam," I said, rubbing my eyes and wishing I dared to pull the curtain back and let some light into the room, "Sam, what's it all about, anyway? How do the two things fit? I don't . . ."

Sam didn't answer at once. Then he said, "You're sure the phone there's not tapped? I'm in a booth, here in D.C."

"Washington, D.C.—what the hell're you doing there?"

"Business. For the union and for us. The sale of our part of Priapus and Steve's part had to be approved by the Justice Department, you know. Sherman Antitrust, right? So . . ."

"It's okay? The same, I mean?"

"Yeah. Sure. I told you—look, I'll get to that in a minute. About this *Pennsylvania thing* . . ."

"*Pennsylvania?*"

"The *U.S.S. Pennsylvania*—that's the ship the Cubans boarded and took into Havana harbor last night. A very special ship, Vanni. A navy spy ship; sent down there to monitor the waters. They sent out some gunboats, boarded her, took her over. And now they got the ship, the crew, and for all I know probably half the *top-secret* shit—all of it, maybe—that was aboard the damn thing. I tell you, there's one hell of a flap on here. Everybody walking around with his asshole puckered."

I sighed. "So they're up the creek. I'm sorry; you know I was for the administration—even if the ungrateful bastards *did* chill me after they got into office. But what the hell's it got to do with *us?*"

"Coming to that." There was another pause; I had a mental image of Sam wrestling to light a cigar in a hot phone booth, and grinned to myself. "See, this *Pensylvania,* it's a real hoo-hah secret ship and all—a real bitch—but it's slow and it ain't got much in the way of guns."

"Yeah . . . ?"

"Well, so, a ship like that, the navy always assigns another ship to be around, out of the immediate area but able to get there in a big hurry, to protect it. That kind of job these days goes to the new gunships. They're real fast, they can operate at sea instead of just on rivers and protected waters, and they're pretty heavy on the armament. Those things got a diesel that can push them along at eighteen knots—and when they need it, a J-57 jet engine can raise the speed to forty knots or better."

"Great." I was *dying!* "I'm glad for them, Sam. Glad! *But what in the hell . . . ?*"

"So a gunship was assigned to protect the *Pennsylvania*. A gunship named the *Olathe*. But when the chips were down, when it was needed, *it wasn't there*. It wasn't where it was supposed to be, Vanni; it couldn't make it to the spot in time and even if it *could* of made it, even at forty knots, it couldn't have done a hell of a lot to stop the *Pennsylvania* being captured because *its guns had been demounted and replaced by cameras*. Vanni, the *Olathe* was being used as the camera ship for shooting the sea sequences on *Boarders Away!*"

Oh-oh. Panic time! "Wait a minute, though," I said, after I had a moment to think. "Look, they can't really hang that rap on the picture. Or on us for getting the administration to lend old Irving the ship. Hell, if it was being used as a camera ship, why in hell didn't the navy send something else to protect the *Pennsylvania?*"

"That's the problem, pal," Sam said, and his voice sounded plenty worried. "See, everyone's yelling for economy in the services, right? So they got a strict budget. To lend Irving the *Olathe,* they couldn't just put that on their records here in Washington. I mean, how's that gonna look to some auditor: 'Ship on Loan to Monarch Pictures.' There'd of been hell to pay. So the Navy just covered the whole thing up. They cut two sets of orders; one for the auditors showing that the *Olathe* was guarding the *Pennsylvania* and the other for real, sending it off to Irving for a bathtub toy. Only, Jeez, you know how paper work is— some asshole thought the phony orders were legit. So when the *Pennsylvania* radioed she thought she might be in trouble, the guy in charge told them not to worry because the *Olathe,* the gunship, was in range and ready to handle things. By the time they found out the truth—well, it was just too fucking late. Fidel and company had already taken over."

"Oh, brother."

" 'Oh, brother' is *right!* Because listen, Vanni: there's going to be a hell of a stink over this. You know, all those

390

guys held prisoner by the Cubans, and they getting hold of our secret equipment and papers and all. Maybe even a congressional investigation, and sure as *hell* a court-martial when—and if—we ever get the crew back. They'll be looking for someone to hang, baby. And if anyone gets wise to what really happened . . ."

"You're *nuts*," I said. "It's *Dahlberg* they'll string up by the ying-yangs. They'll find out the ship was loaned to Monarch, and that'll be that. Hell, keed, it could even be a plus for us, you know, the plans we got for the old fart."

"Yeah, maybe." Sam didn't sound convinced. He sounded worried. "Maybe so," he said, "but that ain't the way Irving sees it, Vanni. In fact, he's threatening to blow the whistle *himself*."

"Huh? He's out of his tree!"

"Not necessarily. I got a call from him this morning; he phoned my answering service out there, and they finally plugged him through to me back here. The way he sees it, Vanni, he can pose as the innocent bystander—at least enough to keep most of the heat offa him. And besides, being head of a studio, he's not so well known to the public. People won't go boycotting Monarch films even if he does have to take the rap. But *you*—you're a *performer*, right? At *you*, every superpatriot out to make a name for himself can throw rotten eggs! And, Vanni—you know how the press'll handle it. You're not exactly their *favorite*, baby! . . ."

Well, shit. He was right. "Okay," I said, wanting that drink worse than before. "Okay, then, Sam. I guess all we can do is sit tight and hope for the best. Maybe no one'll find out if all of us keep our mouths shut."

"Maybe," Sam agreed. "And you're right, it's our best bet. Only, goddamn it, Vanni—that fucking Dahlberg's threatening to *take the whole thing to the public*. Full-blast deal. The works! Public apology from him, and a strong intimation that he had no idea how you were going to handle the matter. He figures he can come off smelling like a rose . . ."

". . . *while I take the fall*." I nodded. Yeah. You know it; that's how it could work, all right. And Irving—say what you will about the old bastard—Irving could bring it off. The guy had maybe fifty years of experience in selling ideas to the public. Oh, he could make it stick, all right. I massaged the bridge of my nose in the darkness, and the broad stirred and moaned nearby. (What the *hell* was her name? Damn if I could remember!)

"So, okay," I said. "He's not just getting hysterical and making threats. Not his style, baby. What's he *want?*"

"He wants *Sadie,* Vanni. The release from us, in writing and *now.* I guess he figures this is the best lever he's ever going to get to pry us loose from it. And he could be right."

"So," I said. "You're the *consigliere.* What do you think, Sam?"

Sam laughed across three thousand miles of wire. "If the FBI," he said, "or someone like them, *is* tapping this call, that oughta clinch it for them: *consigliere,* huh! You know what *I* think, Vanni?"

"I know."

"So—the final decision's yours, Don Giovanni."

I laughed back at him. "Fuck you," I said, "and the FBI, too. I say, okay! Give it to 'em, Sam."

*"Huh?"*

What a *gas!* You know, I think that's the first time in maybe twenty years I ever really surprised the bastard. How *about* that!

"Let him *have* it. I'm with you, kid; give the old fart what he wants and let him think he's got us by the short hairs. You can always afford to kiss an ass today if you know you're going to kick it tomorrow!"

"Well, I'll be damned."

"Probably," I agreed with him. "Look, Sam—maybe I shoulda told you earlier—I already decided to let him release *Sadie* before this came up."

There was a pause on the line and, very faintly, I could hear Sam whistle a tuneless little number through his teeth, the way he does when he's thinking hard and fast.

"Okay, Vanni," he said. "Christ knows I'm not arguing. You know I agree. But—so, tell an old buddy, huh? Fill me in?"

"Two reasons," I said. "First: I already promised Dolly. It's part of the divorce settlement. Not in writing yet, but—you know I don't weasel out of things like that."

"That's the *first* reason . . ."

"And the second—why, Sam, the second is the same reason I figure you want to do it in the *first* place. It's just as important to us as it is to Irving. More, really. Because by the time the gears mesh and the picture's actually showing box-office receipts, *we'll be running the studio instead of him*. Right, *consigliere?*"

And this time Sam really *did* laugh. The big one, from the belly.

"Vanni," he said, "I *love* ya!"

"Yeah, yeah," I said. "So when do we pick out the furniture?"

"Not until you *kiss* me, you little *bitch*," he fag-voiced me back. "Vanni, I wanna apologize. Here I was, all set for an hour of long-distance arguments, and what do you do? I love ya! Ya bastid, you really *do* think like a Siciliano!"

"Listen to that, the half-Yid coming on about Siciliano, yet! No—look, Sam, for real, now: Dahlberg really *could* give us a black eye if he cracks on this, about this navy deal?"

"I dunno. Maybe it could be handled. Maybe."

"Uh-huh. Okay, then: so what's to stop him from doing it anyway when he finds out what's happening with the Monarch stock? You know the kinda guy he is. An agreement, even in writing, wouldn't mean *shit* to him if he's really in a corner. And he's *in* one, where the studio's concerned, even if he doesn't know it yet. By the way, how's that deal coming?"

"Oh, yeah." Sam was all business again suddenly. "I said I'd fill you in, didn't I. No problems, Vanni. That secret tender offer we made to the two bankers, they went for it. Tentatively agreed, now. In writing. And I think Irving's wife is gonna accept the offer, too."

"She can sell? Without Irving's okay?"

"Yeah. Just like that legal secretary told us, the agreement between the two of them only covers his right to *vote* the Monarch stock she holds. She retained full ownership rights aside from that, including the right to *sell*."

"Without notifying him?"

"Without notifying him. So, like the bankers, she's scared —which means she's willing to sell. Monarch stock's at the lowest price in ten years on the Big Board now, and everyone knows it could be worth *bupkis* if we go on holding up the release of *Sadie* because he's short of cash and nobody's going to make loans to a studio that makes a mistake that leaves them in such a crack." Sam paused for breath and, I'd bet, to take a deep one on the cigar. "Besides," he added, "Irving's wife is a pretty weird broad. You know how she got the stock—part as a gift from Irving and part left to her by Irving's sister, Ruth. Margaret's taken a lot of crap from Irving over the years, being farmed out down there in Florida and treated like a dog any time she *was* around and all, only because of Jackie. But she must of hated it— and since the gossip now is that Irving and Jackie may square off any day, she just may jump at the chance to put the old boy down, at long last."

"Right! And by the time Irving finds out we got voting control—since we're buying the stock through dummies the way you set it up—he's already out on his ass. You don't think he'd announce the *Sadie* release too early? I mean, if he did it right now, the stock price'd bounce up there again and everyone could back out of the deal to sell to us at that tender price."

"Not a chance, Vanni. You know Irving—he'll hold off until the day before the annual meeting to get the full benefit of the announcement, figuring a grandstand play'll help him keep the peasants in line. He knows he could have big trouble this year; maybe he even suspects it could be almost as serious as it really is. So he'll play it cool. On the information he's got—which you and I know ain't *enough* information—it's his best shot."

"Yeah," I said, turning it over in my head. "I guess you're right. About the navy deal, though . . ."

"He'll keep it under his hat. For now, anyway. I'm sure of that, if we give him the release. When he finds out we *yentzed* him and he's out on his ass, though—well—after that it's anybody's guess."

"Yeah, sure." I started to yawn again. "Look, Sam, maybe you shouldn't worry too much about that angle right now, anyway. Maybe it's not as important as it seems."

"Vanni, it's *important*. As a performer, you . . ."

"Maybe not," I said, stopping him. "Look—not on the phone, okay—but let's talk when you get back here. Something I been thinking about . . ."

There was a wait while Sam digested that. "Vanni," he said, "what the hell are you . . . ?"

"Not on the phone, *consigliere*," I said. "Later, when you get back. You still seeing Irving in person tomorrow?"

"Uh-huh."

"It won't tip him off?"

"No. Irving knows I represent a couple of the minor blocks of stock for the bankers. And another one for the union. I'll be talking to him, far as he knows, in their behalf."

"You sure it's a good idea, Sam?"

"I'm sure. Vanni—it's always a good idea to give a man one last chance to get out of a jam gracefully, the easy way, before you lower the boom on him. Who knows, maybe he'll go for it. It sure would make things smoother for *everyone*."

"Yeah," I said. "I guess so. Well, then—anything else?"

"Not far as I know."

"Okay, then—*later*, baby."

"I'll keep in touch."

And he clicked off.

I sat still, with the receiver still in my hand, and thought about crawling back in the sack. But the broad stirred again, like she might be waking up, and I decided the hell with it. I dropped the receiver carefully back in its cradle, got up, and walked out of the bedroom.

The light in the rest of the house hit me like a hammer.

Scottsdale is a hell of a spot, really. A blast. You get out here on the desert, and it's like a different world. Good air. Slow pace.

I walked into the front of the house and thought about a drink. But the hell with it—my mouth already tasted like the heel of a bus driver's sock. I reached into the little wet-bar refrigerator and got out a bottle of cold soda. Dry. It went down easy and gave me a good belch.

Still carrying the little bottle of soda, I walked over to the piano and sat down. Johnny Valentine—musician. *What bullshit!*

I didn't even learn to read notes until I was—how old? And even then, it was just the voice. The singing. The piano, out here, was for friends and for bullshitting the public. I could play just enough to fake a background for the voice. The Velvet Voice.

I speared a couple of chords, softly, and hummed along with them. "The Music Stopped." An oldie but a goodie; I wished it had been mine instead of Sinatra's. They really wrote songs, back then—with words that meant something.

The New Sound. Christ—new sound! The New Noise.
Crap music for crap people.

I tried a couple of bars of "Clouds," still just humming.
But even that way, I knew it was wrong. For me, anyway.
All wrong for the Velvet Voice. For Johnny Valentine.

The New Sound—Christ! I hit a hard chord, and pulled
my hand away, quick. Let's watch that jazz, Valentine.
Don't wanna wake the broad in there. And then I wanted
to laugh at myself.

What a yock! Johnny Valentine, the Big Swinger. Would
he come down to the desert alone? Him? No chance!
Johnny Valentine's *always* got a broad, a doll, with him.
Always! Man—that Valentine, he must really be something
*else* in bed!

Yeah! Christ. I couldn't help smiling a little. What a hell
of a surprise the broad in there must of had last night.
What a shock! The Big Swinger brings her down to Arizona
for a couple of days—and the first night, what does he do?

"Listen, kid—forget it tonight, okay? I'm bushed. . . ."
Like some guy married to her a hundred years.

And then, when she decided to change my mind—really
tried—what then? The Big Swinger, Johnny Valentine,
not only couldn't get it up—he went to *sleep,* right in the
middle of the whole scene. Oh, man!

Well, what the hell'd you *expect,* Valentino? You were
going to stay twenty-five years old forever? Yeah. That is
what I expected. That is what I thought. That is what I
wanted.

Twenty-five years old—and fifty years smart. Hah! That's
the hell of it; when you're a kid you could do everything,
but you don't know how; when you're fifty you know how
to do everything, but . . .

Can it, baby! Knock it off!

Maybe if I—if I—oh, Christ, will you please, please,
*please* stop the maybe? Please? I got to stop letting the
mind wander; I got to get down to business. The opening
in Vegas is next week and I'm not ready. I'm supposed to
be out here working on the songs, working on the—on the
—what.

Okay. All right. That's *not* why I came out. I came out
because damn it, I need time. *I need time.* Not for the whole
world. Not for the audiences. Not for Angie. Not for Dolly.
Not for Buddy. I need time for me and I need . . .

*I need love.* That's a lyric. Not a thought, a lyric. Yeah, but it's true, all the same. Love. Johnny Valentine— Giovanni Valentino—needs love. Like every other human in the world.

What in the hell is love, anyway? No, that's a blind alley. It doesn't lead anywhere. I don't have to define love to feel it, do I? Don't I?

Say it, Valentino: *say it!* Ask the question: did you ever love anyone—ever—in your whole damn life? Did you?

My hand had a mind of its own; it struck a chord on the keyboard, and I recognized it at once. The first note of the big one. The one that made Johnny Valentine. I've been a sucker for it ever since, so I couldn't help myself. I began chording along through it. And then I stopped and segued back into the beginning, and began to sing. Really sing— full out, like before an audience—all the way through to the end. It felt good. Jesus, it felt good!

I wished I'd had the tape recorder on. I thought of hooking it up and doing the song again, but then suddenly I was tired and my hangover was a bitch and it was too much trouble—and besides, I knew how I sounded.

It was different. Very different, for sure, from the way it had been the first time I sang it before an audience; the first time I recorded it. The time that gave me my first big success.

That had been a kid's voice. Gift from God, my ma called it. And she was right, too. I hadn't earned that; it wasn't really mine. And—Jesus—the way I spent it, that voice. The one from God.

Who was it said the face you are born with is a gift, but you earn the one you die with? Doesn't matter. He was right, though. And it's just as true of voices as it is of faces. The voice I got now—I earned it. The hard way. Not the kid voice anymore; not the one that swooned 'em. Not the Velvet Voice. A deeper, richer, darker tone. But a man's voice. And mine. *Mine!* Mine because I earned it; trained it, taught it to sing—*really* sing. Most people don't even know the difference, or care.

Christ help me, *I* don't even care anymore. That's it, isn't it, Valentine? That's the whole thing: you just do not care now. Always before, all my life, it was fun. The acting and the money and the broads and all the rest of it, sure, that was the greatest. Show me someone who wouldn't like to have it that way for himself. But the real thing, the big thing, was the singing. Just that. The simple fact of singing before an audience: it was fun.

And now, all of a sudden, it's work. What happened? When did it happen? Who knows. It's been going that way a long time now, and I guess I just didn't notice. What changed? Why did it happen?

*Love.* What a nutty thing. Who'd have figured it? *Love!* That's what there was between me and an audience—an audience that really dug my kind of singing. *Love.* Because that's what it always is, if there is anything there at all. Any spark.

But now it's not fun anymore; it's not *good* anymore, it doesn't *feel the same* anymore, and I *don't want to sing* anymore; I want to do what I almost told Sam, just now, I was going to do. I want to quit—stop performing, stop singing —because I can't *feel* it. I've stopped *loving* the audience —stopped loving to *sing*—and if that's true, if that's happened, then it's time to . . .

## Jack Dahlberg

". . . make a drastic change. I'm sorry, Jackie. These things happen. I'd hoped it wouldn't come to this, but we both know there is going to be a fight—perhaps even a proxy fight—with the stockholders. I've got to do whatever I can. They've got to see that we're taking *steps,* making needed changes, to assure a profit situation during the next year. For several reasons, the most obvious step was firing you. You'll be paid the rest of your annual salary, of course, and you're hardly a *poor* man. I've always seen to that."

He stopped talking, but I didn't answer right away. I needed a moment to get it straight in my head. To make myself believe he'd really said it.

*I was fired.*

It couldn't be true.

*Out.*

It couldn't be true.

Papa had thrown me to the wolves—used me as a sacrificial goat—to try and save his own position. *Papa had fired me.* Me! *Papa* had fired *me.* . . .

Suddenly my mind showed me a series of pictures; some old Russian pictures that had hung on the living room wall at my grandparents' home. I'd been fascinated with them as a child.

They were in a three-frame progression: first a horse-drawn sleigh, with a man and a child in its seat, is being closely followed by a pack of wolves. Second, the man—a fur-wrapped brute—is standing up, facing backward, with the child in his arms. Third, the man has thrown the child out and the wolves have stopped to devour him, while the man and the sleigh make their escape.

Did I say it fascinated me? That's not the right word. Always, I had felt a strange inward tingle when I looked at those awful pictures. Almost a déjà vu. As though I were somehow personally involved with the tragedy depicted. As though I *knew* the people. . . .

"Papa," I said, working to retain control, "Papa, what reasons? You're making a mistake. You mustn't do this."

"I've got to, Jackie."

"Papa, the only money-makers the studio has *got* right now are the ones I personally approved and forced through production. *The ones you didn't want to make.* That's no secret anymore, you know; it's common knowledge. How can you . . . ?"

"That's not true now, Jackie," Papa said quietly. "I made arrangements today—our big picture of the year, *Sadie,* will be released as soon as we can finish the paper work. Which will be before the stockholders' next meeting."

"Papa," I said, while I absorbed that news, "that still won't save us. If they want to vote you out now, they'll do it anyway. Firing me won't help, it only *weakens* your position. Puts you in a spot where you seem to be apologizing. Defending. It won't work."

"It's *got* to work, Jackie."

"Well, it *won't!* Papa, if you fire me, they'll toss you out for sure a week later. If they don't do it right then and there!"

I heard him sigh. Sitting—alone, I'm sure—in his big New York office, I heard him sigh. It was a terribly weary sound, but it didn't get to me at all.

"This new thing—this *Pennsylvania* thing—they thought they could use *that* to force me out. To discredit me. To make it seem like I was responsible for one of our navy's ships being lost!"

What in hell was he *talking* about?

"I don't understand," I said. "What has the capture of the spy ship got to do with . . . ?"

"Never mind, Jackie, it doesn't matter. What *does* matter is that you get rid of that doped-up pervert of a boyfriend you have and I *do* mean David Strauss!"

I gasped. There were too many shocks coming at me to absorb all at once. I *knew* that when David took me home from Len and Nora's party and later moved in with me that it had not gone unobserved around town, but I had hoped it wouldn't have reached Papa's ears all the way back in New York already. It obviously had.

"I thought something was funny when you put him to work in the Valentine unit." Papa continued, brusquely, while I was still trying to come up with something to say. "But what's going on now is a disgrace. I've always kept out of your personal life—Clara *and,* let's not forget, Miss duMain—but when filthy gossip comes in from every side and has the whole board of directors up in arms, then something has to be done. And *that,* my boy, is why I consider it necessary for you to be relieved of your position. Do you understand me now? Am I quite clear?"

I wanted to scream. I wanted to smash the telephone and beat my head on the desk. But I did none of those things. I didn't even speak. I just sat there, numb.

"I assume, then, that I am," he said sharply, when I still did not reply, he hung up.

It was over. Over. I couldn't believe it. My whole life had come crashing down around my ears after that god-awful night at Len and Nora's. Starting with Gaby's call the day after, when I was still barely able to move.

I was pretty goddamned generous, offering to overlook the way she was screwing around with Jeannie at the party —and she laughed! Actually *laughed* at me. Told me it was all true, she and that lezzie were moving in together and —goddamn, I *still* can't think about it.

David was a great comfort to me then, I have to admit that. Playing Nurse Edith Cavell and getting me back on my feet, keeping me from getting depressed about everything. Then—pow!—I made my fatal mistake. When I heard that Clara—*Clara!*—was going around with Gaby and Jeannie, I let David talk me into starting up with him again. I mean, there he was, living in my apartment already,

400

since I hadn't been able to get around much for a while after my encounter with Aloha Shirt, so it just sort of happened one night. I didn't mean it to. Oh, Jesus Christ, no. I spent years trying to forget that *ever* happened. God knows, David was a pest to have around more often than not—never leaving me alone, going off on his crazy tangents. And obviously he was blabbing about us all over town. Diarrhea of the mouth—the more I thought about it, the more I wanted to hurt him. What was clear to me was that he'd just used the whole Gaby and Clara thing to lower my defenses, to manipulate me into bed with him. This time, he would have to be taught a lesson.

Sitting there in the chair behind my desk, I looked at all the buttons in front of me. The buttons that soon would connect to nothing in this world. The buttons that soon would be disconnected. As *I* was disconnected and . . .

## Buddy Valentine

". . . just floating around. Listen, Sandy, I mean it now! It's been wonderful. All this time, Jesus, it's been the most wonderful thing that ever happened to me. But, all right, so I'm a greedy bastard. I don't want to just float anymore, at least I don't want to if you're not floating right alongside. With a string—hell, with a steel chain—holding your raft to mine. . . ."

Damn it—what was wrong? I swear, sometimes I think I'm some kind of a maniac and sometimes I think I'm just plain stupid. But this—this thing of hers of not wanting to get married—was really driving me out of my bird. Really confusing the hell out of me.

Because she didn't exactly turn me down, either. And she wouldn't give me a single counterargument: no fem-lib oration against the institution of marriage; no "I like you, Buddy, but not enough to marry you"; and no guff about not wanting to be tied down or having to give up that flying job of hers if she got married. No way! Hell, she even talked about the idea of having a home, and maybe even some kids of our own and all that. She even talked about that as though it sounded good to her.

But every time I asked her to marry me, it was the same damn answer: *Wait. Not yet. A little more time.*

And no other explanations at all! I tell you, man, it was really bugging me! Not that there was a thing in the ever-lovin', blue-eyed world I could *do* about it!

"My raft," she said, answering my latest merger argument, "digs your raft the most, baby. You know that. And if I were to up and commit marriage with anyone, it would be you. Buddy, if you don't know I *want* to, just as much as you do, then The Hallowell has been kidding herself a lot more than usual. But I just can't—not right now, anyway."

"Sandy," I said, "I love you. Do you believe that?"

She smiled at me and there was a deep softness in her eyes, and she nodded. "I believe that," she said. "And you better believe this, too: I love *you*."

"Then . . . ?"

"I feel lucky," she went right on, "every single time I look at you. Even the times you're half-asleep and grouchy in the morning, or come home from the studio and sit around for hours staring at the wall until I'm not sure whether you've gone off your rocker—or are trying to drive me off mine. I know what love is, Buddy. I never did before, but I do now, and I know that's what I feel with you. That's why I feel lucky. My God, do you know an awful lot of people go through their lives—their whole lives—and never feel that for anyone! How lucky can I get? And the icing on the cake—the real grabber, as far as I'm concerned—is that you love me back. That's the part that really shakes me. Because (forget the way I act a lot of the time; 'act' is the word) I'm just like most people, darling, insecure as hell when it comes to something really big, like love.

"You know, all the time I was a little girl I knew my dad and my brothers and quite a few other people—you might be surprised—loved me. Sure, I never had to question that for a moment. They loved me like a daughter, like a sister, like a granddaughter or a niece. Wow! It was *great!* I used to feel sorry for little girls who didn't come from big, close families and wonder if they weren't lonely and scared a lot. But, Buddy, I was the only girl—in fact the only female —in the whole family, just about. I never knew my mother; she was a black-and-white picture of a pretty lady that stood on my dad's bureau from as far back as I can remember until the day he died. So that left me short one very important item in my life, at a time when I needed it bad:

I didn't have anyone to tell me the things only a mother can really explain to a girl.

"I didn't know anything about the kind of love she'd had with Dad. Sex, sure! I knew the basics before I was four years old; we had pigs and cows and horses and goats and even a couple of sheep once. And a little girl who shares a single bathroom with a flock of brothers and a father just can't help finding out, very early, that men and women are equipped pretty much the same way as the other mammals. The mystery was love. The kind of love people talked about when they meant man-and-woman love. I just couldn't sort it out in my mind, so of course I was sure it was never going to happen to me. I thought I might love a man myself, someday. But I just couldn't believe he'd *love me back.* . . ."

"But you believe I do?"

She leaned toward me, against me, and I thought she wanted to be kissed. But it wasn't that. She just put her face close to mine and touched her cheek against my face, my nose and chin and forehead, and then kissed me lightly, on the earlobe.

"I *know* you do, Buddy," she said. "Please, never doubt that; I *know.*"

"Then what's it all about? The long explanation—if you know it, what is it that turns you off? You're not against marriage . . . ?"

She shook her head. "No *way,* mister!" she said. "No way. And I'm not scared I've made a mistake, either; I don't distrust what I feel and what I believe. I told you (no secrets, right?) about the abortion I got when I was a kid. That was a mistake *I'd* made; you couldn't really blame the boy. I sure didn't. I had just been so curious about the big deal, *love,* that I wanted to see if I could *make* it happen. That's how confused and ignorant I was on the subject. Okay, it was a silly way, a rough way, to learn. But I did learn! Not everything I needed to know, Buddy— I never found out the most important things until I knew you—but enough to know what wasn't love; enough to know the shape and sound and touch and quality of what I was looking for, and enough to keep myself from settling for substitutes. And then—well, and then along came astrology."

I nodded. It still twinged me, just a little, when Sandy

403

talked about it that way; call it a learned response. All my life, the few times astrology was mentioned around me, it was by people who knew next to nothing about it and simply rejected it out of hand as superstition. Nobody took me aside and lectured me; there was no authoritative debunking of the subject. It was simply dismissed as too silly to talk about, and those same attitudes, of course, became mine. Property of Buddy-boy: "Astrology is nonsense! The End."

So it was pure Pavlov when Sandy first broached the subject to me. She sensed how I felt and didn't push it. And even later, when she admitted—no big confession, just a casual nod—that it played a big part in her life, and even had played a part in mine because she trusted it enough to believe it would bring us back together again when I started acting like a prime horse's ass, she wasn't trying to sell me anything.

I had to ask her about it, had to communicate the fact that I wasn't just being polite or making conversation, that I really wanted information. When I finally got that across, she was willing enough. But there was still no kind of salesmanship, not even an unequivocal affirmation of her own absolute faith in it. "It seems to work out," was the most she would say.

". . . along came astrology," she'd said just now. Yeah . . . she hadn't said she'd marry me. No. But she hadn't said she *wouldn't,* either. And she'd said she wanted to; that she dug the marriage bit, the family bit, the whole trip. All of which gave me an idea which I decided to test out, right there and then.

"Okay, baby," I said. "I read you, loud and clear. But we can't go on like this, just exactly the way we are, forever. Every minute changes everything, just a little bit maybe, but it gets changed. So, how many of those change minutes is it going to take? I mean, *when* can you give me an answer? Do you have an idea? I'm not pressing. Honest. I just . . ."

She smiled, then. The big smile; the one that'd really turned me onto her in the very beginning, on that charter jet from New York to L.A. "Not pressing, huh, podnuh?" she said. "Not *much!* But, okay, you're right. What you said. Time—that's all the problem I really have. So I will set a limit."

I held my breath. A month? A year?

"Would you believe . . . *three days?*" she said.

*Would I!*

"Three, at the outside. Two, maybe—but three, to give a margin for error. . . ."

And I guess she'd have gone on for a while. But she didn't get the chance. We were together. We were alone. Love was a big word . . . but not a frightening one, not for either of us anymore.

"Buddy," she said, not long afterward, in a private, secret ear whisper, "Buddy—oh, Buddy . . ."

## Jack Dahlberg

". . . I *love* you, I *trust* you, I *help* you," I yelled. "I save your career after you throw it away using *dope!* And look what happens! Look what you do to me!"

David just stood there with his mouth opening and closing, like a fish out of water. It didn't matter. There was nothing he could have said anyway.

I went on in a rage; I hardly knew what I was saying. "You crazy blabbermouth cocksucker! You conniving little dope-fiend creep! Thanks to you, I'm out of a job. Thanks to you, my reputation's ruined. I should have known . . ."

I had a lot more to say. A very great deal more. But I was winded and I had to pause for a minute. Sitting in my office, alone, after Papa fired me and after my heart stopped hammering on the inside of my chest, I had realized, that in some ways, at least, Papa was *right*—as always.

I had done a good job at Monarch, yes. My program of pictures had been the right one to get Monarch back in the lead, to make it profitable one day soon. And Papa's insistence on big expensive pictures had done a lot of damage; even if *Sadie* was released now, the months of waiting had virtually bankrupted the studio. All that was true.

But Papa had been right. I had failed him, failed the studio and failed myself—all down the line—if my behavior had, as he said, jeopardized Monarch's standing and turned off the bankers. A conservative lot, those bankers. God knows *Papa's* behavior hadn't always been perfect—and he didn't exactly hide his peccadillos—but I had to admit that that scene at Len and Nora's had kept the town buzzing for weeks. Not to mention what filthy stories David had been spreading. Yes, it was David's fault—the whole mess. I'd been so right when I'd dropped him all those years ago; he's never been anything but trouble. I might not be able to salvage my job at Monarch—the scapegoat is never dealt a winning argument—but I sure as hell could see to it that David Strauss didn't mess up whatever other chances I might still have around town. And so I kept my voice icy as I confronted him. *"Get out!"* I ordered. "I don't want you here another minute. Don't even stop to pack your bag, David—I'll have it sent to you."

David found his voice at last.

"Please," he said, his tone pleading and his face terrible to look at, "oh, *please,* Jackie—what *is* it? *Please. Tell* me. What have I *done* to make you hate me?"

"Stop it!" I couldn't bear to go through this scene again, so many years later. Why, oh, why had I allowed myself to get involved with him again. No more! "You *know* what you've done, David. Don't ask me to act out a charade with you. It's useless. I'm ruined in this town, and it's all because of you. It has got to stop this instant!"

But he wouldn't shut up.

"Please, Jackie, please. Don't do this to me. I can't stand it. You're the only person I've ever loved, you know that." He moved toward me, sniveling and blubbering, and all at once, I couldn't stand the sight of him.

I couldn't help myself. I hit him—*as hard as I could*—in the face. He stumbled backward and almost fell, but recovered in time and started to say something to me, then stopped—just *stopped* and stood there looking terrified. At first I thought he was looking at me. But then I could see he wasn't. He was looking over my shoulder, at something that was happening *behind* me.

That's the oldest trick in the book, of course. No one *ever* fell for it in real life, probably, and we'd never pass a script that used a gimmick like that. But nonetheless— *I looked!* I just couldn't help it.

And, of course, there was nothing there; I'd been had by a phony gag that not even a kid would believe. I whirled back, ready to defend myself. But David hadn't moved. He was still standing transfixed, looking at the wall as though he really could see something going on. And from his eyes, he must have seen something terrible. Well, to hell with him.

"Stop that," I ordered. "Don't try to fool me with any of your pervert acting tricks. Go on! *Get out of here before I hit you again!*"

At first I didn't think he was going to move. But he did. Slowly, like in a dream, at first—and then all at once, as though a starting gun had gone off somewhere, he was running out the door and toward the elevator and past it, without a moment's hesitation; and I could hear his feet hammering on the stairs, becoming fainter and fainter. . . .

*Silence.* The blessed, blessed anodyne of silence around me.

I sat down on the couch beside the telephone. It was very quiet in the room. In the apartment. Everywhere. Very quiet. I don't know how long I sat there. The sun went down. The lights of Beverly Hills made patterns in the blue-blackness. There did not seem to be any reason to get up. I did not want to hear any music. Or watch television. In particular, I did not want to watch television.

The time seemed to pass; the time seemed to not pass; the ormolu clock made hour-striking sounds from the big bedroom at what seemed to be rather irregular intervals. The telephone rang once. I think it rang rather a long time.

I thought, for no particular reason, of David's keys to this apartment and to my office. They did not seem very important, either. Especially the key to my office at Monarch; that would be meaningless after tomorrow, in any case. I thought it would be a good idea, though, to get back the key to the apartment. Or have the lock changed.

I wondered if it would be worthwhile to go to the studio at all tomorrow. Perhaps not. Better stay home, the word would be all over town by then. In fact, it was all over town already, no doubt. It would certainly be in the trades by morning. Clean out the office? Clean out the desk? Oh, I could send the . . . sweet GOD!

Suddenly I was standing up. There was a fullness in my head, and my face felt very hot. But I hardly noticed. I stood staring, bolt upright on my feet and nearly rigid, at the darkness and the night-light pattern, but seeing neither. My eyes were focused inward.

Papa couldn't fire me; I could *ruin* him if he tried it! The ocular nerve system, switched from "record" to "playback," gave me a swift rerun—m.o.s.—of the television tape recording locked in my desk at the studio.

Irving Dahlberg, paying Johnny Valentine in unreported company cash to exert political influence in order to obtain use of United States navy ships for the filming of a commercial motion-picture enterprise. Boffo, Papa! A real Irving Dahlberg zinger!

One *hell* of a short subject for the congressional hearings they were also scheduling as they tried to find a scapegoat for the *Pennsylvania* debacle. *Yes,* a hell of a short subject. Why, with a little extra footage spliced in, say, a couple of the rushes from *Boarders Away!* I bet we'd have their undivided attention, particularly if the film was selected to show leader bits and overruns where parts of the camera ship—the *Olathe*—were picked up by accident. The congressmen might be *especially* interested in the *Olathe!* . . .

Oh, yes, *yes!* I was already twisting, ready to run to the phone for a studio long-distance patch-through to New York. But I never got there; I never even moved from my tracks; my feet stayed right where they were. I didn't move, except to relax from that twist. Because I wasn't going to make any such call. No.

And tomorrow—well, tomorrow I would clean out the office myself. And the next day I would burn the tape— burn it, not erase it—right here at home. Alone. *Papa had been right to fire me. I had betrayed his trust.*

He had done the right thing; as always, he had done the right thing. It hurt, but it was right. I knew, he always found a way to show me, that in hurting me he hurt himself far more. He was Papa; the day would come when he would . . .

*Like hell!* The day of forgiveness, the day of acceptance would *never* come again because the truth was that Papa himself was going to be fired. He would not last another month at Monarch, not a month past the board meeting, without me protecting him on this end.

*No, it didn't matter.* He was still Papa; indomitable, uncrushable. He would remain there as head of the studio, and he would see to it that no one could be found who would do the job I had done for him. No one he could hire would run the studio as well as I had. The day would come . . . depend on it. The day *would* come, and we would meet again at the studio gate. . . .

*Not true!* I laughed a little, quietly, at the melodrama of my fantasy. Replace the writer on the Dahlberg project, next time he comes up with a clunker like that! Sometimes these guys just go stale. . . .

Still, everything could turn out for the best, eventually. I would just have to be patient. And exposing Papa wasn't going to accomplish a thing. No. Go to the studio tomorrow. Clean out my desk. Be sure to get the tape, for burning. And before I leave—one little chore that I mustn't overlook . . . *pick up five hundred and fifty thousand dollars in cash*—the Stamp Fund minus Johnny Valentine's quartermil and the even two hundred thou Clara had finally agreed to settle for. For transfer to some safer place. Feeling better now, I smiled at my image, visible in the mirror in the hall.

Suddenly I was hungry. All this mind bending had worked up my appetite. I wandered out to the kitchen, where the clock on the wall said it was already . . .

## Dolly Diamond

. . . *Past four ay-em.* Who the fuck could be calling at this hour?

The telephone rang again in the other room, and the sound, echoing in the quiet rooms, made me feel incredibly alone. I let it ring twice more, hoping it would stop. But it wasn't Dolly's lucky night. It had that I'm-gonna-ring-until-you-answer sound.

All right—all right! I stumbled over a petrified-wood end table (another one of Johnny's little preferences I was going to drop out the window the first chance I got) and finally got the call on about the eighth ring.

"Hello?" Nothing. No answer. But the line wasn't dead; I could hear something, just *barely*. Something. Someone. *Breathing!*

"If this is an obscene phone call," I said conversationally, "Dolly Diamond has a message for you . . . *up your arse, motherfucker!*"

And I was about to hang up when a voice finally came through.

*"Dolly? . . ."*

Oh, for the love of a pig-feathered wombat! . . . "David," I said sweetly. "That *is* you, David, dear?"

"Yes. It's me—listen, Dolly, I got to come over. Right away!"

"No."

"Dolly, *please*. I have got to be with *someone. I have nowhere to go*. It's as bad as before. *Worse*. I just can't make it through this . . ."

"David," I repeated, still sweet. "David, did you hear what I said when you were just *breathing* at me?"

He seemed to need some time to think that over.

"Uh, yes. I think so."

"Well, David, darling, that goes triple for you—and with a *red-hot poker!*"

I slammed the phone down, hard, and then—good thought—lifted it off the cradle again and stuck the whole works in under the sofa pillows. Fuck people who call you at four ay-em! Especially ex-husbands. Let him call his darling Jackie!

So help me—I am beginning to suspect Dolly has kind of shitty taste in men. For *real!* Two husbands so far and no replacement for my own sweet daddy anywhere in sight.

I can't stand *any* of it! *What is it with Dolly . . . does she secretly dig chicks?* No. The hell with it! I never could get it on with a chick; even the few times I really tried. . . .

Well, what, then? How should I know, kid. I just *work* here! And what in hell is *wrong* with this night? Nutty-crawly stuff going on; something in the air—like static, only not. What *is* it?

Who cares—just get Dolly some sleep. Just ship her off to Elsewhere for a few hours. Or she'll really *blow* it. And being the fabulous superstar of some big clunk of a movie isn't going to make one damn bit of difference. Wow. Oh, wow!

The whole *schmear* is really getting to be a weird trip. Something *wrong*. Something. Something bugging me; flying around in . . .

### Sandy Hallowell

. . . the night world. A presence; something else. I worked hard at keeping my eyes closed, but no use. *This was not like The Hallowell.*

I have been known to drop blissfully off in the middle

of a tornado scare, with a funnel knocking things around less than a hundred yards down the road. Bovine, that's me; not easily disturbed.

But all day something icy and insoluble had been growing in the center-of-my-center. *If I were still a little girl it would be time to burrow down under a haunch in Daddy's bed until it's all gone away.*

Well, who am I now? The Hallowell isn't any different; the body got older and the mind got more adept. The distances got longer and the sky got lower. But I'm still me. And *me* is a human being and that means me needs . . . what? Why should I bother to ask?

I turned my head cautiously to peek at Buddy. He had kicked the covers off one foot—as usual—and his head was at a peculiar hanged-man angle off the corner of the bed. He looked like a rag doll discarded by a giant (thank God, Buddy does *not* snore!) and lying there he was just so absolutely *beautiful!*

Am I some kind of weirdo or something? I have seen statues that everybody in the world considers classics— Greek gods, you know—and they were modeled from gorgeous guys, I suppose. But on the whole, I don't think I would want to live with one if it took the notion to come to life; a Greek god just does not turn me on. I get the feeling Apollo would spend more time in front of a mirror than I do. (Also, I bet he would have a perfectly dismal sense of humor!)

Lying there, I looked at my somewhat rumpled love and it hit me for the first time that he did not even particularly *look* like the pretty tentative and apologetic young oaf who had butted me in the stomach and then flopped down in my lap over a year ago.

Nothing specific, really. He didn't cut his hair differently; his clothes were bought at the same places and he hadn't been fitted with false plates or anything like that. But he was a different assembly altogether. And let the record show: The Hallowell was damn well happy with the revised model.

Or, hell—you had a course or two in psychology, girl— maybe the difference was in me. Nuts to analytical thoughts, at least on that particular subject. Don't dissect it, dummy: *enjoy! Right!*

He was sleeping soundly, another improvement. As recently as three months ago, this was the guy who was living disproof of those dreams-last-only-a-moment-or-two theories. If there were an Olympic competition in miles-run-and-hurdled-during-dreams, this was a guy who could have papered the wall in gold medals.

I had made a point of never asking him about those dreams. Just from the little I could catch, watching on the nonparticipant side of the fence, you might say, you could tell they were absolutely nowhere to book a vacation tour. He would literally leap—gasping and terrified—from sleep as many as two or three times every night. Sometimes I was afraid something was gaining on him.

But nowadays the worst that ever seemed to happen was that he occasionally rolled off the mattress headfirst onto the floor—without waking up, mind you—and lay there tangled in the covers looking like an unsuccessful candidate for emperor of Rome.

*Suddenly I couldn't bear to stand there looking at him anymore.* I was embarrassed (thank God he was asleep!) on touching my cheek to find that it was salty-wet. Not that The Hallowell has anything against tears, mind you. In season, a little therapeutic blubbering is absolutely top-drawer. But today was absolutely *not* the time for Sandy to blow her cool. No *way!*

Silent, and wearing the rather fetching suit I got on my first birthday, I made my way to the kitchen and put the coffeepot to work on getting-The-Hallowell-through-the-night. I was glad it was a big pot. This was no time for halfway measures.

What *was* it with the air? Wow. *Bummer!* Nothing you could point to; nothing you could correct. Just—you know the term "weird trip"? Well, mostly I think it's misapplied. The "trip" is seldom really weird. Just stupid. Or downright psychotic.

But "weird trip" was the only really fitting description I could give for what was riding the world—my world anyway—tonight. Truly *weird*. I walked to the window and looked at the Village lights. (The new high-rise buildings that are beginning to ring the place come on like a personal insult to the face of the world. Elsewhere, maybe okay. Maybe necessary. But land isn't that tight in Westwood, and the place was casual, quiet, university-oriented, and a pleasure to the sensibilities before the early erector-set architects got in their licks. I don't like to wish *anyone* bad luck. And I don't really. But, for anyone who had a hand in putting those darn things up, I guess I *do* wish this: I hope you make a million dollars, have it all changed into pennies . . . and dropped on your toes!)

The lights, and the thought about the high-rises, brought me—by what process I wouldn't know—to the subject of today. And it was worth thinking about. Because tomorrow I was going to tell Buddy to get off his duff and forage for wedding rings and churches and marrying-preachers. Only that was tomorrow. And this was (I squinted at the Bank of America clock) 4:22 A.M. today.

I looked at the telephone and considered (a) taking it off the hook, or (b) ripping it out of the wall. Telephones are another bit of progress—like those darn high-rise things—that have a definite and useful place in a world filled with jet airplanes, moon-lander spaceships, sudden emergencies and people. But sometimes I wish Alexander Graham Bell had died in infancy. . . .

I tried a little pep talk-type reassurance: Hey, there, kid . . . you some kind of nervous? Or what? Knock off the teeth chattering and handkerchief twisting. You blind or something? Even with dawn an hour away, a glance at the sky told you this is going to be some kind of day! A real vintage model. Buddy and I will walk in it and talk in it and maybe get bicycles and—well, unless he's got to go to the studio; Sam called last night about something and Buddy didn't fill me in later but all night long he was walking around with canary feathers dangling from his chin.

So, all right. If he does have to go to the studio I'll meet him over in the Valley when he's through and we will use up the remainder of the hours in some scene of gay abandon like, maybe, the swank Big Boy hamburger shop in Glendale, and talk, and go find a park to walk in where stars play games with the leaves, and talk, and—oh—whatever comes easiest to hand (except for a ride down to the beach; this one time, just today, I will turn into a rotten manipulative bitch and find means to keep us away from any body of water larger than the average highball) followed by more talk . . . and then, just exactly one minute after midnight I will calmly inform him that he is practically a married

413

man unless he can outrun a girl who once held the girls' state record for the fifty-yard dash.

Should I tell him what it was all about then? *I wonder.* . . . I know he's pretty much into astrology, now. I didn't coax him or shove him. He asked *me* and even then all I did was tell him what I thought and mention some of the better books on the subject. Say this for the future father of my offspring—when he decides to find out about something he well and truly piles into it. Reading and listening and checking and doodling around with charts and growling at himself when it didn't go like clockwork. And finally deciding he knew what he wanted to know. It's nice to be able to talk to him about it sometimes without wondering whether he'll think I'm some kind of a crazy. But that does *not* mean he will exactly groove on what I've done here.

For one thing, any legitimate astrologer would strangle The Hallowell for acting this way. Tell the truth, I am not really too sold on it myself, friend. But it seemed like the right thing to do when I started . . . and, well, once the train has pulled out it's not usually a good idea to jump off. A feller could get hurt that way.

The bad thing, of course, is that I'm behaving as though I had the notion that astrology was a doctrine of fatalism, that every single event is predestined and that we have no chance of changing the outcome.

I don't think anything of the kind, of course. Only, the way I've handled *this* thing . . . well, anyway, only twenty more hours. After that—well, after that I can maybe relax and start acting a little less like a four-year-old girl hiding under the covers from the bogeyman—and I'd better, too, if I'm going to be much of anything in the way of a wife.

Not that I'm against caution. You check the traffic signal before you cross a street; there never was a world that rewards recklessness. Once in a long while—maybe—it is worthwhile to take the long chance. Just to remind yourself you're not immortal. But in general, entering the cage, unarmed, with a man-eating tiger will do nothing but get you turned into tiger food.

Still, caution can be carried to a ridiculous extreme—like the mother who buttons her child into so many layers of warm clothing that the poor kid can't move or have any fun after she finally lets him out the door to play in the snow. That's the way I'm coming on, and I don't like it one bit. For example, that switch I'd worked with the other stew—what do you call that?

Well, sir, I'd been wondering myself. All right, the chart said today was the day for the fickle finger. Groovy. If The Hallowell can get past it. Of course, water's always dangerous for me. . . . Sun and moon in adverse aspect; Neptune specifically indicating death by drowning (though it *could* come in any mysterious way, including gas, drugs, a poison; it's just that nothing else in the chart seems to give me a heck of a lot of protection on water). And those further progressions I did a few years ago pinning down the specific time of greatest danger. And the time is *now*.

If I were the tight-game type, I guess I would have quit my job, had the household water disconnected, avoided ice cubes in my drinks, and taken as few baths as possible. But a life you try to live like that is no life at all. I'd rather be dead, really dead, than go through a hundred years of the living death of constant fear and elaborate precaution. I will not tremble—not for anything or anyone. The precautions I'd been taking were the most I was willing to take. No more—not a single one more! Because I'd thought of everything.

When the day finally arrived, I found I was flying; scheduled for the LAX-Kennedy run. All right, that's no overocean route, and my air signs are moderately good. Not the greatest, but not a gun pointed at the head, either. All the same, those takeoffs and landings *are* over water. So, feeling a little sneaky and a little silly, I conned my friend Mary Jane with a yarn about relatives in town and got her to switch schedules with me for the week. No big hassle. Not even any need to explain what I'm doing and listen to the guff about "superstition" and all of that.

I realized that the coffeepot had been growling at me for a long time. I got up in a hurry to take the poor thing off the hot burner and was swooping to the rescue when the phone rang . . . and I grabbed it up before the ring was done. The minute it was off the hook, I was sorry.

No matter what the call was about, it was an interruption and I did not want to be interrupted. I wanted to sit still in the morning quiet and think my thoughts out to the end. Also, I was bugged at myself for being such a reflex-ruled type. *Some* people can just let a phone ring itself out.

"Miss Hallowell?"

Damn.

"Yes?"

"This is flight scheduling. Can you be ready for the oh-six-hundred run to Kennedy?"

*Damn.* "I . . . this is my day off. Did the schedule get changed?"

"No, Miss Hallowell. But Mary Jane Handerson's doctor called in to say she turned her ankle roller-skating yesterday, and she'll be laid up for some time. We're having to call-in on emergency . . ."

*Damn!* "Please—I have some . . . company coming from out of town. Isn't there *anyone* else you can get?"

"Sorry. Every other 'available' is already flying except for one. We tried her. But her phone doesn't answer. Be here at oh-five-three-oh, please."

It was the moment when I could have said no. And I let that moment go by. "All right."

And we both hung up.

*DAMN! DAMN! DAMN!*

Illogically furious with myself, the airline, Mary Jane, and the other girl who had sense enough to ignore a noisy talk machine, I stomped back into the bedroom to throw on my clothes. And stopped stomping when I saw that the ringing hadn't roused Buddy.

First piece of luck today! I hadn't mentioned the switch with Mary Jane to him, so he wouldn't be surprised when he found I was gone. No explanations; no nothing.

All the same, that ice finger was back inside me as I climbed into the stew suit, phoned for a cab; and finished stuffing things into the flight bag.

I wished I'd come down with—a nice nonfatal but quarantinable disease—. I wished I hadn't answered the phone. I wished I'd told Buddy why I'd stalled so long about marrying him. I wished . . .

*Of course, there was always that letter.* And that was a good thought to take with me to New York. The letter. I'd spent a lot of time on it, a week ago, and the truth was I never intended it to be read by anyone but me—even though I'd sent it to my brother Ben back in Pennsylvania. With instructions. A hedge against uncertainty.

And now, I felt I had something to add to it. In a hurry, I grabbed a piece of notepaper from my bag and hunted

416

up an envelope. I could say all I needed to say in just a few lines. But suddenly it seemed important to do that.

I finished, just as the cab honked downstairs. I slipped the P.S. note into its envelope, stuck it in my pocket for mailing to Ben from the airport. And closed the door, very softly, behind me.

# The 11th House

*Hopes, wishes, friends, projects, ambitions, associations, and the financial condition of an employer . . .*

---

*Forecast: Word has it that Johnny Valentine will put the Velvet Voice away in a drawer—the very same drawer in which he keeps his millions and all those corporate deals, and now maybe even a newly acquired movie studio.*

*In the Eleventh House there are hopes to be dashed, projects to be realized—and a fateful crossing in the lives of Sandy Hallowell and David Strauss. . . .*

---

### Johnny Valentine

I laid the bit on Sam as soon as he was done telling me how slick everything had come off on the Priapus-Monarch switcheroo.

"Tell the truth, Vanni," he said, and I could hear the satisfaction floating around his cigar and across the coast-to-coast telephone, "I wasn't really convinced till the last minute it was gonna work. That's a hell of a tricky gag to pull, you know. The timing's gotta be right on the line, or *blooey!*"

"Yeah," I said. "It's been a hell of a long time since anyone traded one studio for another in this town. A *hell* of a long time."

He laughed. "It's a hell of a long time," he said, "since anyone went into a studio merger deal with nothing but a losing record company, got the new partner to sign a first-refusal-and-sale-approval agreement, and turned it into $22 million dollars in less than a year, you mean."

*That* figure came as a kind of a grabber. *"Twenty-two,"* I said. "Hey, *hold it*, Dad! I thought you said the best we could expect was—oh, ask for *eighteen-five* and settle for eighteen?"

"That's what I thought," Sam said. "But I got me a piece of news late yesterday—didn't have time to tell ya. Why old Steve's selling right now. Ya know we thought it was just that he'd had trouble getting financing for anything but that damn rock-opera film. Well, Vanni, it was a little more than that."

"Like *what?*"

"He's being investigated, Vanni." Sam's voice was not so happy, now. "So are we—that's how I found out the truth. They're nudging around into both our records because, Vanni, someone's been fooling around with double mortgaging and one thing or another. I guess he wanted to make movies *real bad.*"

That was a stopper. The merger had left Steve in charge of the moviemaking end; we had our accounting people looking over the shoulders of his, of course, and his people were giving ours a little eyeball, too. But we weren't keeping tabs on his day-to-day. Sam was right—the guy *must* have been getting desperate.

"Well," I said, "I'm sorry for old Steve. And I'm sorry he tried a dumb thing like that. But I'm sure as hell *not* sorry to hear we're four mil better off than I'd been figuring. How's the rest of the picture, Sam? Do we have it firm—locked—on Monarch?"

"Made the last contact just before I phoned you," Sam said. "We're *solid*, keed. Even if Irving the Great really has as many proxy votes as he claims, he can't retain control. We got the weight on him. We'll force a majority in the board of directors, and that's the ball game."

"And pick up our markers with the cash from the sale and from the extra fees for agreeing to let old Steve sell at Priapus?"

"And pick 'em all up."

"Those bankers back there been crowding you, Sam?" I asked. "I know those guys are always a little hinky about short-term money; especially when they don't know exactly where you think you're going to get the payoff cash from."

"Oh, a *little*." He sounded casual, but I knew the truth. Old Sam's a guy who likes maneuvering room; he's a dealer and wheeler from way back, but it bugs him to have blue-sky paper out. He'd really slugged this one together. I started wondering about a present—you know—just to show the guy I know he really busted ass and I appreciate it.

And—like that—it zonked me. A real *gas*!

Yeah, and it could click right in with my own plans. I could make the announcement as the Samuel LoCicero Surprise Testimonial Banquet and First Annual Gin Tournament. Hey, that would really bomb old Sam! Two things he likes better than anything else in this world: gin rummy and dago food. And I could get Patsy to let his chef come up to fix the food. *Sure*. And do the guest list myself; all his buddies and mine; everybody having a ball. I could hardly wait to get started.

". . . just made too many mistakes," Sam was saying; I had missed something, thinking about the banquet. What the hell was he talking about?

"Sorry, kid, something jazzed up the phone on this end," I lied. "Twisted cord or something. What were you saying?"

"Irving's wife, Margaret!" Sam said. "That was the thing I didn't have time to tell you. She's definitely going to hold back her proxies so there's really no way Irving can hang in there. You know, Vanni, he's been making a lot too many mistakes lately. Stuff he'd never have fumbled a few years back. Hell, we're probably doing the guy a favor, edging him out, you know? And I think that might be part of why his wife's stiffing him this time; she never did that before, even if he'd treated her like dirt for years. Well— yeah—and also, I guess she's pissed on account of him kicking the kid out of his job, too. Y'know, Vanni, I never thought much, one way or another, about Jackie Dahlberg before all this. But, looking into this whole Monarch setup, now we're gonna have to run the show there, I'm beginning to think the kid was really a pretty damn good studio boss. . . ."

"*Jackie?* You gotta be kidding! You know, Irving—he put the punk in there to transmit and receive orders and make sure he didn't have a mutiny or something, a putsch, while he was on the East Coast."

"It started that way," Sam agreed. "First year or two,

yeah. But the picture changed later. Vanni, you know I found out it was Jack who shoved through that exploitation and X-rated flick policy they went with the past year. And it worked, keed; that's the only place that Monarch made any money at all."

I wondered if Sam really knew what he was talking about. Jackie? He was a kid! Not a hell of a lot older than Buddy. What the hell could *he* know about running a whole studio?

"What's up, Sam?" I said.

"Up?" Sam's round-eyed innocent bit almost jumped out of the phone at me. "Up? Why—nothing. Only like I said, we got to find someone who can handle the job if we're gonna run Monarch."

"And you want to bring *Jackie* back? Oh, balls, Sam! I'd just as soon see Buddy in the job. It would make as much sense. And Buddy can't even keep his own checkbook straight."

"That a fact? Well well." That was a funny answer, and there was something funny, too, in Sam's voice all of a sudden. What the hell was going on, now? He was up to some kind of a damn thing. "Well, then," he said, with his voice still just a little bit wrong, "I guess we'll count Jackie out. I just thought, if we wanted him, now would be the time to say so. Before he makes some other deal, somewhere."

"Sam, you putting me on some way? I mean, you got some kind of a gag going, a rib, that I'm not hep to? Because aside from the fact that he's still wet behind the ears, there's that scrape he got into that has all the tongues wagging. This has to be a gag . . ."

"A gag? No, Vanni. No gag."

"Okay, let it pass," I said. "Hey, by the way, you been to see Irving yet? To lay the offer on him."

"Not yet. Tried to get an appointment earlier, but the girl said he was all full up. I think he's ducking me."

"Figures. Well, do what you can. He would be okay as chairman of the board. Without a strong stock clout he'd be our man; and besides, he's still got a couple of friends left around. He stays as chairman, it doesn't look so much like we crowded him out—keeps everybody happy."

"Well, yeah. But I wouldn't count on it, Vanni. Irving never did anything but run his own show since he was a kid; I don't see too damn big a chance he'll go for it, that chairman spot. . . ."

"Oh, yeah—*another* thing," I said, "what about Steve Pappas?"

"Steve? What *about* him?"

"What's he gonna do now—I mean, he got any plans?"

Sam sighed. "That's the *hell* of it, Vanni," he said. "We did what we had to do here—everything legit; nobody got a fast shuffle. But, in the process, a lot of crap gets moved around and shoved and hauled. And you get breakage that way. I wish we had a chairman job or something like that to offer old Steve. I don't think he's got the slightest idea of what he's gonna do, now he got out of Priapus with a whole skin. And I hate to see it. I mean, Steve's no big, close, personal buddy-buddy. But I known him and worked with him a lotta years. Goddamn pity to see it end this way."

"Yeah. He's not a bad old boy; I always liked him. You're right, too! It *is* a lousy ending for a guy like him—having to get out to keep from losing the whole ball of wax."

"Yeah," I said, "but it's not going to happen to me, Sam! Johnny Valentine's had the best. the whole cake, and thun grabbed off the icing, candles, and platter; I got no complaints, and I can still draw a crowd, right? So I'm going to do what old Steve should of done. Sam, I already had Victor draw up the press release; we'll announce it in Vegas. Maybe the end of next week; I'm quitting, baby! Like, I've had it: Johnny Valentine is officially retiring as a performer."

And I sat there, holding silence to my ear. Well . . . You know, I must of waited a full sixty seconds, and that damn Sam didn't make one sound? I wanted his reaction, and he gives me a forty-eight-bar rest.

"Hey," I finally had to say. "Hey, Sam! You drop dead or something?"

"Uh—no." His voice was controlled and natural. But it had all the inflection of a poker shark's face. "No, Vanni, I didn't faint. But look—Victor's the only one you told so far? No one else?"

What a screwy thing to ask. "No, of course not," I said. "We do it right or not at all."

"Good."

"*Good?* Why *good*, Sam? I mean—look—this is the right time. I can go straight into the business side; I got plenty to keep me busy. More than enough. I'd be crazy to go on acting or singing until they finally stop applauding or buying tickets. And, hell, with that Priapus deal you made, I sure as Christ don't need the extra dough."

"Uh-huh."

"What the hell is it, Sam? What's wrong?"

"Nothing!" He seemed to get hold of himself and some of the briskness came back into his voice. "Nothing wrong, Vanni. But, Vanni, I think you and me ought to *talk* about this."

"Sam, I told ya. I don't need the dough. You, more than anyone in the world, should know I don't. So what would I go on for?"

He waited a second before answering, and I wondered if I was starting another one of those sixty-second breathers. "It's not that, Vanni," he said, in time to stop me from nudging him. "Not the money—hell, you haven't really needed that for ten years or more."

"Well, then? . . ."

"Vanni: the singing, and the acting, too . . . with you, Vanni, it was never the money. Not from the first. Don't you know that?"

"Not the money?" I said. "What you talking about?"

"You'd of sung for nickels," he said quietly. "Or for nothing a week, paid on Friday, if that's the only way you could sing to an audience. It was never the dough with you —it was the singing, the performing, for its own sake. That's what made you worth listening to, Vanni—the love that came through."

Well! Face it—there is no topper line for that; not when he's got you taped and measured. Old Sam! Who'd of figured him to know a weird thing like that, or even less, to say it on a telephone.

"Yeah," was the snapper I finally came back with. "Well, maybe so, Sam. But I'm dropping out, anyway."

"Vanni . . ." He started to say something, but his voice trailed off.

"What?"

"Nothing." I could hear him take a deep one. "Well," he said, "I'm headed over to Dahlberg's office in the Monarch building. And then I'll catch a plane back to the Coast. Anything I can handle for you while I'm out here?"

"Nope. Have a good flight. And let me know what Irving says."

"We'll be in touch."

He hung up, but I just clicked the receiver buttons. I wanted to talk to my lawyer to see how the property settlement with Dolly was coming. But by the time the girl came on the line and asked me what number to get, I'd changed my mind.

"Nothing," I said. And dropped the receiver.

Sam's reaction was something I hadn't expected. I mean, guys retire all the time. Singers, too. What was it about me doing the same thing that had him worried? And should I be worrying, too? Should I?

And then I was tired of the whole scene. It was *my* life and *my* career and *my* voice, and I would play the hand *my way!*

And besides . . . besides, I hadn't really told Victor yet; I was conning Sam about that. I was going to tell him tonight. I'd thought Sam might change my mind or something, I guess, but he hadn't. In fact, I couldn't really tell what he thought. And it didn't matter a damn, anyway.

I'd said I was going to do it. And now I . . .

## Sandy Hallowell

. . . was committed. The jet lifted, smooth, firm and steady, and I flipped the catch to release my seat belt. A full load of passengers would be waiting breakfast before we reached altitude, and the flight deck would want its coffee before *that*.

I grinned at the other stew working first class, a girl I'd never flown with before, and headed forward with two paper cups of coffee. Just before I entered the flight deck, the crew-plate on the bulkhead caught my eye, and I *almost* decided the day wasn't going to be a total loss.

Because the plate said: CAPTAIN—E. J. Malnic. 1st OFFICER—T. E. Newton.

And those two names came in for a little extra benevolence from The Hallowell. They'd been the crew on that charter, over a year ago, when I'd met Buddy.

"Anybody up here drink coffee?" I asked, butt-turning through the door carefully, to keep the coffee in its place.

"Only from your beloved hand, Funny Face!"

Yup. That crew-plate had been up to date.

"You still around, Sneaky-hands?" I needled him, handing him the first cup because the captain was busy with something or other on the overhead panel. "Funny, I thought I heard you'd been arrested for molesting little girls."

He took the cup with one hand, grabbed at me with the other (missed me a mile!) and leaned back into the idiot seat with his usual ersatz nonchalance. "What's wrong with molesting little girls? The littler the better—just as long as they're over eighteen!"

"Oh, the *wit;* oh, the *charm!* What I have *missed* by being reassigned to the A-Crew list. Tell me, Sneaky-hands: with all those millions and millions of people out there, just how did you happen to fall in love with *you?*"

I give Tommy the benefit of the doubt; he *might have* come back with a topper. Score us even. But no one will ever know for sure, because the captain finished his dial-twiddling and claimed my attention.

"Your coffee or the company's, Sandy?" he asked.

I grinned at him. "Mine. Would I poison the only man aboard who can fly this thing?"

"A-hah! I heard that!" Sneaky-hands pretended to be insulted. "Just for that, you get to make *two* laps around the crew table before I give up chasing you when we get to New York."

"He's got a legitimate beef," Captain Malnic said. "I'll have you know our young hero, here, is now a fully qualified and certified and licensed airline *captain.*"

"You're kidding!"

"I'm facting—indeed, I believe you're flying on a historic *last,* Sandy. This New York run is the last Tom's making on that side of the flight deck. Schedules change two days from now, and they'll be assigning him his own run—in the left seat."

This time I actually smiled at Tommy. "I thought I'd never *mean* anything nice I said in your direction," I told him, "but this time I guess I do—and, darn it, there goes my perfect record with you. Congratulations—*Captain* Sneaky-hands!" And I ducked just in time to avoid the elbow he aimed at my ribs.

"Well, then," I said, when I was sure he wasn't ambushing me, "as long as we're handing out the good news—and before I go back to load our passengers with plastic bacon and concrete eggs—I guess this would be the opportune time to announce that today is pretty close to being my last flight—on the crew list anyway."

The captain smiled over at me. "Buddy Valentine?" he said with what had to be the smuggest leer of the century.

*Blush?* Friends, you could have painted a sunset with me. And I'd thought Buddy and I had been so cool, so tactful about our living arrangements. But it had to be all over the line grapevine if Captain Malnic knew. He calmed my fears, however, when he saw my face.

"Don't worry," he said. "Far as I know, I'm the only one around here who has any idea you've even been seeing him. And at that, girl, I'd never have been sure if you weren't such an easy-flustered gal."

"But—how?"

"He flew with me," the captain said. "And you can tell a lot about a man by the way he handles an airplane. The important thing about that one was that he was the stray-pup type."

"Stray *pup!*"

"Yep. Good stuff in him; teachable and willing, all the basic equipment. But like a stray pup, no damn good at all until someone *tells* him he is."

Funny thing. I'd never really looked closely at the captain's face before. I did, now. It wasn't handsome, and it didn't seem likely it ever had been. But the eyes were eyes that *see* instead of just *looking*. And the hands—big, knotted, and blue-knuckled from the days, so I'd heard, when he had been a mechanic instead of a pilot.

"You mean love?" I said.

"Or a word something like that. Stray pups need it to stop being clumsy and timid. People need it for the same reason. And—well, Sandy, back when you were in my crew I marked you down for the type who needs to be needed."

I smiled at him. "Think you're pretty smart, don't you," I said. "Well, I'll put it in writing. You are. I still don't see how you figured it all out from just that, though."

"Well, maybe I was stretching the truth just a leetle," he conceded. "Fact is, I got *some* help from that picture in the paper—the one after he'd been lost in the plane crash. Noticed one of the faces in the background of the Valentine family reunion looked kinda familiar."

"Oh—sure!"

"But I'm still a smart ole geezer."

"But you're still a smart ole geezer!" He and Tommy had finished, and I knew my stew-partner was probably ready to murder me for staying up here gabbing when I should have been lending a hand setting up the breakfast.

"More Hallowell coffee in an hour or so," I promised. "I brought a *big* thermos today."

"Hey, by the way, Sandy," the captain called before I got to the door, "isn't that David Strauss, the actor, mixed up with the Valentine clan some way?"

"Why, yes. He's related by divorce, or something. Why?"

"Oh." The captain nodded. "Well, maybe it doesn't matter. But I was going to tell you—that Strauss guy, he's aboard. Back in the second-class section."

"Oh, thanks!" I said. "Actually, I hardly know him. But maybe I'll go back and say hello when breakfast is done."

But just then the door to the flight deck opened, and the journey back to second-class became unnecessary. David Strauss was standing there looking in at us.

"Why, hello, David! I was just coming back to . . ."

And that was as far as I got before the words stuck in my throat. For David wasn't alone. My stew-mate was with him, looking terrified out of her ever-loving mind, and, peering around the two of them, I could see the passengers twittering and buzzing and making worried motions at us.

The reason, was all too readily apparent.

"Sandy," he said, recognizing me, "I'm sorry you're aboard; I wish you weren't. But it won't make any difference if you or anyone else tries to stop me."

"David! . . ."

"I mean it!" The gun had been half-hidden behind the girl's back. Now he brought it into plain sight; a big, businesslike affair of blue steel with a two-inch barrel and of a caliber that looked *easily* two inches in diameter from where I stood. But what was even more terrifying was the sight of the live grenade he held tightly in his other hand, pin out and ready to explode with the slightest jostle. We exchanged looks in the cabin when we got a load of that;

428

a gun you can deal with, but a live grenade—that's the worst.

"*I want this plane to take me to Havana . . .*" he said. I noticed with horror that both his hands were in constant motion; David was failing to suppress a prime case of the trembling fits.

It had taken a few moments for the true impact of what was happening to hit the captain and Tommy. One minute we'd been talking about David Strauss. His appearance at the door the next minute simply hadn't registered in its true context at first. But it did, now. And the reactions of the two men were typical of each of them.

Tommy Newton edged a foot under the side of his chair and I could see, from the corner of my eye, that he was taking an instep purchase and tensing one arm to throw himself at David.

But the captain reached out, not too swiftly, and touched him on the shoulder. "You fly for a while," he said. The words were casual and the tone was quiet, but the voice was a clear command. Tommy hesitated, then relaxed, and sat back to take the controls.

"Mr. Strauss," the captain nodded, turning to face David, "I don't know you, and I don't even know a great deal about you. But this—well, this is a kind of a pretty damn silly and dangerous thing to do, son."

David turned his head an inch or two to look at him directly, and nodded his head solemnly.

"I know it, captain," he said. "In fact, what I'm doing is a lot more dangerous than you think. But that's my worry, not yours. I'm doing this because I haven't got any choice. Please don't try to trick me or stop me. I don't want to hurt anyone."

The captain shook his head, looking sad but friendly.

"No tricks," he promised. "But one thing we *do* have to do—and right now. That's contact Air Traffic Control and let them know what's happened and give them our new course. That okay with you?"

David hesitated, took a breath, and said, "Yes. Call them. I guess it would be the best thing—oh, and while you're about it, please explain that I'm *not* seeking refuge there, or anything like that. I'm on a mission for my country, a very important one. So they mustn't try to stop me."

That was the moment that I began to shake. And so, at least inwardly, I believe, did the captain. For the very best of reasons.

"A *mission*, huh," the captain nodded slowly. "I *see*. Well, is it secret, son? Or can you tell me about it?" He glanced at me; a quick look that was full of a question: If I knew this man, was I aware that he was out of his mind? And if so—why hadn't I said something?

"Yes," David said, "oh, yes, I can tell you! In fact, the whole world will know, soon. I *want* them all to know."

I was staring, fascinated, at the grenade, now trembling even more noticeably in David's hand. I don't think I'm a coward, really. Not in the usual sense. But I couldn't seem to take my eyes off that grenade. Never mind the gun.

"Well!" The captain wasn't blowing his cool; he just wasn't the type. But I could tell from the fact that he was talking slower and moving more deliberately than usual that he considered our situation even more dangerous for us all than if David had been an ordinary Havana hijacker. "I'm glad to hear that." he said. "But I'll have to admit I'm still a little bit confused, son. Mind telling me just how you hijacking a planeload of people to Havana is gonna prove how loyal you are to your country?"

"Of course!" David nodded energetically. "But you've got it backward: I'm not trying to take people *into* Cuba. Just the opposite. In fact, I really do wish this airplane had no other passengers aboard except myself, though of course everyone'll be released and sent home after we get there."

"Good," the captain nodded. "Good! But now, about this mission of yours . . ."

"Yes," David agreed. "When you make your radio call, and when you talk to the Cuban radio people at Havana, before we land, just explain to them that I'm coming down there to make a deal with Fidel Castro. To pay him ransom for those American sailors he kidnapped and is holding. I'm going to buy them back, understand?"

That time, even the captain showed a little shock. And I only barely managed to keep my expression in line.

"Ransom?" Captain Malnic said after taking a moment to lick his dry lips and to swallow. "Uh—yes. I see how that'd be. Ransom. How—uh—much you figure to offer Castro for those sailors?"

The question seemed to surprise David somehow. "Why," he smiled faintly for a moment, "can you believe it—I haven't worked that out yet! I mean the actual figure per sailor, that is. But I'm sure I can make it high enough to interest Fidel." Suddenly he looked sharply at the captain. "Don't you believe me?" he snapped.

"Yes, *of course!*" The captain's forehead was sweating lightly now. And I couldn't blame him. I guess both of us had secretly hoped that David would have some kind of rational explanation, some real-world contact, some kernel of logic in his idea—something that would let us hope or even believe that he was not what he *seemed* to be. But that hope was gone now. He stood smiling a child's smile at the captain's soothing words of agreement and approval, with the gun and the grenade still shaking and tightly clutched in his hands.

"But—*the ransom*," Captain Malnic tried to nudge him gently back to the present situation, "how much do I tell Castro you can pay?"

"Oh, yes, of course." David looked away from us at the wall. Let's see, that would come to  uh  come to  oh, I never was really good at division if I haven't got a piece of paper. I'm an actor, you know; my agent does all the book-keeping." He smiled, as though it were a good joke on himself. We smiled back the best smiles we could manage. "But tell him roughly twenty-five thousand dollars apiece for each of the men. That ought to be a good enough price for him, don't you think so?"

The captain cleared his throat and nodded quickly. "Sure," he said. "They ought to go for that."

He looked away. I noticed as he turned back to the light that his complexion had gone a waxy gray, with an undertone of green. I had no mirror, and I was glad of it. I know my own color would have been even worse. And I realized, suddenly, that I needed very badly to visit the bathroom.

Human beings are so clownish sometimes. Even then and there I couldn't help being amused at the way basic bodily reactions, which I knew to be the most normal thing in the world, could embarrass me. Embarrassed by the need to urinate. Embarrassed—with blue-steel murder about two feet away. And now, more clownishness, I was having to fight to suppress the urge to laugh. . . .

"I'll make the—radio call now," Captain Malnic said when it became evident that everyone had run out of conversation. "You'll be able to hear all of it," he added. "I *promised*, remember: no tricks from us."

"Yes. Please go right ahead. We mustn't run out of gas."

The captain looked toward the door. "Uh—if I could make a suggestion, Mr. Strauss?"

"Please!"

"The passengers," Captain Malnic nodded at the door, "they're watching, and I'm afraid all this is making them frightened. You see how that could be. Could you just—uh—come inside, here in the flight deck. And close the door so they don't see us?"

David smiled and nodded at once.

"You're right, of course," he said. "No need for them to be fearful."

"Yes . . ."

David extended his arm and motioned the other stewardess past him and inside the compartment. She came, but I could tell her legs were hardly holding her up. Neither were mine. But it didn't show quite as much because I'd had one advantage she probably hadn't—a family of hulking brothers, who'd always just loved an opportunity to use tease words like "sissy" on anyone who showed fear, especially girls.

So I helped her get to a seat, one of the two behind the control positions, and then turned to see what David wanted me to do. He wasn't even looking in our direction.

Tommy, who hadn't entered into any of the conversation and who had been watching David from time to time out of the corner of his eye, saw his turned back and seemed again to be thinking of making like John Wayne.

But, luckily, Captain Malnic saw it too and pinned Tommy's arm to the armrest with one of his big hands. The look he gave Tommy told him not to try *that* again.

David was looking our way once more, and smiling. Stashing the gun in his inside pocket, but hanging on to the grenade, he closed the door to the passenger cabin, walked forward, and I saw what it was he'd brought in with him: a brand-new-looking bag with an over-shoulder strap. Probably made for campers or such, but of bright orange nylon. It was stuffed with something.

"We'd better put *this*," ignoring the grenade, he gave the fat bag a hearty one-handed slap that made my heart stand still, "where we won't forget it. Wouldn't do to try and fob a check off on old Fidel, would it!"

The captain blinked. "Check?" he said.

"For the ransom," David nodded. "Twenty . . . what? Twenty-five thousand apiece for twenty-two men. Funny, you know, that's not as heavy to carry as you'd think? Even in comparatively small bills."

The captain blinked again and eyed the gaudy bag, glanced up at David, and then down again. "Would you," he said in his very quietest voice, "mind just opening the bag a little bit, Mr. Strauss?"

"Opening it?"

"Call it an old man's curiosity. I'd be grateful."

David smiled again. "Oh, sure," he said, "I understand. I'll admit, sir, this is the first time I've ever seen that much cash all in one spot, myself. Funny, though, it isn't really so very impressive. Especially since I had to pack it very tightly to get it in here."

Keeping his precarious grip on the grenade, he pulled the zipper about halfway back and spread the halves of the opening aside, being very careful not to let anything spill out and to brace the bag against the floor. We looked. And if anyone on the flight deck breathed for the next few seconds, well sir, I can tell you for sure it was not The Hallowell!

The stuffing of the bag was money. If it wasn't real, it was certainly the best counterfeit ever produced. And there seemed to be an awful lot of it.

"How much," said the captain, who was the first to regain his power of speech, "how much, exactly, would you say is in there, Mr. Strauss?"

David looked surprised again. "I *told* you before," he said. "Ransom for twenty-two men at twenty-five thousand dollars a man. That's right, isn't it? Doesn't that come to . . ."

## Jack Dahlberg

. . . five hundred and fifty thousand dollars! Yes, a sum like that would make the trip worthwhile. It would even

433

make up for the condescending glances and forced greetings I'd had to suffer on my way into the building and up to my floor.

Somehow it seemed a terribly long time since I'd been there. Almost as if the quality of the light had changed and the trees had grown and I was visiting a scene only vaguely remembered.

Last night was a jumble of images and sounds; a chaotic cacophony I could not seem to unscramble in my head. It had worried me, when I awakened this morning. One of my first actions on any day is a mental review of the previous twenty-four hours—a double check, if you will, on any appointment or other item which might need attention in the coming day.

This morning had been unique in my life, therefore. All I could be sure of was that I had but *one* appointment— with half a million dollars plus—courtesy of a little button in the nose of my father's statue. And that was one appointment I certainly meant to keep!

But yesterday was hazy. I could not bring up a precise mental image of Papa's words or anything else about the manner in which he had told me I was through. Still, there was no mistaking that he had done so, and I understood, with the logical part of my mind—*psychology is no mystical creed*—that I must have spent the remainder of the day in a state of shock probably comparable to that of a man who has survived a heavy blow on the head. Intellectually I could grasp such a thing from observation, label it, and know it to be true. Yet, on an emotional level . . .

"Good morning, Mr. Dahlberg!"

I stopped, astonished and momentarily at a loss, just inside my office door. My chief secretary, Mrs. Czernyk, stood there looking as surprised as I. And very guilty at being caught in my former sanctum.

"I'm terribly sorry," she said, seeming by some miracle to be fluttering all the ample parts of herself in abashed concern. "I really didn't think you'd be in, sir. So I was . . ."

"Yes, I understand," I said. "Don't worry about it, Mrs. Czernyk. It doesn't matter."

The encounter appeared to have deprived the poor woman of what modest bit of mental capacity she usually possessed. Instead of withdrawing immediately and letting me get on with clearing out, she stood rooted to the same spot, watching me in some kind of witless bafflement.

In the end, I had to take the matter in my own hands. "Did you want something, Mrs. Czernyk?" I said in a tone not uncivil, but not exactly chatty, either.

"Oh!" She came to life at last. "Oh, my—no! No, indeed!" And by that time she was in motion, fluttering toward the office door and closing it behind her as she left the room that she had been under strict orders—laid down by me on the day I moved in there—*never* to enter for any reason whatsoever.

Well, enough of that. To work.

There were few things inside my desk that I wanted. (It was really Papa's desk. I'd always had the feeling I'd been just loaned his things to play with.) The tape cassette, the one featuring my father and Johnny Valentine, went into one of the bags I'd brought with me. And an old pen that had been my mother's father's lucky piece (though she said it had *never* held ink or been any good at all for writing). I hesitated with my hand on the drawer that held my pistol. Space in those two bags would be at a premium after I pushed the button that opened the Stamp Fund. I decided against the pistol, but I took two or three other minor items and fitted them handily into my coat pockets. I shut the last drawer with a firm snap, stood up and approached the bust of Papa. (Somewhere, on the far side of my memory, something stirred uneasily. Something related to David. But it was too tenuous to grasp, too far for the reach. And that was too bad, for I had the notion it might be important.)

I stood a while, hand poised, savoring the moment. And then I pushed the button! The lavatory wall slid aside with its usual silent efficiency. I turned to claim what I had decided to call my "severance pay." And damn near screamed out loud—*the space was empty!* When I could, when I was capable of controlling my reactions, I went over to explore the space . . . looking, peering, probing. But not so much as a single stray bill remained. Someone had done a neat and thorough job, a professional job—and one they no doubt knew could never be reported to the police.

*David!*

Standing there, I found myself swimming in a tide of blind,

435

unreasoning, frustrated fury. It was a passion, a rage I had never felt before, a deep, determined and ruthless desire to smash . . .

### Irving Dahlberg

. . . the secret wellsprings of the power wielded by men like Irving Dahlberg; the men who built the Industry they think they can take over and control, but in truth can only destroy!

They think they know these things; they think they have discovered the secrets. They think their computers, or their researchers, or their hoodlum unions can rule the world.

But they know nothing.

In the end, they will always fail.

And in their failure they drag down with them the tower built by superior men.

The words of the ad copy were printed well; hand-set and well displayed in an advertising space proper to attract the notice—and, perhaps, the reading and understanding— of a few thinking men.

I smiled and wished I could call Deac Reese to my office to thank him and tell him he'd done a good job; to go ahead and do a saturation campaign job with it in the trades. But I had already sent an order to kill the ad I'd thought better of and smash the plates. I threw the proof away.

Anyway, I now knew that the fight was over before it had begun. *And Irving Dahlberg was not on the winning side.* Of course, only one of two people in the world knew it as yet; in the forty-odd stories of the building below me, I could be fairly sure not one person knew the truth, or even suspected that such a thing could happen.

Well, good luck to them with the new regime. My instincts, those unique and trustworthy instincts that had made Irving Dahlberg a giant and had kept him in charge of a world he had created, had led me to discover the truth—though, goddamn those no-talent genius robbers, not in time to stop them.

Talking to Bonelli had given me the first warning. That

dago is probably the smartest banker in the business. His spy system makes the CIA look like a cub scout troop. I'd phoned him on a routine matter—just to let him know that the payment on our current note—not one of our bigger ones either—would arrive on time. And heard something different in his voice. What was it? Something very subtle. No lack of warmth, no reservation in his manner. What, then? Ah, yes! *His approach.* He talked to me like a policeman trying to find out how much a suspect really knows.

An hour and seven telephone calls later, I had the answers. Very well. Game to them. Studio to them.

*But victory to me!* Sooner or later. Victory to me, in the end.

Adonai, hear me! I give them a year; a year to cheapen and misuse and misunderstand and misapply and fumble—*and fail.* A year for those *schmucks* to dim and tarnish and finally extinguish the luster of the shining tool created—but not for their use—by Irving Dahlberg. A year to learn that the tools of giants are not for midgets. A year until they come begging me to bail them out!

And then I will be back in this office, in this chair, above these power-pile officers that teem with men who can be trained to do jobs but can never be taught to understand them. This tool, this weapon, this fortress, this tower, this monument, this strength—they are for the man who can control them.

*Irving Dahlberg.* I *am* this creation that I made, and it is *me!* I will not share with thieves. I will not . . .


## Buddy Valentine

". . . even talk to anyone from our side," the *padrino* said. "But I didn't call you all the way from here to gab about Monarch. That deal's set, whether the old bastard will admit it to himself or not. What I called about: if you had to get a production chief—and had to get one in a hurry for some place like Priapus Studios—who'd be your first choice?"

"My first choice," I told him, "wouldn't be worth the effort of saying his name. He's got a setup he likes and it pays him more than Priapus could, even including stock options and even if the stock itself was still selling at a price that would make it worthwhile. Sorry, Sam, but that's the truth. And the same goes for my second choice and my third. If we had some time . . ."

He laughed. "Yeah, kid," he said. "That's the point. If you can wait, you can always grab the best people; sooner or later they all get available. But when it's an emergency all the best are nailed to the floor, because they *are* the best."

"That's how it is," I said. "And it's going to get rough in a hurry, Sam, because Priapus was already in a bad way when you and your hotshot oil conglomerate bought it. The truth is, Sam—I don't know if you know it—but old Steve Pappas was real good at sweeping dirt under the rug. He made everything look okay from the outside but the job wasn't getting done—and it hadn't been getting done for more years than anyone realized."

"Uh—*huh!*"

Funny bit. If I hadn't known that the news I was delivering was *bad*, I'd have sworn the *padrino* sounded pleased! Maybe he just didn't understand how bad the situation had become over there. Not that I had all that much knowledge; I didn't get out of the recording compound all that often.

But he was sure as hell going to find out in a hurry, if he didn't get someone over there to pick up the ball. Pappas had done a real juggling act with the double mortgages; the trick now would be to stop juggling and start building —but not with such a wrench that you smash the whole machine.

"A real mess, is it?"

"Well, yeah. It is." *What the hell was Sam getting at?* I'd never paid too much attention to the rest of the operation. I was too busy on my own job and—I'll say this— Lullaby was in the black and building; the only part of the Priapus lash-up that *was*. And I took a sneaky kind of pride in the fact that most of the people whose music was selling best were people I'd manhandled into our stable, whether the *padrino* knew it or not. Still . . .

*"Then maybe we better liquidate,"* Sam said.

*"No!"*

"No? It can be fixed, then?"

*"Of course!"* I fumbled up a cigarette from the table. Sandy'd dumped a half-empty pack there and put a fresh one in her purse, the way she always does when she's

leaving for a flight. "It would take a little time," I told the *padrino,* lighting the butt with the gold lighter she'd made me take even though she knows I'm so forgetful I quit carrying lighters long ago because I lose them, usually, the same day they're bought. "And there'd be setbacks; you couldn't have the guy sitting on a powder keg that'll blow him away the first time there's a little heat. He'd have to be able to trust you guys to play his game until you can see a real, continuing movement." I grinned at the lighter. Three months I'd hung onto it!

Old Sigmund Freud could of taken lessons from *this* chick.

"And the right chief of production could do all that, huh?" Sam said, and now I was damn well sure he was putting me on; playing some weird Sam-type game on Buddy's head. Well, okay, then; I got time. He wants to spend transcontinental phone money making with the subtle Siciliano number, I got nothing better to do. At least not till Sandy gets in.

"No, a chief of production couldn't," I said. "Because the trouble's not just the studio and it's not just one of the departments or subsidiaries. It's an over-all decay, and you and that conglomerate are the only ones who can deal with it because it's gotta be done on an over-all basis."

"I don't know, kid," Sam said. "That sounds like a hell of a lot of work; I got other things to attend to. . . ."

"Well, *padrino,*" I told him, "it's your problem—and I sure wish you a lotta luck!"

I was tired of the game. I wanted to sit down and play solitaire or fiddle with my sound setup or something. I wanted to be alone and think about Sandy and wish she was back and wish it was tomorrow, because tomorrow was *der Tag!*

Tomorrow, she was supposed to come across with an answer. And I might be wrong about what that answer was going to be. But I damn well didn't think so.

"No," the *padrino* said, and his voice was laughing again; laughing at me: "Nope, Buddy boy, it is *not* my problem."

I decided to needle him a little. "The hell it's *not!*" I said. "Who else engineered the buy-out so as you and the Old Man would have enough cash to *zonk* Irving the Great? And from what I heard this morning, you got it done. Congratulations! But that . . ."

"Where'd you get that?"

Hah! Score one for Buddy!

"It's true," I said. "You know it and I know it, so I plead the Fifth. And don't change the subject, *padrino*. Priapus is still your problem."

"And I repeat: it's not."

"Okay," I said. "Whose, then?"

"*Yours!* And if I was you, kid, I wouldn't let the people around there find out you spend half the day in bed. That sets 'em a bad example—and you got enough trouble without that. Man, are *you* gonna be busy!"

"What? What kind of a trip are you . . . ?"

"I said it's your problem, Buddy. Tex and I decided it a week ago, but I wanted the Monarch deal in the can before we moved."

"But, Sam—I *couldn't* be chief of production! I don't know my . . ."

"That's *right*," Sam said. "Which is why we made you president and chief executive officer of the Priapus Corporation, which we registered today as a holding company. You'll have no direct involvement in any specific project, and you'll be responsible for every damn one of them. Though if I was you, kid, I'd keep a very close thumb on the A & R people at Lullaby Records; don't let 'em go off the deep end too often."

For a second, there, you know, I just damn near banged the phone down in his ear. Because it didn't make one damn bit of sense.

If it was some kind of game the *padrino* was playing, I thought it was a pretty poor one. In fact, if it had been anyone on the face of the earth except Samuel LoCicero, *mi padrino*, I'd have been sure it was a joke.

Because it was Sam, I hesitated. Because it was Sam, I realized it would be a good idea to take it just a shade slow, and check out the scenery, before heading for the hills. He seemed to be waiting, sitting quiet on the other end of that telephone line, listening for some particular sort of response from me. Only I didn't have a clue as to what he wanted to hear. With the *padrino*, it just isn't a good idea to do anything too suddenly; the landscape always seems to sprout booby traps about the time you start feeling safe.

"Okay, Sam," I said finally, keeping the voice neutral and

440

deciding to play it by ear, "you're buying the tickets. I got just one question . . ."

"Shoot!"

"Why me?"

"Why *not* you?"

"The appointment of not exactly successful nightclub singers with no previous business experience and a history of fumbling the ball two yards short of the goal line to head large, complicated industrial complexes is not an everyday occurrence—even in *this* town," I said.

"The number of not exactly experienced *ex*-nightclub singers who can take over and completely reorient the A & R program of a major record company and turn it from a loser into a winner while at the same time organizing and directing the success of a wholly new popular music departure—all this in less than a year—without ever having held a formal executive position or any other visible position of authority—is kinda small, too."

"It could have been sheer luck and a lot of bluffing."

"It could of been a guy finally finding what it is he really likes to do—and is good at."

I let about thirty seconds go by before I said anything else. "A big part of the over-all job will be handling and reorganizing a complicated corporate financial structure," I told him when the major portion of the picture had at last soaked in. "Sam, I don't know enough about that to run a lemonade stand."

"If you did," Sam laughed, "I'd be a little scared of you, keed. Leave that kind of detail work to the people who're hired to do it—and remember the whole thing is back-stopped by the oil company's financial people because Priapus is technically a division of their parent firm now. They're not going to let any major boo-boos happen. And they'll save you a lot of worry over which one of our own people is tapping the till, too."

There was another of those silent waits that seemed to be the major ingredient of this particular conversation.

"Any other objections?" Sam said when it had gone on for quite a while.

"No . . . no, I probably ought to have a couple of hours' worth, but right now—no. Not a one."

"Well, then?"

I couldn't figure out what he meant. "Well, *what?*"

"Are you hired—or not?"

Now it was my turn to laugh. "Hell, Sam, I went on the payroll the first time you asked me! The rest of that was just window dressing—to get my price up."

"Hey, that's right! How much are we paying you, boss-man?"

"You call the shot," I said, remembering a gag I'd heard him use in negotiation, quite a few years back. "If I don't like the price . . . I'll quit, and you can try to figure out what it was I stole on the way out." And that got quite a laugh.

"Buddy," he said, "about one thing I'm real glad . . ."

"What's that?"

"That I'm old enough I won't have to meet up with you in some nice, dark corporate-management alley, say, ten years from now."

"Who needs ten years?" I said. And we both laughed.

"Okay, then, I'm coming back to the Coast tonight and I'll be in touch tomorrow or the next day. Oh, yeah, one thing: you seen your old man lately?"

"No, not recently. Why?"

"No reason. Only—well, no need for Vanni to know all about what's going to happen to Priapus until we make a formal announcement. For now, it's between you and me and the oil company. Right?"

"Sure. Oh—I can tell Sandy?"

"*Her,* yeah. That's quite a woman you got there, young 'un. She in town, now?"

"Back tonight, unless there's a schedule change. But maybe she'll be around a little more pretty soon. . . ."

"Hey, for sure?"

"For pretty sure. I'll know tomorrow."

The *padrino* snorted. "Blow this one, baby," he said, "and I may get them to can you before they even paint your name on the door."

"No argument!"

I started to hang up, but caught myself, and him, in time for a final detail.

"If I hire a production chief before the announcement," I said, "I'll tell whoever it is the offer comes from you. Okay?"

Sam thought for a minute. "Okay," he said finally. "But be sure and let me know who I picked. Just to keep the record straight in case he checks with me. *Ka-peesh?*"

"*Ka-peesh* . . . later, *padrino.*"

And this time we both hung up. And I spent the next thirty or forty minutes staring blank-eyed at the wall.

Scared? Who, me? You just bet your sweet ass! I'd have been even more scared if I hadn't been, though, if that makes any sense. And it does. The hell of it was, it all came on too pat. Too smooth.

And then I stood up and cursed myself. Some executive! Here was Buddy, the corporate kid, sitting around on his dago duff and wondering why the bogeyman hadn't come to get him for daring to do something right and win a game for once in his life Meanwhile, the hours were passing and things were happening out in the wide, wide world and I still hadn't made the first move to siphon up a chief production for Priapus.

I spent about three seconds deciding where to start. Maybe not even that long, really. Because, admit it, how the hell many targets did I have? The *padrino*'d called the number in the beginning: the top men in the field with the long proven records were all working, and they were working because they were the top men.

Which left me with a choice between promoting one of the two or three seasoned hack executive producers still on the lot—which I was not about to do—or going after the only experienced man available, and taking a chance that (a) my own lukewarm feelings about him wouldn't get in the way, and (b) he could pull himself together after the hard-time scenes he'd been through recently.

I picked up the phone to make a direct call, and then realized that as of now the rules of the game had changed. Okay. Right! I dialed the studio and got hold of a woman who worked in the typing pool. I'd used Mrs. Degan a couple of times when I'd needed a secretary for one reason or another. She had a cool head, an eye for detail and—most important—seemed to be able to resist discussing her business with the other girls.

She listened while I explained as much of the situation as I thought she had to know, then agreed to see about finding Jack Dahlberg and making an appointment for him to meet Sam LoCicero. I would keep the appointment instead of Sam, but he didn't have to know that for the time being.

Mrs. Degan asked no unnecessary questions and said she'd call back when she had something definite, or if it looked like Jackie was going to be a problem to run down. Then she switched me back to the board and over to Lullaby, where I arranged for her to use a spare office for the time being. After which I hung up again, and wished to God Sandy was back from New York.

I grinned at myself. Hell, how much fun would St. George have had killing the dragon, if a chick hadn't been waiting around in the neighborhood to tell him he was one hell of a knight and how great it was of him to make her a present of the . . .

### David Strauss

. . . *dragon's head with the far-out gold horns and writhing tendrils growing out of its muzzle.*

It was only that way for a moment; I blinked my eyes once and it went back to being an orange nylon bag stuffed with five hundred and fifty thousand dollars. But it rocked me a little and I peeked out of the tops of my eyes to see if anyone had noticed. Sandy had, I thought.

I wondered if she would say something to the others—the old guy who seemed to be the head pilot, or the rest of them. I didn't want her to. It wouldn't have been fair. Nothing like that had happened since last night when the wall started moving around the way it had there at Jackie's apartment, and I'd done a few tabs of speed to get through the night without sleeping after I took the ransom money from that place he'd shown me in his office. That secret place that no one was supposed to know about.

Jackie wouldn't have shown me that place if he hadn't loved me, would he? No, he *did* love me then, I know he did. He only changed after his father told him what everybody was saying, and that my being with him was hurting the studio. That's when he got angry and had that awful look on his face and was screaming such words—such awful words, in such an awful voice. Well, it'll be all right after this. Everyone will be sorry they said such mean things about me and Jackie, and Jackie will be nice again.

I smiled, thinking about how it would be after I brought that whole crew back home with me. Everyone would apologize. Everyone would be nice to me and try to make up for all the things they'd thought, and all the things they'd done.

*David Strauss, star of stage, screen, television, ESP, and international diplomacy, announces he is ready to forgive and forget!*

I looked at my watch, to see how long we had before we landed at Havana. But my watch had stopped. I must have forgotten to wind it last night. No wonder! I'd had an awful lot on my mind.

Never mind. "What time is it, please?" I asked the captain, and immediately wished I hadn't. Because I could hardly make out my words. My words were slurring and I was out of speed and coming down and now the things it had held away from me, to help me get aboard the plane, were starting to close in. *I have got to hold myself together!*

The captain had evidently understood my question, despite the slurring, and he told me the time. But I was too frightened to remember what he'd said so I only pretended to set my watch, while trying to hold the grenade steady. I had to be very careful. I had to keep them from *finding out*. I had to make sure they all did just exactly what I told them to, or they would get me.

*Have another tab of speed, David, darling.* Thank you. But I don't have another one with me and—oh, God—if only I did! If only I did!

*If only I did . . .*

*You would love me, kid!*

Everything was going to be all right. Everything was going to be all right. Jackie would understand—he wouldn't blame me for taking the money from his office—when he knew what I had done with it. *If only he hadn't been so mean to me.* Why are people that way? Why does anyone, ever, have to be mean and shout and hit and hurt and do such terrible things to anyone else when it just means someone will hurt them back sometime and then they do it back to someone else and pretty soon everyone in the whole world is hurting and hating and screaming and yelling and killing. Why do people have to hurt other people?

Look at the faces of these people in here with me. Hurt. Sandy's the only one who doesn't look like she wants to hurt.

But women *always* end up hurting you, so that doesn't count. Women always hurt you worse than anyone—and they laugh at you when you do things they don't understand, and—maybe that's where all the hurting begins! Yes! Maybe so.

*Why did Dolly have to be so mean when I called?* All I wanted was a place to be. A place where no one would find me until it was time to go to the airport. It's true, I did have that trouble speaking when she answered, at first. I remember, I had that trouble. But I often had trouble, talking to Dolly. When I was looking at her sometimes she would say something and I would try to answer and there would be no sound coming from my mouth.

"That's the final checkpoint. Call ATC and tell them we're on course over the Gulf, now. ETA Havana is . . ."

I stood up. I had let myself half relax into one of the chairs behind the two pilots' seats, and now I edged forward to see the water—the Gulf of Mexico—the only thing now between us and Cuba.

It was so good! *So good!* So good to know that all the pain and fear and all the rest of the terrible things would soon be over. Just a little way, now, across the little mini-ocean, to the beginning of a new life for David Strauss—hero and good American and star of . . .

"Tom—NO!" The captain shouted suddenly, on my left, and I started to look at him but I was off balance—I *had completely forgotten, trying to see the Gulf, that I was supposed to be holding these people at bay with my grenade* —and I tipped sidewise, toward him, and suddenly there was a numbing pain in my right shoulder. I whirled just in time to see that the movement to the side was all that had saved me from having my skull crushed by the heavy nine-cell flashlight the younger pilot had hit me with as he went for the grenade.

I felt the pain and I saw his face, his angry young face so full of hate and coming at me and he was raising the flashlight to hit me *again* and I stumbled backward and tried to regain my balance but it was too late, too late, because the grenade flew out of my hand as I fell and there was an instant symphony chord of sound, unbelievably loud and gratingly harsh, that blossomed immediately into a skyrocket shower of red, red pinpoints filling the air like a tinted fog while the world blew up and the noise of the engines and the explosion and the shrieking all merged into a roar as the hole where the grenade had hit pulled me forward. I fought hard but I was sucked and drawn *whoosh* toward the gaping mouth that the single hole in the world had become, and I fought to stay, fought to stay . . .

Hallelujah!

. . . and then the pressure eased and I was no longer being pulled to the mouth, but it was very hard to breathe and I struggled to stand up again, but half a face was looking at me. The pilot, the young one who had hurt me, was lying still and I was lying on top of him with my face only inches from his, but his face was melted on one side (I knew it was not really that way, but it seemed to be so real!) and his whole head was distorted and I arched away from him, afraid he would hurt me again, but he only lay there with his single eye looking at the mouth in the . . .

Hallelujah!

. . . world and I finally got free, but I could not stand up because the floor of the cabin was tilted so sharply; I looked to see what the other pilot was doing, if he was going to hurt me, too, but he was doing nothing, lying slumped as though asleep and hanging forward in his chair, his face the color of blue candle wax, while . . .

Hallelujah!

. . . and a woman with yellow hair who must have been Sandy was lying on the tilted floor, wedged limply up against the big control panel that was now only half there because of the hole . . .

Hallelujah!

. . . and I wanted to apologize to her, to say I hadn't meant to hurt anyone, all I wanted to do was be nice and be loved and be happy and have everyone be glad I'd rescued the poor sailors, but she couldn't hear me and I couldn't breathe, my lungs were working in a trip-hammer spasm of effort but the world was narrowing at its edges until I could see only a little tiny porthole view of it . . .

Hallelujah!

. . . and even the ever-rising roar of wind and the airplane's engines were beginning to be drowned, now, in the sound as the choir came closer and closer, calling and compelling with their triumphant hymn of praise to . . .

Hallelujah!

. . . all the love and warmth and tenderness and touching and holding and kissing and knowing and blending and being I had missed and needed and tried to find, but apparently I hadn't tried hard enough or looked far enough, but it didn't matter now because I could relax at last and give myself to the music and the devotion as the choir surrounded me at last and caught me up and bore me with them in the oneness of their mighty . . .

Hallelujah!

Hallelujah!

*Haaaaa-Leeee-Looooo . . . JAH!*

# The 12th House

*Exile, restraint, limitation, secret woes or
sorrows, hidden enemies, seclusion,
silent suffering, and self-undoing . . .*

---

*Forecast: For the powerful Valentines and the no longer
powerful Dahlbergs, now is a time for facing secret enemies
and the hidden sorrows within. Sometimes an enemy can
be a condition secured within a person's psyche, which he
surely wishes to acknowledge. But there comes a time for
casting-up, when the mirror of life (the facade) must be
exchanged for the real mirror of self (the soul). Even
lovomaniacs have to face themselves eventually.*

*The Twelfth House is a time of endings, and a time of
preparations for the beginnings that will surely follow as
the interfaces shift and the First House begins once
again. . . .*

---

## Buddy Valentine

The flight from New York back to Los Angeles was
nearly an hour late boarding, and the ticket agent said it
was because it was a "turnaround" flight that had already
made one span of the continent in the dim little hours
before dawn.

He advised us to go up to the airline's private lounge,
where a breakfast of bacon and eggs would be waiting, and
I was about to sit down again because I wasn't especially
hungry but resisted the urge because Mrs. Degan, I had dis-

449

covered, was a lady whose secretarial expertise and discretion were matched only by her appetite. She made it a point throughout any working day to keep herself within what she called "dictating distance" on days when I was out of the office (and sometimes those days, of late, seemed to have a hell of a lot of hours in them). She would *never,* by so much as the twitch of an eyebrow, have betrayed chagrin at the loss of a meal.

But we would be seated side by side on the flight to the Coast—so I could get rid of some of the correspondence she'd brought with her—and it's tough enough to concentrate on things like that without a counter-rhythm of stomach growls into the bargain.

I still wasn't in the mood for food when we got to the lounge, so I told her to go ahead and I would call her if I needed her. She looked doubtful, but went, and I wandered off toward the picture-window side of the room facing out toward the runways.

They had finally officially abandoned the search yesterday. But it had been only a formality, a tip of the hat to custom, after the first day when a piece of the tail-section with the airline's insignia on it was fished up twenty miles off the Texas coast. Nobody could have held the slightest hope after that, and I hadn't, of course. She was gone. No reprieve. No goodbye. No—anything.

It had rained for just a few minutes shortly after we got to Kennedy, and the runways looked like black plastic in the eerie marker lights.

I remembered the hour I had sat in the rented Tri-Pacer two days after the crash. An hour, looking fixedly at the starting mechanism, knowing that if I touched it I would fly the little toy under the weather—there was a low, thick layer at three-thousand—as far as the mountains, and then climb just enough to get into the nothing-grayness; after that it would be just a matter of holding course and altitude. No trouble. No strain. No chance of going chicken at the last moment. I would never see the side of the world until I ran into it. As good a way as any. And I'd had some experience at cracking up small planes, don't forget.

But after that hour, I had climbed back out of the thing and walked, with more gray inside me than above, back to my car for the return to the studio, where I had found Ben Hallowell waiting in my outer office.

He was a huge, solemn man in a conservative non-West Coast sports coat and slacks, the tie knotted so inexpertly that I was sure he didn't wear one very often.

Mrs. Degan, who had already proved herself to be a woman of perception, had already rejiggered my afternoon schedule and Ben followed me into my office without a word, after the initial introduction. I motioned him to a chair—the comfortable one I reserve for people I want to take more than ten minutes with—and it was only then that I noticed he walked with a pronounced limp on the left side. Sandy had said something about one of her brothers' having lost a leg at Iwo, but it had seemed somehow unreal to me, then, that a brother could be so much older than her.

Ben Hallowell came toward the desk instead of sitting down at once. He had a letter in his hand, enclosed in a sealed envelope, which he placed on the desk near where I was standing, and then turned back to the chair. He didn't seem to be much for idle chatter, which suited me.

The letter was addressed to me—just my name, nothing else—in Sandy's hand, and suddenly the world narrowed down to the white, rectangular shape of the folded and pasted paper.

I don't remember sitting down. I don't remember opening the envelope. I only remember that the center of my chest was filled with ice and tight with pressure as I began to read:

Darling—

Although I didn't ask him to, it's my guess this letter will be delivered to you in person by my eldest brother, Ben. He'll do it that way for the same reasons I chose him to hold it for me when the guilties really began to get to me a few days back; he'll hold the letter and never read it himself—and deliver it, if it's to be delivered at all, in person—because he is simply the kindest man left in the world now that my dad's not in it anymore.

I'm writing it all out now because I want to tell you I know I may have made a mistake. It's too late to go back and correct anything. (It always is, really, so that's why it's so important to do it right, if you can, on the first pass.) But I want you to know,

451

here and now, that I didn't hold back because of any lack of love or trust, but because I'm a rotten coward who couldn't *stand* to see you worrying and fidgeting and all the rest. Also, I know all of this may be for nothing because you'll read this letter, if you ever do, on our Golden Wedding Anniversary and probably neither one of us will really be able to remember the silly, frightened girl who wrote it, at all.

But if it does turn up before that time, here's the first thing I wanted to say to you: Buddy, you made the whole trip worthwhile.

If I thought you had any doubt of it, I'd waste a lot of space here telling you how much I love you and how great I think we'd have been together for the rest of our lives. But there are no doubts in me, about anything.

The other thing—the part I'm not proud of—is this:

I've wanted to marry you, darling, since about twenty-four hours after we met, and I'd have tossed you over my shoulder and trotted off, chortling, to my cave except for one thing—my natal chart and another horological one I cast about a year ago both indicate a single, specific, high-peak danger period late this year. It's due about a month from now and is somehow involved with water and, probably, some form of mental trouble.

Most people, I know, would decide right here that the mental trouble must be mine, to pay the slightest attention to such things. But you know what I think, and what I have discovered to be true, about astrology. What I think it is, and what I know it is not.

I've taken what precautions I can. I'm careful around water and don't fly over it. I won't be flying at all, around water or anywhere else, on the peak-influence day, and I'm being darn careful in other ways, too. Not fanatical—that would be a death in itself—but at least not reckless.

But here we come to a kind of touchy point. I said The Hallowell is careful, but not timid; that I believe in influences and probability, but not in predestination. And that sounds fine. But how honest is it when I put off a marriage—and a man—that I want with everything that I am?

And, worse, what kind of person is it that doesn't even tell that man her reasons?

Well, she's this way—at heart a jolly, random type who does not like dirge music or sidewise glances full of concern. I hope I have at least enough sawdust in me to take anything that actually comes. I think I do, because in the main I have always known that life is very iffy and I have busied up my years in good ways.

What I could not face is a life that became, even for the few days left before That Day, a kind of practice funeral—especially not one with you as the chief mourner. There are enough real and certain things to heavy up the air without adding perhaps needless worries to them. So when you became interested in astrology yourself, and developed enough skill to read and cast a chart, I simply hid mine and made a point of never letting you find out the exact hour I was born . . . so you couldn't accidentally find out for yourself.

I think, now, that this was selfish. For if the precautions are not enough and no other solution can be found, then I have failed a very special obligation to you, the duty to let you share a fear of mine and know that I trust you with it as I do with all else I am or have.

But to tell you now, to let you know I was not wholly open, would do more damage, I believe, than it would undo. So the best compromise I can think of is this letter—and I hope it will be enough.

You may be hating me just a little now, and wondering how I could have had so little faith in you. And that is fair; I won't argue about it.

But if the resentment isn't too big, then maybe you'd be willing to do a couple of things that would ease my worry over possible trouble left behind, and that would make a big difference because the main event is all the opponent I need.

I'll say it straight out, darling: it scares me. You know that I accept the karmic debt perspective on living and, considered from that angle, it should not be frightening, since it only marks another step in the process.

But it scares me, anyway. I've felt that way from childhood, and when I look without the editing of the logical approach all I can see is that it's real black out there and it lasts a long time.

I have no remorse, though. And you can help get rid of one regret if you'll do this for me:

Build me no monuments! Whatever clothes or anything else are left around your place—get rid of them the best and quickest way you can and then don't you *dare* sit around the world brooding. If I can be a grown-up, or act like one, it's a cinch you can. So here's what you do:

Find yourself an amiable, warm-centered wench who likes to talk to you and is not hesitant about scratching that part on your back you can't seem to reach, and grooves on touching, being, loving, laughing, and things that are good to think about. Try to pick one of good appetite who thinks you are a man she'd like her kids to resemble and romp the lady with tenderness and affection and if it seems like a really good idea to the both of you, don't you listen when she thinks there's a reason to postpone the wedding.

But now and then, when she's asleep and you're awake, together like spoons with your arms around her and the top of her head propping your chin, breathe deep of the world and close your eyes and just for a moment pretend it's

Sandy, who loved you

The room was moving around a lot and not too well in focus by the time I was done.

I took a breath and lay the letter down and was about to try and say something to Ben, but he was on his feet again, handing me another missive. This was a letter, too, but shorter. More like a note. Sandy had sent a postscript, for inclusion with the other, and it bore no salutation. Only:

It's the Day. I was up early and made the mistake of answering the phone and, of course, it was the line. I'm called for the 6 A.M. to Kennedy and I couldn't get out of it. Well, anyway, it will keep me from chewing my nails.

You slept, thank God, through the call and my dressing and here's what I wanted to tell you: The easiest way to know what you really feel about someone is to watch his face when he's asleep.

I watched yours just before the cab came.

You are my love.

S

And then the dam broke. Through the early moments of fear, through the waiting time, the discovery of the wreckage and the end of hope, I had been able to hurt—but not to cry. Italian families have no taboo against male weeping and I had always, all my life, had that as the final purgative. But this time—no. It was as though the world had filled itself with a hot dry ache, but no water. Now the tears came. And they went on for some time. When they were over, when I could look again and see my surroundings clearly, Ben Hallowell was still sitting in the chair, the eyes that I suddenly realized were very like Sandy's sagging with pain but clear with dignity.

"You loved her?" he said, making it only partly a question.

"Yes."

He nodded, never shifting his gaze. "She lived with you," he said, "and it was good between you and you made her happy. She told me all that in the letter she sent with that first one. She wanted me to know that she'd been happy and that you might need help. Now, maybe—or later—from someone who knew her. I'll go, now, if there's nothing more I can do. But if you ever need to, come see me. I live in Erie. Gave my name and address to your secretary. Come any time. Leave when you want. Her brothers and I—for us, you're family, because she said so."

I didn't know what to say to that. And I had no questions. For then, anyway. So I kept still.

"One thing she may never have told you, nor put in the letter," he said after a time. "It might give you a slant on some of the things she did—our pa was a man who loved just one woman all his life, and when she died he buried himself with her.

"He was a good man and in most ways a wise one. But that was wrong, and it used to hurt Sandy to see him hurt sometimes. So she'd of been pretty wary of letting a thing like that happen to any man of hers. I don't know if that helps or not. Or explains. But it's the why of it, for when you wonder."

He got up and moved over to where I was sitting and held his hand out. I took it. And then he left, with no more words.

And after a little while of looking at the door he'd closed behind him when he went out, I had breathed one breath that was deep and contained the ragged end of a residual tremor—and had picked up the first of the daily reports from the tray on my desk. And there my memory reel ended, halted in midframe by the ticket agent's amplified voice, informing me and my fellow passengers that the plane for LAX was now boarding.

Mrs. Degan joined me at the lounge door, both our tickets in her hand, and we headed down the slight incline to our seats. "Good breakfast?" I asked her as we strapped ourselves down.

"The eggs were powdered," she answered. "You didn't miss a thing."

Without preamble or announcement, the jet's four engines raised their whine into the air and I settled myself for takeoff, my mind already three thousand miles ahead of us in Los Angeles where the near-stagnated cogs of Priapus Studios were just beginning to turn a little, responding at last to the determined efforts of our . . .

### Jack Dahlberg

. . . chief of production. And this time, by God, I know it in a way I could never have known back at Monarch. There, the shadow over the lot would always have been too large for me.

I looked at the hollow bronze sculpture across the room from my desk and grinned. "Right on, mister!" I said to it. Papa's face did not respond. *But then—when had it ever?*

I glanced out the window. There was movement there. Activity. And it was purposeful activity. Our new produc-

456

tion schedule was fully financed, and two of the units were already in production.

Best of all, if the general attitude around the lot was not yet one of unbounded optimism, at least it was no longer the lethargy of despair I'd felt all around me the day I moved in.

Life was filled with ironies, I decided. Who would have thought that after that whole nightmare—David freaking out and being blown to bits and let's not think about the how and why of *that* for too long (it would have happened anyway) and Gaby making a public spectacle of herself around town with that dyke, and Papa turning on me for all the world to see, and the Stamp Fund vanishing (but not before it helped me buy off Clara, thank God for small favors). After all that *shit*, who in the world comes out of left field and, cool as you please, saves my life? The Valentine kid, that's who! Out of left field, all right, but I'm off and running and you better believe I'll just show papa a thing or two about how a studio should be run. Oh, yes. Yessireee!

My very first act as production chief was to have a few rooms whipped into shape in a unit building near the middle of the property. I wanted to set up shop there, where I could keep an eye on the action, not in some big fancy office, like Papa always had. Because I was going to show them all! I had no intention of being fired from this job. Ever. I looked at the bust again and shook my head. Its presence was beginning to irritate me, but there was too much to do to let it get to me. I'd just have to . . .

## Johnny Valentine

. . . get over it. Because there must be more to life than just going around letting the world know you are Public Stud Number One and the Kid of the Krooners and the President's pal and all that jazz. There has just got to be more to life than that. So don't be a klutz, Valentine— don't get all fidgety because you're alone here.

What's so different, anyway? Face it, man . . . you were *always* alone. The difference is, sitting here you *know* you're alone.

Yeah. You know it, baby. No crapping yourself here, Valentine; no coffeehousing with the brain, no filling the place up with voices and faces and bodies and kidding yourself that that makes you unalone. You could turn that stereo up until they hear Blood, Sweat, and Tears all the way to California, and you could fill that glass with enough booze to float the *Queen Mary* and click-clink the ice cubes until you're dizzy and . . . the Big Alone and the Big Quiet would still be right there sneering you down and telling you the truth.

And it's better, baby. You know it—*better!*

For nearly half a century you been singing and balling and yelling and telling and yocking it up to prove a lie. So now—dig this, baby—you are *retired*. Like, *retired,* Dad! And you don't have to crap the troops anymore . . .

You're alone. And it's quiet. And that's only the greatest. Right? *Right.* Right . . .

Yeah. And I am also a goddamn liar. One thing about Scottsdale; one thing about the desert and those mountains and that sun dropping toward them and that clear air and the Big Peace you get right in the kisser just before you hit town and the Big Alone that is all around you . . . they are honest. And, baby, you cannot—*cannot*—lie. Especially to yourself.

So what the hell's the use of sitting here and half-crapping?

Sure, surrounding yourself with strangers doesn't really make you unalone. But why tell yourself you like it better this way? Hey, baby: It hurts! The truth hurts!

Lousy, yeah, to spend half a century kidding yourself—but looking at the way things really are . . . that's no damn fun, either!

Because look how they are.

I got all the money any twenty men could spend in a lifetime, even if they spend dough like I always did, whether I had it or not. Only how much did it ever buy me that I really wanted? The two or three things I really was after—really dug—they turned out not to be for sale. The money buys booze and lies and . . .

*Dolly.* Oh, yeah, *that* was for sale. Not just the money, though. The money, that was only a little extra leverage; the real price on the tag was one I could of read and did read and deliberately ignored, because who the hell can pay *that?* And who says the merchandise was worth it in the first place? What the hell was I doing, trying to kid myself I was her age. What *was* it. A little bitch like that one, what the hell was I trying to prove, what the hell was I after, what the *hell* . . .

And *Buddy*—what's he? A scared, half-phony, mixed-up little-boy-in-man's-clothing. So now he's the bossman at Priapus. Yeah. He's wearing a man's clothes and sitting in a man's office, and Christ, for all I know, he probably thinks he *is* a man, now. And say this for the kid, that chick he had was for men, not boys. And her dying, the way she did and all, that would have turned him into sawdust-and-air if there wasn't *something* inside there besides a boy.

But the hell of it is, there's not enough.

*Not enough!*

How'd he make it into the studio-boss business? Did he go after it because he wanted it? *No.* His *padrino told* him he wanted it. And did he get the job for himself? *No.* His *padrino put* him in there. And can he hold it—or improve the hand—by himself?

No? Yes? You tell me, Father Time . . . you tell me, because right now, on the facts, I say no and I say he's still bullshitting himself and I say he hasn't found out enough about himself, about who he really is and what he really wants and why he wants it and—hell, *everything*—to be *anything* on his own.

He's got a chance. I'll say that for him. He's come a long way and he's got a chance . . . but a chance is all it is, and we'll know what the truth is when the party gets really rough, when the strokes get short. Poor Buddy, trying to imitate a father who's a fifty-year-old child, and smart enough at the same time to see that his old man didn't really give a damn whether he did or didn't.

*Goddamn Scottsdale!* Truthsville—the Big Alone where you look at the Real. It was going to be so great. So great! To be retired, to be quiet, to be free . . . free to think your thoughts and see the important things. So great! Oh, God, what the hell do you do when the truth is that you were a failure as a husband, a failure as a man, failure as a father . . . failure at every damn thing that really matters in this world. And that there is not one fucking thing in this world that you can do about it!

Maybe it's okay to stop, and see the Real when you're a kid. Maybe if Buddy does it—maybe—it will be all right, because he's got the time, he can still change something, he can still do something about it. But what about Giovanni Valentino? What about him?

Can he go back and do it over? He kidded himself that marrying Dolly would give him a chance to Do It All Over. And look, for Chrissake, how that came out. . . .

No. The illusion—all right, it's phony and lousy and a fraud, but I need the illusion. I need to be able to kid myself, to tell myself I am loved because that audience out there is flapping the hands and making the noises. Maybe it's a lie, but I need the lie and I can't do anything else, now; it's too late.

Too late? My God, that fucking retirement speech at Sam's banquet. I said it: final and irrevocable. Permanent. No curtain calls, I said . . .

Well. All right. But there's gotta be an out. Gotta be an angle: something that'll leave me in one piece. A . . . what? Maybe a show . . . something very special, a part that I can say was "just too good to turn down." Something. . . .

I'll call Sam. He'll figure something. He always figures something. Sam . . . he'll laugh. No. Not Sam—not to my face, anyway. But the hell of it is, even if he doesn't, I'll know. I'm not shitting old Sam. He told me it'd be this way. I won't be shitting him a bit. All right. Is it worth that?

You bet your ass it is. *You bet your ass!* Because it's all you got, Valentine. All you got. Screw the money and all the rest. Screw that. I need . . . what I need!

All right. The phone, now. Now. Before you lose your guts. *Now!* Turn off the stereo and call old Sam. Lay it on him—as much of the truth as you got to. A little bit humble, even. A little bit humble, Dad.

Because . . .

### Buddy Valentine

. . . ready or not, here I come.

I'd been able to fall asleep for maybe half an hour or so after we passed over the Mississippi, but the beginning of the letdown toward LAX brought me fully awake. I thought for a minute about having Mrs. Degan get out the work I'd intended to do on the plane, but the time was too short to be worth much now, so I just sat still and did some rubbernecking when we finally got low enough for that, coming over the line of mountains into the L.A. basin.

That was some town down there. There had been rain the day before and I could see the trees moving a little in the wind, even from that height, so the area was clear of smog; CAVU, with the sun shining and whanging back at you from the sparkle of the white stucco they seem to use on any building under five stories. In the distance, far off to the right of the flight path, I tried to make out the group of low buildings that were Priapus—but it was too far. And besides, I would be there soon enough.

My eyes flickered over the houses and commercial corners in the southeast part of town. Places with names like Maywood and El Monte and Montebello and Watts—places I'd never driven through, even though I'd lived in Los Angeles all my life. I wondered about them; wondered if maybe if I'd lived there instead of where I had, if I'd been a garage mechanic or an aircraft engineer or a bus driver or a television repairman or a fry cook or a teacher or a cop—but that was bullshit and I knew it even while I was thinking about all those maybes.

How many people go through life wondering things like that, telling themselves all the maybes?

Not that a part of it wasn't valid. I'd spent some time, since I got the letter, looking at the chart Sandy had made for herself and the one for me. I'd found hers easily enough, all right. And it was there. All that she'd said. But it was still a "maybe," not a "for sure." And so were a lot of the things in my own.

Those maybes—they were the possible. The real. The maybes like being born somewhere else and growing up some other way and actually being some other person, that was the bullshit.

L-O-V-E.

Love. My eyes had been registering the letters for several seconds before my mind turned them into the word. *Love.* Someone had arranged rocks or gravel or something in an open space, a park, I guess, to spell out the word for anyone passing above to read.

L-O-V-E.

It must have taken a lot of work, a lot of sweat, for that

someone—or group of someones—to make a sign like that, one big enough to be seen clearly from this height.

L-O-V-E.

I wondered what that word meant to them. It was the catchword of the times. For sure. Peace and love, baby. Oh, for sure. But what the hell did it *mean?*

Love . . . makes the world go round. Love . . . thy neighbor. Love . . . your magic spell is everywhere. Love . . . and marriage. Love . . . in the afternoon. Love . . . American style. Love . . . and kisses. Love . . . is the answer. *Love* . . .

Suddenly I had said the word too often. Take any word in the dictionary—any word—and say it over twenty times or more, and suddenly it becomes just a sound or combination of sounds. No meaning. No content. No impact. . . . *Love.*

What was that word the *padrino* had used, that time in the Bistro when he really laid it all on me? Love—something. Love-crazy? Love-lovers? Love-seekers? *No.* Love . . . *omaniacs*. Lovomaniacs!

Right. *Right on,* Sam-baby; right on, Sam the *padrino!* You called it, for sure. All the people in the place that day. And all the people who weren't. Buddy included. Lovomaniacs! The *padrino* had called the turn on the whole caboodle; like alcoholics, like nymphos, like junkies—never enough; never satisfied. Lovomaniacs, forever and ever running full tilt through the days and the nights—in pursuit of the *bigger* love, the *truer* love, the *stronger* love, the *hotter* love, the *more* love. Like Dolly the blue-and-white Diamond these days. Making it with every guy on the set of her new movie, in combinations of twos, threes and you name it. In a way, I had to feel sorry for the screwed-up kid. Did she really think that she was gonna snatch some love . . .

Involuntarily, not even knowing I was going to do it, I slipped my fingers inside my coat to touch the corner of the letter. Oh, yes; oh, yes indeed—the letter.

No need to take it out again. No need to read it again. Just touch the edge; ask yourself *what about Buddy,* and the answer is he touches the corner of a folded sheaf of paper. That's his answer. The letter . . . and then—the urge to laugh.

Sandy would have. She'd have laughed her head off at

me carrying a letter around like some sort of talisman. Carry love in your pocket and touch it to prove you're real. Oh, for sure!

I took my hand out of my coat and grinned at it, that hand, and made a mental note—for me, not for Mrs. Degan's book—to find a place to keep the letter and to leave it there until the unlikely day that I began to forget the words. What they'd said and what they hadn't said. And what they'd meant.

*And what about Buddy?* We were low, now, on final approach and the earth was moving very swiftly and I could no longer see for such distances. The horizon was almost back down to human perspective and the city was taking on its normal proportions and the people down below were beginning to be real again, not just abstract ideas remote from Buddy Valentine and his life.

*And what about Buddy?* Well, what *about* him? Come down from the sky; come down to where it's real, to where it's happening, to where you have to live it out, minute by minute and day by day. Come down and look at what's there; at what's *possible*,

*Do that.* Do that, Buddy-boy, because you don't have to; do that because you want to, man. Sure, you can join the lovomaniacs—God knows you've paid your dues; you can live your life as though you were always at thirty thousand feet and it was all abstract and you can be one of the poor, unfortunate, beautiful lovomaniacs, if that's what you want.

But it doesn't even tempt you anymore, does it? A girl you're already starting to forget (God, oh *God*, I don't even have a picture of her, not even a photograph, and no matter how hard I try the day will come, soon, when I won't be able to call up her face and see it there, oh *God!*). A girl you're never going to see or hear or touch again showed you what *real* is, and showed you what happy is, and that's the best and worst thing that ever happened to anyone because now you'll at least know the texture and the shape of what you want and need. But you'll never be able to bullshit yourself again—never be able to rationalize enough—to accept anything else.

*You've paid your dues to join the lovomaniacs—but you can't pass the damn entrance exam!*

The last few airborne yards of space slipped past and

there was a small bump and a faraway howl from the wheels and a rise and then another squeal and a settling and we were down. The jets were reverse-thrusted to brake us and we turned off the runway and soon the airplane would ease up to the terminal ramps and they would make contact and the real living-being world would rush in again—and I realized with surprise that I was eager, I was anticipating, I was ready.

All right, then. *All right!* Ready or not, here I come. Here I come and—win, lose, or draw—it's worth the trip. Who says so? *Buddy Valentine says so.* Buddy Valentine is still alive and he is still in the real world and it may not be the world he picked and it may not be the easiest world and it may not even be the most happy-making world. But it's a world for him; a world for Buddy Valentine as much as for anyone else, and it is worth the trip!

I unsnapped my seat belt and looked at Mrs. Degan, who was doing the same, and the laughter was there, strong inside me, and the words repeated themselves again and again—*it was worth the trip . . .*

# Prime Cusp

*(An Epilogue, continued, as Epilogue)*

Lieutenant Commander Burris Howard Dann, USNR, commanding officer, Navy Oceanographic Vessel (spy-monitor ship) U.S.S. *Pennsylvania*, stood at attention in full uniform, a Cuban infantryman's rifle pointed unwaveringly at his chest. He watched the rest of the infantry squad club kick and beat his crewman, Seamen 2/C Michael M. Digby, to the bricked ground and finally into unconsciousness.

Helpless and unable (by order of the Cuban major who had selected Digby for "paddleboard interrogation" in the middle of the courtyard while the rest of the crew, including the officers this time, looked on) to go to the man's aid or even to protest aloud, the erstwhile captain told himself he should have warned Digby, and the rest of the captive crew as well, of the inevitable consequences of any attempt at resistance.

Digby had got in *one good punch,* though—whirling to take the paddle-wielding soldier full in the face; almost certainly leaving the fellow with a nose permanently canted to windward—before the rest of the squad began hammering him.

And that, Dann told himself wryly, is a hell of a lot more than *you* have entered in the plus column of your personal ledger since the moment you spotted those Cuban patrol crafts pounding down toward you. So far, you have proven yourself perhaps the only totally noncombative sea-com-

465

mand captain in the history of the United States Navy.

*Poor Digby!* Poor Digby? No. *No,* by God! Not poor Digby—*lucky* Digby!

A damn fool, perhaps; he must have known that squad would kick hell out of him if he socked the bastard holding the paddle. And God knows, if they haven't murdered him outright, it sure looks like he stands one hell of a chance to have picked up permanent injuries. A man's never quite the same after treatment like that.

Still—*lucky* Digby, all the rest notwithstanding. Lucky to have the guts—and not to be sadded with the responsibility of an entire crew of men—and so be free to show these spic mothers, these Commie bastards, what a real man is made of. Luckier than his captain, the man whose sphincter had responded when he was undergoing his round of paddling by relaxing and filling his pants in front of the world. The very same captain who now had trouble meeting the eyes of his crew. Yes, I'd trade places with you, Seamen 2/C Digby—trade even at this very moment—only you'd be getting the crappy end of the stick. Yes? Yes! Oh, yes. And who would that fresh-faced smart-ass draftee Digby like to trade with now? Just about anyone in Hollywood, to hear him talking the day they grabbed us. He missed one hell of a chance there, getting captured a week before he was set for a transfer to that electronic camera school out there. In a day or two, according to *his* plan, he would have been paddling his way through all those sun-ripened breasts and buttocks in the land of waterbeds and wishes come true instead of being beaten unconscious by a bunch of Cuban Commies.

Well, I'm with you, Digby. I'm with you. Because right now I think I'd like to be anywhere else in the world—but especially in Hollywood—instead of where I am. And *who* I am. And *what* I am.

Yes, sir! You betcha! Go to Hollywood—soak up the sun, drink up the booze, lay all the girls, spend all the money, have all the fun—and never worry about a damn thing for the rest of your life.

Only—what the hell was that Ortiz was saying last night? Damn! I wish Ortiz could remember a little more of his Spanish from when he was a kid. Only guy in the whole crew who speaks the same language they do here

466

and he can't get but maybe a word or two in there when they talk fast. And do they ever talk fast!

But he *must* have misunderstood what he heard last night over the guard's transistor radio. It's *crazy!* What in the name of hell would a happy, successful, handsome, rich movie star like David Strauss do a thing like *that* for? That damn Ortiz. He sure as hell got that all backward, since according to his brand of interpreting, the guy actually *hijacked* an airliner in Los Angeles and tried to make them fly him to Havana so he could pay Castro five hundred and fifty thousand dollars—*over half a million*—to turn us loose!

Like I say—crazy! A nice gesture on his part, but nutty all the same. And then Ortiz tells us they said Strauss blew up the cabin with a grenade he'd gotten hold of somewhere—something like that—and the plane went down with every poor bastard on board! Hell, he's *got* to be wrong. It just doesn't hang together. Anyway you look at it.

A successful, happy guy like him—he'd never do that. He's got it made! Famous. Big career. A couple of movies and a weekly TV show and sitting around on his ass the rest of the time. Soaking up the sun. Drinking the booze. Jumping all the girls. Spending big money. And having all the fun.


The Cuban squad was finally tiring of working Digby over. They moved away, at the major's order, and for a moment Dann was afraid he and the rest of the crew might be forced to stand there in the sun and watch their crewman die, without being given permission to aid him. After a moment, however, the major nodded and Dann took this as his okay for them to go to Digby's aid.

But there was nothing with which they could improvise a stretcher. The men finally formed two close columns and lifted on command to bear the unconscious Digby to the shady part of the yard, where water and rags could be used to clean his wounds and bathe his face. Dann had little medical or first-aid training, but he knew enough to check Digby's pulse. It was strong and regular. He told the men to keep working and—half-remembering something about treatment for shock—improvised what he could in the way of blankets.

Finally Digby's eyelids began to flutter. "Hey, boy," Dann said. "Digby! Can you hear me, Digby?"

Digby's right eye opened a slit, but the left remained swollen shut. He regarded the captain steadily with his one good eye and the unbroken right side of his mouth quirked upward in what might have been a grin. "Ne'mm'r la'g'uv omme . . ." he croaked.

Dann strained to catch the words, then grinned back at Digby. "Well, he said, "if they *didn't* lay a glove on you, I think you better keep an eye on the referee, because *some-one*'s trying to beat your brains out."

The good side of Digby's face kept on trying to smile, and he opened his swollen lips to say something else. But before he could get it out, the single visible eyeball rolled back in its socket and he lost consciousness again.

Dann wondered if he should try to rouse him. But his pulse still seemed strong and his breathing was regular—if you discounted the snoring effect caused by the smashed nose—so he decided against it. Let the poor bastard sleep. Let him dream, maybe, of being in Hollywood with all that booze and all that poon.

Standing there, the stench from his own trousers hit him. Lacking soap, he had been unable to remove some of the stains—and most of the smell—from that first-day accident.

Well, to hell with it! Dann took a deep breath, well flavored with the scent of his clothing, and held it for a moment before expelling it. If Digby could take what he'd had to take and still try to make a bad joke, Dann told himself; if Digby could do that, his captain could at least stop sniveling to himself about what a rough break he'd been handed.

Okay, all right: *Digby'd still like to be somewhere else.* And so would I, Dann told himself. *And he'd like to be someone else.* And so would I.

But we're not; we're where and who we are and—*who knows, suppose Ortiz was right about that newscast?* In that case, would either one of us *really* have traded places with David Strauss? And, come to think of it, even if Ortiz wasn't right, can we be *sure* we'd want to be in someone else's shoes? . . .

Wishing and dreaming are fine. But, just for right now, I think maybe the captain of the *Pennsylvania* better concentrate on trying to be at least as good a man as Seaman

2/C Michael M. Digby. That's a plenty big enough assignment for one day.

And maybe tomorrow it'll be something else. One day at a time. Get on with it.

But for now—just this minute—I think the captain will have a little look-around, and see if there isn't something he could use to *get that damn smell out of his pants*. . . .

*He moved away, across the now vacant courtyard. And elsewhere, other riders moved in their own eccentric patterns across the face of the lonely mudball, whirling in the eternal cold in its journey around the brightly shining star that maintained their precarious lives in the great Emptiness.*

*And now and then, one by one, a few of the riders stopped and seemed to disappear. And new riders appeared to take their place. And some collided with each other and some circled each other warily . . . and, here and there, two of them seemed to huddle together for warmth and comfort and mutual support against the awful vastness of it all.*

*And sometimes these things meant trouble. . . .*

*Around them—invisible to half the moving dots below—stars blazed in configurations known as Signs and planets moved, predictably and powerfully, through those Signs. And new groupings, new interfaces of power came into being and made their way, almost undetected (and sometimes understood too late), past the Prime Cusp that is the dividing line between the Twelfth and the First Houses of the Heavens.*

*Seaman Digby's broken mouth twitched in a grimace of dreams.*

*The groupings shifted.*

*The captain of the* Pennsylvania *searched for soap.*

*Another small shift.*

*Passengers from an airliner dispersed from the terminal at Los Angeles International Airport.*

*Another movement; another shift; the Prime Cusp was past and a new cycle began.*

*The trouble had ended. The trouble had begun.*

—THE END—

## ABOUT THE AUTHOR

RONA BARRETT graduated with honors from New York University when she was only eighteen years old. After working as a press agent for such stars as Eddie Fisher and Steve Lawrence, she moved to Hollywood to write for motion picture fan magazines. Before entering television, she created a daily newspaper column that was syndicated nationally in 125 papers. Rona Barrett's Hollywood news is syndicated for Metromedia television and seen by millions daily. During 1972, she hosted nationally syndicated one-hour television specials. She is also heard nationally on radio news reports and *Rona Barrett's Hollywood* is her own nationally distributed monthly magazine. Rona Barrett presently lives in Beverly Hills, California.

# RELAX!
## SIT DOWN
## and Catch Up On Your Reading!

☐ THE FRENCH CONNECTION by Robin Moore      (5369— 95¢)

☐ JOHNNY GOT HIS GUN by Dalton Trumbo      (5483— 95¢)

☐ HER by Anonymous      (6669—$1.50)

☐ QB VII by Leon Uris      (6777—$1.50)

☐ THE PATRIOT by Charles Durbin      (6947—$1.50)

☐ JOY IN THE MORNING by Betty Smith      (6984—$1.25)

☐ THE BELL JAR by Sylvia Plat      (7178—$1.50)

☐ THE EXORCIST by William Peter Blatty      (7200—$1.75)

☐ WHEELS by Arthur Hailey      (7244—$1.75)

☐ RAGA SIX by Frank Lauria      (7249—$1.25)

☐ HIM by Anonymous      (7369—$1.50)

☐ THE DAY OF THE JACKAL by Frederick Forsyth      (7377—$1.75)

☐ THE FRIENDS OF EDDIE COYLE by George Higgins      (7504—$1.50)

☐ THE TERMINAL MAN by Michael Crichton      (7545—$1.75)

☐ THE LEVANTER by Eric Ambler      (7603—$1.50)

**Buy them at your local bookstore or use this handy coupon for ordering:**

Bantam Books, Inc., Dept. FBB, 414 East Golf Road, Des Plaines, Ill. 60016

Please send me the books I have checked above. I am enclosing $_____
(please add 25¢ to cover postage and handling). Send check or money
order—no cash or C.O.D.'s please.

Mr/Mrs/Miss_____

Address_____

City_____State/Zip_____

FBB—8/73

Please allow three weeks for delivery. This offer expires 8/74.

# FREE!
## Bantam Book Catalog

It lists over a thousand money-saving bestsellers originally priced from $3.75 to $15.00 —bestsellers that are yours now for as little as 50¢ to $2.25!

The catalog gives you a great opportunity to build your own private library at huge savings!

So don't delay any longer—send for your catalog TODAY! It's absolutely FREE!

Just send us a post card with the
Information below or use this handy coupon:

BANTAM BOOKS, INC.
Dept. FC, 414 East Golf Road, Des Plaines, Ill. 60016

Mr./Mrs./Miss_____
(please print)

Address_____

City_____State_____Zip_____

Do you know someone who enjoys books? Just give us their names and addresses and we'll send them a FREE CATALOG too!

Mr./Mrs./Miss_____

Address_____

City_____State_____Zip_____

Mr./Mrs./Miss_____

Address_____

City_____State_____Zip_____

FC—3/73